Reign of
Shadows

T.S. Colunga

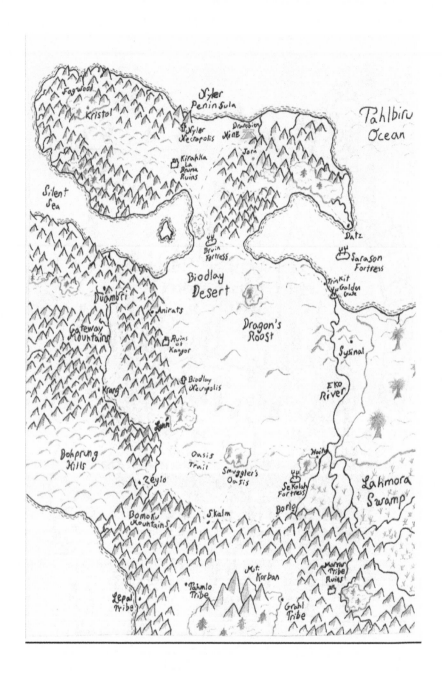

Table of Contents

Chapter 1: The Vigil

Datz, Nyler Peninsula, Alutopek

Rafik stared up at the Black Wall, the few stars shined through like far away candlelight. It wasn't just because of how few stars pierced the ebon dome, but because of his father that he recognized his favorite constellation. Quellor the warrior. Pointing up into the sky, he traced out the warrior, ending on the tip of the spear, which was the north star. Because of the dome it was easier to navigate at night than during the day. Another thing his father taught him. "Seven years." He sighed, scratching patterns into the worn ruined stone tower he sat on.

He imagined a ship coming into view on the horizon, navigating through the dangerous waters leading to Datz. Even in this darkness he could recognize it. The size of the ship, the sails and tattered flag. It was his father's ship. One he was certain he'd never see again. "Some things never change." An older voice laughed from behind him.

"What?" Rafik asked, turning. "Oh, hi Hektor."

"I remember seeing you up here every day whenever your father was out sailing." Hektor said, brushing his grey hair out of his face from the wind. "The other children playing, your mother always with your baby sister. But you sat up here, determined to bring him back by sheer will alone."

Rafik smiled. Those were the good days. When his family was still complete. "Do you know what today is?"

The old man nodded. "I do indeed. Your father was a good man, Rafik. Shame he is gone. We could really use him right now. Fortunately, your uncle, Gorik, is still there for you. For us."

Rafik didn't say a word. The sea breeze was a welcome change to the fires at the city gates. It had been nearly a month since their ruined city went under siege. "Do you think he'll make it back in time?"

"Gorik? Oh, I'm sure of it. The only time he was late was on the trip we lost your father. I don't think that will happen again, but that's a different story."

"What are they waiting for?" Rafik asked, turning his attention to the glowing light of the fires. "They have enough soldiers to overpower us. Anza and I helped count them this morning."

"I'm not sure. But thankful they have waited." Hektor said, scratching his chin. "The king knows we aren't starving." He gestured to the Tahlbiru Ocean. Along the banks were fisherman waiting for their catch.

"What do you think will happen?"

Hektor sighed. He looked over the city in the pale moonlight. It was mostly ruin. Long ago, before the Black Wall, it was a major city with tens of thousands of citizens. Now only 100. "Do you know the legend of that constellation?"

"Quellor?" Rafik said. "Yeah, Dad would always tell me the story whenever he saw me looking up at it."

"He was a farmer." Hektor began, ignoring the fact Rafik had heard the story before. "Nothing great. Had a humble life. A good life. But then a man named Grax arrived and began demanding all his food. Quellor offered a generous portion, but Grax refused, wanting it all. When Quellor refused to give him more, Grax burned the farm and his family as punishment. Grax grew in power, forgetting Quellor. Quellor didn't forget him and helped raise the army to stop him. It was Quellor who defeated Grax. The Gods recognized Quellor and gave him a place among the stars."

"Dad's version was a little different." Rafik smiled.

"Your father was a better storyteller than me. It's probably why he became a sailor, to tell tall tales." Hektor said.

"He did like telling stories." Rafik nodded, a smile slowly growing.

"Us Datians are much like Quellor." Hektor replied. "We will do what's right. King Vanarzir wants to take all the children

8

and force them into his army. We don't agree with that. So, we will do all we can to stop him."

"Even if we die trying." Rafik smirked.

"We're either going to be Quellor, or the destruction that inspires the warrior. But we aren't going to sit by and let the king get away with it. I fear I am veering off course. I didn't come up here to talk to you about the fate of Datz, or constellation stories. I came to collect you."

"What for?"

"You'll see. Come on." Hektor said, tugging at Rafik and beginning to climb down the ladder.

Rafik got to his feet, brushing himself off. He sighed while gazing out on his home. Datz didn't seem like much. In fact, to most it probably looked like a long-forgotten city, slowly crumbling to dust. To Rafik and everyone else here, this was home. He followed Hektor, entering the streets below.

The streets of Datz twisted and turned in all different directions. Rafik couldn't imagine finding his way through the city if the buildings weren't in ruins. Every street now had different shapes of destroyed buildings. The homes that still had people living in them were more intact and had blankets in the windows. But most of those were near the docks. The tower he came from was closer to the city gates.

He followed Hektor, weaving his way through the streets. Then he saw it. Just up ahead. Candlelight and the soft rhythmic noise of a melody on the wind. "What's going on?" Rafik asked, anxious to see more.

Hektor didn't answer. He continued moving forward, walking at a brisk pace for an elderly man. Rafik recognized where they were going but didn't understand why. They arrived at the city center, with a few more than a dozen people huddled around the large pond. They called it the Pond of Memories, and much like the rest of Datz, were the ruins of an ancient temple. The group each held a candle and sang in just above a whisper.

Rafik noticed the dark hair of his sister standing next to their mother. "What's this?" He asked.

Their mother smiled, opening her arms and hugging Rafik. Before she could respond Hektor began to speak. "Thank you for coming out. I know we haven't done this in a long time, but tonight we honor the memory of a great man. Drane. Lost at sea, but not forgotten."

Rafik's mother, Tamra, stepped forward holding a small paper boat, a candle for a mast. She placed it into the pond and pushed the tiny vessel into the water. It drifted to the center of the pond as the candle burned. The small flame burst with light as it touched the paper boat. All the while Rafik held Anza's hand, remembering their father.

The small group watched the boat burn, taking turns sharing their memories of Drane. Rafik wasn't paying attention. He was remembering his own time with his father. Teaching them to read, to sail. Playing pirates and soldiers in and around the ruins. Watching his father hug their mother, telling her how much he loved her. He remembered his jovial smile and booming laughter. He wiped away tears trickling down his face several times. Hektor was just finishing up a memory he had of Gorik and his father testing the waters around Datz. He missed most of it but joined when a few others laughed and smiled.

"Thank you." Tamra said, the last of the boat sinking into the pond. The crowd slowly dispersed, leaving Rafik and his family at the pond. "No don't do that, sweetie."

Anza had picked up a pebble and tossed it into the pond. "You don't want to do that." Hektor said, kneeling to face her.

"Why not?"

"Since the temple collapsed, this pond has been a memorial to all that was lost. Throwing a rock in will disturb the dead." Hektor explained.

"The dead can't come back to life." Rafik argued.

"Throw another pebble in there and find out." Hektor challenged.

"If I do, maybe they'll bring back Dad." Rafik said, kicking loose dirt into the pond.

"Others say there's a door down there. To the land of the Immortals." Tamra said. "One of the two cursed tribes of men."

"Now who is making things up." Hektor laughed. "Either way, don't throw rocks into the pond."

"It's a story Drane would tell." Tamra said. "The world of the Immortals is below us. He and Gorik talked about it all the time."

"The only thing below Datz is dirt." Hektor said.

Tamra sighed. "Let's get you two to bed."

Rafik yawned, only now realizing he was tired. The three started home, leaving Hektor at the pond.

"This wasn't much." Hektor said, catching up to the three of them. He smiled, winking at Anza. "But I hope this has helped."

"It has, thank you." Tamra said. "And I'm glad *she* didn't decide to come ruin everything."

"I threatened Salina if she did." Hektor said. "She can be the rain any other day. But not on special moments like this." His hand lingered on Tamra's shoulder.

Rafik noticed the look he gave his mother and furrowed his brow. Blood almost boiling. "Why did we have a vigil when we haven't since his first anniversary?"

"There is no excuse for why we haven't." Hektor said. "But we'll have one from now on. Every year. Drane, your father, won't be forgotten."

"No, he won't. Right Mom?" Rafik asked, getting her attention. She had a smile he hadn't seen in years on her face.

"No. He won't." Tamra nodded. "Now, take your sister home. Hektor and I need to talk."

Rafik didn't say another word, turning to leave. For the last seven years his mother hadn't always been there for them. Cooped up in her bed, not wanting to leave. Often it was he who took care of Anza. She had been more active recently; yet anger still festered within him when he would see the way she gawked at Hektor. Though he was only 14, he had a feeling tonight wasn't about his father.

11

"Do you think Gorik will be back tomorrow?" Anza asked once they got home. Their home, Rafik nicknamed The Nest, wasn't much. It was one of the buildings without ever having an upper level. There was a cellar, but for the last few years was flooded. All around were cushions and blankets. He remembered gathering the pillows and blankets, making small forts for his sister to play in. There was just one bedroom, and that was their parents. Rafik and Anza slept near the fire, falling asleep to the crackling of flames.

"I hope so." Rafik said. "I'm not sure when the Kylix will attack us, but the sooner he gets back the better."

Anza nodded, taking a sip of milk from a cup on the table. She yawned and gathered up some blankets and pooling them up near the fire. Autumn had crept in seemingly overnight. The days were crisp, but the nights were near freezing. "I miss him."

Rafik gathered some blankets of his own and cuddled next to Anza. "I do too."

"Hey Rafik?" Anza asked, after several minutes of silence.
"Yes?"
"Do you think Hektor will be our new dad?"
Rafik bit his lip, clenching his fist. "Good night, Anza."
"I like Hektor."
"He's not our father." Rafik snapped. He rolled over, his back to Anza. "Good night, Anza."

Rafik woke with a start, noticing Anza was already gone. He scrambled to his feet, looking around The Nest. Anza's giggle echoed from the back bedroom; his mother's voice muffled. Without making a noise he slipped out the window, as the door always creaked. He clenched his fists, thinking of last night. What should have been a good night and memory was tainted. Before he knew it, he was back at the tower, watching the ocean. "Where are you Gorik?" He asked.

He watched the waves crash at the shore and fishermen gather their catches. The salty breeze hit Rafik, and for a moment he imagined himself on the sea with Gorik and his father.

12

An explosive bang jolted Rafik from his daydreams. Another noise came echoing throughout the city. Rafik turned, looking at the city gate. The doors budged with another bang. It was finally happening. His face drained with color. He swiveled around, unsure of what to do. The shouts and screams echoed from those below. Monotony of life under siege had ended.

A handful of Datians climbed the city gates, raining arrows down on the attackers. Moments later they fell backwards off the wall, arrows piercing them. He heard Hektor shout to get into position. But still, Rafik froze. He could only watch with morbid fascination as the city gate bulged again. This time he heard cracks in the doors. Another bang. And another. Then the door burst open, a massive head of a dragon burst through the hole, fires roiling inside its mouth. It took a moment to realize the dragon was just a metal statue as it fell, and the Kylix soldiers poured into the ruined city.

He didn't think anything would be more frightening than the maw of a dragon breaking into the city. Rafik was wrong. The Kylix soldiers dressed like the dead. All metal suits of armor with bones designed into it, making it look as if the dead had risen. Even their helmets looked like skulls. His skin crawled as he watched them flood the city, hacking at even the defenseless.

It wasn't long until the screams of triumph became louder than the screams of the fearful. Rafik hurried to his feet, watching the tidal wave of death come towards him faster than he thought possible. He had to get to Anza. They had to escape.

Chapter 2: Returning Home

Datz, Nyler Peninsula, Alutopek

Gorik heaved a sigh, watching his home come into view. He had sailed around the Nyler Peninsula and across the Silent Sea to the forest city of Emerald. It hid in and around massive trees and along the shore. He always awed at seeing the mysterious and majestic place. But nothing compared to seeing one's home. The feeling of relief and happiness that he would indeed return home always swelled within him. Even if his home, the city of Datz, was more ruin than city at this point. Home was home. No matter its appearance. He had sailed all his life, and the feelings never changed.

Washed away rubble and flooded fortresses surrounded Datz. The most prominent was the spider topped tower of the Sarason Fortress, just south of Gorik and Datz. The closer one got to Datz, the more ruins one had to navigate. Through trial and error, Gorik had completed his chart, marking all the obstacles. To his knowledge, it was the only one in existence.

Steering around one such obstacle, he turned his attention to Datz. Blood drained from his face. Smoke hung over the ruined city making the place look drearier than usual. The black clouds didn't bode well for his family and friends.

"Bastards." He cursed, as he inched ever closer to Datz. He had expected the siege to last longer. Now how was he going to get everyone to safety? Screams of his fellow Datians echoed in the air, along with the shouts of victory from the attackers. Gorik cursed again as he got his ship, the *River Lizard,* to the dock and tied it off. Much like his chart, his ship was one of a kind, with mechanisms below deck to help him sail the *River Lizard* on his own. The gears slowly stopped churning, and the noises of battle grew louder.

He jumped over the side of his small ship and onto the dock, pulling out his sword in one swift motion. Upon landing he wobbled for a moment. He wasn't sure if it was because it had been years since he used it, if he were too drunk, or if his missing left leg kept him off balance from jumping over the side. The thought of his missing leg reminded him of the last time he had used his sword. He had barely escaped, and watched his best friend, Drane, die.

The sailor leaned against the edge of his ship, unhooked his wooden leg, and raised it to his mouth. Taking a couple swallows of his drink, some dribbling down the sides of his mouth, refastened his leg, and got back up. "Guess everything happens for a reason. And I do like to drink." He took another sip before reattaching his leg.

The Kylix hadn't made it this far into the ruined city. He could hear them get closer. It wouldn't be much longer now until all of Datz was taken by the king's army. He hobbled onward, trying to be stealthy, but the rhythmic thump of his wooden leg didn't help. "Don't worry, Drane. I'll protect them." He muttered.

Rafik was still a small boy when his father died. He was told that he had fallen overboard while in a drunken stupor. He didn't believe it, though there was no proof otherwise. His body was never found, as he was lost to the depths of the Tahlbiru. People expected Rafik to be the man of his family. And for seven years he was. He went hunting, providing food. Tried repairing the numerous problems in their ruined home, giving them shelter. Even sailed and fished as well. His mother tried to take care of him and his little sister, Anza, but after their father's death, she was never the same. As if a light had turned off within her.

She was always quiet. Distant. Almost unresponsive some days. Her spending time with Hektor brought some of that light back, but nothing like it was now. The roars of the oncoming Kylix soldiers lit the spark within her again. "Follow me." She demanded in a stern voice Rafik had almost forgotten. She yanked on Anza's arm, nearly dragging her, grabbing an axe on her way out. Rafik followed.

They made their way to a catapult. Tamra and a couple other villagers manned the weapon. They launched stones of different sizes towards the city gates. No one could tell if they were helping, but it felt good to be doing something. Soon both Rafik and Anza were helping to load the catapult.

The group had just launched a handful of stones into the air. Rafik watched them soar in the sky, slowly arcing downward. Anza turned to grab another stone and froze. At the other end of the street were a pair of Kylix soldiers.

"It's ok, baby. Momma's here." Tamra said, kissing the top of Anza's head, and moving to stand in front of her. "I won't let anyone hurt you."

The soldiers looked like the walking dead, with their suits resembling bone. One of the Kylix soldiers held a bow in his hand; an arrow had taken down one of the other Datians working the catapult. Tamra threw her axe at the soldier. The other soldier cut it down in midair with his sword.

"Get in the catapult." She ordered, dashing to the fallen man, and taking a knife from his belt.

"What?" Rafik asked.

"Get in the catapult." She repeated. "Get in the catapult and then keep moving."

Rafik took Anza's hand, and they climbed into the cup of the catapult. Two more Kylix soldiers appeared, taking down the last of the other villagers around them. Their mother smiled at the two of them before pulling the lever. The catapult launched with a 'whoosh.' Rafik held Anza tight as they flew in the air. He looked back and saw their mother fall in a volley of arrows.

The feeling of Anza squeezing him tore Rafik from his thoughts. The cold, autumn wind cut against their face and dug deep into their ragged clothes. He glanced down and saw his home zoom by. The Kylix looking like living skeletons, taking down anything that moved like a tidal wave of death. He looked forward and saw the meadow of grassland fly past and the forest trees grow closer.

Anza screamed as she saw the tree branches reach out to grab her. Rafik bit his cheek, trying to stay quiet. If any Kylix soldier noticed the children flying overhead, they didn't make any motion to go after them.

The two children crashed into the forest, the tree branches scratching and cutting at them, slowing their fall. They finally hit the forest floor, landing on a pile of leaves. Rafik thanked the gods it was already autumn. Nearly all the leaves were now on the ground, cushioning their fall. Though they landed safely, the two appeared as if they had fought off a pack of wild cats. Rafik got the brunt of the fall as he made sure Anza landed on top of him.

Rafik rolled onto his hands and knees, coughing, trying to catch his breath. He shook his head, and hobbled to his feet, brushing off the leaves that clung to him. He smiled, looking at his little sister. Although she was only two years younger than him, he still saw her as the small five-year-old girl who lost her father. She even had the same amber colored eyes as him, too. She helped Rafik up and they both circled the area, trying to get their bearings. Muffled screams and yells echoed in the distance. Neither could tell where it was coming from. And even with the naked trees, they still blocked their view from where Datz was.

"What are we going to do?" Rafik sighed.

Anza groaned. Her long, dark brown hair still had leaves scattered about in it. "Mom said keep moving but didn't say where. I'm more worried about where we're going to go. Everywhere looks the same." She gestured to the forest of barren trees. No matter where she looked, it all appeared identical. Trees going on forever.

Rafik helped pick some of the leaves out of her hair before answering. His own brownish red hair was still spiky and a mess but had nothing stuck in it like his sister's. "We need to get out of here. But we can't go through the forest." His eyes darted back and forth, as if expecting a monster to suddenly launch itself at Anza and him.

Anza nodded. She remembered hearing the stories of the Nyler Forest. A long time ago a group of men went chasing after a thief. The thief taunted them, giggling, and getting away by jumping from treetop to treetop. Tired of the thief's games of

17

evasion, the men burned the forest down until they were caught. The thief refused to tell where his hoard of ill-gotten goods was hidden. Filled with anger, and exhausted from the hunt, the men tortured the thief, hoping to get their treasures back. In the end, the thief died from the torture. The thief was just a child. After that day, the trees that grew back in the forest were said to attack anyone who entered. It's said that the forest was so upset about what the men did to the child, it refused to let anyone enter. Forever hiding the child thief's treasure. Others believe the entire forest is possessed by the spirit of the tortured child. Most believe that is why the Datians became a seafaring people. Better to cross an ocean than to fight off angry spirits.

"I'm not sure if we have a choice." She hated to admit it. Staring into the depths of the forest, she could have sworn she saw the trees twist, getting ready to snatch her.

"There's always another choice." Rafik said.

"If only Gorik had made it back in time." Anza sighed. "We could use his ship."

Rafik looked from himself to Anza. Their clothes were holey and didn't offer much protection to the chill autumn night air. They had no form of protection. They were defenseless if the Kylix found them. But they couldn't stay out once night came or they would freeze. "We need at least a sword or bow. We may be able to start a fire for warmth." He spoke.

"Where are we going to find one, Rafik?" Anza asked in a shrill voice. "We can't go back home. Mom told us to keep moving."

"How often do we listen to Mom?" Rafik smiled, trying to fill the grim air with a joke.

"What are you saying? You want to return home? Just for a sword? How are we going to sneak past the king's men? Let alone sneak back out?" Anza shook her head. "That isn't going to work, Rafik. You should know that."

"I do. I also know we can't stay out here. If we do manage to sneak back in, we don't have to come back this way." Rafik said.

18

Anza tilted her head, looking at her brother, eyes narrowing. "I'm listening."

"What if we sneak back into Datz, steal a sword, or bow, and make our way to the docks? The Kylix don't have ships, so they can't follow us. Eventually they will leave and move onto the next city. Once they're gone, we can come back."

"What if they destroy the ships?" Anza asked.

Rafik shook his head and began pacing back and forth. "No, they won't destroy the ships. The king is up to something, and I have a feeling he will want those ships. Maybe we can find Gorik! He could help us!"

"Gorik isn't even here." Anza said.

"He said he would be back today. We need to at least check. If not, we can still hide in a boat out in the ocean until the Kylix is gone." Rafik argued.

After several moments of silence, Anza nodded. "That could work. You know, if the hundreds of Kylix soldiers don't notice two children sneaking by when they're looking for children in the first place. Or if they notice us and decide two kids won't make a difference and find a way to destroy our boat. And if we die that's the last time that I'll be listening to you."

Rafik laughed. "Obviously. Now, which way back to Datz?" Everywhere looked the same. They couldn't use the sun as the Black Wall didn't indicate where the sun was; it just made the wall glow. They would have to wait until nighttime to navigate through these woods. The thought made his hair stand on end as he could already hear the trees groan and turn, beginning to move to hurt them. He wasn't sure which thought worried him more, dying by the snare of the trees, or freezing, waiting for night to come.

Gorik spotted three skeletal figures of the Kylix soldiers first. Even after fighting them countless times in his life, the metallic suits of armor representing the walking dead still unnerved him. Especially the skulls. The sight of them used to frighten him. It frightened most. But now they just bothered him. Like watching a spider scuttling towards him. Just like tiny spiders,

Gorik beat them with ease. He had sneaked up on them and taken out one before the other two even knew what was happening.

Seeing even one Kylix soldier this far into the city, he knew the entire place had been taken. The children would be rounded up and whisked away to Haitu. And everyone else would either be killed or sent away. He shook his head. He couldn't give up. He didn't give up the last time he encountered the Kylix. With that thought he tapped his peg leg on the stone walkway and turned back to the *River Lizard*.

His ship was safely tethered to the dock. If the Kylix came strolling by it would fall into their hands. He couldn't afford that. He sighed, marveling at the masonry of the archway. There was never a gate, and as far as he knew, there was no need for one. His ancestors had built this dock, and the archway. It was his second home, as his family used to run these docks as well. There was a secret for closure to keep enemies out. Or in Gorik's case, keep them in. Two sconces stood on either side of the archway. If they were both adjusted to turn inward the archway would collapse. For millennia, the docks stood proud and open. The trap never needed. The sailor's heart grew heavy, nodding his head in decision on what to do.

As he turned the last torch inward, he heard a click like a key turning a lock and gears begin to shift. The wall rumbled with a roar of long forgotten machinery. A moment later the archway collapsed. Gorik waved his hands, brushing away the dust, coughing. The entry to the dock was gone. With all the other ruins this city had, it even fit right in. Gorik laughed at the thought and turned. Now he couldn't even get to his ship. Though according to his ancestors, there were secret tunnels branching out from the center of town he could use to escape.

Gorik nodded. It was time to find any survivors and get them to safety. If he could find the tunnels. And, more importantly, if there were still survivors.

Rafik and Anza wandered the forest, hoping they were going the right way. It wasn't nighttime, far from. But both were

20

restless and couldn't just sit and wait. Their thoughts alone kept them wanting to do something. Their home had been conquered. Their mother gave their life to them. They were alone with nowhere to go. Both distracted in thought on what to do, reminiscing about their mother, and for Rafik, his father as well. The two walked alongside each other, walking in sync. Taking a step, they didn't notice the sudden downhill slope.

Both tumbled and rolled down the hill, snapping branches and rustling leaves all the way down. Rafik's fall ended with him rolling headfirst into a tree. He grunted, got to his feet, and brushed himself off. His face paled as he heard commotion nearby. "Hide!" Rafik hissed in a harsh whisper and jumped behind a thick tree nearby. He glanced around but Anza was already hiding.

The air was different. Not from the sudden commotion he had heard. But it felt…fragile. Like a brittle leaf that crumbles to the touch. He then noticed the colors of the world were fainter. The autumn leaves were much duller, and the noise he had heard was more like an echo than a nearby voice. It was like a dream that was all too real. *'That hit on the head really did something to me.'* He thought to himself, shaking his head.

He pushed himself against the tree as the voices grew louder. A moment later he saw out the corner of his eye Kylix soldiers marching down the hill they had just fallen from. The soldiers laughed, not noticing he was just a few feet away. They continued onward, joking about how easy this would be. Others muttered under their breath about the boy who dueled the king, wondering if he had been caught.

Rafik watched them go by. Not one noticed him. He watched the backs of them as he jumped, screaming. A soldier walked right through him. "What?" He shouted, looking around. "How did you do that?" He asked, forgetting he was supposed to be hiding. The soldiers kept marching, not paying attention to him.

"Rafik!" He heard a familiar voice shout. "Rafik!" That voice. It came on the wind but sounded so familiar. "Wake up! Please Wake up!"

Rafik opened his eyes, startled to see himself lying on the ground, Anza crying over him. He spit out her hair, coughing. "Get off me! What happened?"

"What do you mean what happened? I should be asking you that!" Anza snapped, shoving her brother.

"I saw the Kylix marching through here." Rafik said. "They walked right through me. I thought I was a ghost."

Anza scoffed. "You hit your head and just laid there. Nobody has come by."

"That would explain why my head hurts. Guess I wasn't imagining that." Rafik groaned, rubbing his head. A large lump was beginning to grow where he had rolled into the tree. "I saw the Kylix. They were talking about how easy this will be. I think Datz is this way." He pointed toward where he had seen the Kylix march.

"Oh, do you have talent now?" Anza asked, laughing.

"You and I both know that's not possible. Remember? The Black Wall?" Rafik said, pointing upwards at the domed ceiling that shrouded all Alutopek in its darkness. When the sun was at its highest, everything looked to be veiled in twilight. According to legend, King Vanarzir had stolen the people's magic they call talent to create the Black Wall.

Anza shrugged. "That's the only explanation I have. Unless you're going crazy. Might as well follow your crazy vision anyway. We have no better direction to go."

Rafik got to his feet and followed Anza. Could it be true? What she had said. That he now had talent? He had never heard of being able to view another's memories. But she was right. There wasn't any other explanation. He walked mindlessly behind his sister, trying to figure out what had just happened.

The two continued onward, hoping to find Datz before it got dark out and they froze. Just beyond another patch of trees they saw it. The ruined walls of Datz. They had found their way home. "Well, what do you know?" Anza smirked, patting her brother on the back. "Did your vision show you how we're getting out of this alive?"

Chapter 3: Solving a Riddle

Datz, Nyler Peninsula, Alutopek

Before the Black Wall Datz was one of the largest cities in Alutopek. After, it was one of the least populated. Between time and the cataclysm that followed the Black Wall's creation, Datz was in ruin. Walls crumbled. Homes collapsed. What was repaired looked like a shoddy job at best. It was as if the ability to craft and mend had vanished. The wall protecting Datz from the intruders coming from the Nyler Forest seemed to be more intact, though. Until now.

The Kylix tore down the one gate the wall had, along with the surrounding area. It was now a small hill of crumbled stone. A group of Kylix soldiers stood there, guarding the gaping hole of an entrance. "How are we going to get in?" Anza whispered, hiding behind one of the trees. Between her and Datz was a grassy field with nowhere to hide.

"We'll have to climb over the wall somewhere else." Rafik concluded.

Anza nodded, and the two turned to head southward, away from the destroyed gate, but still in the cover of the trees. Not long after losing sight of the entrance and the Kylix that they found a hole in the wall. It wasn't particularly large. Big enough for a raccoon to fit through, maybe. Or two children.

"I'll go first." Rafik said, cautiously craning his neck to look left and right before leaving the protection of the forest. He sprinted towards the wall, slid and skid through the hole. A moment later he stuck his hand out of the hole, beckoning for Anza to come.

She sprinted just as fast, diving for the hole. It wasn't as tight of squeeze as it was for her brother. "Where are we?" She asked, brushing herself off.

Rafik hadn't explored this part of Datz before. Few did. Being a seafaring town, most lived near the docks. The buildings all around him appeared more dilapidated than the others. In front of them were the remains of a large, stone-built farmhouse. Moss grew over the stones while vines stretched across windows. They were facing the rear of the house, with access to the cellar. The chains around the handles had rusted and broken years ago. "Doesn't look like anyone has been here since before the Black Wall. Maybe we can look in here for a weapon, or even some better clothes." He suggested. Their worn and ragged clothes didn't shield them from the chill autumn winds, and if they were to be leaving the comforts of their home, they would need more than rags to wear.

"If anything else, we can hide in there. I doubt anyone would come by." Anza added.

"Just need to make sure we close the door behind us." Rafik said, wrenching open the cellar doors. The chains that bound the doors crumbled once he touched them. He gestured for Anza to head down the stairs, as he closed the door behind them.

"If you did have talent," Anza whispered, her voice echoing. "Why couldn't it be some sort of light? How are we supposed to see down here?" The stairwell was darker than expected. The stale air hung thick and cold. Even though she couldn't see it, she could feel the dust wafting through the air with every step. It was like a tomb, and they were invading it. Anza shivered, trying to shake off the feeling of being watched as she imagined the dead snatching her to join them in the afterlife.

Rafik stayed quiet, running his hand along the stone walls as they descended. Inch by inch, step by careful step, the two made it to the bottom of the stairs. There was no obvious entryway. They started grabbing at the walls, feeling for any kind of handle or hinge to indicate a door. "Right here." Rafik whispered. He felt a round knob jutting out of a smoother part of the wall. He turned the knob, and a crack of light appeared just inches from the two.

The room was large, but empty. Stone columns were scattered about the room, holding up the farmhouse above them. On the far side were more stairs leading to the rest of the house. Two small slivers of windows barely showed the light of the outside world; but was enough to flood most of the vacant room in

24

light. In the center of the room was the only piece of furniture in there. A large wardrobe, nearly the height of the room itself.

The two walked in front of the wardrobe, drawn to it like a moth to a flame. The wardrobe had two doors. Each door was divided in half with a carving in each quarter. In the top left was an eye radiating light like the sun. The top right had a sword that was plunged into a skull. The bottom left had what looked like a bag with random objects strewn about. In the bottom right was a chalice with a moon hanging over it. Along the center of the wardrobe were three locks, chains wrapping around the entire wardrobe.

"Speak three names to find my opening."

"What?" Anza asked, looking at her brother with a scrunched brow.

"That's what it says." Rafik repeated, pointing at the wardrobe. He pointed at the base of the wardrobe. A single sentence carved into it. "Speak three names to find my opening."

Anza wasn't paying attention anymore. She was examining the carvings. At first glance each one looked like a basic carving. As if a caveman was responsible for the graffiti on an otherwise pristine piece of furniture. But the more she looked, the more details emerged. The chalice was now rimmed with jewels and shimmered with a liquid inside it. The eye seemed to be following her, moving on its own accord. Anza reached up, trying to touch the eye. A jolt of electricity pulsed through her, sending her back into one of the stone columns the moment she touched the eye.

"Anza!" Rafik shouted, dashing to her side.

Gorik arrived too late. Any surviving adults were chained and shackled. Some had their heads bowed in defeat, others watched helplessly as the Kylix soldiers loaded the children into caged wagons. In the middle of it all was a man Gorik had only heard of. Taller than most other soldiers, wearing the same skeletal armor as the rest. But resting on the skull helmet, between two curling horns, was a crown with four gems. It was the war crown only the king would wear. King Vanarzir.

25

"Ya shire." He cursed in a dead language he knew little of. *'If I just had a bow!'* The king was saying something to another soldier, but the sailor couldn't hear him.

He skulked around more, hoping to find survivors that weren't captured. After sneaking around several buildings, and away from the captured children, he found a group of Kylix soldiers guarding a small group of people. Strange, they weren't with the rest. He inched closer and recognized why. There were three of them. The city's leaders. One of them was even his friend, Hektor.

"Well, Shallon, let's hope your gift is as good as you say it is." He muttered to himself. The sailor reached into one of his many pockets and pulled out some coarse black sand. He threw it at a nearby torch, causing it to explode with a bright flash. Four of the nine soldiers went to investigate.

Gorik limped forward, revealing himself to the remaining five. One of the soldiers shouted for the others to come back. Gorik threw another handful of the black powder in their faces. The soldiers charged him with swords drawn. The sailor tried his best to defend against them. He hadn't fought this many at once in nearly seven years. The rush was exhilarating, and he found himself fending them off with skill he thought was long forgotten. One soldier who Gorik had knocked down swiped at his peg leg. An instant later Gorik was on his back with six swords at his neck.

"Chain him up with the others." One of the Kylix soldiers said. "I'm sure the king will be interested how he made that explosion."

Gorik nodded to the three leaders, smiling. "I'm back." All of them had the same muddled look of surprise and disappointment. "You just wait." He smiled. "I may be a cripple and a drunk, but I'm not stupid."

The three scoffed at the comment. "You could have fooled us." Salina, one of the leaders, snapped.

"Don't you have children to terrorize or a man to sneak a love potion to?" Gorik retorted.

Salina glared at him. His friend, Hektor, let out a small chuckle. "At least you're back to die with us." He said.

"I wouldn't have it any other way, old friend. Though I hate to ruin your plans. I'm not planning to die today." Gorik smiled.

"Shut it!" One of the soldiers yelled, kicking Gorik in his leg.

Anza got to her feet a moment later. Her whole body felt numb. "What happened?" She asked, although she was fairly certain about what had occurred.

"You touched the wardrobe." Rafik said. "I'm not sure what happened, though."

Anza looked back at the wardrobe. "There is something hiding in there. If we can think of three names, maybe it will open?" She suggested.

"Alright. I'm Rafik of Datz, son of Drane. That's three names, right?" Rafik asked. He glanced at the wardrobe, but nothing happened.

"Maybe a girl has to give three names?" Anza suggested. She clapped her hands together and stood in front of the wardrobe. "My name is Anza of Datz. Daughter of Drane." They waited several moments, but still, nothing happened.

"This is pointless." Rafik groaned. "Let's just get upstairs and look through the rest of the house. Forget about this cursed closet."

Anza shook her head. "Why would someone charm a closet to shock you if you touch it? No, there is something in there. We just need to find three names. Could be the owners of this place?"

"Or whoever is in the closet." Rafik smirked.

Anza glared at her brother. "That's not funny."

"Well, if there was someone in there, or whoever lived here, it had to have been before the Black Wall." Rafik said. "No way of knowing now."

"There has to be a clue. No one would take this much time to carve into the wardrobe those images, lock it up, and leave a riddle at the bottom. Why not just leave it in a corner, instead of the middle of the room?"

Rafik shrugged. "They're terrible decorators, maybe?" He joked.

"Maybe the names are on the locks?" Anza guessed.

"No!" Rafik yelled, swatting Anza's hand away. "You're not getting shocked again. If you're that interested, let me try." He took a deep breath, closed his eyes, and reached for the uppermost lock, wincing as he anticipated to be flown across the room.

Nothing.

Rafik opened one eye. The mysterious jolt that sent his sister across the room didn't hit him. He was still holding the lock. Yet something was different. Just like back in the forest with his vision the colors seemed hazy. Out of the corner of his eyes he saw a man standing on either side of him. Rafik gasped, jumping back, falling through a third man. The three didn't notice him.

He looked around the room, trying to find Anza. And just as before she wasn't here. The room was just as barren, but brighter as two of the men were holding torches. The man to the left of Rafik stood straight and tall. Bags under his eyes were the only sign of how tired he truly was. Rafik imagined he could be some sort of knight for how he stood. But where his armor was, he couldn't tell. He wore thick leather, torn in places from a recent fight. His thin black hair was matted down as if he was wearing a helmet just recently.

The man to the right of Rafik didn't look much different than the one on the left. Tears streaked his face, his lower lip trembling. The two could have been brothers, Rafik thought. But this one seemed older. His hair was graying along the sides. A tattoo of a dragon coiled around a sword was on the top of his left hand. Once Rafik noticed the tattoo he was distracted by the insignia until it was covered up by the man's other hand. He had seen that emblem before. But where?

Finally, after a long moment of silence the man in the middle heaved a sigh of relief. Rafik moved so he could get a look at him. A dark, wide brimmed, pointed hat sat atop his head. A beard came to a point just above his hips. His frazzled and matted whitish silver hair was dirty and reached to the middle of his back. His bulbous nose was crooked, and his black eyes showed no hint of emotion. "It is finally over." He sighed again, turning away from the wardrobe. Rafik noticed he was holding an old and gnarled crook in one hand, and a thick, leather book in the other. Rafik recognized him instantly for what he was. A wizard.

Rafik's eyes widened and a smile grew on his face. The thought of an actual wizard excited him. Talent was taken away from everyone 200 years ago. Witches and wizards were said to be gone long before that. "When is this?" He asked himself, looking around the room.

"Can we really trust it here?" The man with the dragon tattoo asked. His voice was deeper than Rafik had expected, startling him.

"Yes. We have been through this, Sarafin." The wizard said in a strong voice that betrayed his quivering and aged body.

"But only three locks? To hold away such power? And in Datz of all places? It doesn't make much sense is all I'm saying." Sarafin replied. Even with trembling lips he spoke firmly.

The wizard turned to look back at the wardrobe with the three locks. The doors were carved with the pictures Rafik recognized from his time. "If we don't tell anyone how to unlock this box, no one will get in. These pictures tell you what is in here, but no answer for the key. So, unless you or your brother plan on telling someone, it is more than safe."

"The sword created by evil rests in its scabbard for an ageless slumber. The eye of the king who stood up to the others. A chalice of which any who drink will become one with the shadows. And a bag that has no end." Sarafin's brother interrupted. "These shouldn't be hidden away, Izamar. They should be destroyed."

The wizard, who Rafik realized was Izamar, twitched at the sound of his own name. "Never speak my name again, Furen. No one must ever speak our names again. The sword can never be broken, and the eye can never be truly destroyed. If the chalice

29

breaks, a new one appears at the original's birthplace. And the bag can't be dismantled. They are all safer here and left forgotten." Izamar scowled. "Now, we must go and never return to this place."

Sarafin led the way up the staircase leading out the cellar. He had finally stopped crying, Rafik noticed. Furen was next, standing as straight and tall as ever. Before Izamar left he pointed the crook at the base of the wardrobe and burned letters into it. "Speak three names to find my opening." He muttered to himself. Then, as he turned to leave, Rafik's vision went dark.

"Good." Anza said, holding her hand out for Rafik to take. "You're awake."

Rafik shook his head, realizing he had indeed been shocked. He was lying on the ground, several feet away from the wardrobe, just like Anza was when she had touched it. "You won't believe it but-"

"You had another vision?" Anza asked with an even tone. No hint of surprise in her voice. "I figured after you were talking in your sleep. Saying 'that's a wizard' over and over."

"I did." Rafik nodded, looking at the wardrobe. "And I know how to open this. I think I know the three names." He moved to face the wardrobe and read the inscription. He remembered his father, reading the phrase. Not for what it said, but for him reading it. When he was alive, he tried teaching him and Anza how to read, saying it was the most important thing he could ever teach them. Rafik hadn't read much in the last seven years, he was amazed he still could.

"Did you find out what's in there, too?" Anza asked, excited.

"Yeah. Not sure if we should open it. But we need a sword. And there is one in there." Rafik said, pointing to the picture of the blade. He cleared his voice and spoke firmly. "Izamar." Anza cast him a funny look with the name. A moment later the center lock clicked open and a figure appeared to Rafik's right. He looked exactly as Rafik had seen him.

The wizard stared at the two children. "You're just a boy." He muttered softly.

"How did you get here?" Anza snapped, taking a step back, holding up her hands in fists.

"One of you said my name." Izamar said. He nodded at Rafik. "I'm guessing that was you. How did you learn of it, young one?"

"I-I saw it in a vision. You and two other men." Rafik answered.

"You saw me in a vision?" Izamar asked skeptically. It was as if a light went on in his head. "Awe, so you have talent, do you?"

"What? No. Nobody does anymore. How could I have gotten it?" Rafik asked.

"Unless you are a natural born wizard, boy, you have talent. Psychometry, by the sound of it. The ability to glimpse the past through certain objects is a great gift. But I digress. I must ask you; do you really want to speak my name?"

"I'm trying to solve the riddle." Rafik said. "And if there is a sword in there, I need it."

"That wardrobe holds dangerous secrets that are better left forgotten. Surely you can find a sword elsewhere?" Izamar asked.

"The king who stole everyone's talent is attacking this city. My sister and I need to escape and be able to defend ourselves. If we're lucky, even stop the king." Rafik said. He tried hiding his surprise at what he had said. The memory of seeing his mother fall flashed in his mind, and any doubt vanished. Yes, he had to stop him, not just run away.

"Well, if you are determined to get into this wardrobe, don't let anyone know you have these treasures. When the third lock is opened everyone will be noted to your presence. When that happens, run. And run quickly. Try not to use the artifacts in here. Each one is cursed." Izamar explained.

Rafik nodded. "If I can, I will return them to the wardrobe."

Izamar shook his head, heaving a sigh. "I doubt you will be able to. But good luck, young one. You will need it in the journey to come."

Before Rafik or Anza could reply the wizard disappeared in a wisp of orange smoke. Rafik grabbed the opened lock and removed it from the chains. Again, he stood straight and said a name. "Sarafin." The upper most lock clicked open.

Just as where Izamar was, Sarafin now stood. He still looked just as tired as before. Although this time, his hands were gloved and resting on a pommel of a large broadsword, stabbing into the ground. And just like Izamar he, too, was surprised to see Rafik. "Just a boy summons me? I knew this was a terrible idea."

"Izamar told me not to use these objects in here if I can avoid it. Why?" Rafik asked.

"Ah, so you have already spoken to the wizard. Very well, boy. Take what you wish. I haven't the slightest idea how you managed to find our names since we removed them from all of history. Do what you wish."

"Wait!" Rafik snapped as Sarafin began to fade.

"What is it?" He sighed.

"The tattoo on your hand. What is it?" Rafik asked.

Sarafin's jaw dropped. "How did you discover my name without finding out about the Soniky?" Not waiting for an answer, the warrior vanished in a cloud of orange smoke, leaving Rafik and Anza alone once again. This time it left them with a chill.

Questions swirled around both of their minds as they stood there in silence. Both felt they were uncovering something that no one in ages, if not longer, had known about. How did he get talent? Who, or what, is the Soniky? How could the three keepers of the closet erase themselves from history? How are these items so deadly? Rafik took the opened lock from the chains, dropping it to the ground. "You ready?" He asked, turning to Anza.

She nodded, clenching her fists, eyes wide. Any moment now they would see what's inside the wardrobe.

Rafik whispered the last name, Sarafin's brother. "Furen."

32

The younger of the brothers appeared with his arms folded, leaning against the wardrobe. He was the only one that didn't look surprised at seeing Rafik and Anza. "I hope you know what you are doing, and it isn't anything stupid." Furen said, looking around the room.

"I'm not planning onto." Rafik said. "I just need a sword."

"If you need a sword then you have already done something stupid." Furen argued. "Enough blood has been spilled by those four relics, boy. In my day kings waged wars for these. We locked them up to make the world a safer place. So, again, I say I hope you know what you are doing. A prince once took the bag to rescue his mother from an evil ruler. Both died horribly, and a war started because of it. The sword was crafted to destroy evil, but it only absorbs it. The darkness will flow into the user like water into an empty vessel. They will succumb to its power and be nothing but a slave to the blade. The chalice steals your soul for unholy powers, and the eye should be left alone unless you want to invoke the wrath of the Four Kings."

"The Four Kings? That's just a legend." Anza said.

"If they're just a legend I guess the wizard's plan worked better than I thought." Furen said, a look of surprise growing on his face. He turned to face the wardrobe. "I was the last one you called, huh? Be prepared."

Faster than a room going dark from an extinguished candle, Furen vanished like the other two apparitions. The cloud of orange smoke billowed from nowhere, filling the room. Rafik waved his hand in front of him, brushing the smoke away. He grabbed the last lock, dropping it as the chains clattered to the floor. The orange smoke began to glow, as if it was fire. It glowed brighter, almost pulsing as it swirled around the room, condensing itself. The orange, now turning bright yellow, smoke coalesced just above the wardrobe. With a large crack like thunder the smoke shot up into the air in a beam of light.

"Guess that's how everyone gets notified." Rafik said.

"That's one question answered. Just a thousand more to go." Anza nodded. They both reached for the doors of the wardrobe and gasped. They weren't expecting to see someone inside it.

Chapter 4: The Mentor's Mirror

Datz, Nyler Peninsula, Alutopek

The boy and girl staring back at Rafik and Anza looked equally shocked. When Rafik moved, so did the boy. When Anza spoke, so did the girl. It took a moment of staring from one to the other before realizing it was a mirror. It had been years since either had seen their own reflection. Mirrors weren't that common in the ruins of Datz.

The inside of the wardrobe seemed much emptier than Rafik had anticipated. The back had the mirror reflecting the room. But only four objects rested inside. A small black bag was folded up and resting on the floor of the wardrobe. On top of the bag was a silver chalice with a large diamond shaped black jewel embedded into the center of the cup. Rubies lined the rim, giving it the look of blood. Inside the chalice was a bright ruby the size of a large marble. The more he looked at the marble the more he heard strange whispers filling his head. And resting next to it all was a sword. Its hilt was covered in a pattern of forest green and yellow jewels. A dragon's head jutted out at on each side of the guard.

Rafik reached for the sword, grabbing it by the scabbard. Anza pushed him to the side and reached for the chalice. She grabbed the marble out of the cup, and sudden visions of wars, people screaming, and violence filled Anza's head. She dropped the marble back into the chalice and grabbed the bag. Her eyes widened as she unfolded the common cloth that was the bag. The opening was easily wide enough to fit around a grown man's shoulders. She reached inside, searching for the bottom, but her hand just sifted through air. Curious, she poked her head into the bag; a moment later she was sucked in. The bag fell to the floor, not a trace of Anza remained.

The chalice clanged on the ground, the marble rolling away. Rafik spun around, searching for Anza. "Anza?" He asked, walking around the wardrobe. There was no sign of her. Making his way back around, he scooped up the marble and chalice, and heard a faint shout coming from the bag. He yanked the bag off the ground, expecting his sister to somehow be hiding underneath it. The muffled shouting seemed closer.

It sounded like his sister. Before Rafik could open the bag on his own an arm pulled on him. Rafik shouted, throwing the bag as far away from him as he could. A bulge suddenly appeared from within the bag. Anza came crawling out a moment later. "Rafik, come here." She said with a bright smile on her face.

"What happened?" He asked, staying rooted where he was.

Anza took the chalice with the marble from Rafik and returned to the bag. "Check this out." She opened the bag and crawled inside. Again, the bag rested on the ground without a trace of his sister being inside.

"What the…?" Rafik muttered, tilting his head in confusion. He inched toward the bag, unsure of what to expect. "A bag with no end. Interesting." He opened the bag, peering inside, eyes furrowed, and saw nothing but darkness. "Where are you, Anza?" He reached his hand inside and felt it being yanked. A moment later, he was sucked into the bag. Rafik held his breath as light emerged and he fell onto a stack of hay. He got to his feet, brushing himself off, and looked around. Beside him was a ladder leading to a trap door he knew would be the way out of here. Opposite the ladder was a writing desk. A portrait of a strange, ugly, and angry looking man hung above the desk. A bookcase stood on either side of the desk. Anza sat in a chair, smiling.

"What do you think?" She asked, marveling at this room. There was nothing else in this room, but the fact that it existed made them both look around in confusion and wonder. "A secret room!"

"What is this place?" Rafik asked.

"The bag with no end." Anna smirked.

"This room doesn't go on forever." Rafik argued.

Anna laughed. "No, but a whole lot more room than any other bag I know of.

He walked over to the portrait and noticed a note etched into the wall. The lettering at the base, titling the portrait seemed off. He wasn't sure if the letters were of a different language, or too weathered he couldn't read it. Either way, he couldn't decipher what it said. Losing interest in the portrait, he stole one last glance at the ugly man before turning his attention to a nearby bookshelf.

On one of the shelves, he found two glowing rocks. He recognized them instantly from one of the fairy tales he had heard growing up. There was a cotton white stone with a yellow streak in it as if it were lightning. He knew this stone instantly for what it was. It was the fabled lightstone. Squeezing it emitted a light that would never fade. The harder one squeezed, the brighter the light. Next to it was a dark blue stone with lighter blue particles within it. This was the waterstone. This one gushed out water. And just like the lightstone, squeezing it brought on its powers. Water would gush out of every part of the stone.

Rafik snatched both stones, his eyes wide. He always wondered what they were like. Both were incredibly light, and with their touch a slight tinge of electricity coursed through him. "Do you know what these are?" He asked, handing them gently over to his sister. The fairy tales never said how fragile they were. "They are the Element Stones."

Anza nodded, holding the two in either hand. "Yeah, we have a full set. See?" She said, pointing to the other bookshelf. Rafik's smile grew. One was bright orange with yellow and red particles swirling around and fading in and out as if it were breathing. This was the Firestone. It emitted flames from the stone when squeezed while protecting the user. And the last one was the Airstone. A sailor's dream, as Gorik would say. It was transparent, could barely be seen, almost as if it were a trick of the light. Squeezing it created a bubble of breathable air.

Each stone was said to have infinite power. Though no one had ever owned one that he knew of. Let alone all four. "Whoever had this bag last must have gone through a lot of trouble to find these." Rafik said, taking the stones back from Anza and placing them reverently back on the shelf.

Anza opened her mouth as if to speak when they heard a faint banging noise. Both shot their glances upwards towards the trap door of the ceiling. "What's going on?" She asked, trying to look out the trap door her brother was climbing the ladder too.

Rafik inched forward, poking his head out. He looked around the room, gasping as he noticed the stairs. Three pairs of feet were coming down from within the rest of the home. He grabbed the sword and retreated into the room within the bag. "Quiet." Rafik whispered, holding his finger to his lips. "Someone is down here."

Anza's face went pale. She heard the men stomp down the stairs, cursing and laughing. Rafik stood at the top of the ladder, ready to attack. He looked down at the sword in his hands, still in the scabbard. He undid the strap holding it in place and grabbed the hilt. The sheath fell to the floor below and Rafik soon followed from the weight of the sword.

It felt heavier now. Colder. His vision began to fade, much like before. He shook his head, thinking of Anza, trying to concentrate on the moment, not be lost in memories from the sword's history. As he fought back the vision he gazed at the sword, eyes wide and mouth agape. It was no longer an extra weight holding him down. It was like an extension of his arm he never thought he needed. A dark voice whispered into his head, demanding cooperation.

Rafik shook his head again, but the voice persisted, getting louder. More menacing. "Rafik, are you alright?" Anza asked, grabbing her brother's shoulder. "Rafik?"

"Yeah." Rafik muttered, shaking his head. "Just feels weird." He gazed at the blade. It was shimmering shadow, like midnight taking a solid form.

"There's nothing down here." Shouted one man, tearing Rafik away from his wonderment of the sword. Rafik could barely hear him.

"There has to be something." Another voice tried to reason. This one sounded older, stronger. "A beam of light doesn't just suddenly appear out of nowhere."

"Can you imagine if it's that kid? If we capture him the king will give us almost anything we want." A third voice asked. This one softer, more feminine than the other two.

"I doubt he will be here. He hasn't been found yet, and it has been nearly a month. He's probably dead." The first voice said. "King Vanarzir left him pretty burned up. Try coming back from that."

"You never know. That's why we need to search everywhere. Remember? King's orders." The older man replied.

"Rafik! They're Kylix soldiers!" Anza squealed in a high pitch whisper.

"What was that?" The woman asked. Rafik heard her step closer to the bag, but they hadn't noticed it yet.

"I didn't hear anything." The older one said, stepping closer.

"What's that by your feet?" The other man asked.

Rafik gripped the sword tighter, waiting for them to open the bag and discover them. The moment never happened. "Look what I found." The woman said, picking up the bag. "There isn't anything in it, though."

"Well, whoever was here must have dropped it. We went in through the front; they must have escaped through the back." The older man growled.

The two children felt a shift in the room as the woman carried them away. Rafik tried to poke his head out, and the woman slouched from the sudden weight. He quickly ducked back into the room, and onto the floor, waiting for them to enter. He gripped the sword with both hands, the dark voice insisting on controlling Rafik.

He shook his head. "Get out of my head." He whispered. "Get out of my head."

'If you want to live, you won't tell me that again.' The voice snarled. A pulse, almost like a shock, went from Rafik's hands up to his head. *'Don't fight me.'*

"Are you okay?" The first man asked.

"Yeah, just seemed like there was something in here for a moment. Lost my balance is all." The woman said. She flipped the bag upside down and shook it, but nothing came out. "Must be my imagination."

"Someone got to the celebratory drink before we finished, I see." The older man joked.

"Hey captain, we need to watch her. I think she's going crazy." The first man laughed.

Rafik heard the two push each other back and forth, but nothing within the room moved. He looked around and allowed his mind to wander. How was this possible? The stone walls seemed ancient and worn. The only thing strange or showed any sign of personality was the disturbing portrait behind him.

He turned to look at the portrait of the ugly, bald man. His red eyes were in the shape of a cat's. His nose narrow, and cheeks full as if stuffed with food. A thin line was drawn for a frown, and little fuzz running along the jaw. His ears were lower than the average man's, almost ending in a point. And his pale skin seemed to have a slight tint of violet. No matter where in the room Rafik or Anza stood, it looked like the man was watching them.

"That thing freaks me out." Anza whispered, noticing that her brother was now looking at the portrait instead of the trap door.

"Me too." Rafik agreed. He walked over to the portrait and took it off the wall. It was surprisingly light for the heavy frame it was set in. He put the picture down, leaning it against the shelf, the portrait facing the wall. Behind the portrait was another mirror, the same size as the picture. The two looked in it and found the distorted reflections of themselves. A strange fog of yellows, reds, and blues swirled around in the mirror, hiding the children's images. A silhouette of a figure emerged from the fog. Rafik could make out the pointed hat and the gnarled crook in its hand.

"Is that a wizard?" Anza asked, both her and her brother's head cocked.

"Izamar?" Rafik whispered. The wizard suddenly appearing in full view a moment later, angry.

"Don't say my name!" He ordered in a loud, booming voice. His eyes narrowed, darting between the two children.

"SSSHHH!" Rafik and Anza said at the same time.

The wizard looked around, startled at being silenced in such a manner. "Young one. It's you." He sighed, after noticing Rafik.

"What are you doing here?" Rafik asked, glancing back at the ladder, hoping his captors hadn't heard the wizard.

"Shouldn't you be dead or something?" Anza asked.

Izamar laughed. "This isn't just a mirror, young ones. It's like a gate of sorts. It conjures spirits who can help you. If they have been in contact with the mirror, that is. I called it the Mentor's Mirror."

"How can you help us?" Rafik asked. He still held the sword in his hand. The deep and dark voice growled from within his head. It hated Izamar. He could feel it. Rafik fought back the urge to slash at the mirror, shattering it.

Izamar shrugged. "You tell me. One of you summoned me here."

"What? No we didn't." Anza snapped.

"One of you must have. Even if you didn't realize it." Izamar said. He looked from one child to the next. "I'm guessing it was you." He pointed at Rafik. "You found the sword. How do you like *Blaridane?*"

"Blaridane?" Rafik asked, looking down at the sword. "That's its name? Maybe I did? We are being taken. By Kylix soldiers."

"Think you can cast a spell on them or something?" Anza smirked, imaging the skeletal soldiers turning into actual skeletons and crumbling to the ground.

"Unfortunately, we can't interact directly with the physical world from the Mentor's Mirror." Izamar sighed. "We can only give advice and teach. Or just keep you company."

"What the...?" The woman's voice said in bewilderment behind the two children before falling and crashing to the floor.

Without thinking the dark voice within Rafik roared. He spun around, sword at the ready. *'KILL!'* It shouted. Rafik fought back, screaming, tearing his own body away from the charge.

"Rafik?" Anza asked.

"It's the sword." Izamar explained. "He's fighting the command of the sword."

The woman shook her head, getting to her feet. Shouts from above echoed into the room. "Two more children for the army." She smirked. A moment later another soldier fell from the ceiling, crashing onto the woman.

Anza stood petrified. Flashes of watching her fellow Datians fall earlier ran through her mind. The skeletal armor looked so real. Especially the skull helmet.

'KILL!' The voice repeated within Rafik.

"No!" Rafik shouted, startling Anza.

'If you want to protect your sister, you will obey!' The voice demanded. Rafik turned to his sister. She couldn't take her eyes off the two Kylix soldiers. Her eyes large and round, hands visibly shaking.

"Fine." Rafik nodded. He closed his eyes and felt the cold embrace of the spirit in the sword take over. He could feel its movements from ages ago. He saw the memories of every fight the sword fought in. Not one was lost.

"What? Where are we?" The man's voice said. The two appeared so similar in their armor Rafik couldn't tell them apart. The man got to his feet and looked at the children. "Well, well, well. Look what we have here. We have a magic bag and two more children for the army. King Vanarzir will be pleased. Even if it isn't that kid we're after."

"We aren't going anywhere." Rafik snapped, his voice deeper than usual. His usual calm brown eyes were burning with hatred and anger. "Anza, stay behind me."

"You think you can stop me?" The man laughed, taking out his own sword. "Just because you have a fancy sword doesn't mean you are going to win. It's about how you use it."

"Is everything alright?" A voice shouted form above.

"Yeah, Captain. We just found two more kids trying to hide." The man hollered back.

"Is either of them Xeo?" The captain asked.

"No." Rafik yelled back. He felt the energy surge through him, pulsing outwards from the sword. The power he had! He could get used to this. He screamed, charged forward, slashing his sword at the man as the woman rolled to the side and out of the way. Rafik hacked at the soldier, blocking every strike with his own blade. Rafik tossed the blade from one hand to the other, spun around and swiped, getting the soldier in the gut.

The soldier shouted in pain as it cut through his armor like a hot knife through butter. "You know what you're doing. I'll admit that." He said. The soldier produced two knives sheathed on the small of his back. "But you won't win." He lunged forward, close enough Rafik couldn't use the sword.

Rafik watched as his own body move on its own accord. The sword was controlling him now. He could only watch as he took a step back, turned the sword around so the hilt was up and ducked. The man sprang forward, trying to close the gap, and Rafik shot up, jamming the hilt into the open wound on the stomach. The soldier screamed in agony until Rafik twirled the sword around and in one swift motion moved it across the soldier's neck. He fell to the floor, not making another move.

The woman stepped forward, trying to catch Rafik by surprise. Rafik spun around, blocking the blow just in time. She attempted to kick him as the blades were locked. Rafik stopped resisting, causing both blades to shift and her to lose balance. As she regained control Rafik slashed at her.

Anza screamed, watching the soldier's head fall to the floor faster than her body. The trapdoor above opened, and the captain fell into the room. Not wasting time, he dashed over and grabbed Anza, a knife at her throat. "Rafik!" She cried.

Rafik turned, the anger burning brighter in his eyes as he saw his sister in the skeleton's clutches. He was indeed a captain. A green cape draped over his left shoulder and a small circle of

43

thorns atop his skull indicated his rank. "No, you aren't Xeo." The captain said. "Now drop the sword, or she dies."

"Ya shire." Rafik cursed. A swear word he had picked up while sailing with Gorik and his father. There was nothing more he wanted than to keep his sister safe. The voice roared with anger within him. *'Forget the girl! Kill him!'* Rafik fought the urge to charge forward, dropping the sword. The moment the sword left his touch the voice stopped, the power gone, all the hatred and anger that welled inside him evaporated. He fell back against the wall, knees weak and arms shaking. The sword clattered to the ground, and he stared at it. He wanted nothing more than to grab it again and feel that power.

"Smart choice, boy." The captain said, releasing Anza and shoving her towards Rafik. He pulled some rope from one of the fallen solder's belts and tied the two children up. "Just in time for the executions. You can watch before we ship you off. Don't try anything funny." He said, glancing at the mirror before climbing the ladder and leaving the room.

"What are we going to do?" Anza asked once the trapdoor shut.

"I'm not sure yet." Rafik said, already trying to get loose from the rope.

"I didn't know you knew how to fight like that." Anza said. "That was amazing. I've never seen someone move like that."

"That's because it wasn't him." Izamar said, reappearing in the mirror. "It was *Blaridane*."

"The sword?" Anza asked. "How?"

"There is an ancient technique mixing the skills of a magician and that of a smith. It's called Blood Metal." Izamar explained. "Blaridane is a sword forged of blood metal. A piece of both smith and witch or wizard reside in it. Because of this, it holds the memories of them both."

"Is that what I was seeing?" Rafik asked. "When I allowed it to take over me, I saw things. But not like my own visions. They were like…"

"Your own memories." Izamar answered. "Yes. You will have several of the memories. Probably even learned some skill using the sword as well. Only the one who crafted the item of Blood Metal can truly control it. If any other does, they slowly get possessed until there is nothing left of the host. You needed a sword, young one. But I urge you to find a new one. One that won't take your soul."

Rafik nodded, staring at the blade. The edges glinted with crimson now. "I don't want to touch that thing. Izamar, can you help us get out of here?"

Izamar shook his head. "I fear I cannot. But I can suggest to maybe look around. I'm sure there is something here you can use to cut through the rope?"

The two were tied back-to-back in the middle of the room. Their legs weren't bound, but their hands and necks were. "We could use one of his knives?" Anza suggested, jerking her head toward the ladder where the first soldier fell.

"I have a better idea." Rafik smiled. "Here, let's get up." They pushed against each other's backs as they slowly made their way to their feet. Anza followed as Rafik took the lead, heading to one of the shelves. He raised his foot to the shelf, kicking it. The airstone and firestone clattered to the ground.

They both lowered themselves to the ground. Rafik reached blindly at the firestone, finally grabbing it. It was warm, like a midsummer day's heat gently radiating. He squeezed the stone just for a moment and heard Anza yelp.

"You're burning me!" She shouted. "Stop!"

"What? Oh, sorry." Rafik said, instantly dropping the stone. The firestone granted the user protection from the flames. Nobody else. "What if we both grabbed it?" He grabbed the stone and pressed it against Anza's palm. They both pushed on the stone, and a fire roared to life. A moment later the ropes were gone.

"Great job!" Izamar smiled gleefully. "I would have gone with Anza's idea myself, but I like the way you think."

45

"I've always wanted to use the firestone." Rafik said. "Controlling fire would be amazing. Can I trade my talent for that?"

Izamar shook his head. "You don't have a choice in what you get. Be grateful you have talent at all."

"Well, now what?" Anza asked. She couldn't stop staring at the bodies on the ground. Flashes of watching her mom fall to the Kylix kept creeping in.

"Now we wait." Rafik said, glaring at the door in the ceiling. "Wait until we can escape." He turned his attention to the two bodies on the floor. His face paled. He had done this. He had never killed another person before, let alone two. Even if the spirit of the sword controlled his body at the time, Rafik had allowed it. He began to lose himself in his own thoughts, trying to grapple with what he had just done.

Chapter 5: Under the City

Datz, Nyler Peninsula, Alutopek

Gorik's vision blurred, lifting his head. He assumed some time had passed. When he was captured it was bright out. But now it was dark, the only light coming from torches. He knew he had fallen asleep but didn't think for that long. He noticed the guards who captured him were still close by. That was a relief. If he wanted to escape, they had to be nearby. The sailor finally tried to move, and noticed he was in chains. "That's new." He whispered to himself. His hands were behind his back and even his neck was chained to his waist so he could barely look up. His legs were free, as his peg leg prevented him from being shackled.

The sailor was sitting against a brick wall in the center of Datz. Books and legends say the center used to be a beautiful temple dedicated to the gods. Now it was little more than a large pond with jutting stones out of it, all resting in a massive crater. The Pond of Memories. Next to him were the city leaders who all concealed their fright well. Although Gorik could tell otherwise. Countless sailors had the same look of foolish bravery while on the seas and coming against a ferocious storm. He was glad to see he was sitting next to his friend, Hektor, though. It was the only one of the city leaders he liked.

Coincidentally, Hektor was the only one of the city leaders who tolerated Gorik. Unlike the sailor who was short and bald, Hektor was rail thin, tall, and a head full of messy grey hairs. His crooked nose and narrowed eyes always gave off the look of a permanent scowl on his face. Most everyone knew it was the exact opposite. He was one of the most lighthearted people Gorik had ever met.

Next to Hektor was Salina, the only woman on the council, and true heir to rule over Datz. She still appeared young and her vibrant green eyes and smooth skin perpetuated that belief. And beside Salina was the oldest of the three, Zarohm. Zarohm was the eternal pessimist. His wrinkled face and pitted eyes scared children and intimidated most adults.

"Did I miss anything?" Gorik whispered.

"Hey!" One of the guards yelled at him, kicking his foot and peg leg. "No talking."

Before Gorik could make a witty reply, he noticed people shuffling into the town center. With his head chained down he couldn't see who, but it sounded like several dozen. Those that were leading the way were barefoot and in tattered clothes. Gorik figured they were all prisoners the Kylix had captured. And behind them was the unmistakable armor of the Kylix soldiers. The sailor glared at the soldier's feet, wanting to leap out and stop them all. Concealing his anger, Gorik smiled. He would get his revenge soon.

One soldier stepped forward, calming the mumbling voices, and clearing his throat. "Another victory for the great King Vanarzir!" He shouted. Rounds of cheers and applause echoed around Gorik. "And to the victor goes the spoils. I am newly promoted Commander Jinuk. And our great king needs your children to build his army. You went against him. If you would have graciously accepted his request, you would live and be honored as parents of heroes. Now you are all traitors and must be punished as such. According to Alutopek law, all traitors must be put to death."

A gasp came from some of the prisoners. Others began sobbing even more. Gorik had expected this when he got caught. But hearing it confirmed was still unnerving. The prisoners were quickly silenced, and Jinuk continued. "The leaders shall die first as they were the ones who could have put a stop to this. But our king isn't coldhearted. There is time for redemption. King Vanarzir has declared that anyone who can give reliable information about the boy named Xeo, or the mysterious rider who helped him escape, shall be spared. Otherwise, your life is now forfeit. Now, bring up the first leader. The old one."

A Kylix soldier grabbed Zarohm's arm, hoisting him up. He dragged him to where the speaker was standing, Zarohm struggling the entire way. The former leader was pushed down to his knees. Commander Jinuk removed his helmet, revealing a smug grin, staring coldly at Zarohm. "So, do you know anything about Xeo and his whereabouts?" The commander asked.

Zarohm smiled and nodded his head. "Yes." He finally answered. He turned his head so he could glare up at the Kylix soldier standing above him. "Xeo is destined to overthrow King Vanarzir. Anyone who says any different is a fool. He's on his way to be king even as we speak."

Commander Jinuk nodded, and without warning another stepped forward with a large axe. In one swift motion Zarohm's head fell to the floor and rolled away from the collapsing body. "Any more stupidity like that and all of you will die." He yelled. "Give me the next one. Maybe she will be more cooperative."

"Wait!" A voice shouted, pushing his way through the crowds. Gorik's eyes full of hope drained in an instant. It was just another Kylix soldier, although this one had a dark green cape draped over his left shoulder.

"What is it, Captain Bohdin?" Jinuk snapped.

"Commander Jinuk," The captain said between tight lips. "Where is the king? I have found something he should be interested in."

"If it is the new purse you are sporting, I doubt the king cares about your newest piece of fashion." Jinuk snapped. A small fit of laughter erupted from the crowd. Even Gorik smiled. "This is why you are still a captain while I'm now commander."

"No, it's what's in the bag." The captain said, ignoring the insult. "Look in the bag."

"What could possibly be in there that warrants the king's attention?" Jinuk scoffed.

"Just look." Captain Bohdin insisted, the note of aggravation apparent as he opened the bag.

The sailor couldn't believe what he saw next. And neither could anyone else as they all gasped with astonishment. As Commander Jinuk began to investigate the plain, black, bag he was sucked in. The bag didn't grow any larger, and he didn't fall out of

49

the bottom of the bag either. He was just gone. The prisoners and soldiers all began muttering, asking what they had just seen. As the murmuring and whispering began to evolve to shouts and of confusion, Jinuk's head popped out of the bag. His body was soon to follow along with a young man Gorik recognized instantly. His messy brown hair with the tint of red, the fierceness in his stare and hint of mischief in his smile was just like his father's.

"Before anyone asks," Commander Jinuk began, a look of amazement on his face. "This isn't Xeo. But this bag and its contents, including this boy and the girl still down there, is particularly important indeed."

"I told you." Captain Bohdin said. "Now, where is the king?"

"You there." Jinuk said, pointing at a soldier in the crowd. "Go fetch the king. Tell him I have found a great gift for His Majesty."

"You?" Bohdin yelled. "I found it."

"I oversee this attack. And what you or anyone else finds under me belongs to me." Jinuk yelled.

Captain Bohdin growled, throwing the bag on the floor.

Gorik saw the chance he had been waiting for. In an instant he sprang to his feet and ran into one of the Kylix guards who had subdued him earlier that day. Gorik didn't stop and continued charging forward until the soldier lost his footing and stumbled. Gorik tilted his head as he was running into a torch on a nearby wall. He hit the torch, knocking it off and embers flew into the air. Embers scattered into the air and drifted. Some landed on the soldier where the black powder Gorik had thrown earlier. He dropped to the ground as a tremendous explosion obliterated the nearby wall, startling everyone from the sudden commotion. He glanced up and saw a smoking bottom half of the Kylix soldier.

The sailor scrambled to his feet and tackled another of the guards, sending him into the chaos. A burning bit of debris hit the soldier, catching his armor on fire the black sand had settled from earlier. Kylix soldiers stared at Gorik, unsure of what to do. The two he had touched seemingly caught fire from nothing.

"Stop him!" Jinuk shouted, pointing at the sailor.

Hektor had managed to wriggle himself out of his chains and helped Salina out of hers. He dashed to his friend and got the chains around Gorik undone. Gorik looked up at his friend astonished. "Always be prepared." He laughed, showing several small pins in his hand.

Gorik smiled and nodded. "We need to get to the pond. Swim to the bottom and find the tunnels.

Hektor looked at his friend in bewilderment. "No one even knows if those tunnels actually exist. And you want us to just swim to the bottom?" Before Gorik could respond he noticed the Kylix soldiers surrounding them. It was either the pond or fight through a heavily armed wall of soldiers. "To the pond!" He shouted. Salina and Gorik nodded, all three of them sprinting towards the pond. Kylix soldiers barred their way. Hektor slid to the ground and rolled the same time Salina tried to jump over them. Some were focused on Salina while others to Hektor. The confusion caused all of them to be knocked over and the two city leaders got away, dropping into the water. Some soldiers jumped in after them.

Gorik stayed and fought, getting a sword from one of the fallen soldiers. He helped others get into the water, making clear pathways for others to escape. During a moment of reprieve, Gorik grabbed a piece of timber from one of his many pockets. He struck it against his peg leg and the piece of wood lit up. Gorik tossed it at a group of Kylix soldiers who all winced, expecting it to explode. With the focus on the burning wood, he fished into another pocket, grabbed the last of his black powder, and tossed it at the already dying flame. Another explosion went off, this one blasting Gorik back. He landed just feet from the pond's edge.

"Where are you?" He mumbled to himself, looking around, trying to find Rafik.

Once the commotion started, Rafik jumped back into the bag as Captain Bohdin lunged for him. A moment later Rafik reappeared with Blaridane in hand. Anza crept out soon after, fists clenched. Rafik swiped at the Kylix soldiers, fighting back four at once. He heard the call to get to the pond and made his way towards it. The power of Blaridane flowed through him. He felt like a marionet as it controlled his movement.

One soldier tried sneaking up on Rafik. Anza pushed out her fist, screaming, sending a gush of water into the soldier. "What are you doing?" Rafik snapped, spinning around.

"Saving your butt." Anza replied, shooting water at another solider and scooping up the bag with her free hand. "You're welcome."

"You should be in the bag."

Anza shook her head. "If you're scared you can get in the bag."

"Ya shire." Rafik cursed. "Just stay close to me. Come on."

The captain got to his feet and started for Rafik and Anza. Jinuk grabbed the captain's shoulder, yelling at him. "This is all your fault! Look at what happened! I had complete control and order until you arrived."

Bohdin roared, watching Rafik and Anza jump into the water and out of sight. "We can still get them. Tell everyone to surround the pond. Some go in after them!"

Gorik noticed Rafik jump into the water, a look of pride on his face as he watched his niece and nephew defend themselves so well from the Kylix soldiers. Satisfied, he went in after the children.

Jinuk cursed. Not only would he have to report that Xeo was still out there, but that all their prisoners had gotten away, and a riot was now happening. He had ordered his soldiers to do as Bohdin suggested, surround the pond. Arrows at the ready. Captain Bohdin was one of the few high-ranking officers who went after Rafik and the others.

Legends say that it was ages ago, when Salina's ancestors were the sole ruler over Datz, that the center of the city was a great temple. It was a wonder that most marveled at as people went in and out of Alutopek. It was said to be as tall as a mountain and evoked such beauty that some just stopped and stared in wonder, gazing at it. Beneath the temple was said to have tunnels leading to all over Datz, some leading to a whole other world.

Depending on the version of story, the temple collapsed from marauders, an earthquake, or a king who wanted the gods to be forgotten. In all versions, the results were the same. The temple was destroyed. The ancient Datian builders removed most of the rubble but left its foundation as a memorial to those lives lost in its collapse. What is known, is that when the Black Wall was formed a tsunami ravished Datz, flooding the memorial. Most dubbed it the Pond of Memories, though, as it always evoked a kind of reverence and self-reflection.

But not today.

The confusion erupted everywhere. Datians scattered into the streets, while others listened and jumped into the pond. The soldiers jumping in after them sank, while the villagers waded in place for further direction. Other soldiers shot arrows, and the remaining villagers dived into the pond, following one another blindly.

Gorik was positive the tunnels would be there. There were enough stories about them. But doubt trickled into his mind as he swam deeper into the depths. Even if there were tunnels, how many would be able to hold their breath long enough to find them?

The pond was murky, and hard to see one's hand in front of their face. Random stones stuck out like teeth from a larger animal. Rafik felt a tap on his side. He looked down to see his sister's hand holding something. It looked like a bubble in her hand. Rafik smiled as he realized what it was. He nodded, and she squeezed the stone.

Anza squeezed, and a surge of water pushed away from her hand. As the water pushed away a bubble of air surrounded them. Instead of floating, Rafik fell to the bottom of the bubble, splashing on the new surface. "This is crazy!" Anza shouted with a smile, watching a Kylix soldier swim towards them, fall through the bubble with a scream, and splash to the water below.

"How is this possible?" Rafik asked. The bubble provided air, but they could only see as far as the air went. The murky depths were still too dark, they couldn't even see the shapes of others as they came crashing through the bubble.

Anza held the air bubble above her head, squeezing tighter. The bubble grew and other Datians joined them. Any Kylix soldier trying to get in was pushed away. Rafik held his sword in the air, poking at anyone with armor to leave the bubble. They slowly descended, holding the airstone tighter.

Gorik and two Kylix soldiers exploded from the side of the bubble. Rafik and Anza burst into laughter seeing his face. Gorik was the first to reemerge, cursing and thanking the gods for the bubble. "How-how is this possible?" He asked, in awe after calming down. He stuck his hand out of the air bubble and felt the cool water surround it. "Just when you think you've seen everything."

"Thank Anza." Rafik said, smiling at his sister.

"Hi Gorik." She waved, giggling as the bubble shifted.

"Every sailor's dream." Gorik gasped. "An airstone."

"The other three are in the bag." Anza said.

"Sounds like we have some stories to share." Gorik said.

Anza squeezed with both hands and the bubble grew. The group drifted to the bottom, sinking into the mud on the ground. They pushed out the soldiers, crowding around Anza as they walked blindly. "Where are we going?" She asked.

"There should be a trap door of some sort." Gorik answered. Leads to the tunnels.

"We could just stay here in this bubble. Wait until the Kylix think we're all dead." Salina suggested, pushing her way through the crowd. She looked Rafik up and down and scoffed. "How the son of a drunkard found something so valuable is beyond me."

"I found this one, thank you." Anza said, returning the glare.

Rafik's brows furrowed as he strained to not use the sword. The voice in his head from Blaridane screamed to slash at Salina. Imagining it felt good. The urges to actually do it were getting stronger. "No." He whispered to himself.

"Do you know how long they'll be in the city, Salina? Until then we will just pop our heads up to check where they can pick us off. Great idea." Gorik said. "No, we need to find these tunnels."

"And what are we going to do if we find the tunnels? If they even exist?"

"Get away from the Kylix." Rafik said.

Gorik smiled. "The boy is right."

"We're listening to a child now, is that it?" Salina spat, cutting off Rafik and Gorik from saying anything else.

"How someone so bitter and so lonely makes perfect sense to me." Gorik said, stepping between Salina and his nephew.

"Of course you would defend him. A dwarf with a gimp." The venomous glare she gave Gorik could almost be felt by others.

"That's enough." Hektor snapped, stepping out of the crowd. "Gorik is right. We can't stay here. Sitting here for who knows how long. Whether you like it or not, we are all stuck down here together. We need to find these tunnels."

The voice of Blaridane screamed through Rafik as he locked eyes with Salina. He gripped the sword tighter, wanting to give in to this temptation. How fast he could strike her down. He imagined it so clearly in his head.

"What would we do if we go through the tunnels? If they exist." Salina asked, her calm tone betrayed the feeling Rafik knew she was having. She might not have a cursed sword tempting her to murder, but he knew that's what she was contemplating. The look in her eyes gave it away.

"The *River Lizard* is here. I destroyed the entrance to the dock so the Kylix can't get to it. One of the tunnel pathways should lead to the dock. I can ferry everyone to the Sarason Fortress until the Kylix leave. And then from there to safety." Gorik explained. "I did just get back from Emerald."

"What did they say?" Hektor asked.

"They are offering us refuge. We just need to get there." Gorik said.

Hektor nodded. "I say we go with Gorik's plan."

Several others from the crowd spoke up in agreement. "I'm with you, Gorik." Rafik said. "Anza and I are."

"Well, I guess that settles it. If you're the one with the airstone," pointing to Anza, "And you're coming with me, I can't imagine everyone can hold their breath for very long." Gorik laughed. "I guess the next step is finding the entrance."

Anza stifled a laugh, watching Salina scowl, her face crinkle even more than usual, before slinking back into the crowd. "I've missed you, Uncle Gorik."

"It's good to see you two. I think all of us are happy you're here."

Anza smiled, straining to pull her foot out of the thick mud. It was like walking through tree sap. "Why don't you get in the bag?" Rafik suggested.

"I can handle this." Anza said, nearly falling over with another step.

"You're as stubborn as your father." Gorik sighed.

Anza flashed a smile at Gorik, her face growing red.

By now the Kylix had stopped finding them. Every so often a fish would swim into the bubble and fall to the bottom, swimming away. They slowly inched along, keeping their eyes peeled for any sign of a door. "How are we to find it if there's all this mud?" Salina asked.

Gorik had wondered this. He hoped the door wasn't buried. Not wanting to give her the satisfaction of knowing she may be right; he ignored her comment. "Just stop complaining and keep looking."

The crowd wandered, searching for any clue of a hidden entrance. The seabed was littered with algae covered stones, crumbled walls, and even an archway. Seeing any of it through the murky water was hard enough. Even if they did find it, who was to say they would recognize it in the first place? Where there wasn't stone, it was thick sand, sucking in every step like a vacuum. Gorik compared it to the swampland of the Lahmora Swamps. Twice Rafik had to step over a soldier or Datian who had recently drowned. Looking at them unnerved Rafik. He wanted to let go of

56

Blaridane but didn't want to be caught off guard. Seeing the bodies seemed to intensify the sword's voice.

'You can't get rid of me.' The cold voice snarled. *'It is too late now. You need me.'*

'Yeah, well, if we don't find a way out of here, you'll be lost to this pond forever.' Rafik replied to the voice.

The cold of the voice retreated. Rafik wondered if he had scared it off. He couldn't imagine a possessed or evil sword would enjoy rusting away into nothing. *'You're going the wrong way.'* The voice said, suddenly appearing.

"Excuse me?" Rafik asked. Gorik turned to look at him, but Rafik shook his head, dismissing him.

Blaridane showed Rafik another memory. It was being carried through a torch lit hall, to a great doorway. The doorway, however, built into the floor. The memory faded and Rafik saw the hall the memory had shown him. He was going in the opposite direction. "I think it's this way." Rafik said, grabbing Gorik's shoulder. "It's the other way."

"How do you know?" Gorik asked.

"Kind of hard to explain. But trust me. It's the other way." Rafik said.

"Rafik has talent now." Anza beamed.

"Talent! Really?" Gorik asked, patting him on the back.

"No. Well, yes. But that's not how I know. I think." Rafik said. "I don't know, really."

"Everyone let's turn around. I believe the tunnel entrance is in the other direction." Gorik shouted. "Got a little lost. A bit murky down here." The crowd muttered in agreement. It was worse looking down here in the darkness than searching through a vat of honey for a piece of copper.

A few Datians laughed. Hektor smiled. Salina made a sour face at Gorik and glared at Rafik.

It wasn't much longer that they had found something. Glints of gold shimmered on the seabed. Covered in algae, a few stones resting atop it, they almost missed it. The sword's voice screamed in Rafik's head, causing him to stop. It was then that they noticed the noise. When stepping on the ground it sounded as though there was something hollow beneath it. The group scrambled for the entrance, scraping away algae and moving the stones. Finally, resting below them were a pair of doors. They were carved with half circles capping off the ends of other half circles.

"I know that mark." Gorik said, pointing at the doors. "Immortals."

"Excuse me?" Salina scoffed. "You believe in those fairy tales?"

Gorik ignored her and looked at Rafik and Hektor. "A long time ago this symbol was used for the Immortals. But then thieves used it to mark a home with value. It's a well-known symbol for treasure amongst sailors."

"Stop marveling at the doors and just open them." Salina snapped, bending over, and grabbing at the handles. They didn't budge.

"No, they're locked." Gorik said, ignoring Salina's tugging. "Follow the pattern." He traced his finger along the largest half circle. There wasn't a line connecting the ends, just another semicircle covering the end. The half circles slowly got smaller as the ends multiplied. It was a sign Rafik had never seen before, but one that mesmerized him and others.

"What are we looking for?" Hektor asked, tracing the symbol with his finger.

"Something that is off. It doesn't match." Gorik said.

'It's right there.' Blaridane said. Even without pointing, Rafik looked in the direction he felt the sword urge him to. Sure enough, one of the smaller half circles was turned, so it wasn't capping the one that came before it.

"Right here." Rafik said, pointing at the spot in the carving.

"Good eye, Rafik." Gorik smiled.

"I could have found it if I wanted to." Salina said.

Gorik ignored her. He put his finger in the carving and applied pressure. The noise of stone scraping against stone echoed around the bubble. The small half circle shifted and began to rotate. Once in the correct position it locked into place and a loud click signaled their success. Salina pulled at the doors, and with ease, they both opened.

An unnatural darkness seemed to radiate from the entryway. "This looks friendly." Rafik sighed.

Salina glared at him and Gorik. "Lead the way." She hissed.

Rafik stayed back with Anza, waiting for everyone to make their way into the darkness. "Get in the bag." He ordered.

"What?" Anza snapped, letting go of the airstone as the two entered.

"I have a bad feeling about this place." Rafik said, closing the door as water filled the void the bubble left.

"I can handle it." Anza said, pushing her way past her brother. "I'm not a little girl."

Rafik noticed her trembling hands, and the slight twang in her voice. "No, you're my little sister. And I couldn't live with myself if I let something happen to you. I'll get you if anything exciting happens. Until then, get in the bag."

Anza stared up at her brother. She opened her mouth but noticed the stern stare in his eyes. This wasn't an argument she was going to win anytime soon. Truth be told, as she saw the darkness radiating from the tunnel entrance, she didn't want to take a step further. "You better get me if something happens. I don't want to miss anything."

"I promise." He held the bag open as Anza disappeared into the secret room within. It still confused him how any of this was possible.

Within the secret room of the bag, Anza waited. Being alone in here sent a shiver down her spine. The mirror had ghosts, and there was a portrait of an ugly man that appeared as if it wanted to tarnish her soul. She tried looking around, but her eyes kept getting drawn to the two Kylix soldiers her brother had killed.

There they were. Motionless. Lifeless. It was strange to think not even a day earlier they were both alive. They had lives of

59

their own. Families. Friends. Would they even know what happened to them? Would they care?

The thought of her mother kept entering her mind as she stared at the corpses. Like the soldiers, yesterday she was alive. Now she was gone. She had sacrificed herself to save them. Anza furrowed her brow, unsure of how to feel about that. She had sneaked a glance as they were jettisoned out of Datz, watching her mother's last moments.

Unlike Rafik, who was fearless, she was full of it. She remembered her mother holding her close as thunderstorms raged in the middle of the night. Waves would crash into homes and wind threatening to topple everything in its path. She would hold her and tell her, "All storms pass. Be the mountain that stands firm through it." She wondered how long this storm would last. And like the mountain, she intended on staying strong.

The Kylix soldiers scared her. Even the darkened tunnels frightened her. And losing her brother, like she had just lost her mother, petrified her. As hard as she tried to resist, tears trickled down. She cried for her mother who had given her life. They were foolish enough to believe in the stories of the forest and walk back into the lion's den. Now they were beneath the pond, in long forgotten tunnels, and in the unknown.

"Why are you crying?" A voice asked. Anza looked up and saw the wizard, Izamar, once more.

"What? I...nothing. I'm fine." Anza said, feeling silly for about to confess to a stranger all she had worried and feared.

"Crying over nothing isn't something I would personally cry over, but, then again, times have changed, I suppose." Izamar sighed, smiling.

Anza returned the smile and looked at his twinkling eyes. "You would laugh at me." She said, looking back down at the floor.

"Little girl, I have seen monstrosities in my lifetime. But the thing that breaks my heart most is seeing a child cry. There is no reason they should be. So, tell me, how can I help?" The wizard asked.

60

The young girl looked up at Izamar, noticing the sincerity in his black eyes. The half-smile gleamed safe and protecting. She didn't remember much of her father, but she imagined he had those features. "C-Can I see my mother?"

Izamar bowed his head and sighed. "She never interacted with this mirror. Unfortunately, not." He shook his head. "But I think I have an idea. Stay right here." Before Anza could respond Izamar vanished. She stared at the mirror a moment before hearing something rustling.

Tentatively, Anza crept over to the shelf. Inch by inch, body quivering. She jumped back when she noticed the portrait move. Anza bit her lip and grabbed the portrait, turning it around. The ugly man shifted within the frame and looked at Anza. "I can help you." He said in a deep, scratchy, voice. Anza fainted; her jaw agape.

"We're safe." Rafik muttered, repeating it to himself. Descending a dozen stairs, Rafik looked around the group of Datians. Before the Black Wall Datz was one of the largest cities with tens of thousands of residents. After the Black Wall there was maybe only a 100. But now, all that was left, were maybe a few dozen at most. "Well, what's left of us."

"Thank you, boy." Hektor said, clapping Rafik on the back. Others thanked him as well. "If you and your sister didn't have that stone, we'd all be dead."

"Where'd you get that stone? And the bag for that matter?" Salina asked, eying Rafik. She reminded Rafik of a snake. The way she spoke and slinked around. Though he imagined most snakes would be friendlier.

"Found it." Rafik said, wanting to be as vague as possible. "In an old farmhouse."

"Let me see it." Salina snapped. "I've never seen such a thing. If you found it within Datz it belongs to me."

"Aye, it could go for a high price." Gorik said. "Hold onto it, Rafik. You never know what a thief looks like until it's too late."

"I am no thief!" Salina yelled.

"I can't let you see it." Rafik said, pulling the bag closer to him. "It's dirty."

Salina scoffed. "You're as bad of a liar as your father. Hopefully, you won't become a drunk, too."

Rafik lunged forward, screaming. He didn't need urging from Blaridane. Nobody speaks ill of his father. He screamed, cursing at Salina. Blaridane cooed, encouraging the wanted violence.

Gorik and Hektor pulled Rafik back, refusing to let him go. "That's enough, Salina." The sailor said sternly. "Drane was a good man. Everyone knows that."

"Yeah, he was…until he picked up a bottle." Salina laughed. "Trust me."

"I didn't know you were one of *those* kinds of girls." Rafik snapped, spitting at Salina's feet. "Just a bottle and you'll get with anyone?"

Salina's face turned red. "You twist my words."

Gorik held in a laugh. Hektor smirked. "That's enough. From both of you. We need to find our way out of here."

"Do you even know where we are going?" Salina snapped, once Rafik was released and calmed down. "Or are we stuck in this labyrinth forever?"

"That keeps us away from the Kylix if we were." Gorik laughed. "Of course, I know my way! We need to make it to the docks."

"And where is that?" Salina asked.

Gorik looked around in the darkness. Everywhere was the same. He tried recalling the stories he had heard of the tunnels. There were tunnels all over Alutopek. They were considered nothing more than a myth to some.

"Gorik," Rafik said. "I have another stone that might help. I'll grab it and check on Anza. Do you mind holding onto my bag to make sure no one steals it?" He glared at Salina as he said it.

"You have more surprises than me!" Gorik laughed, grabbing the bag. "I'd be happy to."

Rafik was getting used to the peculiar and dizzying feeling of getting sucked into the bag. He nearly landed on his feet this time, too. What he wasn't used to was seeing his sister lying on the ground, paler than usual and barely breathing. "Anza!" He shouted, hurrying to her side.

The second Rafik touched her she began to stir. "Wh-what?" She whispered in a soft, weak voice. Her eyes flew up and in an instant. She bolted upright, knocking her brother over, and screaming his name.

"Anza," Rafik said, holding his sister. "Anza, you're just fine. You're safe. I'm right here. Always will be."

"That picture. The one of the ugly man. He talked to me." Anza said between deep breaths, pointing at the portrait.

"Pictures don't talk, Anza."

"And dead people don't randomly appear in the mirror, too!" Anza snapped.

Rafik sighed. "You have a point. But, if the portrait talked, I would have noticed, too. Maybe you shouldn't be down here alone. Gorik says he knows where we're going."

Anza shrugged. "Maybe. It seemed so real."

"It always does." Rafik said. He helped her to her feet as she walked to the ladder. Rafik turned to the shelf and grabbed the lightstone. Anza had placed the waterstone beside the other two. He stared in awe at them. "That fairy tale was right. These things are life savers."

Anza glanced back at the portrait and saw the ugly man wave to her. She shook her head and turned back to the ladder. "It can't be real."

Gorik hobbled over, nearly falling from the sudden weight of the bag. Fortunately, it was Anza this time who was relatively light. "There you are." Gorik beamed. Everyone behind Gorik gasped at the sudden appearance of Anza and Rafik. The three ignored the stares. "Now that we aren't running for our lives, let's get a good look at you."

"Hello again, Gorik." Anza said, hugging him tight. She had known Gorik longer than her own father; even saw him like one. In her memories of her father, Drane, picking her up as a baby were being replaced with Gorik's face. She knew it wouldn't be much longer until she had forgotten his face completely.

"I promised to protect you and your brother. I'm not going to go back on my word now." He hugged Anza before turning to Rafik. "After all this, and you get a moment, we need to talk."

"About what?"

"Your father." Gorik answered.

"If it's about what Salina said, I don't care. I've heard worse." Rafik said, turning and glaring at the dark-haired woman.

"No, you need to hear something about him that only your mother and I knew." Gorik said. "Speaking of which, is she in the bag, too?"

"No." Rafik and Anza said at the same time, staring down at the ground.

"I'm so sorry, kids." Gorik said, pulling them in closer. "I should have been there."

"Are we going to stop and have a tea party?" Salina shouted, her voice echoing throughout the dark chamber. Rafik gently squeezed the light stone, giving off a small light he could just see things a few yards away. "We don't have time for this."

"The Kylix doesn't know about these tunnels. This is probably the safest place than anywhere else in Alutopek from them." Gorik assured them.

Hektor stepped forward from the group. "Friends." He shouted, pausing, and looking around, peering into the darkness at those who were still hidden. "Those skeletal soldiers are gone. They had got what they came for. But we Datians don't go down so easily. King Vanarzir tried destroying us with the Black Wall and failed. He tried again today and failed. They may have our children. And he may have taken our home. But we are resilient! And we stick together. We can rebuild and take back our home. And take back our children!"

The crowd cheered in agreement, drowning out the negative thinkers like Salina. "Thank you, friends. And I will do all I can to lead us to safety." Gorik assured them.

"What makes you think we want you in charge? You can't lead." Salina snapped.

"Well, let's see, Salina." Gorik said, scratching his chin. "I have a ship that we can use to get to safety. I was the one who shouted for us to get to the tunnels. I was the one who allowed us a chance to escape. And last I checked, there was an opening on the council."

Salina glowered at Gorik, hatred spilling from her eyes as she stared from Gorik to Rafik. "Lead the way." She said through gritted teeth. "Lead the way into the darkness. And hopefully it will kill you." The last bit she muttered to herself.

"Gladly." Gorik smiled. "Now, Rafik, how does this work?" He pointed at the glowing stone in Rafik's hand.

In his other hand was Blaridane. He couldn't bring himself to let it go. He needed its knowledge. Its protection. The voice purred in agreement with his reasoning. "Just like the stories." He said, holding up his hand. He squeezed harder and a wave of light surged through the cavern. The walls were rough, the ceiling jagged. In some areas of the wall they were smoothed. Sconces resting on them.

"Torches." Hektor smiled.

"Everyone take those." Gorik insisted. "That way you don't need to use that magic rock of yours."

Rafik smiled, pocketing the lightstone.

It wasn't long after that they came to a dead end. It was a wall just like any of the others. Rough, jagged as if carved by an axe. Everyone searched the walls, looking for any sign of an exit. Some even looked up at the ceiling, trying to find something. Anything. Salina voiced her opinion about how pointless this was several times while searching for anything. It was during one of these outbursts she shoved Gorik, pushing him into a stalagmite. The tip bent backward, showing a hidden compartment.

65

Gorik reached inside, found a lever, and pulled. The dead-end wall growled to life as stone scraped against stone. A doorway opened, runes revealing themselves above the entryway in purple light. "Well, for once your anger actually helped, Salina." Gorik laughed. "Congratulations."

Salina scowled, making a face at Gorik.

"And here I was about to give up." Rafik smiled. "I guess the lesson is; if you ever hit a dead end, just knock everything over."

Hours passed with no sign of any sort of life. It was quiet, the only sounds coming from them. They were making slower progress as fatigue crept upon them. The adrenaline of the day's events began to fade. Their legs grew heavier as they trudged forward.

Three more times they came across the secret doors. Each time runes were revealed that no one could read. Gorik recognized the occasional rune, but not enough to understand what it was saying. Each doorway led to a massive domed cavern. The last of which had other tunnels branching off in different directions. The entire place felt unreal. Like they were in another world. More of those strange runes were etched into the walls now. Rafik was comforted by the fact that he wasn't the only one who didn't know what they said. In one hallway the entire length was etched with runes and pictures. People with wings and heads of birds were prominent in the carvings.

It was when they came to the fourth and final mechanized door that they came across runes they could read. In the center of the domed cavern was a monolith of a stone. The boulder was carved expertly in the shape of a pyramid with a sphere balancing on the tip. Rafik recognized the sphere as the world of Amlima. He saw the familiar shape of Alutopek, the Rantyak Islands, and the other lands he had only heard of. On the pyramid were the mysterious runes etched into the base. And along the sides was the warning Salina read aloud.

"Turn back now, or life is forfeit." She repeated even louder. "What do you think it means?"

"It means someone doesn't want us down here." Rafik answered.

Salina glared at him.

"We can't just stay here." Hektor said. "Or even turn around. The doors closed behind us. Didn't check to see if we could go back through them."

"Whoever wrote this has been gone for at least 200 years. I think it will be alright." Gorik said. He pulled the stalagmite he recognized as one hiding a lever. The back wall of the domed cavern rumbled open.

Rafik had pulled out his lightstone. The shadows from the new room appeared to seep out. As if the darkness itself tried pushing them away. He noticed others having the same look of worry and apprehension on their faces. Whispers of evil spread across them, and no one moved forward.

"Everyone link hands." Gorik said. "None of us will get lost if we link together."

"Do you want to go back in the bag?" Rafik asked, turning to Anza.

Anza paused, remembering the portrait. Before she passed out, he said he could help. And she *knew* it had waved to her. She had to see if he could. And she had a feeling Rafik wouldn't let her if he were with her. She nodded. "I think so."

"Get in the bag. I'll protect us." Rafik said, smiling. He sheathed Blaridane, much to the sword's protest, and opened the bag for Anza to climb into. She smiled and a moment later disappeared.

"If you want, you can go in there, too." Gorik said, placing his hand on Rafik's shoulder.

"I'm not afraid of the dark." Rafik replied.

"Well good." Gorik laughed. "That makes one of us."

"If you're so brave, and you have that fancy lightstone, why don't you lead the way?" Salina challenged.

"Well, if you want something done right, you have to do it yourself." Rafik said and started into the darkness not waiting for a reply.

Even from within the hidden room Anza could feel the darkness. Everything seemed to get darker, and much colder. She could now see her breath and shivered uncontrollably. She sat down on the chair and turned to the picture. The ugly man had changed position, staring at her with a malicious grin. All his teeth ended in a point.

"Who are you?" She asked.

"They used to call me Skage." The picture replied.

Unfazed, Anza kept staring at the ugly man. "What do you want?"

"I want to help you, Anza. Every girl needs her mother. And I can bring her back to you." Skage said.

"How?"

"I'm what you call a necromancer, Anza. I can bring the dead to life." Skage replied.

"Prove it." Anza said, skeptical.

Skage nodded, muttering something under his breath. The two Kylix corpses on the floor began to move. The one with no head screamed in pain, asking what was going on. The other got to her feet, panicking. Anza stepped back against the wall, face pale. A moment later the two soldiers disappeared in a cloud of black smoke. Not a trace of them remained. "My power is but a fraction of what it was while in this picture. But I am the greatest necromancer the world has ever seen."

"How come I haven't heard of you?"

"Would you want to tell a story of a man who could summon monsters at will?"

"Why would you summon monsters?"

"Same reason why I would summon your mother. To help others."

"That doesn't help anyone!" Anza shouted. "Monsters don't love like a mother does."

"No. But a monster can scare you into doing something that needs to be done. Much like a parent does. A monster can protect one from danger. Much like a parent does." Skage reasoned, his smile twisting with mischief. "One man's monster is another man's hero."

"Are you going to summon any monsters?"

Skage laughed, making Anza's skin crawl. Something about him didn't feel right, but at the same time she felt drawn to him like a magnet. "Only if you want me to, Anza."

"So, you can bring back my mother?"

"Of course! But if I do now, she will end up like those two soldiers. You don't want that, do you, Anza? If I use more of my power, she would be stuck in this picture instead. Forever. For her to reenter this world, I need to be in this world."

"How can you get out of the picture?"

Skage smiled a toothy grin. Anza wanted to look away but couldn't. "I need you to find something for me, Anza. Can you do that? Find something for me?"

"What's that?" Anza asked.

"A talisman." Skage sighed. "A talisman hidden in the Sarason Fortress. If you find it, I can help you."

"What does the talisman look like?"

"It's called the Kymu-Guiden Talisman. It looks like a spider with a diamond body and ruby studded legs, encased in a small pentagon shaped stone. Anza, I need you to find this for me. Can you do this for me? For your mother?"

Anza felt something touch her shoulder, and Skage's voice whisper in her ear. She finally nodded. "I will get it for you."

"Good. And in return I will bring your mother back." Skage said. "I promise, Anza."

Anza looked at the portrait long and hard. She saw the ugly man, but now his image didn't frighten or disturb her. She saw something else. Hope? "You can count on me." She smiled.

"One more thing, Anza." Skage said offhandedly. "Don't let your brother know about our little deal. He wouldn't understand."

Chapter 6: Labyrinth of Shadows

The Dark Tribe Tunnels, World Beneath the World

There were so many twists and turns that even Gorik was beginning to lose track on which way they were going. The darkness was thick, like a fog. The torches some held only illuminated a small area around them. Even when Rafik tried squeezing the lightstone harder it couldn't pierce the permanent shadows. The only time it seemed to get lighter was when they would come across a fork in the road.

At one fork they saw a plume of fire, an echo of shouting, and then silence. With how dark everything was, it was impossible to tell how far away it was. The shadows even dampened the noises to faint echoes when speaking to somebody just beside you. Gorik rubbed his eyes, wondering if he had seen what had happened. The darkness felt colder after that. Like a looming threat in a dream. "Alright calm down, calm down." Gorik yelled before anyone could begin to panic. Though he yelled, his shout was carried like an overly loud whisper. He had seen fear like this in their eyes once before. Seven years ago. He didn't want a repeat event. Especially with Rafik and Anza here. "This darkness is unnatural. It is playing with our fears. We must keep moving."

"Which way?" Salina scoffed. "You have a map of this place, too?"

"Always left." Hektor interrupted. "Always choose left." The group nodded and moved forward. At each fork in the road Hektor would repeat what he said.

"Why?" Rafik asked at the fourth one.

"Superstition." Salina answered, the venom thick on her lips as she glared at him.

"In ancient stories it always seemed to be that the correct passage was on the left." Hektor explained. "This is an ancient place. It must be left."

Rafik nodded. Before today he would question his elder's sanity. But before today he never thought he'd see the four

70

elemental stones from fairy tales. Let alone everything else that had happened. His mind began to wander, thinking of whether he had talent. How else could he explain what he saw? But it made no sense. The Black Wall was proof that all forms of magic were gone. Forever.

Lost in thought, Rafik didn't notice someone in front of him until he walked into them. "Oh. Sorry." Rafik said, noticing it was Salina.

"Ssshh." She hissed, narrowing her eyes even more than usual at him.

Before Rafik could respond he heard a faint noise. A rustling of chains. He thought he had heard that earlier, but this time it had echoed. Just as suddenly as the noise started, it had stopped. They all froze, waiting for the noise to return.

Nothing.

"Alright, let's keep moving." Gorik said, clapping his hands together.

As they all began inching forward, slower than usual, the noise picked up again. It was several minutes later, and more unnerving noises, they all agreed to investigate the sound. The chains sounded as if they were getting closer one moment, farther the next. "We should see what it is." One man said, stepping forward. He held his torch high and walked toward the noise.

Soon the man faded from view, only his light shined like a lone star in a blackened sky. Then in an instant the light was gone. Everyone stopped, staring at where the light had just been, all wishing by sheer will alone he would return. The chain rustling had ended, and nobody spoke. Finally, the light reappeared. The faint outline of the man could be seen. "Nothing!" He shouted. "Just more tunnels."

The chains rustled, clattered, and whistled, being flung into the air. The light fell to the floor and the man screamed. The torch extinguished and the screaming stopped abruptly. It was obvious now that whatever had the chain was hunting them. The chains began rustling once more. Creeping closer. Everyone stood still, not daring to move. Color was gone from their faces. Something was out there. Rafik envisioned a dragon. Gorik a minotaur. Others imagined other hideous monsters attacking them.

"Wh-What was that?" One woman finally asked from the crowd.

"We shouldn't be down here."

"What should we do?" Another asked.

Even Salina and Hektor were speechless. The looks of fear written on their faces told it all. "If you are having a nightmare, don't stop and watch the monsters. Move forward into the light." Rafik said. "My father told me that. Now come on before that thing gets brave enough to come after us." He gripped Blaridane, getting fueled with the blind violent rage as courage.

Gorik nodded. "He's right. It shouldn't be much further." He limped next to Rafik, patting him on the back. They led the group deeper into the tunnels. The sound of chains followed them.

The rustling chains grew louder, and the tunnels became colder. The lights dimmed, torches flickered in and out. A deep voice echoed in the passageway in a strange, unknown language. It was a combination of clicks and whistles and deep guttural sounds. Like ravens arguing with dogs.

"What's it saying?" Rafik whispered. He was thankful there wasn't much light. It hid his pale face. Even in this cold he was sweating.

"I can't tell." Gorik sighed. "But whatever it is, it's smart if it can speak so much."

"Maybe it's like a parrot?" Rafik suggested. "Just mimics what it hears."

"If that were correct than that thing is old. Archaic even. No one speaks the ancient language anymore."

"But you know it." Rafik argued.

"Yes. My adventures required me to learn some of it." Gorik said.

A sudden scream came from the back. And another as chains whistled through the air. Everyone shouted and ran forward, trying to escape the chains that pulled them into the darkness. Gorik pushed Rafik against the wall, getting him out of the way of the stampeding, panicked crowd. The sailor took a step and got knocked down.

"Keep to the left! Keep to the left!" Hektor yelled, trying to ensure the crowd stayed together.

"Are you alright?" Rafik asked, helping Gorik up.

"I've been hurt worse." Gorik said, brushing himself off. "Fortunately, only one person stepped on me and my wooden leg didn't snap."

"I hope they know where they're going." Rafik said, looking forward into the darkness. The group had disappeared, leaving them behind.

"There is one more fork in the road. After that it comes to a dead end with a ladder." Gorik said, glancing behind them.

"How do you know? Nobody has been in these tunnels in ages." Rafik said.

Gorik shook his head. "No, nobody has gone through the tunnels from the temple ruins in ages. Did I ever tell you how I met your father?"

Rafik shook his head.

A smile lit up on Gorik's face. "Well, let's keep walking, and I'll tell you all about it." He glanced behind them. The faint sound of chains could be heard. If Rafik had heard it as well he gave no notice. "It was at a market on my family's dock. Somebody was shouting about a thief who had just stolen something. Well, nobody steals, let alone if it cuts into *my* family's profits. So, I chased after him.

The thief was fast. It wasn't long before he was gone. But I didn't want to give up. I heard a banging on a nearby ruined door. It had just been closed, and not too subtly either. It was a trap, I knew it. I pulled out my sword, kicked open the door, and there was your father. Sword drawn. Four small children no older than Anza was when we lost your father were huddled behind him. Their eyes wide with fear as they nibbled greedily on the food Drane had stolen.

Unbeknownst to me were soldiers who had followed me. They entered the door. I turned to see who it was, and Drane

73

kicked my back, shoving me into the soldiers, as he and the kids took off. The kids got away. But I found Drane, just as he jumped into a shadow in another nearby ruin. I lunged in after him and went rolling down a hill. We ended up in these tunnels. Soon after we became friends that day, trying to make our way out of this labyrinth of darkness. Several times we tried mapping some of these tunnels, but that familiar chain noise kept us from exploring too much."

"I never heard that story about my father." Rafik smiled. "He doesn't sound like a drunkard."

Gorik laughed. "Your father was a great man. Always helping those he could. Even if it put him on the road to danger." He sighed, trailing off, looking off as the memories filled him.

"So, you recognize this tunnel?" Rafik asked, breaking Gorik out of his reminiscing.

Again, Gorik laughed. "Recognize it? Boy, look around you. There is nothing to recognize. Our map was horrible, and it seemed like the tunnels always shifted and changed, like a living maze. But Hektor is right. As long as we keep to the left; we will find our way out."

The two continued walking in silence. Gorik fondly playing through the memories of his best friend while Rafik imagined his father playing the part of a hero. For so long everyone told him he had been lost at sea, because he was drunk, he was beginning to forget all the good he had done.

The faint glow of lights could be seen just ahead. Their anxious whispers began echoing back to them. A faint outline of a ladder was at the edge of all the lights. They had made it to the end of the tunnels. "We made it!" Rafik smiled as Gorik pointed out the ladder.

"You expect us to climb this?" Salina snapped as Gorik and Rafik joined the group. She grabbed the ladder, shaking it. Thin wiry cables looped around half rotted pieces of wood making up the ladder rattled against the back wall of the tunnel. "I've used rope ladders before. This is a death trap. Look at the wood! I doubt this could even hold a child."

"Unless you want to find out what that thing is that's hunting us you will." Gorik said. "Now hurry up, before it catches up to us again."

Salina opened her mouth to argue when the familiar rustling of chains came from behind them. "We're trapped! And it's your fault!"

"My fault?" Gorik asked.

"Yes! Your fault." Salina snapped. "We could have gotten away if we ran from the Kylix instead of jumping into a pond and being hunted by some monster in the dark."

Rafik brandished his sword and turned around. "Start climbing." He ordered. His voice harsher than usual. He didn't wait for a response, but faced the darkness, stepping into it and putting the lightstone in his mouth. Grabbing Blaridane with both hands, the shadows engulfed him as if he ceased to exist.

"He has more guts than the lot of you." Gorik snarled and followed Rafik, revealing a hammer the Kylix had failed to take from him.

Several grunted and voiced disdain. The sudden venomous voice of Salina filled the darkened air. "Out of my way! Do you know who I am? I'm first." She began climbing the rope ladder, not looking back.

"Rafik?" Gorik called out. "Where are you?" A small light began to glow not far from him. It emanated around Rafik's head like a halo as he stared at the ground. Just on the edge of the light was a tip of a blackened chain. When Gorik bent over to examine it the chain slithered away like a snake.

Rafik gripped the sword tighter. Memories of Blaridane fighting in previous battles flashed before him. Fast enough he couldn't make out the details, but enough that he felt as if he was learning from them. He was going to catch this thing. And he was going to kill it. He knew he could do it. The voice of the sword filled his head, encouraging him to kill.

A moment later a chain whistled through the air toward Rafik. He crouched, pivoted, raised his sword, and twirled it downward. As it stabbed the ground, he grabbed the end of the chain. It was like any other. The metal was smooth and cold; the links were large. Nothing strange was apparent. The very tip of the chain began wriggling. Startled, Rafik dropped it.

A second chain whistled through the air, and a third one. Each one tangled around Rafik's legs. Gorik howled and leapt into the air. His hammer pounded into the chains, crushing them. The chains still wriggled with unnatural life. A fourth chain wrapped around Gorik and yanked him off his feet, throwing him into the wall. Another chain appeared, coming towards Rafik. Without thinking Rafik ripped the sword out of the ground and swung it around. The chain wrapped around the blade and tried to take it away. Rafik held on, being dragged toward the source of the chaos.

The light from the stone extinguished once Rafik's mouth gaped open. He saw the source of the chains just as the light went out. Its eyes were that of a man's, but where his nose and mouth should have been protruded a large beak that curved downward like a parrot's. And he could just make out two stubs hanging off his back at the shoulder blades. The figure raised its hand to block the light, and he noticed on each finger was a chain. What looked like feathers were mixed into its hair. Rafik regained composure fast enough to clench down on the lightstone. The light turned on once more and the figure turned to escape, cursing in a voice that sounded scratchy, unused, and like it was drowning.

The figure fled into the darkness, releasing Gorik and howling. Gorik ran up to Rafik, panting. "Are you alright?" He asked, checking his own body where the chains had entangled him.

Rafik fought back the urge to follow the monster. The voice from the sword screamed at him. *'Coward! After that thing! Blind it and stab it in the heart!'*

"No." Rafik said, shaking his head. "No. I'm not doing that."

"Doing what?" Gorik asked, placing a hand on Rafik's shoulder. "Rafik?"

Rafik scowled, shrugging Gorik off him. "I'm fine." He wasn't sure what surprised him more. The creature's face or the power of the sword. If it wasn't for Gorik he would have gone after

76

that monster like the sword wanted. He glanced down at the blade, wanting to drop it, but not wanting to at the same time. This sword gave him power. He knew he could defeat anything with Blaridane.

'Then listen to me!' Blaridane screamed in Rafik's head. *'Follow me!'*

Gorik watched Rafik pace back and forth, his knuckles white around the sword. He had never seen a sword like that before. Black steel, the edges of the blade crimson. It glinted with an unnatural beauty. "Rafik. Come on. We got to be going."

Rafik shook his head, fighting away the voice. "I-I'm fine. I'm not sure what I saw."

"They say these tunnels are cursed. That thing could be the source of it." Gorik said. "But we know its weakness, thanks to you. Light. Now come on, before it decides to come back."

"What was that?" Rafik asked, as they made their way back to the group. He had sheathed Blaridane but left his hand on the pommel.

"If I had to take a guess," Gorik said. "I think that was an Immortal. One of the cursed tribes of men."

"How did they get cursed?"

"According to legend, they watched the world burn."

The two returned to the ladder with cheers. "We thought you were a goner." One said.

Hektor stepped forward. "We weren't expecting to see either of you again. But fortunate both of you are safe."

"I, for one, am glad I'm not dead." Gorik smiled, clapping Rafik on the back. "Thanks to Rafik."

Rafik repositioned the bag on his shoulder, thankful he was still holding it. "Yeah, me too." He spoke. With shaking hands and resisting the voice, he let go of the sword sheathed at his side.

"Hey!" Salina shouted from above where the shaft of light poured into the cavern. "Enough of the tea party, we have a problem up here."

"If it isn't one thing it's another." Gorik muttered.

77

"The Kylix is breaking through the wall to the dock."
Salina shouted down.

"Ya shire." Gorik cursed. "We need to hurry to my ship!
Hurry! Everyone! Climb!"

Chapter 7: Chalice of Lost Souls

Datz, Nyler Peninsula, Alutopek

The Kylix soldiers digging out the rubble shouted to one another to work harder. They had heard Salina, and it sparked a frenzy within them. Shouts of finding and killing them echoed down into the tunnels. Before hearing Salina's shout, they only tore at the wall halfheartedly. Joking and reveling in their victory. Now they yelled with vigor and anger. How dare anyone make fools of them. "Over here," and "I found them." They cursed, scowled, and made obscenities at Salina and the others.

"Come on, hurry up!" Salina shouted down the tunnel as she pulled another person out. The tone of panic replaced her usual sound of venomous hatred.

"Don't panic. Don't panic." Hektor insisted, helping another climb the rungs of the ladder. "Panic causes mistakes."

Rafik felt the nervous surge of energy. It was just like when the Kylix first showed up at Datz. A heavy silence. People pale, eyes wide. A fervor to do something, but nobody able to do anything. "You'll have enough room for all of us, right Gorik?" He finally asked.

Gorik looked from person to person, not saying a word. "We'll make room. We'll make room."

More shouts from above echoed down into the tunnel, encouraging everyone to go faster. "After you." Hektor smiled, gesturing for Rafik onto the ladder. Rafik nodded and climbed. The rungs were moist and more than once he nearly lost grip. Hektor urged him to keep moving. Gorik cursed, slowly bringing up the rear with his peg leg.

Rafik thought he heard Gorik mention his father once in his grumbling. The Kylix had nearly broken through. With their armor it looked as if the dead were crawling out of their graves. He fought back a scream and reached for his sword. The moment he did his fears disappeared. Blaridane roared to life in his head, seething with anger. *'Kill! Kill!'* He didn't fight the voice this time.

Rafik roared, charging to the front of the crowd. A few other Datians with swords followed. Others threw rocks.

The Kylix pushed through, finally toppling the wall and rushing towards the Datians. Rafik screamed back, his sword clashing against theirs. He allowed Blaridane to take control, and watched as his body danced around the Kylix, slashing, and hacking as he went. It was like an elegant ballet being performed through him. He was merely a puppet for the power of the sword. Its thoughts were becoming his thoughts. Its motives were his motives. He wanted nothing more than to destroy and to kill. And it felt good.

Gorik led the others to the *River Lizard*. A large splash rocked the boat as he made his way over the side. Another crashing noise beside Gorik caused him to jump. The post his ship was tied to had shattered. Gorik cursed, spinning, eyes darting everywhere, looking for the source. The Kylix was using the catapults. He noticed a handful of soldiers in a far tower loading a catapult. "Ya shire." The *River Lizard* started drifting away from the docks now. He turned to Datz, helping others climb aboard. "Rafik!" He shouted. "Rafik, we're leaving."

Rafik turned and saw the boat already moving. "I thought you weren't going to leave me behind?" He said to himself, kicking back another soldier. An anger he had never felt before roared within him. How dare Gorik betray him! His blood boiled and the violence he craved was now aimed towards his uncle.

'Forget him. We can take them.' Blaridane's voice screamed, trying to pull Rafik's attention back to the battle.

Rafik shook his head. "No. We need to protect Anza." He grabbed the bag with his free hand, making sure he still had it. He turned, running back to the docks.

'We can destroy them.' The sword argued. *'You can be a hero. Let them leave. We will win.'*

"But Anza." Rafik said. "I'm not going to risk her life."

'She's safe in the bag. Toss her to them. Be a hero. Kill the others.' Blaridane insisted.

"Go on!" Hektor said, shoving Rafik. He had found a sword and was fighting off the last of the Kylix. He shoved Rafik again harder towards the boat. If he didn't leave now, there'd be no way he could catch the ship.

For a moment he lost grip of Blaridane and the voice stopped. He could think clearly again. He shook his head, starting for the *River* Lizard. Rafik glanced back just in time to see Hektor being circled like a pack of wolves trapping their prey. Rafik stopped, turning back to Hektor and felt the bag hit his hip. No, he had to protect his sister. *'Forget your sister! Kill!'*

"I'm sorry." He whispered, sheathing the sword, and turning to face the ship. "I'm not risking her life." Another boulder crashed a few feet in front of him, making a gaping hole in the dock. He jumped the gap and sprinted to the *River Lizard*. Gorik held out his peg leg and Rafik grabbed hold. Gorik and the Datians on board helped pull Rafik up. They were finally safe. The last boulder hit the sea behind them, signaling being out of range. They had escaped the Kylix but lost their home.

"That was close." Gorik sighed, reattaching his leg. "Anyone missing?"

"Nobody that matters." Salina said, shoving her way through the crowd. "I'm surprised this bucket hasn't sunk from the weight."

Gorik shook his head. "If you aren't happy with my ship, let alone the escape, you're more than welcome to swim. I'll even give you a little push to get you started."

"Hektor." Rafik said. "We lost Hektor."

"But he was behind me." Gorik said, peering through the crowd. There was no sign of his friend's face. He looked back at the destroyed dock and only saw the Kylix soldiers cheering and snarling.

"He helped me get away." Rafik said with a twinge of guilt. If he wasn't arguing with Blaridane, maybe they both could have made it.

Gorik nodded. "Don't you ever do that again."

"Do what?" Rafik asked, taking his eyes off the icy water.

"You're as reckless as your father."

Rafik smiled. "But I'm not a drunk yet."

"No." Gorik sighed. He opened his mouth, then noticed Salina still standing there. "I had no idea you knew how to fight like that." He patted Rafik on the back.

"I didn't. It's this sword." Rafik said. "Anza and I found it along with the bag."

"Let's see that." Gorik said, grabbing the hilt of the sword. He screamed, yanking his hand back. "That thing shocked me."

"Well, it's supposed to be a cursed sword or something." Rafik said. "Does me fine. This a new ship?" He added, trying to change the subject. Fear grew in him that Gorik would take Blaridane. He looked up and down the ship. Last time he was with Gorik he had a ferry that could only fit maybe 20 people. This one was much larger and had two masts. It fit the surviving Datians, though Rafik wasn't sure how many were left.

"Aye. She's called the *River Lizard.* I won her in a bet in Syro." Gorik said. "Let Shallon borrow it, but he returned it when I was in Emerald. If you go below deck, we have the supplies we needed before the Kylix attacked.

"I think you may be a little too late for that." Rafik said, forcing a laugh. He glanced back at his home, now overrun with the Kylix. He had lived there his whole life. Gone on a few trips with Gorik and his father to nearby towns and cities, but Datz was his home. Now it was gone. Along with his life. If the king, or anyone who supported him, found any of them they would be sent to the Kylix stronghold to be trained as a soldier. Or just killed. He looked up at the Black Wall. There was nowhere he could really escape to while under here.

'Is that so bad?' The sword's voice asked. *'You have no home now. We make a great team. We could be the best.'*

Rafik shook his head. He didn't want to leave Gorik. Or anyone else on this ship. Except for Salina. Why she was always so bitter confused him.

"At least we are well prepared." Gorik said, pulling Rafik from his thoughts.

"So, what's the plan now?" Salina asked, her hands folded and foot tapping.

"Well, follow me." Gorik said. He crossed the deck and up to the wheel of the ship. Next to the wheel was a table with a chart of the surrounding area. The infamously detailed map was lying in plain sight.

It surprised Rafik that he had left such a valuable item out in the open. He gripped his bag closer, thinking of Anza and the Elemental Stones inside. "Why'd you leave the chart out?" Rafik asked. "Aren't you worried about someone taking it?"

Gorik laughed, taking the knife that was holding the chart on the table. "No, anyone who gets on my ship is friend, prisoner, or dead. I have no need of hiding it."

Anza began climbing out of the bag, Rafik nearly falling over from the sudden weight. "You need to warn me when you're getting out." Rafik said. "I feel like my arm is going to fall off."

"Sorry." Anza said, obviously not caring. "Are we sailing?" She turned to Gorik, smile wide. She ran to the side of the ship and watched as it cut through the water. "I like this much better than those tunnels."

"Aye, we are." Gorik smiled, taking a deep sniff of the salty air.

"I've never been sailing." Anza giggled, rocking back and forth. The waves of the Tahlbiru Ocean rocking the boat.

"It isn't all fun." Rafik said, holding his sister steady.

A moment later Anza's face turned a pale green. "I'm going to be sick." She hurried to the side of the ship where a couple others were doing the same.

"Well," Gorik said, tracing his finger across the map. "We are just leaving the docks here. Here is the biggest ruin, the Sarason Fortress, and beyond that are the ruined towers and sharp rocks. If we get passed all of that we have a choice. We can make port in Trinkit, Syro, or even Sampra if we head east. But Shallon did agree to offer us refuge in Emerald. And that's heading west. How long we would be given hospitality there I'm not sure. The people of Emerald aren't really known for being friendly. But, with the Kylix moving eastward to collect children, it may be the safest place to be. Salina, as much as I hate to say this, but you're the last city leader left. What do you say?"

Salina's eyes widened, her malicious grin growing. "You know…if it were up to me none of this would have happened. We could have traded the little brats to make our city great again." She glared at everyone who would meet her gaze before continuing. "But that decision is behind us. We are all wanted now. I say we stop at Trinkit. Those who want to avoid the Kylix can get off there. We can recruit others there to help fight."

"I thought you were against fighting the Kylix?" Gorik asked, not hiding the look of surprise on his face.

"The Kylix took *my* home. *I* am finally the sole leader, just as it should be. But the king doesn't care about me. I want my city back."

"How are we going to do that?" One man said from the crowd, overhearing them speaking. "We are going up against a trained army. We were being hunted by a monster with chains and nearly died. They have swords, spears, and arrows! What do you expect us to do against a whole army?" Others mumbled in agreement.

"We can't just sit still and let the king do what he wants. He just destroyed our home. Took *your* children. Took our future." Salina snapped, stepping forward and facing the man. "Do you just want to give up? Just let King Vanarzir win, and you'll never see your children again. And you'll be less than a nobody. Just someone without a home. Without a purpose."

"We can rebuild somewhere else!" The man argued. "Keep our heads down and make a new home."

"Again, without your children." Salina said. "I am fine if you want to leave them with the king. We'll take back our city, make a home of it. And when your children are fully trained soldiers, they'll come to take back Datz in the name of the king. And they will either kill you, or you kill them. Do you want that?"

No one answered her. She was right.

"Alright then." Gorik said, clapping his hands together. "I may know somebody who can help." He limped back to the chart, tracing a finger across an imaginary line. "Trinkit is a dangerous place. It isn't the Kylix we have to worry about there, yet. It's the bottom of the barrel for scum. Stopping there, letting people leave there, would be a mistake. I only suggested Trinkit because my contact is currently there. I think."

"Who is your contact?" Rafik asked.

Rafik and Gorik's eyes met. He smiled and winked as he answered. "Let's just say an old friend." He tapped his peg leg a few times, chortling.

"You're telling us it's dangerous and we shouldn't go, but we need to?" Salina asked, shaking her head.

"No." Gorik said, ignoring her tone. "I'm explaining the reasoning for my plan. We can leave everyone at the Sarason Fortress like we originally planned until we know the Kylix are gone. We can then go where we want without them trailing us. In the meantime, there should be a small boat I can row the rest of the way to Trinkit. The Kylix won't be able to touch anyone there, and we aren't getting into anymore danger."

"How do we know you won't just leave us?" Salina asked.

Gorik sighed. "You'd really think I would just leave? I could have done that a half dozen times by now if I wanted."

"I do." She spat.

"Well, for one, Rafik and Anza are staying at the Sarason Fortress. Two, I'm not leaving anyone behind. I set out to save us all, and I intend to do that. At least those that are left."

"But the Sarason Fortress?" Salina asked. "Can't we all just stay on the ship?"

"No." Gorik said. "Much like the city of Kristol, Trinkit has its own guard. They search all incoming ships and register everyone on board. We don't want to leave a trail of where we are going, do we? I doubt the rumors of the Sarason Fortress are true, anyway. Besides, it would be better than staying in Datz now. Or, at the very least, you can stay on the ship while docked at the fortress."

Everyone looked back at their home. The creation of the Black Wall couldn't destroy the city. But now smoke was rising from it once more, and more of it appeared to have fallen to ruin. Even the most heartless of refugees on the *River Lizard* shed a tear. They could see the skeletal soldiers setting fires and crumbling buildings. Datz was no more.

"We will stay to the north eastern wall of the Sarason Fortress." Gorik said. "The Lizard will be hidden from view from Datz or Trinkit. The Kylix will think we sailed far away. They don't have a navy. Never heard of one at least."

"I'm sure you haven't heard how the king stole everyone's talent, but he did." Salina mocked.

"Alright, I'll rephrase. I know the Kylix doesn't have a navy."

Rafik took a step back tuning out the ensuing argument. So much had happened. His mother was now gone. His home gone. All that he had left was Anza and this sword with a voice of its own. He wondered about his sword fighting skill. His possible talent. That thought froze him. Talent. He had hardly used it, and yet he knew it would be life changing. It already had been. "I'm getting some rest." He said, cutting into Salina and Gorik's bantering. "Nobody but Gorik, Anza, or I touch this bag."

He put the bag on the ground in front of Anza's feet, opening the flap. In one motion the bag bulged and deflated as Rafik was sucked in. Anza stayed out, gazing at the Sarason Fortress. Legend had it that a powerful being constructed the fortress. Topped it with the sign of the god of death, a spider. It looked so realistic it unnerved most who sailed to Datz. The fortress consisted of five towers. One in each corner, and one twice as tall as the others with the spider in the center. After the Black Wall, though, the fortress collapsed. All that was left was the central tower and two walls leading out from it, and into the sea. Even the tower was beginning to sink and topple over.

"That place is creepy." She muttered to herself, her skin crawling with goosebumps. All the children's stories she heard of the fortress told of the spider having glowing red eyes and would

86

take away misbehaving children. Nobody knew what was inside the fortress if anything. The few who dared to enter never returned to tell the tale. Anza grabbed the bag, patting it. "Don't worry, Skage. Your talisman should still be there."

The room felt different as Rafik entered. It seemed gloomier. Darker. Shadows cast out in parts of the room it hadn't earlier. As he circled the room, trying to find what was different he found the portrait of the ugly man wasn't facing the wall. Not thinking, he picked it up and turned it around. The shadows didn't go away, but he didn't feel like someone was watching him.

"Do you know who that is?" A voice asked just in front of him. The sudden voice caused Rafik to jump and he pulled out his sword, scanning the room in a near frenzy. Blaridane's voice screamed to destroy whoever was ambushing them.

He found the source of the voice a moment later and relaxed while Blaridane continued to scream for blood. It was the mirror, and Izamar was standing in there once more. "You scared me, Izamar."

"Don't say my name." He scolded, paused, and took a deep breath. "I guess it doesn't matter much anymore, does it?"

Rafik shrugged. "Guess it depends how many more magical locks you have lying around. What were you asking?"

"Do you know him? That portrait you held." The grey wizard asked.

"Can't say I do." Rafik said, shaking his head. "But he is one ugly man."

"His name is Skage, a former apprentice of mine. After I taught him all I could he went to take the test and disappeared."

"What test?"

"The sorcery test, of course. Haven't you heard of the Witching Towers?"

"Only in fairy tales." Rafik answered. "Are you telling me they actually existed?"

"Oh yes. Not sure why you haven't heard of them, but they do indeed exist."

"Stories say the last of the wizards tore them down and scattered whatever was inside them across all of Amlima."

"Well, in my time they were still around." Izamar said. "And it was Skage's turn to attempt the test or die trying. But he disappeared. No one heard from him in years. Then, whispers of a Necromancer cropped up in Datz and the rest of the Nyler Peninsula. The Jewel War was just ending, and no one wanted another one. So, we wizards tried to keep it a secret. We found Skage, though. He had been twisted and turned into what is in that portrait and had truly gone mad. Drunken with power I was surprised to see he had. Whatever gave him his power turned him into what you see now."

"You stopped him, though, right?"

"If I hadn't, we wouldn't be having this conversation now." Izamar said. "Something was off about him. When we last fought his movements seemed jarred and stiff, as if someone was controlling him. I still believe he was someone's puppet, but I don't know who, and have no proof of it."

"Why are you telling me this?"

"Because he swore he would return. And I fear he already is trying. The shadows seem darker now in this room. This room grows darker as evil becomes more prevalent"

"It might not be him causing it. The king is doing some pretty horrible things right now. Besides, it's just a story." Rafik said, trying not to let what Izamar said bother him. "What does it getting darker have to do with him returning anyway, and not somebody else?"

"Life is light, Rafik. Life can always thrive in the light. In the darkness, though, only monsters survive. The more powerful the necromancer the darker their life becomes. Raising the dead is an unnatural ability. A mockery of life itself. And Skage had become a powerful necromancer in the end. I'm sure his deeds still far outweigh your king's."

"It's just a story." Rafik repeated.

"Maybe. Maybe not." Izamar sighed. "Where is your sister?"

"On deck with our uncle." Rafik said, gesturing to the ladder. "Why?"

"She was missing her mother, and so I found something to help. Though I guess that gift can wait."

"I was wondering if you could help me." Rafik asked after what felt like a lifetime of silence.

"How can I help, young one?"

"You said I have talent. I need to learn how to use it."

"Ah yes, psychometry, right?"

"If you say so." Rafik laughed, shrugging. "All I know is I see the past when I touch things."

Izamar nodded. "That's what it's called. Being able to glimpse things that have been. As if they were memories of the inanimate. How can I help?"

"I don't even know how to use it. Or how I got it. I just touch something, anything, and it comes to me." Rafik explained.

The grey wizard laughed. "Yes, you have undeveloped talent. When did this start?"

"This morning." Rafik said, still surprised it hadn't been that long at all.

"Talent comes in one of two ways. Either when you are born, or sometime while growing up. Usually when something tragic happens and the body tries to protect itself." Izamar said. "Where the talent comes from is anyone's guess, though I have an idea."

"Looking into the past saved me?" Rafik asked, the hint of skepticism was obvious.

"It must have." Izamar laughed. "How else would you be here now?"

"When the Kylix attacked Datz our mom helped us escape. Ended up in the forest and we couldn't find a way out."

"Until you glimpsed a memory." Izamar said, continuing as Rafik nodded. "Rafik, psychometry is a fickle thing. Most wizards haven't mastered the art. Even I haven't. But I do know enough that I can help. To master anything, you need to know the basics."

"Alright, well, it's called psychometry and I can see the past through objects. What else do I need to know?"

"When you were a boy what is something you made? Something that took a lot of time and effort into creating." Izamar asked.

Rafik scratched his head, thinking, for a few seconds before answering. "I made a doll for Anza once. It took months to make it for her."

Izamar nodded. "When one puts a lot of time and effort into something, or there is an emotional trauma tied to something, it gets imprinted on the object. With your talent, you can glimpse into that moment. If you master it, you can view the smallest of memories and the object's entire life. Where it's been. What it's witnessed. But that takes years of practice."

"How can I master it?"

"Practice, and effort. Challenge yourself. If you touch something with a strong tie to a moment you should feel something. A tingling just behind the eyes. The stronger the moment the easier it is to recall it. Then, as you get stronger in your ability the tingling can be felt in even the most mundane of objects. Learn secrets beyond your imagination. But first, try something that is immensely powerful. That ruby I had locked away in the wardrobe. Try that."

Rafik nodded and the grey wizard vanished from the mirror. With a quivering hand, he grabbed the ruby still at the bottom of the chalice. Izamar was right. A tingling just behind the eyes was growing. His vision blurred. Flashes of light blinded him until he was back in a memory.

"Have you heard of the Sarason Fortress before?" Gorik asked Anza, staring at the ruined marvel. Waves crashed against the walls and towers still poking above the sea. "We don't talk about it much back at home."

Anza shook her head, feigning ignorance. The talisman she had to find was in the Sarason Fortress. "No." She said, realizing Gorik wasn't paying attention to her.

"The ancients built it to control the sea. Royals have lived there, including some old kings and even King Emerald himself. The main tower, the one with the spider, were said to have been built by mindless servants enslaved by an evil wizard. Legends say he built is so the world could never sneak up on him. But he was overthrown not long after.

In recent history, though, it was used as an outpost for the Kylix to control the supplies that came in and out of Alutopek. But with the creation of the Black Wall, it sank beneath the waves. All that remains is what you see before you. No one has set foot in there since. My great -grandfather was part of the Kylix and was posted there for a time."

"Is there any treasure there?" Anza asked almost as suddenly as Gorik finished talking.

If Gorik was suspicious of the immediate response, she couldn't tell. "Oh, I would imagine. The Black Wall was created so suddenly that nobody had time to escape the rushing tide. I'm sure there is more than just treasure down there. Ghosts, more like it."

"While we are waiting for you can I explore the fortress?"

Gorik turned, brow scrunched, looking at Anza. "Oh no. It is much too dangerous. No one is allowed in there. Even the Kylix avoid the fortress."

Anza nodded and yawned, stretching. "Well, I'm going to go see what Rafik is up to." She handed Gorik the bag. He opened the top and took Anza's hand, helping her get sucked into its depths.

He stared at the bag once she disappeared. It wasn't anything special. A dark cloth bag with an unusually large mouth. He reached in and couldn't feel the bottom. As he looked inside, he felt the suctioning feeling and whipped his head away. "I need a drink." He sighed. As he turned, he noticed something. A reflection in the water. It was just barely there. On the horizon between the Black Wall and spit of land between Datz and Trinkit. The actual land couldn't be seen, as it was getting darker out. But there, running along the coast, were campfires. "This isn't good."

"What's wrong?" Salina asked, squinting at the fires Gorik was staring at.

"Those fires." Gorik said, pointing to the coast. "It's the Kylix. They are careless and make them burn bright and tall."

"So what?" Salina asked.

"They know we are out here and are waiting for us." Gorik explained. "We're stuck behind the Sarason Fortress, otherwise they'll know which direction we go in. Then they can hunt us down."

"Wasn't that the plan? You even said we have supplies." Salina said.

Gorik nodded. "Yes, but I was hoping they wouldn't try keeping an eye on us like this. That fortress is cursed. After what happened in the tunnels, I don't want anything else like that to happen to us."

"Isn't this ship faster than the Kylix being on foot or horseback? We could outrun them."

"Yes." Gorik said. "But the key to a good outlaw is misdirection. When everyone is expecting you to go right, you go left. We can't do that if we are constantly being watched."

"Sure we can." Salina said. "The way I see it, the plan is the same. We wait behind the fortress, you row to Trinkit and back. I know you can hide from them."

"And then what? We can't wait forever behind here." Gorik said.

"You said it yourself. We have the supplies. We can wait long enough. In the morning we should be able to tell if they are staying there or not."

Gorik nodded. She had a point, as much as he hated to admit it. He turned to Salina and smiled. Salina took a step back. "It's surprisingly nice to be on the same side as you."

Salina's puzzled look turned to a malicious glare so fast it was as if a whole other person had replaced her. "Oh, Gorik. I just want what is rightfully mine. But I still hate you. And those two brats of your friend's. We may be working together, but as soon as you're of no use to me you can expect my knife in your back."

"Did I ever tell you how I lost my leg?" Gorik asked, his tone unusually gleeful for just being threatened.

"No."

"I didn't think so. Every time you hear my peg leg clunking, every time you see me hobble back and forth, know that I am always willing to do what it takes. If anything happens to those two not even the Black Wall could come between me ending you. And I'll make sure your end is as horrible as you are of a person. Holding onto a generation long feud. Your family would be ashamed of you if they were still around. Which is why I'm sure you probably had them killed, didn't you?"

Salina rushed forward, grabbing the collar of Gorik's jacket. The sailor laughed, holding up his arms and spreading them, breaking her grip. He grabbed his sword and pointed it at Salina. She glowered at him, not saying a word.

"You pathetic little worm." She finally said through gritted teeth.

"No one tries to attack me on my own ship. Not even you." Gorik said, sheathing his sword and turning his back on her. "Now, if you'll excuse me."

Salina lunged for Gorik, grabbing his shoulder. He shrugged it off, continuing to walk away from her. The bag slid off his shoulder and Salina yanked it away from him. "Don't try anything foolish in Trinkit, Gorik." She warned.

The sailor looked from the bag to Salina. He could feel the look of hatred searing into him. "As soon as Rafik comes out he'll take the bag."

"Yes." Salina smiled. "But he and his sister will still be with me. So, I suggest you hurry."

They had finally made it behind the Sarason Fortress. As it grew nearer everyone gasped at the sheer size of the remaining central tower and the spider atop it. Even so close it looked real. The thin hairs on its legs and body. The spray from the wind now dripping from its fangs as if it were venom. The only thing to give it away were the dull, lifeless eyes. Gorik steered the ship in closer, throwing a rope around a stone column and tightening it. Just beyond, if one jumped from stone to stone, was a dark entryway. It reminded Gorik of the entryway to some of the tunnels. Where not even light could escape from.

Beyond the tower was a wall, connecting one of the outer towers. Along part of the wall were small row boats in varying states of disrepair. Gorik hopped from one stone to the next, not wasting time. Salina and a few others shouted for him to be safe. He ignored them. Getting to the Sarason Fortress was easy. It would be rowing there and back that would be the difficult part.

Anza landed on the floor gracefully like a cat. She was getting used to going in and out of the secret room. Rafik was standing next to the shelf, not moving. His fist clenched around something she couldn't tell. Although concerned, she crept towards the portrait of Skage and turned it around. The moment their eyes met the bust of the ugly man came to life.

"Did you get it, Anza?" He hissed

Anza shook her head. "We are at the Sarason Fortress, but I can't get inside. The people I'm with won't let me."

Skage nodded. "When you found this bag did you find a chalice?"

Anza nodded. "Yeah, we were warned not to use it."

"Well, if you want to see your mother again you will have to. Drink from it and you will be able to sneak by anyone. You will be more than invisible. It will be as if you didn't exist to others."

"You mean like a ghost?" She asked, her interest piqued.

"Exactly like that." Skage said. "Now go find me that talisman so I can bring your mother back, Anza. And don't talk to me again until you have it." With that Skage fell silent and motionless once more.

Anza found the chalice near the shelf Rafik was standing in front of. He was staring off into space, not even acknowledging she was there. She glanced down at what he was holding and noticed the ruby. She realized he must be having another vision. Brushing past him, she grabbed the chalice and the waterstone. "Have fun with your visions, I'm saving Mom." She pecked a kiss on Rafik's cheek and squeezed the stone above the chalice, filling it with cool water. She moved the chalice to her lips, resting it there. Should she drink the whole thing? Or just a sip? She glanced at Skage, wondering if she should ask him. Shaking her head, she tilted the chalice and took a small sip.

She stood there, frozen, unsure of what to do. Then it happened. A feeling of cold washed over her. Then emptiness and sorrow consumed her. She was nothing. The chalice clattered to the floor and Anza took a step back, gasping for air. As the panic subsided her breath returned. "That's so weird." She said, holding out her hand. She could see it, but also the table beyond it. She was transparent. Turning to her brother, she walked right through him. Anza giggled and turned to the ladder, fearing she would be trapped. She grabbed the first rung as if nothing had changed. "I'll be back, Rafik. I promise."

Chapter 8: House of Spiders

Sarason Fortress, Tahlbiru Ocean, Alutopek

The sky was pale blue. A color he had never seen in the sky before. Storm clouds rolled in and a cold breeze brushed against Rafik. He was surrounded by pink water, and he stood on an island with six others. Beyond the small island and the pink water was a shore lined with Kylix soldiers. The faint smell of burning caught on the breeze as it turned.

"It is finally over." One man said, his eyes a glowing dark green. His skin pale and he stood taller than the others. He turned to the one woman that was here and kissed her. Even Rafik was surprised with how handsome he was.

She smiled before turning to the man on the ground. "You had so much potential, Ruby."

"Don't call me that." He snapped, spitting on the ground at her feet. "My name is Roobino."

"Yes." The woman smiled, a hint of song on her voice. "A name that history will forget."

"Kristol, how could-"

"It's Queen Kristol." She said, cutting Roobino off. "I am Queen Kristol. You're nothing."

"I'm a king!" Roobino said. He tried getting to his feet but another with icy blue eyes stopped him from getting up.

"Former king." The green-eyed man laughed. "And not a very good one. Even your own wizard turned on you."

He gestured to a man standing aside from everyone else. His head bowed, but Rafik recognized the robe and staff. "Izamar?" He asked, though nobody answered.

Roobino turned to the wizard. "Why?" He asked.

Izamar smiled, winking at Roobino, but not saying a word.

"Safsil." Roobino said, looking up at the icy blue-eyed man keeping him down. "You're next. Emerald and Kristol are going to get you next."

Rafik guessed the one with the vibrant green eyes was Emerald. He stepped forward, laughing at Roobino. "No, he won't be next. We've made a deal."

"A deal?" Roobino asked. Again, he tried getting up, and again, the one called Safsil pushed him down onto his knees.

"Yes. After this we are going to conquer the Rantyak Islands. I'll have Alutopek and King Emerald and Queen Kristol will have the island chain." Safsil explained.

"I think we have talked long enough." Emerald said. "Sarafin!" He ordered, snapping his fingers. "My most loyal soldier."

Rafik gasped, seeing the sixth man. He had seen him before. The tattoo of the dragon wrapped around a sword still on his left hand. He pulled out a small knife from his belt and turned to Roobino.

"Please, Emerald!" Roobino said, fighting back tears.

"Roobino, I sentence you to death." King Emerald said. "Go on." He nodded.

Sarafin turned from Emerald to Roobino, knife at the ready. In one motion he threw the knife at Safsil's foot, spun around pulling out another knife, and held it at Emerald's neck. Izamar stepped in, waving his staff before banging it on the ground. The words he spoke Rafik didn't understand. It froze Kristol, Roobino, and Safsil in place.

"Your tricks don't work on me." Emerald laughed; his hands still raised. He glared at Sarafin. "You are going to pay."

Sarafin shook his head. "For years you have allowed needless bloodshed. Betraying others for your own gain. It didn't matter to you so long as you were the one left on top. So many people died. You murdered my family! I've been planning this for years. And now it is finally happening. Thanks to you Alutopek is united under one king now. And I am going to make sure it's the right man. Not a monster."

Emerald laughed. "You? You are going to be king?"

Sarafin shook his head. "No. My want for vengeance makes me no better than you. It is up to Izamar here to find the rightful king."

The smile faded from Emerald's face. His glare narrowed. "You are going to pay."

"Yes. But not from you." Sarafin said. Emerald threw a punch as Sarafin ducked. Izamar clapped his staff against the back of Emerald, immobilizing him.

The wizard spoke several words Rafik couldn't recognize. He gasped, as he saw the four kings begin to turn to stone. Kristol gasped, Roobino began crying, Safsil stood calm, and Emerald snarled with anger. Only their eyes remained with color. They glowed with light before finally becoming a dull color. Safsil's eyes turned to sapphires, Emerald's to emeralds, Kristol's to a pure white crystal, and Roobino's to rubies.

"What did you do?" Sarafin asked?

"Stopped you from adding more blood on your hands." Izamar sighed. He reached for Kristol's eyes, popping the stones out. "They will remain like this forever until these stones return to their eyes."

"Well," Sarafin said. "They'll never find him." He pushed the statue of King Emerald. It splashed into the pink water and sank into the depths. As Izamar took the rubies from Roobino's eyes the memory faded.

Rafik gasped. The serene pink waters were replaced with the familiar drab stone walls. "Welcome back." Izamar smiled.

"Th-that was…they were…" Rafik said, still shaking the feeling of the vision out of him.

Izamar nodded. "The Four Kings, yes. The Jewels of Alutopek, as they've been dubbed."

"And you were there." Rafik stated more as fact than question.

"I was." Izamar said. "Sarafin and I were working together for years in trying to find a way to stop King Emerald. He was cunning, ruthless, and the trait all four of them shared, bloodthirsty."

Rafik stared at the spherical ruby. He'd never believe that it was once an actual eye. Let alone one of the eyes of Alutopek's most famous kings. He wanted to grab it again, investigate more of the former king's past.

"That feeling, the tingling." Izamar said, pulling Rafik away from his thoughts. "That is what you are feeling for when trying to use psychometry. A memory just wanting to escape. Everything has a memory. You just need to find it."

Rafik nodded. "I want to see more."

"Of course." Izamar chuckled lightly. "That is the curse with psychometry. You're shown just enough to crave more. To go back. And to know infinite knowledge of the truth is at your fingertips. Whole groups of seekers have been formed obsessing over the hidden knowledge. Be careful, Rafik. It isn't unheard of to be lost to the powers of psychometry."

"Why did you have me use the ruby?" Rafik asked, setting it down. "Roobino's eye."

"Because since that stone was once part of a living being its imprint of a memory would be much stronger." Izamar said. "Anybody with a trace of psychometry could view the memories."

"I could have just used this." Rafik said, holding the hilt of his sword and hearing the voice enter his mind.

Izamar's eyes widened. "Blaridane." He said softly. "I actually got the idea of what I did to the Four Kings from blood metal. We could have used blood metal, yes. But not Blaridane."

"Why?" Rafik asked.

"The origins of Blaridane are unknown. Just when you find its birth, there are clues that it is even older. What is known that it is twisted, and so ancient it has gained a mind of its own. It taints the user, slowly possessing them."

Rafik shook his head. "Then how come I'm not possessed?"

"Possession doesn't happen instantly. It takes time. But you are holding it, using it, the process has already begun. Drop the sword, boy."

He moved to unclasp the sheath but froze. He needed the sword. What if there was danger? His sister needed him. And he could still learn how to fight with Blaridane. More so than if he had any other sword. "No." Rafik said.

"But there are so many other swords out there." Izamar reasoned.

"No." Rafik repeated. "I need it."

Izamar sighed. "See. It has already begun. My only hope for you is that you lose that sword."

"And if I don't?" Rafik asked. He felt his blood boil, heat swelling within him as he clenched his fists.

"I won't teach you anymore until you do." Izamar said.

Rafik stared at the ground, thinking of what to say to the wizard. He couldn't give up Blaridane. But he needed Izamar. He had to learn how to control his talent. It would be easy to lie and say he no longer had the sword, hiding it from Izamar. But was it really wise to be lying to a wizard? Even if they were stuck in a mirror. As he wondered, a twinkle of light shimmered out of the corner of his eye. He stooped down, picking up the chalice. He looked around for any sign of Anza, but she wasn't here. Rafik cursed, seeing the portrait of Skage turned back around. He turned it back to face the wall and looked at Izamar.

"Was Anza down here?" He asked.

Izamar shrugged. "While you were in a trance I wasn't here."

"Ya shire." Rafik cursed again. He turned to the ladder and left.

Salina screamed, falling over. The bag she held suddenly bulged, toppling her over. The flap opened but nothing came out. She balled up the cloth bag and threw it across the deck. If it was going to try and cripple her, she didn't want anything to do with it.

100

Soon after the bag bulged a second time. Rafik crawled out of it, confusion written over his face as he looked around.

"Have you seen Anza?" He asked Salina, still appearing visibly shaken.

She shook her head, slowly regaining her composure. "No. Just you. Everyone else is below deck."

"Where is Gorik?" Rafik asked.

"Gorik just left us here. I haven't seen your sister since she crawled into that cursed thing." Salina said, glaring at the bag and then at Rafik.

"What? Why doesn't he have the bag? Why did he leave us?"

"Because he is selfish. I doubt he'll be back for any of us." Salina said.

"He is not selfish." Rafik snapped. "He may be a lot of things, but selfish isn't one of them."

Salina sighed. "I took the bag. I took it to ensure he comes back. Gods know he loves you and your sister. Haven't the slightest idea why."

"Anza wasn't with Gorik?" Rafik asked, ignoring Salina's goading.

"No." Salina said. "I saw him leave myself. It was just him."

Rafik's heart beat faster. His imagination racing with dangerous events that may have befallen his sister. The Kylix snatching her. The monster from the tunnels taking her. Dragons in the sunken fortress ready to devour the unknowing. His hands shook, and voice cracked. "I-I lost my father seven years ago. I watched my mother give her life for Anza and me just yesterday. I'm not losing my sister too. She's missing, and I need to find her."

"She's in the bag." Salina said. "She hasn't come out of there."

Rafik shook his head. "There isn't anyone else down there, and there aren't any hiding spots. She's on this ship, or in the fortress."

He began searching the deck for his sister, yelling her name. A few of the Datians below deck emerged, asking what was going on. Rafik explained, and they confirmed she wasn't below deck. They all faced the Sarason Fortress.

"She isn't in the fortress." Salina insisted. "We would have heard her get off the ship. Do you really think she could even make it there safely? Probably fell overboard."

"No." Rafik said, shaking his head. "She's alive. And I'm going to find her."

He got to the port side of the *River Lizard* and climbed over the rail. He jumped down, steadying himself. "Get back here. No one is to leave this ship." Salina ordered.

"I'm going to find my sister." Rafik said. "You can stay back. I don't care. Anybody coming with me?"

Several others moved to the rail to climb over. Some mentioning finding Anza, while others just wanted to get off the ship. "No. I am in charge!"

"You are the city leader of Datz." Rafik said, turning back around to face her. "But we aren't in Datz anymore. You are the leader of nothing." He and the others began jumping from rock to rock, slowly making their way to the entrance. Periodically they would scream Anza's name.

Salina paced back and forth on the *River Lizard*, cursing Rafik. No one talked to her like that. As the last of them entered the fortress she climbed over the rail and onto the rocky shores. She was going to make him pay.

From the coast, and back home in Datz, the Sarason Fortress just looked like a black dot on the horizon. Even the spider just seemed to be a lump on the end of a stick unless one squinted to make out the spider. But up close, it was another story. The spider, even with its lifeless eyes, looked real and ready to attack. The tower it rested on was built with black stone. As Rafik got closer to the door his stomach churned. He had to find his sister, but everything in his body was telling him to turn the other way. It didn't help that the black entrance emanated darkness. It was like the tunnels above water. Nothing good could be in there.

He pushed forward, entering the shadows. Passing through it was like going into another world. The tower was at a tilt, sinking slowly into the ocean. But the floors here were level. Stranger still, torches were lit. Behind him the darkness still glowed with an unholy light.

Rafik yelled, and his voice echoed around the chamber. It was a round room, torches and statues placed against the wall under a stone archway. Topping each keystone was a spider. Rafik saw a trap door he believed to lead to the lower levels. To his left, though, was a spiral staircase leading to the rest of the tower.

"Anza!" He shouted. He paused, waiting for a response, but no one answered.

The first of the Datians began to emerge from the dark portal. Some had the same look of curious wonder as Rafik. Others of fear. Those afraid made a sign of protection across their heart and began to explore. Rafik opened the trapdoor and shouted for his sister once more.

Nothing.

He took a step on the staircase descending deeper into the tower. Others followed him. The stairs spiraled around the tower once. The new room lit up as Rafik entered. Elegant tapestries hung on the wall, and an ornate rug ran from one end to the other. There were no windows, but the smell of the sea wafted in. There were doors on either side, and a large set of double doors on the other end of the room. Everyone scattered. Some marveling the tapestries while others tried the doors.

One room was filled with armor, another swords and spears. A third had bows and quivers of arrows. Others were empty shelves while the last one on the right was devoid of anything. Through all the rooms there wasn't any sign of Anza.

Rafik turned to the double doors. A silver lining traced around the edges, and just like the arches on the above floor, a spider stood guard over them. It took Rafik and one other man to pull open one door. It scraped across the floor, growling. The hinges creaking with every movement.

Beyond the doors was another portal of darkness. The tendrils of shadow wafted into the room, giving Rafik chills. Streaks of purple light emanated from it. His stomach dropped and he began to sweat. Whatever was beyond there, it wasn't safe. He clenched his teeth, thinking of Anza and grabbing hold of his sword. No matter what, he'd find her.

With Blaridane's added courage, Rafik stumbled as he walked through the veil of darkness. A sudden cold shot through him entering the new darkened room. The only light came from the purple and black glowing behind him. This was the room he was expecting upon entering. The room was tilted, walls crumbled. There were doors leading to other rooms, but halfway across the room water lapped at the stone floor. He went to the first door and opened it.

More weapons. But these ones less refined. Green rope bound jagged rocks or shells to long poles. If Rafik didn't know better, he would have thought the rope was seaweed. The blades were rimmed with reds, purples, and dark greens. Each one looking sicklier than the last.

He left the room and turned back to the rhythmic tide of the water. His hair on the back of his neck stood straight up. He squinted into the murky depths but saw nothing. It felt as if something was watching him. Turning away from water he noticed others finally enter this part of the tower. Beside the black and purple portal was a peculiarly large well that was boarded up. Rafik leaned over the edge and peered through the cracks. Nothing. A reflective light of shimmering water at the bottom of the well sparkled as a fellow Datian held a torch over the ledge. Why a well was so high up in the tower didn't make any sense.

"Maybe they used it for something else?" The Datian suggested, obviously having the same thought.

"Maybe. No sign of Anza, though." He said, shaking his head."

"I think she went up the stairs instead." The man said, pointing back at the portal. "I don't think she would want to go through that."

Rafik glanced at the black and purple portal as he walked through it, giving him the same chills as before. Before going up the stairs Rafik returned to the room with the swords. Although he had Blaridane, he took a couple knives, stuffing them into his belt.

Anza marveled at her new-found ability. When she left the *River Lizard,* she slipped on one of the rocks and landed on the water. It was like landing on the softest of feather cushions. She didn't sink, and it felt like the water just moved aside to accept her. As she got to her feet she was just as surprised to find she could walk across it.

She made her way to the entrance, wonder in her eyes. Before she had drank from the chalice it looked dark and foreboding. Although the darkness was still there, it didn't have the menacing quality. Like a famous portrait missing a portion of color.

"Now where are you, talisman?" She asked herself upon entering. Anza turned to the spiral staircase on her left and went up them. "Might as well start at the top and work my way down."

Everything looked the same now. A few doors, a long red rug with black and gold trim. Portraits or torches stood between each door. The only difference was who was in the portrait. The corridor slowly turned, winding upward at a steady incline. Dust covered the floor, but she didn't stir it up. Her feet just pressed lightly against the ground but were as if she never even touched it.

Once or twice, she thought she heard faint echoes coming from below, calling her name. Each time she shrugged it off, believing it was her imagination. Onward she went, not deviating from the main path. Every portrait she glanced at it felt as if the person inside was going to lunge at her. Some were dressed in Kylix armor, others in elegant robes.

Finally, after what felt like it coiled upwards for far too long, she came to the end of the hallway. The stones closer to the ground were more weathered and discolored than the upper half. It was obvious to her that where she stood now was once the very top of this tower. At the far end of the hall was a bust of Skage, in the same pose and scowling facial expression as the one in the portrait back in the secret room. His glare pierced through her, as if he could see her, even though she was invisible.

There were no windows or doors at the end. The only way through was back the way she came. She looked down at the floor to find any hint of a door, but none was found. She then looked up and gasped. Dangling from the ceiling where a chandelier would usually hang were two large, intricately carved wooden doors. How she didn't notice them before, she wasn't sure. Each door had a carving of half a spider. When closed, like they were now, it was one giant beast that looked surprisingly convincing. From the abdomen of the carved spider was a white chain hovering just above her head. Anza jumped up, trying to grab it, and missed.

With a running start she leaped into the air, caught hold of the chain, and pulled. At first nothing happened. When Anza was just dangling there, holding tight of the chain, she yanked again. This time the doors pulled open and a horde of bats shrieked and flew towards her. Anza cowered to the floor, the bats just inches from her. They screeched flying past her, and down the corridor.

As the cloud of bats disappeared, Anza noticed in the center of the hallway was a small, spiraling staircase. She got to her feet and stepped on it. The moment she did it began to rise back into the hole the spider doors exposed. The spider doors closed behind her with a resounding clank. Anza prayed to herself that not only would she be safe, but also be able to leave.

Rafik heard the screeching of the bats and yelled his sister's name. Looking at the ground he didn't believe anyone else had been up here. The dust hadn't been disturbed, at least. He knew it stood to reason that it probably meant his sister wasn't up there, but he still had to check. He couldn't give up on her. "I'm coming." He shouted and ran towards the noise of the shrieking bats.

He remembered one day while exploring in Datz a cloud of bats came out of nowhere, swarming her. If she was anywhere near these ones, he knew she'd be frightened. It relieved him that he didn't hear a familiar scream of hers, but also worried him even more. Where was she? If she didn't scream, then something else caused the bats to suddenly disperse like that.

Who would have been hiding, and living, in the Sarason Fortress? Would they accept strangers, or try to kill them on sight? He grabbed the hilt of Blaridance moving forward, finding calm in its familiar scream of bloodlust.

"Where are you, Anza?" Rafik asked himself, continuing forward. By now others had caught up to him. Some wielding weapons, others still as defenseless as before. They didn't talk, just continued upward.

All he could do was check each room as he continued upward. Every room was decorated in some elegant fashion or another. Not one gave any sign that it was in a ruined tower. What was worse, there was no sign of Anza.

"Maybe she did fall overboard?" Rafik heard someone murmur. He shot them a glare, refusing to even consider the thought. She was alive, not drowned in the depths of the Tahlbiru Ocean. He closed another door, continuing his search.

Anza was taking each step carefully. Even with her ability to see in the dark, thanks to drinking from that chalice, it was hard to see. This darkness wasn't natural. The stairs were narrow and uneven as if this part of the tower was hastily put together. She tripped on one stair, not paying attention, and fell. Pushing herself up she realized why they were, in fact, uneven. Each step was a myriad of bones varying in shapes and sizes. The thought that she was walking over the dead unnerved her, but she kept moving forward.

There weren't any windows to peer out of, or portrait or carving to keep her entertained. It wasn't long before she grew bored and started to count the stairs spiraling upwards to who knows what. Several minutes, and 983 steps later, she made it to the top. Anza groaned, looking back down the stairwell. Once she finds the talisman, she will need to go back down them. Even on normally level stairs it wouldn't be any better.

The stairs ended onto a long platform. At the end was a set of spider shaped doors like the one she had opened to get here. Halfway across the platform there was a spider carved into the ground, and on the walls. From the ceiling hung a statue of one. Each spider seemed so real she caught herself waiting for one to move or growl. A moment of hesitation later she began her way to the doors, careful not to step on the carving on the floor.

The doors were bigger up close. She ran her hand along the spiders. There weren't any handles to pull. She pushed against the door, but it didn't budge. Trying again, putting her weight in it, it didn't even rattle.

Anza looked around, wondering how to get in. Something told her the Kymu-Guiden Talisman would be behind those doors. There wasn't a sign of a keyhole on the spider either. She turned, trying to find some sort of clue to get in.

Anza started feeling the carvings, hoping for a secret button. She whipped her hand back, feeling the first one. It had actual coarse fur on its body. It felt real, and the last thing she wanted to do was to pet a spider. She turned to the one in the center. It had to be there. This one also had fur, though it didn't bother her as she pretended it was just a rug. She shook her head after combing through the fur. No keyhole or clue to show how to get inside.

The last one, hanging from the ceiling was hard to examine. It hung above her head higher than she could reach from jumping. It dangled downwards as if on a web. She imagined their dark eyes glaring down at her, waiting to strike. A moment later she averted her gaze, turning her attention elsewhere, as for the briefest of moments it appeared alive and waiting to attack. Her imagination got the better of her when she noticed drool on the spider's mouth and pincers. She hurried away from where it could attack her and found herself in front of the large spider door once again.

She ran or hands over it, squinting in some areas, even scratching parts as she examined it. She thanked the gods these doors didn't appear as realistic as the other arachnid decorations in the room. It was just a basic shape of a spider's head, body, and eight legs. She traced her hands across the door and found a thin, nearly invisible, string coming from its abdomen much like the first door had the chain. She pulled on the fine wire and could hear gears turning and what sounded like a lock shifting positions.

The door stayed shut.

Anza screamed in frustration, stamping her foot. "Why won't you open?" She said, banging and pushing on the door. The echo of her hitting the door was her only reply. "Guess I'll turn back, start looking in all the other rooms I passed."

She let out another scream, this time from fear. The spider carvings on the wall had emerged from off the wall. And the one on the floor had risen, glaring at her with bright red eyes. She sprinted to the wall, wanting to avoid the spider in the center of the room. The spiders on the wall were held up by a pole in the center. Seeing this, the look of realism faded from her mind, and she examined the spider once more. The spider rotated around a pole in either direction. When it was facing towards the door there was more mechanical clicking. It retracted back into the wall, and another bolt echoed. Anza moved to the spider on the opposite wall and did the same.

All that was left was the one in the center of the room now. She avoided its glowing eyes and was surprised that it was now standing taller than a horse. Anza pushed on the spider, but it didn't budge. She pulled on it, but nothing happened. She tried lifting it, kicking it, adjusting the legs, but nothing changed. Scratching her head in confusion, Anza looked up and saw the spider dangling from the ceiling. It had lowered itself as well. Hanging from its mouth wasn't saliva, like she had imagined, but a white metal key. Anza climbed the top of the spider on the floor and jumped. Barely able to reach the key, she snatched it from the spider's 'web.' Once the key was free another lock unbolted.

Anza took the key to the door, but still no keyhole to be found. She had solved one puzzle and got stuck with a new one. She turned to face the last remaining spider. It looked real. From the glowing eyes to the thin hairs on its legs. Its mouth appeared ready for its meal, which Anza hoped wouldn't be her.

She circled the spider, looking for any sign of where to put the key. When none was found she climbed on top and combed through its fur. Still, nothing was found. Frustrated, Anza screamed and hit the spider. A hollow sound emanated from the statue. Anza jumped, sliding off the spider's body and fell on her back. She groaned and rubbed her eyes. A cloud of dust had plumed from her landing on the floor. Her hand wasn't as translucent as it once was either. The power from the chalice was fading.

"I should have taken more than a sip." She said to herself. She rubbed her eyes, waving her hands to try and clear up the dust. Then, she saw it. On the belly of the spider was a small hole. It looked out of place on an otherwise realistic spider. It was the exact same shape as the key she got from the dangling spider. With shaking hands, Anza slid the key in.

Even more gears roared to life, churning, and growling. If Anza didn't know better, she would have thought she had awoken some monster. The last bolt came loose and before Anza could get out from under the spider it sank back beneath the floor.

Anza screamed for help as the room disappeared.

The spider came to a stop, and Anza looked around. She was in a small crawlspace. There was only one way to go, forward. Praying this wasn't a trap, she began crawling. The room slowly grew big enough that a child her size could now walk upright. There was another small, spiraling staircase that led to a trapdoor. She pushed open the trapdoor and gasped. The walls were lined with books, tables, and a coffin. Beside the coffin was a massive suit of armor. Not like the Kylix skeletal armor, but plain metal. It looked menacing, and she didn't want to go near it. In the center of the room was another spider, carved into the floor. A pedestal sprouted from its center. On the far side of the wall was the spider door she was trying so hard to open just minutes ago.

"Oh. It's the exit." She said to herself, shaking her head. "Now where's the talisman?"

Anza had wandered the circular room several times now. There was a chest next to the door. She filed through it but found no talisman the one Skage had described. There was another bust of Skage. The menacing suit of armor stood guard next to the coffin she was still hesitant on approaching. There was an old robe that the priests of Rhine-Pa would wear. And there was another robe she always imagined witches or wizards in fairytales would wear. On another part of the room was a table against a wall with thick books stacked on top of it. She rummaged through it, wondering if there was a secret compartment.

Still nothing.

She was beginning to believe it wasn't anywhere in this room when she noticed a lever hiding between two bookcases. She pulled the lever and a ladder descended from the ceiling allowing the upper level to be reached. She had noticed the upper level earlier but didn't notice any sign of reaching it.

The loft area was just a walkway circling the room. Her heart sank, realizing it was filled with even more clutter than below. More books filled this area. A table she came across was littered with loose papers and quills. Chests were stacked atop one another, and furniture was shifted around making reaching it seem more like a maze. Anza sighed, looking from one end of the room to the other. She knew she was close; she could feel it. She just wondered how long it would take to find it.

Chapter 9: A Girl Full of Poison

Trinkit, Biodlay Desert, Alutopek

Gorik turned his head upward to the night sky. It was his favorite time. He could peer into the darkness and fool himself into believing the Black Wall wasn't there. Stories were told that the night sky was littered with stars. As if a black canvas had been punctured nearly to shreds and put over a light. Now only the brightest of stars shined through. He could see the navigation star, and his favorite constellation. He remembered Drane telling the story of Quellor to Rafik around a campfire one night and smiled.

"You should have seen him down there, Drane. You would have been so proud. Of both of them." He choked back a tear, now focusing on the floor of his boat. "Pull yourself together, man."

A flash of light struck in the distance. The rumble of thunder came soon after. He cursed. The last thing he wanted to do was row a boat in a rainstorm in the middle of an ocean. He turned around and gave a sigh of relief. Trinkit was growing closer.

Before the Black Wall, the people of Datz expanded to Trinkit. It soon became a seething underbelly of corruption. Somehow, they survived the Black Wall while Datz was destroyed. There was no sign of ruin, and the docks didn't have any hazards to sail around. He wasn't surprised it was becoming what Datz once was.

He allowed himself to look back at the Sarason Fortress. "I should have fought harder." He said to himself, thinking of Salina with the bag hiding two children. "Now you're stuck there. With her." He always avoided looking at the massive spider. In the religion of Rhine-Pa it was the symbol for death. It never made sense to him why it was here, in a city that revolved around sailing, traded goods, and money. He always assumed it was a long-forgotten secret. The legends and stories only a deterrent to the truth. In either case, he hated the statue.

"Oy!" A voice shouted at Gorik. "Wha' choo doin' ou' this late?"

Gorik kept rowing, ignoring the call. A moment later an arrow landed just in front of his feet, a rope tied to its end. A ship sailed towards him, a sailor with a bow glaring at him. Sailors from the ship began pulling on the rope, towing Gorik in closer.

"Are ya deaf?" A sailor shouted at him.

"What? No, I was distracted." Gorik said, getting to his feet. "Who are you?"

"We'll ask the questions. Who are you?" One of the sailors on the ship shouted back.

"My name is Gorik of Datz. I just escaped the Kylix. The king has taken Datz. All that's left of us are on the Sarason Fortress. I've come looking for aid."

"Soun's t' me is tha' we 'ave a traitor. You, Gorik o' Datz, are under arrest fer treason."

Gorik cursed under his breath. He wasn't planning for this. There were few people who supported King Vanarzir in Trinkit. Just his luck to have found one. Acknowledging defeat, and praying the gods hadn't deserted him, he raised his hands into the air and lowered his head.

The sailors brought him on board, tying him up. "What should we do with him, Captain?" One sailor asked.

The captain stepped forward. Gorik looked up but couldn't see any distinguishing features. His face was hidden behind a wide brimmed hat and the darkness of the night. "You three. Take him to the Trainer. He will handle our little friend. The rest of us will go to the Sarason Fortress."

Gorik's face paled. He could go to the Trainer; that was fine. But the ones he left behind wouldn't be prepared for new attackers. He said nothing, unsure of what he could say. *'Least I'm still on my way to Trinkit.'* He thought to himself.

Gorik was surprised at how fast he and his captors had arrived at Trinkit. Either they were incredibly fast rowers, or he had gone farther than he thought before getting caught. He liked to believe it was the latter. There were two guards at the dock, and a new stone wall was put up just behind them. "That's new." Gorik said out loud as he was shoved out of the boat.

"Shut up." One of his captors snarled.

Trinkit had always been known to house the lowlifes, thieves, murderers, and the generally unsavory people within society. The guards of Trinkit were well armed, and more dangerous than the Kylix. Their only weakness was money. They would serve and protect the highest bidder before they protected their own mother. With the fall of Datz after the Black Wall Trinkit picked up the pieces. It was a strange cocktail of legitimacy mixed with the criminal underbelly seething to the top.

But last time Gorik was here there wasn't a wall blocking the rest of the city from the dock and Tahlbiru Ocean. There was one good thing about the Black Wall. Violence had reduced drastically after that. War was but a whisper. There wasn't any need for other walls, until recently. The sailor scrunched his brows, looking up and down the dock to see what else had changed. These walls didn't look like anything the Kylix soldiers or King Vanarzir's architects build. No, this one was built hastily. It wouldn't hold up to most large waves, let alone a well-placed kick. It was no wonder the guards were standing in front of the wall, rather than on top.

"Why are there walls here now?" Gorik asked one of the guards.

"I said be quiet!" His captor said, kicking Gorik in the back of his knee. He collapsed to the floor, his peg leg breaking off. His captors were nice enough to let him pick up the leg, as they were all laughing too much to stop him anyway.

"Monsters." The guard on the left replied. "They come every new moon."

"And then disappear as the first light of the sun glows off of the Black Wall." The other guard continued.

"What are they?" Gorik asked, ignoring his captor telling him to stay silent.

114

"We are taking this prisoner to the Trainer. Is he still here?" His other captor asked, cutting off the guard from answering Gorik.

The guards nodded. "Yes. Until tomorrow."

Gorik was shoved in the back and ordered to continue forward. He walked past the guards and into the rubble that passed as an entryway from the wall. Aside from the wall, the city looked the same. A heavy haze hung over everything making what lied in the distance appear distorted. The smell of alcohol, tobacco, and mixed perfumes wafted through the air in a sickening mixture. "I see it hasn't changed much." He noted, seeing men stumble from one tavern and into another. Scantily clad women walked the streets, calling to others. Walking past one alley he saw two men dueling with swords, insulting one another.

The group turned down the infamous Pirate's Alley. On one end was a jailhouse, rarely used except to lock up the highly dangerous until they had calmed down. On the other end was a temple. It was the one building in Trinkit that wasn't vandalized or in any form of dilapidation. Everywhere between the two were taverns, brothels, opium and gambling dens, and an inn. If someone couldn't find what they were looking for in Pirate's Alley, it didn't exist.

In the middle of Pirate's Alley was a familiar tavern. The Silver Shark. A weathered sign swayed back and forth in the shape of a shark with the tavern's name. The arm of a man hanging out of its mouth pointing to the door.

The smell of alcohol was stronger inside the Silver Shark. The hooting and hollering deafening, and if one paid attention they could hear music being played somewhere. All the furniture had seen better days. Fights occurred almost nightly. As a result, the tables and chairs were just nailed with the scraps of wood they could piece together. Even the lights were dimmer inside as tobacco smoke wafted through the air.

One of his captors walked up to the barman, and he pointed to a man in the far corner of the Silver Shark. "We're in luck. He is still here. In the far corner." His captor said upon returning. They shoved Gorik deeper into the tavern.

Gorik noticed shady characters sitting in wait. He knew most were killers. Murder for hire. Few approached these men without their purses much lighter and someone dead by morning. In the farthest corner was a hooded figure that looked like the rest. An emblem of a skull on the back of his hood gave away who it was.

"Samron?" One of his captors asked.

"Aye." He responded without looking up and taking a drink from his mug. "What do you want?"

"We found a rebel out at sea. Says they were fighting off the Kylix in Datz and ended up on the Sarason Fortress."

"Did you, now? Leave him." Samron ordered.

"What do you want us to do with the others at the fortress? Our captain and crew are heading there now."

"If they return," He said, taking another drink. "Then I'll decide. But I'm sure they're already dead. You know what lurks in those waters. Untie him before you leave." He brushed his hand, shooing them.

One man knelt and freed Gorik from his bonds. They nodded towards Samron and left. Once out of earshot Gorik sat down, yanked the mug from Samron and took a long swig. "Hello Samron."

"Long time, Gorik."

"About seven years, give or take the day."

"What are you doing, getting caught? Thought you were smarter than that. Haven't even heard from you since Drane's death." Samron said in an authoritative whisper with a hint of anger.

"Well, I wasn't sure if we could do what you believed. Especially after what you let happen. But I do now." Gorik said.

"You believe, or forced into it?"

Gorik laughed. "A little of both to be perfectly honest."

"I can't imagine you came here to say hi to me. What do you want?"

116

"The Kylix have taken Datz. I managed to get the few survivors to the Sarason Fortress. I was hoping you might be able to help."

"Well, what do you expect me to do with the old and weak?" Samron asked.

"They lost their homes, are willing to stop the king, and get their children back."

"A lot are. But few who are put to the test are capable of such a feat. The rest just gets in the way." Samron took another drink and let out a deep, satisfying breath. "And you want me to waltz into the Sarason Fortress and then meet with the Kylix who are campaigning, with the king might I add, and say 'it's okay, they're with me?'"

"No...well, not exactly." Gorik said. "There is this boy there you might like." He paused, staring Samron into his eyes still hiding beneath the hood.

"I should gut you right now." Samron snapped, cutting off Gorik. "Just because of what happened gives you no excuse to insult me like that. And you know me better than to suggest something like that."

"Which is why I wasn't." Gorik said, raising his hands in surrender. "Old friend, you misunderstand me. He has talent."

"How do you know?"

"He told me, asking me about it. And has some old artifacts hidden away and forgotten to prove it." Gorik said.

"Very interesting." Samron nodded.

"No, the interesting thing is that it's Drane's boy."

"Does he know the truth about his father?"

Gorik shook his head. "No. But I'm sure he will find out on his own if he isn't told soon."

"Have you heard of Xeo?" Samron asked, changing the subject.

Gorik nodded. "Just what the Kylix said when conquering Datz."

"Two interesting things happened in the Nyler Peninsula." Samron said, leaning in close to avoid the local eavesdroppers.

117

"Go on." Gorik insisted, leaning forward as well.

"In Kristol, a boy who wasn't captured by the Kylix strolled into camp, demanding the king. He challenged him to a duel."

"That wasn't the best move." Gorik laughed. "I like his spirit, though. Shame he is dead."

Samron glared from within his hood. Gorik went quiet not a moment later. "As I was saying, he challenged the king to a duel. The king agreed, and the boy was getting the better of him. The king pushed him into the campfire they were fighting around. At the same time a mysterious rider charged into camp, hoisted the boy up onto horseback and disappeared into the night. The boy who fell into the fire, that is Xeo. The king wants him, and fast. Whispers are beginning to spread that King Vanarzir isn't as invincible as we once believed."

"Very interesting." Gorik nodded. "And no one can find the boy?"

"Or the mysterious rider." Samron said. "The Kylix lost track of him after he hid out in the Nyler Necropolis. They tore apart what was left of Jorn and the dransbian mine. That's why the Kylix held off on attacking Datz; and ransacked it once they did."

"As far as I know, he never made it there." Gorik said. "What's the second thing?"

"We have a queen." Samron said.

"Excuse me?"

"A queen." Samron said. "One man stood up to the Kylix in Kristol once they arrived. Went face to face with the king. The king killed him and heard a scream from nearby. It was a young woman. The king had just killed her father. She agreed to go with him so long as the people of Kristol were left safe. The king, smitten with her beauty, agreed. He would call off their attack and she would be his queen."

"How do you know this?" Gorik asked.

"I was there." Samron said. "Very few know yet."

"Then why are you telling me this?"

"The king was convinced that taking her as a queen would help calm the other cities in the east to not raise arms against him." Samron said. "Though I doubt that will be the case. Not with Xeo out there."

"Again, why are you telling me this?"

"Because it's time! It's time, Gorik." Samron insisted.

"That's what you said last time. And I lost my best friend and my leg. And the king is still sitting there in his throne." Gorik said.

"This time it's different, Gorik." Samron said. "People are going to rally behind Xeo. If a boy challenged the king and survived, anybody could."

"I came to you asking for help." Gorik said.

"You were coming to me before being captured?" Samron asked, taking a drink. "You're losing your touch."

"No, just distracted. I don't have my best friend to watch my back."

"I'm surprised you knew I was here." Samron said.

Gorik shook his head. "I still know how to read what's written in silver, Samron."

"I see." Samron chuckled. "I'll help. But you will help me in return."

"Fine." Gorik said, thinking of Rafik and Anza. They needed to be protected.

Samron smiled. "Then we have a deal. Take me to him. I might be able to help if the Kylix haven't tried to attack them yet. There is one thing I must grab before we go."

Gorik nodded. "I'll find us a ship."

"One last thing. How'd you find the letter saying I was here?" Samron turned to ask.

"I found Shallon. He showed me the letter. He had lost his stone. Plus, I heard the king sent someone out ahead of him to find the ones with talent and bring them in before his army arrives. And their next stop is Trinkit. If you haven't been killed for being a traitor, I figured it was you."

"Yes. I'm glad not everyone abandoned me seven years ago." Samron said.

Gorik bit his lip, not wanting to insult his old friend who was about to help him.

"You know," Samron said, clapping Gorik on the shoulder. "One day your luck is going to run out."

"If it does, I'll take a gamble. Maybe I'll get lucky." Gorik laughed.

Samron shook his head and turned up the stairs that could be rented out above. "I'll be down in a minute."

"I'll meet you back here." Gorik smiled, clapping his hands. "Time to go find a ship."

Gorik's eyes widened. His mouth agape, and his body shook, hairs standing on end. He had just watched his hand shrivel as he shook the girl's hand, greeting her. His heart raced, knee wobbled, and he felt as if he were to collapse at any moment. The girl touched him again and the poison within him was gone. His hand returned to normal, heart slowing, and strength returning. "Who are you?" He gasped, breathless.

"Gorik, this is Ziri." Samron said, resting his hands on her shoulders. "She has talent of poison. Can cure anyone from it as well."

The sailor stared at the girl, eyes wide, mouth agape. Her light brown hair shimmered red in some light and her bright pink lips and icy blue eyes popped in contrast to her ghostly pale complexion. If poison was a person, it would look like Ziri. "Nice to meet you." She whispered. As she spoke a puff of reddish pink smoke left her mouth as well.

"Where did you find her?" Gorik asked, not taking his eyes off the girl.

"Right here, actually. She was being used as an enforcer until she managed to run away. She hid in the cellar of the Silver Shark. I was able to convince the barman and Ziri here to let me take her for a better future." Samron said. He squeezed her shoulders and smiled. "I'm not leaving her."

120

"Well, what's the plan? I found us a ship."

"We go to the fortress, get the boy, and leave."

"What about everyone else?" Gorik asked. "You can't just leave them there."

"It appears that I am." Samron laughed. Gorik glared at the trainer. "No, once I have the boy, I can tell the Kylix soldiers everyone else is dead at the fortress. Proof being Ziri and her talent. Then you can take everyone to wherever you all choose."

"But Samron, they want to join the Soniky. They want to fight." Gorik said a little too loud. Patrons nearby turned to look at them.

Samron shoved his hand to Gorik's mouth and glared at him. "Don't you even mention that to me when I'm in public." He hissed. "You should know better, Gorik."

"Sorry sir." Gorik said once Samron released him.

"They can wait until I come to them. Until then, you can train them. Take them to Rayz or even Syro." Samron said. "I'll be there in a few weeks."

Gorik nodded. "Fine. Let's go." He moved to the side and gestured for them to move forward. He didn't want that girl behind him. He had heard of a girl who could kill with her touch living in Trinkit. He thought it was as believable as an alcohol that offered eternal life. He watched Samron take her hand without hesitation. Gorik tried to remember a time when Samron showed fear and failed.

The same guards were at the dock, and bid them safe traveling, reminding them that there were only 12 days until the new moon. Samron waved it off and climbed into the ship Gorik had provided. It was more of a small ferry than a ship, but it would do. "Why are they talking about the new moon? And what's with the wall?" Gorik finally asked, hoping for a better answer than the one he received when he first arrived.

"Supposedly Taktors have been attacking. I personally haven't witnessed it." Samron said.

"Taktors." Gorik laughed. "You mean the sea people who are hellbent at killing anything on land? The supposed monsters of the deep. I thought they were extinct. If they even existed at all."

"The very same." Samron said. "I heard they even have a weapons cache on the Sarason Fortress."

"I saw one." Ziri whispered. Gorik wasn't sure if she was intentionally whispering, or if that was as loud as she could go. "They're real."

"Girl, I'm a fisherman and sailor. I know my fair share of tall tales, and told some myself, I might add. But Taktors, if they even existed at all, are extinct. No more. Gone. Dead." Gorik argued.

Ziri shook her head, narrowing her eyes at Gorik. Her icy blue eyes gleamed in the moonlight. "One day the truth will show you what's right." With that she sat at the bow of the ferry, away from the other two.

"Where'd you get this one?" Samron asked, patting the side of the boat, picking up an oar. "Not bad for a last-minute pick up."

"Won it from a kid in the Silver Shark." Gorik said. "Barely old enough to drink, let alone gamble at the same time."

"You took advantage of a child?" Samron asked.

Gorik smiled, scratching the back of his head, and looking away from the Trainer. "Yeah, not my proudest moment. He can have it back once we're done with it. Says he built it himself, too."

"Guess we'll see how well she manages." Samron sighed. "It'll do."

The three set sail, back to the Sarason Fortress. Ziri looked around in wonder, dipping her hand into the chilly water. Gorik stared at the spider topped tower looming ever closer, hoping everyone was still safe.

A faint echo of shouting and the clanging of swords caused Rafik to pause. "We're under attack!" A man ran up to Rafik, shouting.

"The Kylix?" Rafik asked, grabbing Blaridane.

The man shook his head. "Looks like mercenaries of some kind."

Rafik nodded. "I still need to find my sister. The rest of you can go fight. I'll join you when I find her."

The group he was with nodded and turned to leave with the man who came to warn them. A nightmare swirled around in his head. Even when holding Blaridane it started to overcome him. He envisioned pirates sweeping the fortress. The trained killers taking anything that moved. And he fell before he found Anza behind the next door. The last thing he would see is them kicking open the nearby door, finding his sister, and her screaming. Wiping away the cold sweat and taking a deep breath, Rafik bit back the wave of fear. He had to find her.

'You doubt me.' Blaridane snarled. *'After everything we've accomplished.'*

Rafik shook his head. "No. I doubt me. You can't control me for every battle. I won't let you."

If fear could laugh, he just heard it. The voice from the sword chuckled. *'You are strong boy, but not enough to stop me.'* Without realizing, Rafik raised his free hand and punched it into the wall.

The boy bit his lip, trying not to curse and give the sword satisfaction. "After this I'm getting rid of you."

'After this you'll already be gone.'

At least the Datians had found weapons, he tried to think, tuning out Blaridane's eagerness for bloodlust. If it wasn't for that they wouldn't stand a chance. He continued up the inclined hallway, hoping there was an end. He was following his sister's footsteps he had finally found, but they continued onward. Minutes later he rounded the corner and came to the spider door on the ceiling with white chain dangling from its abdomen. He had noticed the chain immediately and ran at it. He jumped, grabbed the chain, and yanked as hard as he could. The skinny spiral staircase lowered. Rafik didn't waste any time. As it rose back into the ceiling, he climbed the stairs two at a time. "I'm coming for you Anza."

Anza had sifted through papers and made her way in and out of the randomly placed furniture. She pulled away a couple of chests and looked through its contents, but to no avail. There were diagrams of animals, recipes for potions, a jar containing a silvery substance, and instructions on spells and rituals. In the bottom there were even gold coins, squished quills, and small clay pots. The talisman was still missing. She was beginning to think that it wasn't here. Someone else must have found it. She brushed away her hair, heaved a sigh, and swept the books on the nearby shelf onto the ground. "What the…?" Anza said, leaning into the now empty shelf. A hole was hiding on the wall behind the books. Inside the hole was a wheel.

She reached in and turned the wheel. The now familiar sound of gears churning roared to life. A metal platform extended from the loft as a pole descended from the domed ceiling. Anza inched out onto the platform, arms out balancing like she was on a tight rope. She made it to the pole, the end of the platform widening slightly.

Touching the glass sent a shiver down her spine. The pole moved up and down. On the end of the pole was a glimmer of glass that caught her eye. She held the glass to her eyes and smiled, gasping. "That's amazing." The pole was a telescope, extending to the top of the dome, and what she thought was probably the eyes of the spider. She could see the Kylix in Datz, still celebrating their victory. A small crank was attached to the side of the pole. Turning it rotated where she could see. The spider turned and she could see a boat making its way to the fortress. She could see Gorik clearly but didn't recognize who he was with. She turned the crank again, but nothing happened.

Anza hit the side of the pole and heard a strange clanking noise. She turned back to the eyepiece again and gasped. A sparkling spider took up the entire view. She pulled at the crank, hoping for a miracle. How can she reach it when it was on the other end of the telescope? Pulling the crank was the trick. A hissing sound made Anza jump back, nearly falling off the platform. Popping out of the eye piece was a small compartment. Looking inside confirmed what she believed. She had found the Kymu-Guiden Talisman.

The Kymu-Guiden Talisman was just as Skage had described it. A pentagonal shaped stone with a diamond spider in the center. Its legs were thin and made of ruby, making it more like blood veins rather than legs. It was cold to the touch, and she could feel the power within it pulsing.

"Now to get you back to Skage." Anza said, tossing the talisman into the air and catching it. She turned to leave when she heard banging on the door below. Something was trying to break in. Anza's eyes widened, her heart racing. She should be the only one up here. Who was that? She darted back to the walls, grabbing a sword from a nearby table. It was half rusted, but it would do.

Down below the suit of armor next to the coffin creaked to life. Its movement was rickety like someone stumbling awake. It wobbled its way around to face Anza, each step a little more graceful than the last. The armor lifted an arm to its helmet and lifted its visor. A grotesque, half decayed face stared back at Anza. "You aren't Lord Skage." It gurgled as if more liquid was in its lungs than air.

"No, I am Anza." She replied. "Who-who are you?"

"A loyal servant to Lord Skage. You summoned me?"

As if on cue the door rattled once more. Anza nodded her head. "Something is trying to break in, though."

"Lord Skage?" The suit of armor asked.

Anza shook her head. "I doubt that. He's stuck in a portrait."

"Enemies." It snarled through a gurgling voice.

"I don't know." Anza said. "But we are going to find out." She glanced at the suit of armor, trying to avoid staring. His posture was that of a royal, but that was where any sort of humanity ended. What she assumed was a man's face decayed under the helmet and reeked of rotten flesh. "How long have you been in there?"

The suit of armor shrugged. "Lord Skage sent me to my death before they broke in. That way I could serve him upon his return. When it was the right time."

"Right time for what? And who broke in?" Anza asked. The pounding on the door getting louder.

If the suit of armor knew the answers, he didn't give any. Standing there silent for several moments he finally spoke up. "You hold the talisman. You must be a servant of his too. Until his return, or the talisman is no longer yours, I will serve you." He lowered his visor and began to stomp towards the door. Whoever was trying to break through was going to meet the head of his hammer. The thought excited the reanimated corpse. It had been a long time since he had gone to battle.

Chapter 10: A Worthy Opponent

Sarason Fortress, Tahlbiru Ocean, Alutopek

Salina had a spear in her hands and a knife hidden in the small of her back. Both came from the weapons cache in the sinking portion of the armory. The colors of poison on the blades enticed her more than the better crafted ones. Using the spear, she stabbed a fish in the water. Its skin began to burn and bubble. She smiled, imagining using it on all of those she hated. It was finally time to find Rafik, and anyone else who opposed her. Boisterous yells echoed, causing her to pause on the stairs.

Three men charged at her, screaming. Salina twirled the spear, stabbing at one. He stepped to the side, but not without it glancing across his arm. The man yelped in pain, dropping his sword. His arm went limp and the surrounding area of the wound began to bubble.

"Who are you?" She said, not taking her eyes off the other two.

"Mercenaries. Purchased by the king." One answered. "Here to help collect strays."

"Unless you have a better offer?" The other said.

"I don't have any money on me-"

"Then no deal." The first man said, cutting her off.

Salina shoved the spear forward, the men trying to take a step back. The one she had injured lost his balance, falling into the other two. As they tried to regain their balance Salina turned and ran upwards, deeper into the tower. They followed, screaming at her, cursing, and snarling. She sprinted faster up the stairs.

Rafik banged on the spider door one last time. He didn't understand how a door could have no knob when the hinges indicated it would pull out towards him. There was nothing he could grab onto to pull them, either. He tried searching the rest of the room, including the spiders on the wall, floor, and one from the ceiling. He couldn't find any sort of clue that would help him enter.

He heard the fighting getting closer. Either everyone else was dead, or they were all hiding. In either case it seemed like he was on his own. Rafik glanced down at his bag. He could easily just hide in there and avoid the whole confrontation. Or he could try to fend them off like everyone else had tried. He always had a feeling he wouldn't live long. But before he found his sister? Rafik couldn't accept that. He would stay and fight like his father would have, but he would make sure he would win.

He tightened his grip on Blaridane, turned, and waited for his attackers to arrive.

The former leader of Datz started to believe the hallway would never end. It was a nightmare come to life, running down an empty corridor with no end in sight. But just as her legs began to burn, her lungs contracted, and heart nearly pounding out of her chest, she rounded the last part and found herself at the end. A domed room with a spider engraved door on the opposite end. In front of the door, sword raised, was Rafik.

Just her luck. When she finds her prey, she can't do anything about it. "They're coming." She said between breaths to him. Rafik nodded, but otherwise didn't move. She looked around and noticed the bag off to the side. It was just any old dark clothed bag with a flap cover. And yet so many possibilities.

Before she could say anything else, or regain her breath entirely, her pursuers arrived. She could finally take a better look at them as in this room it was much lighter than in the hallway, she had first confronted them in. There were nine men. One of them was the one she had scratched. His other arm had gone limp now, too. He wouldn't be a problem. But the others, maybe.

The others seemed very much the same. Unlike the skeletal armor the Kylix wore, they had rusted pieces of scrap metal tied together. Five of them, including the one she wounded, all looked the same. Bald, tall, broad shoulders, with a sour face like they smelled something rotting. The other four looked similar, but at

128

least had different hairstyles. One even looked much more feminine than the others, and Salina thought was a girl for a moment. But they all appeared equally imposing.

The one red head of the group stepped forward. "Fancy spear you have there. Drop it, and we will kill you swiftly. Try and fight, and we will make sure you beg for death."

"Not if I do to you what I did to your friend." Salina spat. She walked over to Rafik and stood next to him.

"Two against nine is hardly a fair fight." Rafik shouted as they began to spread out and circling them.

"Which is why you should give up, boy." The red head suggested. "You don't have to die. She does." He nodded towards the man who was scratched, now teetering back and forth, his legs wobbling.

"I meant for you." Rafik smiled. He pulled his hand out from behind his back and threw several of the knives he got from the armory. Only two hit somebody. One of the bald men in the leg, and the red head in the foot as he jumped out of the way. Before the last of the knives hit the ground, the rest screamed, charging for attack. Rafik gripped Blaridane, hearing the comforting violence of its voice echo in his mind. The power of the sword surged through him, allowing it to take control.

"Wait, stop!" Anza shouted. The animated corpse in armor stood still at the command. She could have sworn she had just heard her brother's voice. And if he was out there then she didn't want him hurt. A moment later she heard the all too familiar sound of fighting. Flashes of watching her mother fight popped in her head. Fighting back the terrible memories, she looked back at the suit of armor. "I'll open it."

The suit of armor didn't say a word or even move. It stood still. Frozen, waiting for its next command. Anza crossed her fingers, hoping the spider door wouldn't be another puzzle. There was enough of those already. She breathed a sigh of relief, discovering there weren't any tricks. A slight nudge, not even a push, and the doors began to creak open. She wanted to sneak out and see her brother; help him fight.

Anza gasped, seeing nearly a dozen men attacking Salina and Rafik. She hadn't expected so many trying to stop them. They looked different, too. Not Kylix soldiers or Datians. And Rafik and Salina fighting together was a surprise in and of itself. As she reached to close the doors, she noticed the bag off to the side. If she could get to the bag, she could rescue Skage and he could help.

This time Anza took a deep breath, pushed both doors open and ran towards the bag as fast as she could. Just as Anza was entering, she hollered back to her armored minion. "Stop them!" And disappeared.

Rafik spun around, hearing his sister's voice. He saw the bag bulge and then shrink once more. Before he could act on his discovery one of the men thrust his sword forward. *'No!'* Blaridane screamed, regaining control of his body. *'I'm in control. I fight. Don't ever do that again!'* The sheer anger and venom in the sword's voice weren't like anything he had heard before. It was getting stronger, and he felt his mind cower to the will of Blaridane. Rafik's body parried the attack, tripped him, and attempted to stab his attacker. His foe rolled to the side, sprang to his feet, and came for Rafik. Before the mercenary made it, however, he was struck from the side with what looked like a boulder that was flung across the room. As the man was swept aside, his screams of agony echoing the chamber, he saw an armored figure in the doorway he was trying to open earlier.

The armored figure held out his hand and a massive hammer flew back from across the room. He pointed it at Rafik and began walking towards him. "Ya shire." He cursed under his breath, taking a step back.

It seemed like all the fighting had stopped once the armored figure appeared. Rafik noticed the other bodies crumpled to the ground. He was positive Salina and he hadn't killed anyone yet. Which meant this armored one did. The figure took another step towards Rafik, hammer already raised for attack.

Rafik jumped out of the way as the hammer hit the ground, sending shards of rock and a cloud of dust into the air. "I was hoping you were on my side." Rafik groaned.

'I can take him.' Blaridane said. 'Easy.'

Rafik could feel Blaridane itching to fight the armored figure. He tried fighting the urge, beginning to feel his grasp slip in controlling his own body.

'Finally, a worthy opponent.' Blaridane growled.

Rafik resisted taking the step forward. "What if we lose?" He asked in a strained voice. Salina eyed him, not knowing who he was talking to.

The sword let out a soft chuckle in his head that made his hairs stand on end. 'Then I have a new host. A new champion who is worthy of wielding me.'

"Sounds like you win either way." Rafik said, shaking his head.

'I always win.' Rafik felt a violent push on his mind before losing control to Blaridane. He felt his legs slip, almost as if they were numb, before losing the feeling altogether. His arms were no longer his. He tried to scream, but his mouth wouldn't move. He could only watch. Blaridane was in control. The sword had won.

Chapter 11: Losing One's Soul

Sarason Fortress, Tahlbiru Ocean, Alutopek

Anza hurried to the portrait and turned it around. Again, Skage came to life upon making eye contact. He eyed Anza suspiciously before smiling. "I'm guessing you have the talisman?" He asked.

She nodded, holding it out for him to see. "Yes. And I need your help. My brother is in trouble."

"Why would I help him? He hasn't done anything for me. Or even you." Skage snapped.

"Of course he has. He has protected me." Anza argued.

"You mean he has held you back." Skage countered. "Not letting you reach your full potential. If he wasn't there to supposedly protect you then you would know what you're truly capable of, Anza."

"No. He loves me. He wants to protect me and is going to die doing so if we don't help." Anza said.

"Then so be it. That's how loyalty should be paid. With their lives."

"He's my brother." Anza shouted. "If you don't help me then you will never get this stone. And you will be stuck in that picture forever."

"Then you will never see your mother again." Skage said, defiantly. "Your choice, Anza. Make sure you choose the right one."

"So be it." Anza said. "I'm going to help my brother." She turned, dropping the talisman on the ground and grabbed the water and firestones. On the third rung of her climbing the ladder she heard Skage's voice.

"Stop, Anza. Fine. I'll help." He said. The sound of defeat evident.

"Thank you. What do I need to do?"

"Grab the other two stones." Skage instructed. "Pour the water into the chalice. Next, make a burst of light, ensuring the light touches the water. Put part of the airstone in the cup and let it bubble. Remove it, and then heat up the water with the firestone."

"Is that it?"

"For now." Skage said, nodding.

With shaking fingers Anza did as she was told, filling the chalice with water. The same one that made her invisible. Once she heated up the water, she turned to Skage. "Now what?"

"Now, repeat after me. *Byta kuduhlli fro sah.*"

Anza repeated the line to Skage, making several pronunciation mistakes.

"No. It is *byta kuduhlli fro sah.*" Skage repeated, emphasizing the parts she had mispronounced.

"Those are funny words. I wonder what they mean." Anza said before trying to say the phrase again.

Skage nodded after the third try, confirming she had said it right. "Good. Good. Now, while holding that talisman, take a sip of water, and then we need to say the phrase at the exact same time. Once finished, drink the rest of the water, keep holding the talisman the whole time."

Anza nodded and took a sip. She felt the familiar tingle go through her as before. She stared at Skage and began to say the words in unison with the portrait. She then drank the rest of the water. An instant later her world went dark.

The last thing she heard was Skage's blood curdling laugh. "That phrase, Anza. It means switch places with me."

Everything was dark. Nothing could be heard. Touch was nonexistent. Even the dank smell in the air was gone. She floated in a void, unsure if she were dead. It was worse than a nightmare, yet there was an unexpected calm about her. A moment later she could feel her eyes open, but the darkness was still there. What seemed like hours passed before light even began to enter. Everything was fuzzy, like looking at something from underwater. Slowly, ever so slowly, things began to return to how they were.

Anza could see something lying on the ground. The ladder reached up high to the doorway. The table off to the side was taller than she remembered, too. In fact, everything was. She tried to get up but hit her head on the ceiling. Glancing to either side she saw nothing. By leaning forward a bit she could see more of the secret room. Something stopped her from leaning forward too far.

Turning around, she saw the backdrop of Skage's portrait. She could touch it. The silk red curtains moved with her touch. Her face paled as realization donned on her. Anza screamed. She was stuck in the portrait. She now recognized the shape that was lying on the ground. They were legs. And she could only assume they belonged to Skage.

Rafik could have sworn he had heard the muffled scream of Anza. He was positive she was in the bag again. *'What could frighten her in there?'* He thought to himself as he ducked from another swing of the armored man's hammer. He dove, rolled, and sprang back to his feet when the hammer struck downwards at him. The hammer crashed into the ground, sending dust and shattered tile into the air. Once back on his feet he jabbed his sword forward, taking one of the bald men down who tried attacking him. It was just he and Salina against all of them. His mind was free to worry about her, as Blaridane was in control. He couldn't even feel what his body was doing.

Salina was off to the side, aiding in the fight every so often, otherwise watching Rafik fend off the attackers. Why everyone was trying to attack him, he couldn't understand. Not even a dent was made in the suit of armor. For it being a possessed sword, he felt like it hadn't done much in taking down this great warrior. He ducked once again, dodging the hammer. The hammer hit another of the mercenaries in the stomach, sending him flying across the room. The thought made Blaridane roar. *'You would be dead already if it weren't for me.'* Rafik didn't answer.

One mercenary jumped on the suit of armor's back. It slammed into the wall. The man gasped, letting go of the figure. The armored warrior turned around, bringing the hammer down on their head. It was now just Salina and Rafik against this unstoppable force.

He looked around the dark domed room. The spider hanging from the ceiling swayed back and forth from the commotion. The spider in the center was banged up and almost unrecognizable. Bodies of the fallen were strewn about, each more horrific than the last one Rafik had seen.

His stomach churned, and he felt bile build up within him. *'I don't think so.'* Blaridane shouted in his head. *'This is my body, now, and I am not weak.'*

Rafik's stomach settled as the spirit of the sword pulsed within him, taking back control.

Anza noticed the shape in front of her twitch. First his legs, and then fingers. The sporadic movement eventually made it up to his face. His mouth twitched, and eyes fluttered. A moment later they flew open, revealing the red cat eyes. He hobbled to his feet, grabbing hold of the table for balance, and laughed. In his hand was the talisman Anza had found for him.

"If it wasn't for you, I'd still be stuck in that frame." Skage said, nodding in thanks to Anza. "I thank you, Anza, for your sacrifice."

Anza glared at the necromancer. "You tricked me."

Skage shrugged his shoulders. "Of course! How else was I to get out of that portrait? If I had wanted to, I'm sure I could have helped you, too."

"My brother will stop you." Anza said.

"So many have tried. Only one has succeeded. And I'm sure he's dead now." Skage laughed. "Seeing as you're stuck in there, I'm guessing you don't need this anymore?" He picked up the chalice and tossed it into the air, catching it. He marveled at the detail of the dark cup before stowing it away inside his black robes. "It's so good to be back!"

He paced the room, looking at his reflection in the mirror, a wicked smile on his ugly face. "So you don't go too crazy in there, I'll tell you the one rule. You cannot communicate with people, or even move while they're around, until they have made eye contact with you." Skage explained.

"It won't take long. My brother will find me." Anza said.

Skage smiled. "Not if he thinks you're me." He leaned over and picked up the frame of the portrait, turning it around. "So long Anza. And thank you once again for your help." He laughed, climbing the ladder, and leaving her behind.

Anza screamed, but as the dark wizard left the room her screams fell silent. Her voice couldn't escape the confines of the frame.

Rafik's eye widened. The sword clashed against the hammer, but the blade didn't break. The suit of armor moved so fast he was always on the defensive, even with Blaridane controlling him. He finally found an opening and thrust his sword. The armored figure pivoted and swatted Rafik with his free hand, sending him sprawling across the floor. The suit of armor hadn't said a word, and Salina was still hiding in the shadows.

She was watching. Waiting. For what, he wasn't sure. But he knew it wasn't anything good for him. He saw glimpses of her moving out of the way, using the spear she had found like a staff.

The suit of armor stomped towards Rafik and stood over him. He panted for breath. Everything that had happened up until now began to weigh down on him as he lied there. Blaridane retreated into the sword, allowing Rafik to feel everything. *'Good luck, boy.'* The sword taunted. Fatigue seeped into him. His body ached. His mind muddled as he reclaimed what was lost. At the last moment he noticed the suit of armor, standing over him, hammer raised. He rolled to the side as the hammer came down right where he was a moment before. The suit of armor blocked his escape by sticking out its foot. Rafik reached out, placing his hands on the suit of armor, and tried to pivot around him. His talent had other ideas as another vision ensnared him, taking him out of the battle.

It was in the very room he was in now, although brighter. More torches were lit, and statues of spiders decorated the room more than it did in his time. A silhouette of a figure in robes stood

136

in the spider shaped doorway. The suit of armor kneeled, head bowed, in the center of the room.

"You have been loyal to me, have you now?" The figure asked in a tone that gave Rafik chills.

Without looking up the suit of armor responded. "I have, my lord. I am your most loyal servant."

"And you wish to serve me however you can." The figure said, more of a statement than a question.

"I do, my lord. But I fear we have lost."

The figure laughed. It was a horrible sound like a wolf's growl mixed with the dying screams of a hunted deer. "Maybe today. But tomorrow is a new day."

"My lord, if I may?" The armored man asked, looking up. The silhouette nodded. "I don't see a way any of us can make it out today."

"Oh, my loyal servant, how stupid you are. You will survive." The figure stepped forward out of the shadow of the doorway. Rafik gasped. He recognized the ugly man the moment he saw him. It was Skage, the necromancer Izamar told him about, and of the portrait in the secret room. The dark wizard pulled out a familiar looking sword. Green and yellow jewels around the hilt, with dragons stretching out for the guard. The edges of the blade glimmered in an unnatural crimson. He raised the sword and held it next to his staff. With a steady hand the two objects touched the armor. The person within the armor screamed for just a fraction of a second before everything went quiet. A silvery light glowed on the end of the staff. Skage twirled it around before launching it into the room with the spider shaped doorway.

Seconds passed and no one moved. Rafik didn't dare to even breath, fearing the wrath of the dark wizard. The suit of armor began to stir. Its movement was shaky as it teetered to their feet, nearly falling over. It looked at its hands, trembling. "What did you do to me?" The frightened voice echoed in the chamber.

"My former mentor told me once of the most heinous and vile of people. The leader of this group was so terrible that after he was defeated all records of his name were wiped away. His legacy

137

reduced to stories told around the campfire. He became known as The Forgotten One. He could strip one of their soul and harness it for his own use. It is an act considered even worse than raising the dead. You see, in raising the dead, you animate life with a fragment of your own soul. If you're talented enough, maybe even theirs. But The Forgotten One was stealing souls. Fusing them and using them to boost his own strength. Well, my loyal servant, I took your soul. I saved you from death because you cannot die until your soul is returned to you." Skage explained, a devilish smile on his face. "Now you will serve me always and forever."

"Yes, Master." The suit of armor replied. He followed Skage into the room his soul was sent to. The spider doors closing behind him.

Rafik awoke from his vision with a start. A shadow out of the corner of his eye caught his attention. Fearing it was the suit of armor, he scrambled to his feet, and turned, just in time to see the hammer swipe at him, taking out his legs. He was too slow to raise Blaridane in defense and collapsed once more. The sounds of his bones breaking echoed in the chamber. The armored figure took a step forward, putting his foot on Rafik's chest so he couldn't get away.

"Enough!" The shadow he had seen shouted. The armored figured took a step back, getting off Rafik, and stood at attention. "Give me back my sword!" The figure raised its hand and Blaridane was ripped from Rafik's fingers and flew across the room.

An emptiness filled Rafik as the voice faded. "Master." The suit of armor said, kneeling.

The figure nodded and turned around. "Come. We have much to do in extraordinarily little time." He walked into the room and disappeared.

As the suit of armor followed, he swatted Rafik one last time in his side with his hammer. Rafik landed on his stomach, groaning, gasping for air. His stomach ached, his chest felt like it had caved in, and his legs felt as if a butcher had ground them up in a meat grinder. Blood trickled out of his mouth.

Salina stepped out of the shadows, clapping to Rafik. A malicious grin on her face. "You lasted longer than I originally thought. You have spirit kid. But I don't think you will last much longer."

Rafik tried to ask for help but nothing came out. Every breath he could feel his stomach constrict and ooze out life. He reached for Salina, his arm trembling. A moment later he dropped his arm, sighing.

"The war has started, boy. And I believe we found our new king. I will give him that bag you found as a peace offering so our people can survive. Unfortunately for you, I don't believe you're one of the survivors. We don't need heroes. We need people who will do what they're told." She raised the spear into the air in front of Rafik's eyes and stamped it into the ground beside him. "I've seen what this spear does. It's boring now. But I have this knife. Has a green edge instead of purple. Let's see what this does, shall we?"

Salina kneeled, hunching over Rafik, and inched the knife into Rafik's side that wasn't crushed by the hammer. The effects were immediate. Rafik groaned, almost squealing in pain. Black lines grew outwards, spreading across his body. With a little twist she yanked the knife out and threw it across the room. She turned, walking away, smiling at Rafik's pain. She scooped up the bag and knocked on the spider door.

"Rafik!" A voice shouted from across the room. Salina turned to see Gorik with a man she had never seen before, and a small girl she thought looked diseased.

"Gorik! You're back?" Salina asked, whipping around to face him. Her eyebrows raised, and tone of voice several pitches higher.

"What happened?" Gorik asked.

The man she didn't recognize whispered to the girl. She nodded and ran to Rafik's side. She took his hands in hers and kissed his head. "He's dying." She said in little more than a whisper.

"What are you doing?" Salina gasped.

"She is drawing the poison out of the boy." The man explained. He pulled what looked like a stick from inside his cloak and unfolded it. It tripled in size, and he attached a string from one end to the other. He grabbed an arrow from behind his back and placed it to the newly formed bow.

"What are you doing? I haven't done anything." Salina said, raising her hands as the man pointed it at her.

"Where I come from a person who doesn't try and help a dying child is usually the guilty party." The man said.

Rafik tried to say something, but only muttered a guttural growl before passing out. "Is he dead?" Gorik asked.

The girl shook her head. "Not yet. I got all the poison out. If he doesn't see a healer soon, he will be."

"Gorik, Ziri, start taking him back to our boat. I'll meet you down there." The man said.

Gorik and Ziri nodded. They carefully hoisted Rafik up and began moving down the stairs. Once gone from sight Salina's demeanor changed. Her spear, instead of held like a staff, was now ready to for attack. "What are you going to do to me?"

"I recognize that spear, and I know you poisoned him." The man said. "Drop it, and I won't kill you where you stand."

"Let me go with you." Salina said. "Let me go wherever you are going, and you have yourself a deal."

The man thought about this for a moment before nodding. "Drop the spear and we have a deal."

Without hesitation Salina dropped the spear. She didn't think it was going to be this easy. "Tell me, who are you anyway?"

The man laughed. "You should have asked that before agreeing." He put away his bow as he got closer to Salina, tearing the bag from her shoulders. "You are in the presence of Samron of Haitu, originally Borlo. Master trainer of the Kylix army, and in high favor of King Vanarzir."

Salina's face paled. Before she could move Samron grabbed her hands and tied them behind her back. "What are you doing?"

"Taking you prisoner." Samron said. He shoved her forward, not saying another word, and scooped up the bag and spear.

Gorik heaved a sigh, noticing that most of the Datians had hidden from the mercenaries. Most, he had noticed, of the attackers were dead in the chamber he found Rafik in. As he and Ziri took him back to the ferry he tried to imagine what had happened. His legs were mangled, side stabbed, and his breathing was short and ragged. Rafik's wounds didn't match anything he noticed in there. Except for maybe the side wound. He had an inkling of suspicion that Salina was responsible for some of it.

The surviving Datians slowly trickled out of their hiding spaces as Gorik and Ziri grew nearer to the dark portal. One replaced Ziri as the rest whispered and murmured how brave Rafik was. They left the fortress, not looking back, and helped maneuver Rafik onto the ferry.

Samron soon followed, Salina bound in front of him. Several whispered, but no one questioned what was happening. "See that boat?" He said, pointing to the one the mercenaries used. "Use that one. Sail anywhere you want. But don't follow us. We are going to Haitu. And I doubt any of you want to go there. We leave the *River Lizard* here."

Gorik's eyes widened. That wasn't part of the plan. He lifted his head and Samron gave him a look to stay quiet. He nodded, turning his attention back to Rafik.

No one argued that. Haitu was home to the Kylix soldiers. It was where they were all trained, and where most of them would be. It was the largest Kylix stronghold in all Alutopek. Sure, that's where all the children were going, but there wasn't a way to get them back once they had gotten into the city.

Gorik thanked some and waved to everyone goodbye as his fellow Datians sailed into the east. He, Samron, Salina, Ziri, and

141

Rafik were heading south. Deep into Alutopek. "He's part of the Kylix." Salina said.

Gorik smiled. "I know." But didn't say another word about it. "What can we do for Rafik?"

"All the poison is out of him." Ziri whispered.

"He only has one choice of survival now." Samron sighed. "I'm sorry, Gorik. But we need to take him to the Kylix."

"What? No. There must be another way. I didn't tell you about Rafik so you could hand him over to be part of the king's army!" Gorik yelled.

"I understand. But we don't have a choice in the matter." Samron said. "They have the best healers. And, if anything else, the Kylika can heal him."

"Who?" Ziri asked. "I've never heard of them."

"They are King Vanarzir's best soldiers." Samron explained. "You'll learn more about them soon enough."

"Samron. This is Drane's son." Gorik tried to reason. "He deserves better from you."

Samron shook his head. "I'm sorry. But if you want him to survive, we don't have much else of a choice."

Gorik glared at the Trainer. Finally, he nodded, and stared to the south. It wouldn't be long until they encountered the Kylix that had camped out on the coast. "When we get closer, I'm hiding in there." He gestured to the bag now resting at Rafik's feet. If Samron was surprised or confused, he gave no notice.

"Can I go in there?" Salina asked.

Samron glared at her. "No."

Salina hovered over Rafik. The look of disdain all over her. "I should have killed you a long time ago." She whispered in a low tone nobody else could hear.

Samron came towards her and noticed Rafik. "You know," He said to no one in particular. "If he survives this, I have a feeling he is going to be one of the greatest warriors Alutopek has ever seen."

Back at the Sarason Fortress Skage watched the two boats leave. One to the east, the other to the south. Where they were going, he wasn't sure. Didn't really care, either. He noticed the Black Wall and wondered what all he had missed during his absence. *'Only one way to find out.'* He thought to himself. It was fortunate Anza had not only found the Kymu-Guiden Talisman, but also took him straight to his old home. If she hadn't his plan would be delayed much longer, possibly indefinitely. He placed the talisman back into the slot in the telescope and chanted a series of words even he could barely hear.

Outside the fortress the eyes of the spider began to glow. A first time in more than millennia. The people still within the fortress who had fallen began to wake, screaming an unnatural sound. Their movements jarred and shaky, as if they were controlled by an unseen puppeteer.

Skage marveled at the machine in front of him. Forged from the best smiths and architects during his time, the massive dome he stood in was the interior of the stone spider. Its eyes connected to a powerful telescope whose sight could be amplified by the magical artifacts he had collected. He fingered the snowflake pendant around his neck, thinking of all that he had obtained. His plethora of magical artifacts had to be the largest Alutopek had ever seen. Now most of it scattered to the four winds. What was missing? He had made sure the Kymu-Guiden talisman was hidden, but the other snowflake he should have had was missing.

To his knowledge, there were four of those. And he owned them all. One was safely around his neck. The second was safely hidden near the coffin. A third snowflake had to be here somewhere. The dark wizard fished through one of his several trunks, tossing around artifacts and books, before finally finding it. He peered through the telescope, trying to get his bearings. The fourth should be here, in a different compartment than the talisman. He opened it up, only to reveal an empty slot.

"Where is it?" He hissed.

"Where is what?" The suit of armor gurgled in reply.

"My snowflake pendant. It was here." Skage said. He bobbed up, down, and around the telescope, hoping the snowflake had fallen out. Nothing. "No matter. We'll find it. I still have three."

He placed the Kymu-Guiden Talisman in its respective slot and marveled at this contraption. Anywhere the spider's eyes looked he could see. And with the Kymu-Guiden talisman, and his own magic, he could watch over far more than just the Tahlbiru Ocean. But far beyond, across all Alutopek. Every nook and cranny, dark cave or forgotten swamp, he could peer into.

He was searching for somewhere particular. He didn't know the customs and culture of today, but in his time, and ancient times, the dead were stowed away in great tombs. Cities for the dead. Each region had one. He turned the spider, slowly scanning across the land before he found it. The Nyler Necropolis.

The thick city walls were topped with spiders, guardians of the dead. He began chanting again, this time louder. He concentrated, imagining the dead waking. It was a feeling he had gotten used to and reveled. His consciousness reaching out, stirring the bodies, giving them life. He was a god to them, as they writhed in anger from being woken. And they would serve him forever.

The bodies twisted and contorted as they awoke. Some screamed while others creaked and hobbled to life. All the dead within the silent city moved, with only two thoughts in their simple minds. To serve Lord Skage, and to defeat anyone who tried stopping them.

The guardians of the city, tasked with keeping the living out and ensuring the dead stay that way, blocked their path. The horde of the dead surged forward, slowly defeating them, and the newly deceased guardians joining their ranks.

As the last of the dead rose to life, Skage placed the snowflake pendant into the notch on his telescope. It glowed with power, giving off a small hum. He could now look away, the pendant freezing the magic from fading.

"And so." Skage said to his armored servant below. "It finally begins."

Chapter 12: The Golden Gate

Golden Gate, Biodlay Desert, Alutopek

Thunder rumbled as they left the Sarason Fortress. Small pellets of rain grew larger, the storm growing. Winds churned, nearly capsizing the ferry. The little light of the stars gleaming through the Black Wall disappeared behind storm clouds. Gorik turned back to the fortress. "Was the spider always like that?" The usually dead eyes glowed red and had turned direction. He could have sworn it faced Trinkit and the Eko River before.

Salina shook her head. "I don't think so."

"I'm guessing that's not a good sign." Gorik said. "What happened up there?"

"Those mercenaries ambushed us." Salina said.

"Why were you even in the fortress? I told you to stay on the ship."

"I tried telling him," Salina said, pointing at Rafik. "But he wouldn't listen. He couldn't find his sister."

"What?" Gorik gasped. "You mean she isn't in the bag?"

Salina shrugged, glaring at Samron. "I wouldn't know. I'm not allowed in there. He went after her and the others followed."

Gorik opened the flap of the bag and jumped in.

"Wow." Ziri gasped.

A moment later Gorik climbed out. "She isn't down there. Samron, we have to turn back."

"She is probably safe with the others sailing away from here." Samron said.

"I think she fell overboard." Salina said.

"She wouldn't leave her brother behind. She is still at the fortress. We didn't see her with the others, and they left the same time we did." Gorik said.

Samron shook his head. "We can go back and look for her, or we can save Rafik."

"Ya shire." Gorik cursed, looking from the fortress to Rafik's broken body. "Fine. Did you see what happened to him?"

145

"He and I fought the mercenaries." Salina said. "Then a giant suit of armor came out of another room and attacked Rafik. A hideous, robed man appeared out of nowhere, and he called for the suit of armor back, closing the doors behind him. That's when you arrived."

"You fought?" Gorik asked, eyes wide. "With, not against, Rafik?"

Salina nodded.

"You forgot your part in hurting the boy." Samron said. "But we can save that for later. This robed figure. Have you seen him before?"

"No." Salina said, shaking her head. "But he and that armored giant are still at the fortress. I could point him out in a crowd anywhere."

"Please be safe, Anza." Gorik whispered, clutching the side rail of the ferry. "Stay hidden."

"Well, whoever it is, I'm sure they are responsible for the glowing eyes." Samron said. "And I'm positive that isn't good."

"What are they going to do from inside a tower?" Salina asked. "They don't even have a way to get off that island."

"The *River Lizard* is still there." Gorik said. "If we aren't going back, we can think about the fortress later. What are we going to do here?" He pointed southward.

The monument grew as they approached. Before the Black Wall it was called the Golden Gate, as it glistened from gold plating and radiated light. Only patches of gold remained now. The rest either looted or fallen into the Tahlbiru Ocean. The Golden Gate was a stronghold spanning to either side of the Eko River. It was what the Datians used to control what came in and out of Alutopek. The gates had remained closed since the Black Wall's creation and lay abandoned. But now Gorik could see Kylix soldiers standing guard over it.

"Gorik, you can hide in the bag." Samron said. "The children are safe with me, and Salina is my prisoner."

Without further prompting Gorik crawled into the bag, leaving it at Rafik's side. The waters churned more the closer they approached. Samron marveled at this ancient feat of engineering. Two massive towers on either side, with an expanse connecting the two. Halfway down the bridge portion of the fortress separated into columns, which could control what came through. As the ferry came nearer the columns raised into the upper part of the gate. If a Kylix soldier was calling to them, he couldn't tell. The storm was swirling above, gaining in strength, drowning out any voices they could have heard.

"I'm not happy I'm arrested." Salina said. "But I hope they will offer us some clean clothes or a fire to sit by."

"Even if they did, we're not taking it." Samron said. "That boy needs to get to Haitu as soon as possible, no thanks to you. We aren't stopping."

Salina nodded. "Shame. A hot meal would be nice. I hope they don't insist on searching the ferry. And what's in it." She glanced back at the bag.

"If you even mention Gorik, or that bag's ability," Samron warned. "Ziri will show you her talent."

"It's not healing? What? Is she going to heal me to live forever so I can think about my actions?" Salina laughed.

"No." Ziri said taking Salina's bound hand. "I can cure, or poison, whoever I want. This is the poison I took out of Rafik."

Salina felt the burning flow through her. It climbed up her arms, spreading like a spider's web. She felt it crawl up her arm, the burning sensation intensifying as it got to her heart. With every beat it coursed through her body, the burning growing. As the pain became unbearable, she felt it retreat. Leave her feet, her neck, and return to her hand. The searing pain disappeared, and she felt better than before.

"I can make a poison enter you so fast you can't react and hold it there so you're in agony forever. With just a touch I can make you collapse where you stand. I am one girl you don't want to get on my bad side." Ziri said.

"Where'd you find her?" Salina asked, stepping away from her, eyes narrow, as she checked her hand.

Samron ignored her. The ferry had now passed under the entryway. He could see Kylix soldiers on either side of the riverbank. Behind him were even more. Although he trained them, he never liked seeing the uniform. The skeletal armor. It unnerved him, and he always thought it was mocking the dead more than being intimidating.

"Who goes there?" A voice hollered from above the storm. From within the fortress walls the voices echoed off, allowing it to be heard over the weather.

The trainer froze. He recognized that voice. The nasally nuisance and pestering of a voice. Sure enough, on the western riverbank was one person he couldn't stand. Jinuk. Though, it appeared that he was more than just a foot soldier now. He was a commander. How that was possible he guessed was through blackmail and not valor. "Trainer Samron." He yelled, glaring at him.

Commander Jinuk returned the glare. "Ah, Samron. Off being a traitor, I'm guessing?"

"Watch your mouth!" Samron yelled. "I will not have you question my character again. No matter your rank, you have no authority over me. How a sniveling coward like yourself became a commander is beyond me. No wonder King Vanarzir is recruiting children for soldiers if he is promoting the likes of you."

Jinuk turned to a Kylix soldier who nodded. He walked to the shore and began throwing a rope to the ferry. "Yes, do you like my new promotion? For aiding in Kristol. I even took charge of the siege on Datz while the king left. He trusts me. More than he trusts you, I'm sure. And now I'm commander over the Golden Gate until further notice. As the commander of the fortress, you are coming ashore and can be my guest."

"No." Samron said. "We have a wounded child on board. I need to get him to Haitu."

"We have healers here." Jinuk insisted.

Samron shook his head. "I'm not going to risk a child's life, Jinuk. I trust the healers in Haitu."

Jinuk nodded and signaled for a soldier down the river. They pulled on a crank. A metal grate began to lower into the water. "You're staying for at least a night. Let our healers check the boy. You and I can...catch up."

Samron cursed under his breath. "Ziri, take the bag. Don't let anyone look into it."

Thunder echoed, growling across the sky. Samron looked up at the rumbling sky, fearing it was warning him. He didn't get to where he was without being cautious and superstitious.

Once out of the boat the Kylix soldiers swarmed. "We'll need to check everything. Make sure you aren't hiding anything."

"You really think I'm a traitor?" Samron smirked.

"For seven years." Commander Jinuk replied. He noticed the bag slung over Ziri's shoulder. "I don't recognize this girl. The boy, though..."

"Ziri came with me. As you know, I'm trying to find those with talent. She is one of them. Same with the boy." Samron said.

"I recognize her, though." Jinuk said, stepping in front of Salina. "How did you survive diving into the water? We stood guard around that pond for a solid hour."

"I held my breath." Salina smirked.

"As you can see," Samron interrupted as Jinuk opened his mouth. "She is arrested. Under my authority. I am taking her to Haitu."

Commander Jinuk nodded, scratching his narrow chin. His thick glasses appeared too large for his scrawny figure. "Very well, Samron. I'll play along. Take her to the jails. Take the boy to the healers. Samron and the girl, we'll find you rooms to stay in. But you with me, first, Trainer."

"I'm going with him." Ziri spoke up. She took a step towards the Kylix soldiers hauling away Rafik. One soldier turned, swatting her. Ziri caught herself and hurried to her feet, yanking on the soldier's hand. The soldier screamed, ripping off his glove and scratching at his hand.

"It's like needles!" He yelled, scratching harder. "What did you do to me?"

"Ziri." Samron said, giving her a look.

Ziri grabbed the soldier's hand and the pain went away. "I'm going with him." She said sternly yet still in a whisper. The soldier nodded.

Salina stayed quiet, the Kylix hauling her away. Samron watched his prisoner being taken one way and Rafik in another. Commander Jinuk ushered him away from the others. "You'll see your friends soon enough." He said.

Samron bit his tongue.

Rafik screamed when he opened his eyes. This had to be a dream. He knew he was being taken by the Kylix to be healed. But he wasn't expecting to see birds. The Kylix healers wore masks with long beaks covering the nose and mouth, a slight curve at the end. The eyes looked empty and soulless. They wafted a bowl of smoking incense in front of his nose and he grew tired. From what he heard before falling asleep, the stab wound Salina inflicted was the least of his worries. The last he remembered hearing was them wondering if he would ever walk again.

His dreams weren't pleasant. He fought the armored man again, Skage watching. Every time Rafik managed to beat him the necromancer would bring him back, making him larger than before. If he tried to retreat, Salina would try and poison him. All the while his sister's screams echoed throughout the chamber. He prayed Gorik, his mother, or father would be there to help him, but the help never came. Blaridane's voice echoed throughout the fight, urging to kill everyone. The cold, heartless voice of the sword was his only companion. Relying on that, he managed to beat the suit of armor. Again, and again. Each time the suit of armor would rise, his prayers ignored, and Blaridane was his only solace to save his sister.

He awoke with a start, the thunder grumbling. He sat up, panting, sweating. His sides were bandaged, and he took comfort that his legs seared with pain. At least he could still feel them. "You're alright." A soft voice said beside him, holding his hand.

Rafik turned and saw a pale girl. She seemed his age, but thinner. Frailer. Her bright pink lips looked like they were dripping with venom. "Who are you?" He asked.

"I'm Ziri." She smiled, squeezing his hand. "I cured you back at the fortress. I was told to stay by your side."

"Who told you? Where am I?" Rafik asked, rubbing his head. The last he knew what happened was Skage and the armored figure retreating, taking Blaridane. "Where's Anza?" The emptiness was obvious to Rafik, but it wasn't the longing for his sister. It was for the sword. He needed it back with him. To hear its voice. To have its confidence. "Where's Blaridane?"

"One at a time." Ziri laughed. "Let's see. By whom? Samron. That's Gorik's friend. Where are you? I think Samron said this place is the Golden Gate? It's a Kylix fortress. Is that your sister? Anza? Gorik mentioned her. He says she's probably still at the spider fortress. And Blari-who? I don't know what you're talking about."

"What? I have to find her!" Rafik gasped, pulling the covers off him. "You all just left her there? We need to go get her!"

Ziri pushed him back down, replacing the blanket over him. "You need to rest. You're in no shape to even walk, let alone go on a rescue mission."

"Why are you whispering?" Rafik asked, annoyed she was forcing him to stay.

"I can't talk louder than this."

"Why not?"

"My talent." Ziri said, looking down and away from Rafik.

"You have talent?" Rafik asked. "I think I do, too."

Ziri turned to face him again. "What can you do?" A glint of hope in her eyes.

Rafik shrugged. "I don't remember the name. Psycho-something, I think. I have visions of the past. When I touch things, I can see where they have been and who has interacted with them."

"Oh." Ziri said, not hiding the disappoint in her voice.

"I know it isn't the most exciting power. I'd love to be able to move things with my mind or fly. But I didn't think it was *that* boring."

Ziri shook her head, smiling. "It's not that. I-I just hoped you were like me."

"What can you do?" Rafik asked.

"I can cure anyone from poison or inflict it." Ziri said. She squeezed Rafik's hand, biting her lip. Rafik thought he could see her fighting back a tear.

"What's wrong?"

"I'm a monster." Ziri said.

"You aren't a monster, Ziri!" Rafik insisted. "That is an amazing talent. If I could trade you I would."

"Really?" Ziri smiled. "Why?"

"You can cure people. Have you tried healing the sick?" Rafik asked. "That's a type of poison, right?"

Ziri shrugged. "I never tried. Before Samron found me, I was an enforcer for the barman at the Silver Shark. Those who couldn't pay their debts I had to visit."

"Well you should. You could save so many people, Ziri. And protect others, too." Rafik said. "You should be proud!"

"Tha-thank you." Ziri said, smiling wider and squeezing his hand. "You're the first to tell me I'm not a monster. Even Samron said I could bring down an army. I don't want to do that. I don't want to be a killer and a monster. I just want to be me."

"Before my dad died," Rafik began, looking into her eyes. "He would always say there is a monster in all of us that always wants to get out. If we feed it greed, selfishness, and anger it grows until we can't control it anymore. But there is another creature inside us. And if we feed it kindness and selflessness the bad monster can never control us."

"I like your dad." Ziri smiled.

"I do too." Rafik laughed. "So, do you know what's wrong with me?"

"A little bit." Ziri nodded. "Your ribs are broken, and the stab wound on your side is stitched up. The healers are worried,

152

though, that your insides are bleeding. I'm not sure what that means. Blood should be on the inside of your body. And your legs are broken. A lot. One bone is completely shattered."

"So...I can't walk?" Rafik asked.

"For now." Ziri said. "They wanted to cut them off, but Samron insisted that you can make it to Haitu. There's someone there that can heal you. I think she has talent like us."

"I'm not going to Haitu." Rafik said. "It's bad enough I'm here. I need to save my sister."

"If you want to walk again you are." Ziri said. "And I'm going there. If I must go then you do too. Friends stick together."

"We're friends?" Rafik asked.

"I-I thought we were." Ziri said, hurrying to her feet, looking down at the floor. "I mean, if you want to?"

Rafik laughed. "I like you, Ziri. Of course we're friends. But as my friend, you need to help me find my sister and escape the Kylix."

Ziri nodded. "Samron said he has a plan but hasn't told me. I think Gorik knows."

"Where is Gorik?"

"Right here." Ziri said, handing him the bag. "He won't come out until we've left this place."

Rafik laughed. "Probably a good idea. He's wanted by the Kylix."

"Same with that Salina woman." Ziri said. "She's locked up."

"She's here?" Rafik gasped.

"Yeah, Samron arrested her." Ziri said. She began to tell him what he had missed from when they had first found him until now. "Were the red eyes glowing when you were there?"

"The spider?" Rafik shook his head. "No. That has to be Skage. He's back. I don't know how that's possible. But it sounds like he has."

"Who is Skage?"

"An ancient necromancer." Rafik said. "Does anyone else know he's returned?"

Ziri shrugged. "I don't know."

"We need to tell somebody." Rafik said.

"Tell somebody what?" A voice asked, entering the room. Two men entered. Ziri greeted one, Rafik guessed was Samron. An older man with darker hair and deep wrinkles. His nose was jagged as if it were broken in more than one place. The other in Kylix uniform with a weak chin and thick glasses. "Ah, you're awake."

Rafik nodded.

"Nice to finally meet you, Rafik." Samron said. "I'm Samron. Now, what do you need to tell us?"

Rafik smiled, happy he had deduced correctly who he was. "Skage has returned."

"I'm sorry, who?" Jinuk asked.

"Skage. A necromancer." Rafik said. "He's in the Sarason Fortress."

"Magic is gone thanks to the Black Wall." Commander Jinuk said with pride, puffing out his chest. "You're delusional."

Rafik shook his head. "I saw him."

"If I listened to every child, I would still be combing through Fogwood and Kristol looking for Xeo." Jinuk snapped. "Even if a necromancer did return, he would have no power."

"I do." Rafik said.

"Same with me." Ziri chimed in.

"They have a point." Samron laughed. "We need to get you to Haitu."

Rafik shook his head. "No. We need to stop him. And I need to find my sister."

Samron placed a hand on Rafik's shoulder. "You are stubborn, just like your father. That's what got him killed."

"You know my dad?" Rafik asked.

"Don't you know all adults know each other?" Samron smirked. "We have to take care of you first, Rafik. The healers did all they could to put you back together, but whatever attacked you did a good job of it. A couple of your ribs are broken, and the healers couldn't set them. Your legs are broken. One bone even shattered to bits. If you want to walk again, let alone live

154

comfortably, your only hope is a girl in Haitu. She has a talent of healing."

"Isn't he bleeding from the inside?" Ziri asked.

"No." Samron said. "They thought he might. If he were, he would already be dead."

Rafik shook his head. "I can't leave her behind."

"You won't." Commander Jinuk smiled. "We'll find her. You'll see her in Haitu in no time. Serving the king in the Kylix army like all children should be."

"We will be leaving soon." Samron said. "Don't think of it as leaving her behind. If you need to take care of yourself first, you need to. You aren't good to her dead, you know."

"I'm not good to her enslaved, either." Rafik argued.

"You have my word, Rafik. Once we get you healed, we will find her." Samron promised. He turned to Commander Jinuk. "If I may, I wish to speak to these two. Alone."

"Oh." Jinuk gasped. "Yes, of course, because this is your fortress." He opened his mouth to continue his rant but saw Samron's face. There was a look about him. Dangerous. Like a pot of boiling water with the lid about to pop. "Alright. But I'm posting a guard at the door. Don't want any funny business."

Gorik woke with a start as Samron fell on the floor of the secret room. He was balanced on one leg, knife at the ready, swearing. "You dare sneak up on me?" He shouted.

"Relax, it's me." Samron said, groaning, rubbing his back. He looked around the room in marvel and confusion. "How this room is possible is beyond me."

"Yeah." Gorik said. "Could have come in handy seven years ago."

"You can't keep throwing that in my face."

"Why not?"

"Because how stupid are you?" Samron shouted. "Jinuk told me what happened in Datz. Rafik just filled me in what happened after. Jumping into the water like that."

Gorik smiled. "They didn't see that coming."

155

"For good reason, Gorik." Samron said. "If it wasn't for those kids finding an airstone you would all be dead."

"No. Some of us would have made it." Gorik said. "Do you think anyone would want to live as slaves or prisoners of the king? And most of us were going to die anyway. It was a risk we were all willing to take."

"It was a risk you were willing to take. Everyone else just followed, hoping they were backing the right horse. You can't keep praying for luck to swing your way."

"What else was I supposed to do? Let everyone die. Especially when Rafik appears. I promised to protect him." Gorik said. "He and Anza mean the world to me."

"And you put them in danger, too." Samron paced back and forth. "If you ever make a foolish decision like that again, and you happen to survive, I will kill you. I won't tolerate someone who gambles with others' lives."

Gorik began to laugh. "You're one to talk. Every battle, every war, you are gambling with others' lives. You are training them, only to lead them to the slaughter. Tell me how you're better."

"I'm not. But you were supposed to be better than me." Samron said.

"Did you come down here just to berate me?" Gorik asked.

"No." Samron said, shaking his head. "Tell me what you know of the necromancer Skage."

"It's just an ancient Datian legend." Gorik said. "He was the one who built the spider on the Sarason Fortress. His powers were so great he could raise the dead across all of Alutopek."

"What happened to him?"

"Nobody knows." Gorik said. "When they stormed the spider-topped tower he was gone. Not a trace of where he went."

"According to Rafik," Samron said. "He's back."

"Anza!" Gorik said, looking up at the ceiling. "She's stuck there."

"That's what Rafik thinks. I need you to go back to the Sarason Fortress and rescue her. Before Skage, or Jinuk, get to her."

"That's a great idea. I'll just crawl out of this magic room in the middle of a Kylix stronghold, commandeer one of their boats, and leave through the front door. Nothing could go wrong."

"Are you done?" Samron asked in a flat tone.

"Just one more thing." Gorik said. "When I get to the Sarason Fortress, should I politely ask Skage to go back to where he's been all this time, too?"

"Once we leave the Golden Gate you can sneak back around." Samron said, ignoring Gorik's sarcasm.

"And then what? The Sarason Fortress is on an island. Remember?"

"Use some of your luck you always seem to have. Maybe a whale will befriend you and let you ride its back."

"You want me to sneak into the fortress, avoid this evil wizard, and save Anza?"

Samron nodded. "Think you can handle that?"

Gorik smiled, the mischievous grin he always wore when with Drane. "I'll find a way."

Chapter 13: Death Comes Knocking

Golden Gate, Biodlay Desert, Alutopek

Rafik learned it had been a week that they stayed at the Golden Gate. He hadn't woken up until the fourth night. On the fifth day was when he could move again. The healers had done the best they could. At least he knew he wasn't dying. His legs, though. "I just hope I can walk again." He said for the hundredth time to Ziri. From the waist up he appeared fine, a bandage wrapped around his ribs. But his legs were a different story. They burned with pain with the smallest of movement.

"That's why we're going to Haitu." Ziri replied for the hundredth time, not showing any sign of being annoyed. "Then we can save your sister."

"I hope she's alright." Rafik said, looking out the window towards the Sarason Fortress. The spider's eyes hadn't stopped glowing since they left. He was positive he had seen Skage. The Kylix and Samron didn't seem to believe him, though. With not being able to walk, he hadn't checked the portrait in the bag, or even gone down there to see Gorik.

"If she is anything like you, she is." Ziri said. "I can't wait to meet her. She seems like a sweet girl."

"You'd love her." Rafik smiled, eyes lighting up. His eyes darted upwards and noticed a sword hanging on the wall. Thoughts of his sister faded. Blaridane was gone. The emptiness within him felt stronger this time. His heart ached from losing his father. He hadn't had much time to think about his mother sacrificing herself. But the thought of abandonment echoed within him, revealing how empty he was without the sword. It was cold and left him wanting. He needed Blaridane. To hear its voice, feel its power, and have that courage. This time he would be ready and could fight off Blaridane from taking over. He was sure of it. He just had to get the sword again.

"You alright?" Ziri asked, cutting off his thoughts of longing.

158

"Yeah, why?"

Ziri nodded, gesturing to his hands. He was wringing them, nearly making them bruise.

"I'm fine. Just miss something."

"You mean someone. Your sister?"

"What?" Rafik asked, being pulled from his thoughts of Blaridane again. "Oh, yeah. I do. Did you hear that?"

"Hear what?" Ziri replied.

There wasn't anyone else in the small room. His bed could barely fit in here. When he first woke up, he thought he was stuffed in a closet more than in a room for recovery. There was a window behind him, with a ledge Ziri sat on, that towered over the road from Trinkit and northwards to Datz. But the air was calm, not even a whisper came from outside. That voice, though. It sounded so rough. So...evil.

"Blaridane." Rafik muttered, hearing the voice again.

"What?" Ziri asked.

"Nothing." Rafik said, shaking his head. It was a slight whisper within him. Nothing more.

"Doesn't look like nothing." Ziri said. "You look worried."

"I might not be able to walk again. Of course I'm worried." Rafik snapped. "Just leave me alone."

"Sorry. Just trying to help."

"I don't need your help!" Rafik yelled. "I don't need you. I don't need Gorik or Samron. I need...I need my sword."

"We didn't find you with a sword. We'll get you a new one." Ziri said, placing her hand on his shoulder. "It's alright."

"No! It's not alright." Rafik said, gritting his teeth, wincing as he tried shrugging off Ziri's hand. "I don't want a new sword. I need *my* sword." Blaridane called to him, as if it was still in his hand. His hand itched, and the craving grew inside of him. He *needed* Blaridane. Even if he couldn't walk again, he could stop Skage, save Anza, do anything with the sword. Flashes of him standing on a mountain, sword raised, crossed through his mind. He saw himself fighting off monsters and saving entire villages.

159

He was no longer in the small closet sized room but on a battlefield.

Seemingly a lifetime later the urge began to subside. The images faded back into the forgotten corners of his mind where dreams resided. The dark and unnatural voice disappeared, and he could hear his own thoughts once more. There was something else. A sniffle. A cry.

"Anza?" He asked, spinning around. He hadn't remembered lying on the floor and couldn't recall how he got there.

Ziri shook her head, rocking back and forth in the fetal position on the window ledge.

"Ziri, what's wrong?" Rafik asked, climbing back onto his bed.

"Yo-you." She said between sobs.

"What do you mean? What happened?"

Ziri looked up, eyes scrunched. "What do you mean what happened?"

"I remember talking to you about hearing something. Then I woke up on the floor." Rafik explained.

Ziri shook her head. "No. You yelled at me. You said horrible things and began thrashing around like you were a monster."

"Are you sure?" Rafik asked.

Ziri nodded. "You scare me."

"I don't remember." Rafik said.

"You were upset about losing your sword."

Rafik nodded. Just the thought of the cursed sword made his fingers itch. "It was a nice sword."

"But enough to go crazy over?" She asked, helping Rafik climb onto the window ledge.

"I'm not going crazy." Rafik said without an ounce of conviction. He could feel his mind slipping. Between wanting to save Anza and needing Blaridane he felt like his mind was being consumed by wanting the impossible.

160

"Not if I can help it." Ziri said. She pulled Rafik in close, the two of them watching out the window.

"What's that?" He pointed to the ground far below, a peculiar shape moving towards them. The sun was inching higher, making the Black Wall glow in the east casting everything in a curious and distorted light.

The two squinted, trying to make out the shape. They recognized a cart being pulled. But the thing pulling it looked jarring. Unnatural. "I think…" Ziri said, trailing off. "I think that's a person."

Rafik tilted his head, squinting harder. As the shape grew closer, he nodded. It was two Kylix soldiers pulling the cart, to be exact. They were both walking like their ankles were broken. Every step was a limp with them nearly collapsing. From a distance it looked like a snarling feral animal pulling the cart. "I wonder what's in the cart."

"Probably treasure from Datz. There were a couple carts like that yesterday." Ziri said. "Nothing different in this one, I'm sure."

"Except the way they're walking." Rafik said. "That doesn't look right."

Ziri shook her head. "No."

The cart approached closer on the road leading to the Golden Gate. The soldiers didn't speak or make any motion they were in pain. A crunch and cracking of bones resounded the closer they got. The doors to the Golden Gate opened, allowing them entry. Ziri helped Rafik off the ledge, and to the balcony overlooking the inside courtyard of the western fortress.

The cart was pulled all the way to the river's edge. Some Kylix soldiers shouted at them while others barked orders. All were ignored. One man stomped over to the cart pullers, stating that he didn't appreciate being ignored. He grabbed one of their shoulders, turning them around. In one swift motion the newly arrived soldier turned and stabbed the man in the stomach, piercing through the armor.

161

"Traitor! Killer!" Soldiers yelled, taking out their swords. The soldiers standing guard on the walls now had their bows aimed at the treasonous Kylix soldier and his companion. The two stood there, not making eye contact with any, but staring off into the distance. They tilted their head, like a dog's after hearing something they're unsure of from their master.

Rafik turned, noticing the spider was now facing them, rather than at Datz. "I have a bad feeling about this, Ziri."

"Drop the sword." A soldier said, inching closer to the two. Again, the two cart pullers didn't respond.

Seconds later the soldier who was killed began to stir. At first, he gasped for breath. The next moment he pulled himself up to his feet. He snarled and began to scream. Everyone took a step back from the newly risen soldier.

Samron and Jinuk stepped out of a nearby room, looking towards the commotion. Before Jinuk could bark an order the canvas of the cart flew into the air. A horde of soldiers sprang forward attacking anything in front of them. As one fell, they would wake seconds later to fight their former comrades.

The few who managed to defend themselves from the surprise attack hacked limbs and the treacherous soldiers kept moving, unfazed by the loss. Jinuk screamed for retreat as Samron ordered for torches. Arrows rained down on everyone within the fortress. Just like from sword fighting, the arrows had no effect. With some still in their skeletal armor, they just bounced off.

"We need to get out of here." Rafik muttered, face going pale. He watched the battle below. He recognized a couple soldiers from the pond back in Datz. He had pushed them out of the air bubble. Their looks on their faces didn't change from the death face they had now. Others had burn marks. One didn't have a head but slashed away, trying to hit anything. If the situation wasn't so serious, he would have laughed as the headless soldier tried sword fighting a lamp post.

Ziri nodded. "Where's Samron?"

Rafik shrugged, taking the bag that was by his bedside. "I don't know, but we need to get to the boat and get out of here."

162

A fire erupted nearby. The living tried defending themselves but with each fallen they soldier became a new enemy that couldn't be stopped. Fire arrows now rained down on the soldiers. Those that were raised from the dead kept attacking, unaware as their own bodies burned.

The undead soldiers began spreading throughout the fort. One approached the two children, snarling. Ziri lunged forward, grabbing the soldier's arm. She closed her eyes, brows furrowed. The soldier screamed an unnaturally high-pitched wail and swung down at Ziri. Rafik threw the pillow from his bed at the soldier's face. It gave enough time of a distraction for Ziri to let go and step away.

"What are you doing?" He asked, wishing his legs could work. He still had all the memories of sword fighting from Blaridane and knew he could take them on if he could just stand.

"Trying to poison them." Ziri snapped, pushing the soldier over.

"One is missing a head!" Rafik said, trying to keep his voice steady. "I don't think that will help any."

Ziri nodded. "Worth a shot." She grabbed Rafik from beneath the shoulders and dragged him. As they made their way down the stairs to the docks Rafik, his legs hitting the ground with every step. "I'm sorry." She repeated after each time his leg hit the steps.

"Just keep going." Rafik said, shaking his head.

The high-pitched screeching of the undead grew louder. Rafik covered his ears, but it didn't help. On the last step a soldier noticed the kids and came towards them. Ziri screamed. The soldier swung his club, only to be blocked by the shaft of a spear.

Samron had appeared. The trainer kicked up the spear, jabbing the soldier, pushing him back. "Get to the boat." He ordered.

"We're trying." Rafik said, yanking a sword out of a recently fallen soldier just as they began to come back to life. Ziri kept dragging Rafik as he defended them from the soldiers who noticed their escape.

Samron hurried to the southern entrance and found the wheel to open the gate leading to the rest of the Eko River. Slowly, inch by inch, the gates on the river opened. Rafik turned in time to see Jinuk jump into the river and swim away, escaping the slaughter of the fortress. A small swarm of the undead soldiers surrounded Samron.

Another fallen soldier reached the boat once the children were on there. A second one jumped onto the other end, cornering them. "Rafik." Ziri said, choking back her fear in her whisper of a voice.

"Don't worry, Ziri." Rafik said. "Just stay close to me."

Ziri crouched into the fetal position, leaning against Rafik. The fallen soldier Rafik was facing raised their sword, screeching. It swung down, and Rafik managed to deflect the blow, but couldn't attack back. Blocking another blow Rafik swung the sword at the soldier's legs, cleaving them off. The soldier fell into the river, wailing and thrashing as if nothing happened.

The one behind Rafik took a step forward. Ziri screamed again. The soldier fell into the water as someone else jumped onto the boat, shoving them overboard. "You were going to leave without me?" Salina asked, just as pale as the children. "Let's go. Anywhere is better than here." She leaned over and untied the rope from the dock. She began to row down the channel, getting closer to the southern gateway.

The undead soldiers screamed even higher, throwing anything they could at the three of them. Samron jumped into the water near the ferry as it passed, Salina helping him into the ferry. A handful of other Kylix soldiers still living managed to escape. Samron watched as the dead screamed in victory. The high-pitched noise echoed and grew louder, piercing their ears. They all continued southward, trying to escape the unnerving noise.

"What happened back there?" Salina asked as the Golden Gate faded from view. Echoes of those screams could still be heard as the wind blew. Every time any of them closed their eyes flashes of what had just happened entered their minds.

"I...I don't know." Samron said, glancing back.

"I told you." Rafik said. "That's Skage. He's a necromancer."

"What's a necromancer?" Ziri asked.

"Someone who can summon the dead." Salina answered. "He's just a legend."

"Obviously more than that." Samron interrupted. "As much as I don't want to believe it, I'm afraid Rafik is right."

"How can we defeat that?" Salina asked, closing her eyes, and shivering again.

"My poison didn't work on them." Ziri said.

"Same with fire or beheading them." Rafik said.

"I don't know." Samron said. "But we will find out."

The group was now deep into the Biodlay Desert. Even with the muted light of the Black Wall it was bright. In every direction was sand. Mountains of sand. The air was dry, and the heat made Rafik feel like he was inside an oven. The occasional gust of wind whipped up wisps of sand but offered no relief to the relentless heat. There wasn't a cloud in the sky, and the only sign of water was the Eko River they were on.

"Is anybody going to help?" Salina asked, sweating more than the others. She was rowing the boat as Ziri sat next to Rafik. Samron paced from the front of the boat to the back. At each end he would stop and stare, trying to see something just beyond the horizon.

"We can take a break. Row us to shore." Samron said, not breaking his pace. For most of the Eko River, it was a lazy and calm current. However, it flowed northwards to the Golden Gate, so getting to Haitu required constant rowing.

"Gladly." Salina sighed, turning course, rowing the small ferry up onto the riverbank and jumped out. She dunked herself into the Eko River, coming back up after several minutes.

"Aren't you worried she'll get away?" Ziri asked.

Samron shook his head.

"Where will I go? Back to get killed and turn into one of those things, or to Haitu to be killed?" Salina snapped back before Samron could respond.

"You could escape into the desert." Rafik suggested.

"No one has ever survived that." Samron said. "The Biodlay is the largest expanse of nothing in all Alutopek. Probably in all Amlima. The only safe route is on the Eko River and the Oasis Trail."

"What's the Oasis Trail?" Rafik and Ziri asked in unison.

"It's the only safe passageway through the desert. On the eastern edge you have Haitu and the Eko River. With an oasis dotted here and there one can make it westward to Lynn, and the Gateway Mountains. It's a dangerous road. If the heat won't get you, thieves will." Samron explained.

Ziri jumped into the water next, splashing Rafik and Samron. "Wait for me." Rafik smiled, dragging himself to the boat's edge.

"Hold on a second." Samron said, stopping Rafik. "Get Gorik out."

Rafik nodded and opened the bag, taking it off his shoulder. "Gorik. You're safe now."

A moment later the bag enlarged and Gorik crawled out. "Blazes it is hot out. What happened to letting me out near the Golden Gate?"

"Why would we have done that?" Rafik asked.

"While you would be going to get healed, Gorik is going back to save your sister." Samron said. "You didn't think I'd just let her be stuck there? Especially now."

"What's happened?" Gorik asked.

Rafik and Samron recounted what had happened at the Golden Gate. "And that's why we didn't let you out until now." Samron finished.

The sailor shook his head, squinting back to the north. "Anza, I sure hope you're safe."

"You and me both." Rafik said. "Here." He tossed the bag to Gorik.

"Why are you giving me this?"

"To keep you safe. You could hide in there. From the heat and maybe Skage's soldiers." Rafik said. "Plus, once you have Anza back, she can stay in there until it's safe."

"I think she's feisty enough she could take care of herself, you know?" Gorik said, giving Rafik a parental look.

"I know. But she might die and turn into one of those things." Rafik argued. "She needs to be safe. Make sure she is in the bag."

"You know, your father always wanted that." Gorik smiled, looking into the distance. "Locking you two away somewhere so you can't grow up. And I'll tell you the same thing I told him. You can't protect her forever."

Rafik smiled. "I can try."

"That was your father's answer, too." Gorik laughed. He hugged Rafik goodbye, promised he'd rescue Anza, and jumped off the ferry. He floated down the river a way until he climbed onto shore and out of sight. Rafik watched him fade from view before moving again.

"He'll be fine." Samron sighed. "I've known him for a long time and he never fails."

Rafik nodded. "I remember seven years ago I was sitting on the docks, waiting for my father to return. I saw the sails in the distance. I jumped up, excited that they were finally home. As the ship grew closer, I saw Gorik. He smiled, throwing something towards me. I had no idea it was his peg leg. He made me smile, jumping towards me demanding his leg. He put me in a good mood before telling me my father died. He said my father was drunk. Slipped overboard. Gorik will do whatever he can to protect Anza and me. I know he'll be fine. I know if he can get to her, she'll be safe as well."

Samron nodded. "He's a good man."

"Can we stay here?" Ziri asked, splashing the two still on the boat.

Samron looked north and south before answering with a smile. "I think we deserve a rest. Why not?"

"What about me? The healers at the Golden Gate said I was bleeding on the inside." Rafik reminded Samron.

"If you were, I'm certain you would be dead by now. The only thing I'm worried about is your legs." Samron said. "Healers anywhere but Haitu, Detnu, and Lynn aren't known for their accuracy. I once had one tell me I was going to die when I was just hungover."

Rafik smiled and looked down at his legs. His demeanor changed. Just a week ago he could walk. And now he could only drag himself and rely on others. He couldn't tell if the pain was going away, or he was slowly learning to live with it. Samron scooped up Rafik and threw him into the river before he could respond. He bobbed to the surface and began to swim. He was surprised to find that his legs didn't hurt but floated behind him.

"If you can still move, you aren't useless. You just have to think outside the box." Samron said, jumping into the water beside him.

Chapter 14: The Sandstorm

Biodlay Desert, Alutopek

"Ya shire." Gorik cursed again. He had never liked sand. If he could live all day on a boat out at sea he would. He looked up once again and saw nothing but the grainy eye sore he was doomed to walk. There was no sign he was getting any closer. If it weren't for Rafik and the others gone from view, he would have thought he had only gone mere inches.

The sailor looked behind him and saw the evident proof of his journey. Along his footprint was a line in the sand from his peg leg. When trying to use it to walk he would sink deeper into the scorching sand. Instead, he just dragged it behind him.

He could hear the little drink he had left slosh around. The noise called to him, his mouth growing drier by the second. He wasn't desperate enough to drink that river water. The Dragonborn of the Bomoku Mountains were known to toss the dead into the Eko River for one of their rituals. It wasn't often, and even rarer for the corpse making it this far north, but just the thought made him think twice. No, he would drink from his leg, and hope that would be enough. Deep down he already knew it wouldn't be.

The sailor tried ignoring how dry his mouth and throat felt. "Find a distraction, Gorik." He told himself, looking around at his surroundings. Sand everywhere. The only change was the long expanse of the Eko River. He could barely make out the opposing shore if he squinted. Even then he believed it to be a sort of mirage. Watching the river, he imagined jumping in and floating down to the Golden Gate, like one of the Dragonborn corpses. It would definitely be the fastest way to get there.

Unfortunately, even that wasn't an option for him. According to legend and local rumor, a giant lizard lived in the waters and devoured those that don't belong to the desert. He wasn't sure if the stories were true, but he didn't want to find out any time soon. For his entire life he believed the legends of Skage were just stories. Now he wasn't sure what stories were true or not.

As the light on the Black Wall began to fade the hot desert began to shift. He could see his breath now and began to shiver. He was surprised by the sudden cold and tried looking for shelter. Not surprisingly, it was all sand and no sign of a cave or even a rock to hide under. Gorik threw down the bag beside the riverbank and climbed in, silently thanking Rafik. He wasn't a fan of the heat of the desert, but he didn't want to freeze to death either.

Falling into the bag was an experience he still wasn't used to. This was the first time he didn't try landing on his foot and nearly snapping his peg leg. He used his hands and rolled upon landing. It didn't feel the best, but at least he would be able to walk still. The room was quiet and empty, almost giving off an eerie feeling. He couldn't place it, but it felt as if someone was down here with him. His skin prickled, and hair stood on end at the thought. Now wasn't the time to scare oneself with ghosts when there was a necromancer on the loose. He unscrewed his leg and took the last of his drink. Although he was out, at least he would get a goodnight's sleep. Moments later he was in dreamland, alone in the room, snoring loud enough to wake a slumbering dragon.

Gorik crawled out of the bag just before the light enveloped the Black Wall. It was a peculiar time when it wasn't night, but not the familiar twilight of the day. He stretched, drank a handful of water from the river, wishing it was only water, and continued northward. Halfway through the day he began cursing again, missing his leg. The alternative wasn't worth it, though. *'I'd be dead, too, if I didn't cut it off.'* He thought to himself, the memories of that night filling him.

He hadn't thought of that night in ages. He shook his head and pushed that memory out once again. The day dragged on. Every minute was the same as the last. Sand ahead of him, and behind. Sand to the left and a lazy river he couldn't see the other side of to his right. More than once he thought if it wasn't for his peg leg dragging behind him, he would have thought he was walking in place.

Another day passed, and he still hadn't come any closer to the Golden Gate. His stomach growled, as he only had water since arriving in Datz the day of the attack. He didn't have the tools with him to fish. And if he did, he didn't want to stop. He needed to save Anza. Especially if what Rafik and Samron were saying had happened. Which he did believe. Seeing the apparent fear on their faces wasn't something that could be faked.

By the third day he could see it. A black spec in the distance. The river had narrowed so he could see the other side. Not to his surprise, more sand stretched along there as well. The spec didn't seem to be getting any closer by the end of the day. Gorik crawled back into the bag that night, falling asleep before he had even rested his head.

The sailor awoke to a monstrous growl. He scrambled to his feet, nearly tumbling over, before realizing he was alone in the room. As he scrambled across the room, looking high and low for the source of the growl it happened again. His stomach. He had been ignoring the pain and hunger, and now it was screaming at him.

As he started the climb up the ladder he paused. Gorik turned around, investigating the mirror. His face was gaunter than ever before. "Look at you," He said to himself smirking. "You're wasting away. You should probably eat something." He climbed the ladder, shaking his head, and left the bag.

It wasn't much longer after this that Gorik noticed something. Coming from deep within the desert was a large cloud. It blew over an entire dune, shrouding it in the dust cloud. The cloud moved towards him faster than he had expected. The growl of the cloud roared towards him and thunder rumbled. Gorik looked around, trying to find shelter. He couldn't hide in the bag. It would get buried and he'd never get out. He ran forward, as fast as he could. If it came to it, he would jump into the river.

The spec had grown larger now. He could make out details of the Golden Gate. But the storm was nearly on him. There, just ahead, was a large stone. A red boulder that stuck out of the sand like a sore thumb. Gorik pushed himself harder and dove into the shadow of the stone as the sandstorm reached him.

He had never been in one, and never wanted to again, either. Sand swirled around him. Loose grains scratching him across his face. What startled him most was lightning beginning to strike, and thunder roaring. One bolt got exceptionally close to him. Praying the stone would protect him, he climbed back into the bag for shelter.

The storm couldn't be heard from within. The only thunder came from his growling belly. "There has to be food in here somewhere." He said aloud, beginning to look around.

On the table were loose papers he had found in a secret compartment on the underside of the desk. On either shelf there were the elemental stones, but no sign of food. Glancing in the mirror, he didn't notice anything near the ladder either. Out of the corner of his eye he saw it, though. He had spent days in this hidden room, probably weeks, but never really snooped around. But there, beside the desk, was the backside of a picture.

"I swear if that is a picture of food I will scream." Gorik grumbled. He grabbed the portrait and turned it around, dropping it just as quickly with a gasp. "Anza?"

As soon as their eyes met, she came to life. "Gorik! Gorik can you hear me?"

"What, yes of course I can." Gorik said, smiling. "Is-is it really you?"

"Yes, I'm trapped in here, and don't know how to get out." Anza said.

Usually Gorik would have made a quip about the definition of trapped being exactly that. But in this case, he started to laugh. "You've been with us this whole time? In this bag? Oh, that saves me so much time and trouble."

"What do you mean? What's going on?" Anza asked.

Gorik shook his head. "According to your brother a man named Skage is raising the dead."

"Is Rafik alright?" Anza asked, cutting off Gorik's explanation.

The sailor nodded. "As good as he can be. He can't walk. My friend is taking him to a healer. What are you doing in there?"

Anza fell silent, turning to stare down at her feet. "Well, I-I got tricked."

'Tricked? By whom?"

"The man in this painting. He promised me he was going to help bring back Mom." Anza explained. "But once he was out, he left me here."

"Who was this man?" Gorik asked after several seconds. He already had a guess who, but prayed he was wrong.

Anza turned away from him as she answered. "Skage."

"Skage? The one who is now raising everyone from the dead as if they were just sleeping? He was in there? And you got him out?"

"I'm sorry, Gorik. I didn't know he was a bad man." Anza said, beginning to cry. "I just wanted Mom back."

Gorik sighed, leaning against the desk, drooping his head. "If you and your brother had just stayed on the boat none of this would have happened."

"I know, I'm sorry."

"Sorry doesn't cut it this time, Anza." Gorik yelled. "Your brother nearly got killed. Countless people have been attacked and killed, only to be brought back to life to kill others. Skage isn't a bad man, Anza. No, he's evil. Pure evil. Even the king seems like a nice guy compared to what he can do."

"I know, and I learned my lesson."

"Well, least you're not stuck at the Sarason Fortress." Gorik said after several minutes of silence. He would pace back and forth, pause to open his mouth, and look at Anza, only to continue pacing. Even his stomach had quieted down. "We need to get you out of there. Then we can find your brother, get you two to safety."

"Am I in trouble?"

"We'll figure that out after everything has been taken care of. Now, how do we get you out of there?"

173

"I don't remember." Anza shrugged. "I had to use those stones, drink from a cup, and say these funny words."

"Do you remember what the words were? Where's the cup?"

"No." Anza said. "It's a language I've never even heard before. The words were hard to say. And he took the cup with him."

"This isn't good." Gorik said. "Magic is gone. Has been since before King Vanarzir. All that was left was talent until the Black Wall. And I doubt there is anyone with the ability to remove people from pictures." Gorik said in a frenzy. "And the only person who has magic is the one who got you in there."

"There is another." Anza said. "There's Izamar."

"Who is Izamar?" Gorik asked, trying to keep his tone level.

"Do I know you?" A calm, elderly voice asked from the mirror.

Gorik screamed as the wizard appeared beside his reflection. "Who are you? Gods, I hate magic."

"You called my name." Izamar explained. "I don't know who you are. But this is the Mentor's Mirror. I am here to help. Tell me, how did you find my name?"

"Anza told me it." Gorik said, holding up the portrait.

"Hi, Izamar." Anza said, waving sheepishly.

"Anza! What happened?" Izamar gasped.

"I was upset that you couldn't help me. When you left, I met Skage. He promised he could help instead." Anza explained.

Izamar shook his head, his grey beard swaying back and forth. "Anza, Anza, Anza. Impatience and ignorance are many a man's folly. I hope you have learned your lesson."

"That's it?" Gorik asked. "I would have thought wiser words and a lot more anger from some wizard. Do you know who this Skage person is?"

"I should say I do. He was my apprentice for a time." Izamar said, his glance towards Gorik left the sailor unimpressed.

174

"What?" Gorik said, unsure of what else to say. "I've never heard of you."

"And for good reason." The wizard said, stretching his arms. "I removed myself from history to keep this room safe and Skage away from the outside world. And it worked until Rafik had discovered it."

"How can we stop him? And get Anza out of here?" Gorik asked.

"When Skage was about to be defeated he disappeared. I didn't find him until a year later, hiding in a portrait. It was of his own design. I don't know how he did it, but the answers should be at my library." Izamar said.

"And where is that?"

"I call it the Dragon's Roost. It's a lone mountain in the middle of the Biodlay Desert."

"Well, that's convenient because that's where I am. In a middle of a sandstorm in the Biodlay." Gorik said. "Lucky for me there was one, otherwise I wouldn't have found Anza until I was already at the Sarason Fortress."

"Where are you in the desert?"

"About a day away from the Golden Gate."

Izamar scratched his head. "I don't know where that is. It was probably built after my time."

"It's a fortress at the mouth of the Eko River." Gorik explained.

"And you said a sandstorm caused you to come in here?"

Gorik nodded. "Nearly got zapped by lightning before I did."

Izamar smiled. "You're hiding behind a stone?"

"I am." Gorik nodded in agreement.

"I bewitched that boulder to always remain above the sand. It's a marker. If one gets too close to the Dragon's Roost without my permission, then a violent sandstorm kicks up in the area. It's a four day's walk into the desert from that stone."

175

Gorik's stomach rumbled and he tried to ignore it. "So, I'm nowhere close to it? That means someone else was. Did Skage know where the Dragon's Roost was?"

"Of course. He was my apprentice." Izamar said.

"This isn't good." Gorik said. "He's already trying to get there. That's why the storm kicked up."

Izamar frowned. "If he tried, he wouldn't get through the storm."

"If I go there, we can get Anza out of the picture and find a way to stop Skage, right?"

"If there is a way, it would be there."

Gorik sighed. "I am hungry. Sorry, Anza, but before I go waltzing into the desert, I need to find me some food. I'm sneaking into the Golden Gate to find some, and then we'll go. Unless you can summon some?"

Izamar laughed. "I could have, yes. But from the Mentor's Mirror I can only teach and advise. I cannot interfere with the physical world. I may be able to once we're at the Dragon's Roost."

"Well, wish me luck. Last I heard the Golden Gate was filled with Skage's minions." Gorik said.

Walking through the desert after the storm was much easier. He had found Anza and didn't have to sneak into the Sarason Fortress. All he had to do was get to the Golden Gate, steal some food as fast as he could, and get out. Stealing food was always much easier than finding someone. Especially when the guards are undead and don't need the food.

He patted the bag, knowing that Anza was safely inside. A weight had been lifted from him, knowing she wasn't missing. Gorik laughed, imagining Rafik's face when he learned Anza was with him the whole time. "Well, Rafik, you got your wish. She's safe."

Sure enough, by midday the next day Gorik had made it to the Golden Gate. It was just as quiet as the desert. He wondered if the newly arisen dead made sound or communicated with one

176

another. His face wrinkled as the foul stench of death wafted through the air. But he had made it. His stomach growled more than ever, his arms and legs shaky.

The Golden Gate was a black mark on the golden sands. It stretched across both shores of the river. Gorik looked up to the parapets but saw no guards. The gate Samron had opened was still open. To the side of it was a small doorway.

Gorik looked down at his shaky hands. Between the heat and the hunger, he felt as if he could fall asleep the moment he closed his eyes. *'Probably shouldn't swim.'* He thought to himself, dragging his peg leg to the door.

If he thought it smelled terrible walking up, it was horrendous inside. The sudden powerful odor caused Gorik to take a step back. He took a deep breath and entered the fortress. There were bodies everywhere. Some on the stairs, half hanging off the upper levels. Others were scattered across the ground. All of them looked like they were on the losing end of a battle, but the victors were nowhere to be seen.

It wasn't long before Gorik had to take another breath. He coughed and continued through the fortress. Every room there was a body of a fallen Kylix soldier. Their skeletal armor looked almost like a burial shroud. "This isn't as terrible as they said it was." Gorik laughed. "I'm still living, at least."

After entering several rooms and wandering around he found the kitchens. It was based on the lower east side of the Golden Gate with a chute to the Tahlbiru Ocean. The fireplaces were dead, and the place had an unnatural cold to it. He kept an ear open for any sort of sound but only heard the clunking of his peg leg upon the stone.

The first cupboard was empty. Same with the second. Gorik gasped, opening the third one and a Kylix soldier fell out. He stepped to the side as the corpse collapsed where he was standing. Just as his stomach growled again, he checked the cupboard and found a bowl of fruit. His mouth watered, snatching the bowl, and eating, tearing off junks like a ravenous boar.

After he had his fill there were three apples left. He tossed them into the bag and kept searching. In other cupboards he found rancid meat, and more fruits and vegetables. With the current smell, he wasn't that interested in meat, and took all the fruits and vegetables he could find. He tossed them into the bag and turned to leave when he caught something out of the corner of his eye. A wheel of cheese. He tried lifting it, but the giant wheel was too heavy. It still rested on the table, not even showing a budge. He grabbed a knife and started cutting off chunks when he heard it. A door locking.

Gorik snapped his head up, looking back at the door. It had closed. A corpse stood guard beside the door but showed no movement. After several seconds of staring at the door he returned to the cheese. It had to be his imagination. A couple more pieces and the clinking of armor echoed in the room. The sailor grabbed another knife, looking around. The corpse by the door was gone. He opened the shoot and glanced out the window. The spider atop the Sarason Fortress was staring at the Golden Gate, its eyes glowing.

He turned and an undead Kylix soldier screamed, waving a sword about. Gorik stepped closer, ducked, and stabbed one knife into the soldier's gut. He jumped to his feet and used the other one to slice across their exposed neck. The soldier screamed again, unfazed by the damage. He shoved the soldier and bolted for the door.

Two other corpses began to stir, trying to trip Gorik as they got to their feet. He kicked open the door, balancing on his peg leg, and ran out of the room. The fortress was alive with more screams. He saw two soldiers hobbling towards them from out of the darkened corridor. Gorik turned and ran back into the kitchen, jumping over a counter and sliding across another. The dead were now behind him, all giving chase. He made it to the chute and climbed out.

Instead of jumping he clung onto the ledge, inching himself over. The waters of the Tahlbiru were always ice cold. Jumping in there, even if he survived, would be a death sentence. The soldiers

178

stared down into the water and stood still. Gorik continued climbing across the ledge, hoping not to make a sound.

As he got to another ledge one corpse howled and closed the chute. All around him he could hear the stirring of the dead. This was a trap. He clung onto the bag, and climbed around the Golden Gate, slipping several times because of his leg.

The dead hadn't noticed him, but they didn't fall back asleep, either. They stamped, skulked, and prowled around the fortress, screeching every so often. The noises disturbed him. But the disjointed movements as if they were puppets on string, he would see passing by windows did even more so.

The night grew longer when he finally inched his way across the last of the Golden Gate. "I never thought I'd be so happy to be on sand." He said, tapping his peg leg on the loose ground. The dead hadn't noticed. He climbed into the bag, leaning it against the wall of the Golden Gate, and went to sleep.

Chapter 15: Change of Plans

Sekolah Fortress, Haitu, Biodlay Desert, Alutopek

Rafik screamed as hard as he could. His lungs ached, dragging it out longer. A moment later the scream echoed back and Ziri laughed. It was one of several canyons lining the Eko River. According to Samron, 'eko' meant repeat in an ancient language, and was how this river got its name. Because of these canyons.

"Will you two stop?" Salina snapped. Her voice echoed back much to the enjoyment of the children. Even Samron smirked as she cursed.

"You should enjoy it." Rafik said, smiling. He had regained some strength, and able to drag himself around the ferry at a quick pace. "When we get there, you're going to prison."

"And you'll be forced into the Kylix." Salina spat. "Your fate is worse than mine."

"Samron said I won't be joining them. Just go in, get healed, get out." Rafik said.

Ziri looked down, the smile she had watching Rafik faded.

"And you trust him? He's one of them." Salina said, glaring at the man.

"He's Gorik's friend." Rafik argued.

"Yes, that's why he's not here. He's Gorik's friend. Not yours." Salina said. Her voice hadn't lost any sense of venom to it. "You're a foolish boy and deserve this if you actually trust him."

"That's enough." Samron said. On most days he stayed quiet, not saying a word. It was Salina who decided when they would stop for the night or have a break. Since Gorik left he hardly said a word to anyone. Something Rafik noticed. He tried asking him questions but he either grunted or ignored them.

All the canyons were the same. Smooth red rock, scraping the sky without a ledge to stand on. There had been a cave or two with birds flying out, but without climbing continuously there wasn't a way to get to them. But on this one, high up, just before the lip of the ledge, Ziri spotted it. "What's that?" She asked in her

180

regular whisper. Within the canyon her voice reverberated louder than her original statement. She pointed up at the peculiar markings.

"Those are petroglyphs." Samron said, holding his hand up to cover the light emanating off the Black Wall. "Ancient drawings from a long time ago. Before history, even."

"What do they say?" Rafik asked, noticing them. If he squinted, he could just make them out. There were fires, water droplets, swirling lines, and a mountain.

"Nobody knows." Samron said. "If anyone could read and decipher them, they would be famous. For all we know, they could have just been drawings from children no older than you two."

"How did they get up there?" Ziri asked.

Samron shrugged. "Another mystery. Some mountains even have fossils of fish in them."

"No way!" Salina scoffed. "How did fish get on the top of mountains?"

"It was ages ago." Samron started, staring into the river. "The first age. The Age of the Elements. The gods had created this world and gave life to the elements themselves. But they waged war with one another, putting all Amlima into chaos. In a single night, the world was flooded, and the next mountains throttling rivers. Fires scorched the air and wind tore away at rock like butter. Nothing could survive the constant battle. The gods ended it. And we can see proof of this from the fossils of fish on the mountains. Even this desert is proof that the living fires burned the world and left this scar."

"That's just a myth." Salina laughed as Rafik and Ziri stared at the red rocks with newfound awe. "That never happened."

"Alright." Samron smiled. "How did fossils of fish get on top of the mountains? Let alone turn to stone?"

"I don't know. Birds." Salina said. "Birds caught the fish and dropped them."

"Birds?" Samron said, biting back a smile. "All over the world birds just dropping fish of all sizes on mountain tops."

"How did they become fossils?" Ziri asked.

181

"Sometimes when we bury the dead," Samron began "The bodies turn to stone, and become one with the earth. We've seen this in the case of fossils. The living element of earth still claims what it can for its own. That's why our ancestors built the cities of the dead. So, when it is time for our souls to return to our bodies, we aren't imprisoned in stone."

The desert air was cooler in the canyons. Salina would row just a little slower to enjoy the cool air. Even if it meant listening to the children screaming for the echoes. The current was faster here, as the river narrowed to fit into the canyons. Even if she wanted to go faster, she doubted she could. As the current slowed, and the cooler air began to rise, she missed it already. Without warning, leaving the canyon and the desert sky beat down on them. It was relentless. Even at night, as they camped by the river, she felt like she would freeze. It never failed that she would pray for the desert air to warm her at night, and to freeze her during the day.

"Is Haitu this hot?" She asked after leaving the canyon.

Samron shrugged. "Sometimes hotter. With all the people close together. But we'll be indoors most of the time. We won't have the burning air right on us."

"I wish I had the talent over cold air." Ziri said, swirling her hand in the air before shoving it straight into the sky. "I'd make this place perfect."

"If you had the talent over cold air," Samron laughed, "You'd be a goddess to these desert dwellers."

Night soon fell on them as they neared another canyon. Samron announced it would be the last canyon before Haitu. They would be there tomorrow. Even Salina was relieved by the news. Rafik dragged himself onto shore, lying next to Ziri and staring up at the few stars piercing through the Black Wall. They looked different here. The stars he was used to had stayed north of them. Samron dug a pit and managed to start a fire from the few loose bits of wood that were left on the boat.

"Not much of a fire, but it'll do." Samron shrugged. He had been fishing most of the day off the back of the boat and caught a couple. It wasn't much, but at least they wouldn't be sleeping with empty bellies.

By now the routine was made. There wasn't much splashing and playing in the water like there was the first day. Salina would steer them to shore. Ziri and Rafik would find a place and lay down to rest. Samron would make a fire and cook. Salina was asleep before anyone most nights and woke up as the light of the Black Wall began heating up the sky.

The final canyon before Haitu was different than the others. Each side was potted with caves. One billowing smoke out. "Is someone in there?" Ziri asked. Her voice didn't echo as much as in the other canyons.

Samron nodded. "I believe so. Hello!" He shouted

The group stared up at the cave entrance with anticipation. Nobody answered, but the smoke stopped. "Somebody is in there." Salina said. "And I think they're hiding."

Rafik bit his tongue, wanting to insult her for stating what everyone was thinking. "Are you going to report him?"

"No." Samron smiled.

Passing the smoking cave, Rafik marveled at the canyon. It amazed him that there was so much more than Datz and the surrounding sea he was used to. He had heard stories of other places but seeing them was another thing entirely. His heart sank, thinking of home. He turned, looking longingly northward. There wasn't a sign of his home behind him. His thoughts turned to Anza. How scared was she? If Skage found her, did she get away, or become one of his minions?

His thoughts changed again. His fingers itched to grasp it, again. Feel the cold steel in his hands. His mind lingered, looking for that other voice. The cold, violent voice that offered bravery. That would make him a warrior. He needed Blaridane. Rafik shifted where he sat, scratching at his palms and arms. "How long until we can go home?"

Samron scratched his hairy chin. "It shouldn't be long. Taking a page out of Gorik's book, and hope to smuggle you in. Once you're healed, we can get you out of here."

"And if I mention that you're doing this?" Salina asked. "You can't threaten to kill me. I'm sure that's already going to happen to me."

"You won't." Samron snarled.

"Yes, she would." Rafik said. "She hates me."

"Fine." Samron said. "Ziri will poison you. Just enough for you to suffer and be on the brink of death. Too weak to say anything. Once Rafik is safely homeward bound, she'll cure you. Just in time for you to be executed."

Salina's face soured.

"I'm not going back?" Ziri asked.

"Not yet." Samron said, shaking his head. "But you will."

Salina scoffed, but didn't say anything. The boat ride was quiet, as she rowed them closer to the desert city of Haitu. She jumped, nearly dropping the oar in the water as Ziri let out the loudest scream she had heard from her.

Rafik laughed, screaming as well, making the echoes louder.

"It was fun the first time." Salina snapped, covering her ears. "It's getting ridiculous."

"I thought you'd enjoy the last little bit of freedom you had." Rafik smirked. In the last couple days, his spirit lifted as Ziri tried cheering him up.

"It would be a lot easier to enjoy if you were quiet." Salina replied. She steered the boat around another bend and sighed a relief as the canyon gave way to more mountains of sand. "Now you two can shut up."

The sand dunes were higher here than other places. Mountains of sand with the occasional gust of wind picking up wisps of it. Ziri tried screaming, but there wasn't an echo, just a glare from Salina. Heat beat down on them, slowly cooking them. The only one who didn't seem to have darker skin from being out in it all day was Ziri. Everyone else had burned or got a slight tan. It wasn't much farther until the mountains slowly flattened out into a long expanse of nothing. "What's that?" Ziri asked, pointing out into the distance. From where they were it looked like stones stacked to knee high levels scattered about as far as the eye could see.

"It's the Well Field." Samron explained. "Supposedly a long time ago water was pulled out them all, and the city stretched even farther into the desert. I've been in some of those wells and I didn't see any sign of a water. Or that the city was larger than it is now, for that matter."

"Can we check it out?" Rafik asked. He remembered the wardrobe he had found. Maybe he could get lucky and find more treasures. If anything, he could practice using his talent. He hadn't been able to since back at the Sarason Fortress. He worried that his talent had slipped, and it was just a onetime thing. More than once he had to convince himself Ziri's power wasn't like that, so his shouldn't be either.

"I don't think so." Samron said, shaking his head. "No one is allowed in there. King's orders. I almost lost my head when I was caught."

"Really?" Rafik asked.

"Yep." Samron said. "The king even came and interrogated me personally. When he determined I didn't find anything he let me live. So long as I served the Kylix, that is. I agreed in a heartbeat. I kind of value my life."

"I wouldn't have." Rafik said. "I would have challenged him like that Xeo kid did."

Samron laughed. "It's not that easy. If it were, I'm sure everyone would be challenging the king to a duel. He is over 200 years old."

"That's just a story." Salina argued. "No one lives that long. It's unnatural."

"King Vanarzir has." Samron said. "I've been to the Hall of Records in Haitu. Next best thing than being in the Great Libraries of Detnu. And he was born over 200 years ago. Outlived his wife, sons, and grandchildren."

"What happened to his family?" Rafik asked.

"Nobody knows." Samron said. "Even in the Hall of Records it doesn't say. They just vanished and no one heard from them again."

"I bet I could find them." Rafik said holding up his hand. "Just give me something of theirs and I could find them all."

Samron laughed. "You just might. Maybe if you meet the king you could suggest that? Unless he doesn't want them found. Then you might be in trouble."

Rafik's face paled. "I thought you said he wasn't killing anyone with talent?" Ziri squeezed Rafik's hand, the look of fear on her face apparent.

"I did. But you have an interesting talent, Rafik. You can uncover secrets that some might want left forgotten. You could end up getting hurt advertising your talent." Samron said.

"What's the point of having talent if I can't show it off? I mean, I don't have a cool one like Ziri where I can poison anybody I want." Rafik said.

"No. You have a talent that could crumble an empire, not just kill a king." Samron said.

Rafik didn't respond to that. He stared down at the water, wondering what Samron had said. He could reveal secrets, but would anyone believe him? He could easily make up his visions and would anyone know?

As if he could read minds Samron spoke up. "Ever heard of the Bantrita?"

Rafik nodded. "Storytellers, right?"

"They are now, yes." Samron said. "The Bantrita were once record keepers. They could glimpse into the past and write it exactly as is. Their records are in the libraries of Detnu. But King Vanarzir outlawed them. Those who resisted died. Those who complied became glorified storytellers."

"Oh." Rafik said, unsure of how else to respond.

"What I'm saying is, why would a king outlaw accurate history unless he was trying to hide something?"

"And that's why you're taking him to the Kylix." Salina said. "To turn him in and you get some big reward."

186

"An interesting theory, but no." Samron said. "I am taking him to the Kylix so he can be healed there and walk again."

"And then what? A child can't just walk out of the Kylix, I'm sure." Salina said. "He's going to be stuck there. You can't smuggle him out like you say you can."

"There's always a way out." Samron said, smiling. "There is one girl, she sneaks out nearly every night. I'm sure Rafik can escape. Especially if I am helping him."

"So, are you for or against King Vanarzir? I've never met someone who is serving the king but seems to be plotting his downfall." Salina asked.

Samron's demeanor changed. He stood up straight and became much more rigid in his voice. Any tone of joviality was gone. "You watch your tongue. I do serve the king. But I am a human and will do what's right."

Salina smirked but didn't say another word. Rafik noticed the conversation was over and he turned his attention back onto the water. The current was nearly nonexistent now as Salina was able to cut through the water much faster here.

"Why is the current gone?" Ziri asked after nearly an hour of silence.

"We're getting close." Samron replied. They turned another bend and found themselves entering one more canyon.

"I thought you said that was the last canyon." Salina said with a big sigh.

Rafik was already itching to scream as loud as he could within the canyon. "Because it was." Samron said. Haitu's harbor is built within the canyon. The ancient people of Alutopek carved the entrance out of the stone itself."

Moments later echoes of people shouting and hammers hitting anvils deafened them as they entered the canyon. Even Rafik and Ziri covered their ears. Samron laughed at their sudden shudder. "Is it always this loud?" Rafik yelled, trying to be heard.

Samron nodded. "Just on the river."

Kylix soldiers stood guard. One was barking orders, telling where each boat on the river had to go. As the soldier saw Samron he shouted, "You know where to go." And pointed southward in an arcing motion.

Samron gave a thumbs up and told Salina to keep rowing. Rafik watched the hustle and bustle as people got on and off boats. There was a large expanse of cleared out stone that small shops stood on. Merchants shouted prices and bartered with people who were interested. On the far side was a massive wall with arching entryways. Between the four arches were giant statues that Rafik thought looked familiar but couldn't quite place it. The figures towered over everything, and inscriptions were half worn on the base.

"Welcome to the City of Sand." Samron said, clapping Rafik on the back. "Ever thought you'd be in Haitu?"

Rafik shook his head. "I didn't even think this many people existed."

"Can we explore?" Ziri asked, hanging off the side of the ferry and gawking at the people on land.

"Not yet." Samron said. "We need to stop at the Kylix stronghold first. The echoes faded to muffled noise as they continued down the river. As the harbor faded a statue of a Kylix soldier was engraved into the wall. Rafik looked up and saw the wall guarded with Kylix. Towers reached into the sky with a bridge connecting some of the shorter ones together. Spires topped each tower with the familiar flag of Alutopek.

A small dock protruded outward, big enough for just the ferry. "I would have thought the Kylix would have a bigger port." Rafik said.

"They do." Samron said. "This wall isn't actually rock but camouflaged like it."

Rafik nodded, squinting at the rock, trying to see through it. "I can't tell."

"That's the point." Salina said.

The trainer wrapped the rope around one of the posts and called for the Kylix. The three guarding the entrance stepped forward. "This woman is under arrest for attempted murder." Samron said. "Take her away."

Salina glared at Samron. She muttered under her breath, getting to her feet. "Don't touch me." She spat, yanking her arm away as the Kylix soldier tried reaching for her. She walked in front of the Kylix, disappearing into the stone of the Kylix stronghold.

"This one, her name is Ziri." Samron said, putting his arm around her and smiling. "She has talent. Take her with the other Kylika."

The second Kylix soldier held out his hand and Ziri took it. She waved goodbye to Rafik, promising to see him soon. "What about him?" The last soldier asked.

"You never saw him." Samron said. "I am taking him to my office. Bring Krista. Don't tell anyone."

The Kylix soldier nodded. "Yes sir. Commander Jinuk arrived yesterday. He's shaken up but mentioned you might be coming." Before Samron could say anything else the soldier turned to leave.

"That coward made it, huh? Locked himself in a closet until I opened it back at the Golden Gate. Then took off like a scurrying mouse. Now, Rafik. Welcome to the Sekolah Fortress. Home of the Kylix." He said with a sigh, placing his hand on his shoulder. "I know you can't walk, so I'm going to carry you. I don't want anyone to see you, though. So, I'm placing a blanket over you. You'll have to trust me."

Rafik nodded and grabbed a blanket from the ferry and wrapped himself in it. "They'll still know you are carrying a person, though."

"I know. I can say it was Ziri. She's new here too." Samron said. He scooped Rafik up and stepped off the ferry as three more Kylix soldiers appeared to stand guard.

The trainer took him through the Sekolah Fortress, greeting some and yelling orders at others. Nobody asked what he was doing, and they addressed him with 'sir' and 'lord.' Climbing several stairs and turning countless corners, Samron unlocked a door and opened it. Samron placed Rafik on a bed telling him he could take off the blanket now.

189

Rafik had tried memorizing the route, but with the twists and turns, it didn't take long for him to give up. He removed the blanket, eager to see if he were in a jail cell or not. He imagined that's how they kept all the new children until they learned to behave. Across one entire wall was a map of Alutopek. A desk off to the side. Beside the bed were a table, and a shelf of books. He didn't notice any windows. "Are we in a dungeon?"

"What?"

"There's no windows." Rafik said.

Samron shook his head, smiling. "Good observation. No, we are in one of the towers. This room isn't on any map of the fortress. Can't exactly have a window in a room that doesn't exist."

"Guess not." Rafik said.

Samron opened his mouth to speak as someone knocked on the door. "Sir, it's Krista."

"Enter." Samron ordered.

Rafik's face paled. It was a Kylix soldier, he recognized from the body armor. The helmet wasn't what he was expecting, though. Thick horns curled up and around the skull, ending in points near the mouth like mountain goat horns. The eyes were narrow and the skull slim, ending in a snout. The jaw filled with serrated teeth. He couldn't tell if the skull was a sort of wolf, fox, or even a small dragon. It was a mishmash of so many different animals. The skull unnerved him. As the skull looked at him, he froze.

"Who is that?" The soldier said.

"Krista, you are here because of your talent." Samron said. "What you see in this room you will not speak about. To anyone. You understand."

Krista nodded. "I understand."

"Good. You can remove your helmet." Samron said. "Krista, this is Rafik. Rafik, this is Krista. She is one of the elite soldiers of the Kylix army called Kylika. She has the talent of healing."

She removed her helmet revealing a face opposite of the skull helmet she was wearing. Her skin smooth and soft, blue eyes with a golden ring in them, looking like a sunflower in a warm summer's day. They were mesmerizing. She looked to be the same age as Rafik, too.

"H-hi." Rafik said, holding out his hand. "I'm Rafik."

"Well, you're a smart one." Krista spat. "He already told me your name."

"Krista, be nice." Samron ordered.

"He looks fine to me." Krista said. "You know I can't heal stupid, right?"

"That's enough!" Samron yelled. "It's been a long journey and I've had enough of your attitude."

"Yeah well, I heal everybody. You need me." Krista sighed.

"You know, this army managed just fine without a healer like you. I'm sure we can handle fine again without one." Samron said. "Give me anymore of that attitude and I'll make sure you get punished."

Krista glared at the trainer for several seconds before finally bowing her head. "My apologies, *sir*. How can I heal him?"

"This boy can't walk. Healers at the Golden Gate did what they could. Said he's also bleeding internally, but I have my doubts."

"I see." She said, leaning over and putting both of her hands on his face. Rafik flinched. "Don't be such a baby."

"I wasn't." Rafik said. "Your hands are freezing."

"Is he one of us, or one of the others?" Krista asked.

"That doesn't concern you." Samron answered. "Now heal him."

"No, he isn't bleeding anywhere." Krista said after a moment. "His legs are broken." She moved her hands from his face to his legs. Her hands moved up and down, sending small sharp pains within Rafik. Like tiny birds nipping at his skin. He felt his legs snap and contort like a spark went off inside him and

191

he could feel his feet again. He could move his feet without any pain.

Rafik got to his feet, jumping in place. "I can walk!" He smiled.

"Hooray, it's a miracle." Krista said in the most monotone voice he had heard.

"You remind me of somebody." Rafik said. "I hope you change before you end up like her."

"And? Where is she?"

"In the dungeons below. Awaiting trial." Samron answered. "Thank you, Krista. If I hear word from anyone about this boy here, you might end up sharing a cell with her. You may leave."

Krista nodded, biting her lip as she placed the skull helmet back on. She lunged at Rafik and laughed as he flinched. "Pathetic." She laughed, closing the door behind her.

If only he had Blaridane! He would cut her down where she stood. His mind growled with longing for the sword. "I don't like her." Rafik said.

"Few do." Samron said. "She is born to my second in command, Mahlix. He was so panicked when Krista was born, he hid her away. The king came here with a girl one night who had the talent of fire. He proclaimed that those with talent are no longer to be killed on sight. They are to be taken and raised as the Kylika. Elite killers, basically. The next day Mahlix brought Krista in. King Vanarzir was so happy since she had the power to heal. He gave her, and Mahlix, special privileges. Although I am now lord of the Sekolah Fortress and the main trainer, it is Mahlix who gets most of the recognition."

"I'm sorry." Rafik said. "You deserve recognition if you did the work."

Samron smiled. "You sound like your father. No, I am happy with the arrangement. I don't get bothered. And it gave me the opportunity to travel Alutopek and find others with talent like you and Ziri."

"How did you know my father?" Rafik asked.

"Well," Samron said, heaving a long sigh. "I probably should have told you before you could walk again."

"Why?"

"Because you will get angry." Samron said. Before he could elaborate more there was another knock on the door. Samron answered the door. No words were said, he was just given a letter. Rafik couldn't make out by who, but he assumed it was another Kylix soldier. "But that is a story that will have to wait. I need to meet with Jinuk." He said after reading the letter. "Stay in here. I'll be back soon."

Rafik examined the map of Alutopek. He had found the capital, Detnu, on the western side of the Gateway Mountains. His finger traced along the Oasis Trail from the city of Lynn to Haitu, and then up the Eko River. At its end was the Tahlbiru Ocean. And just north of that, his home, Datz. Even the Sarason Fortress was marked on the map. To the east, beyond the Eko River, were jungles and swamps he had only heard of. The whole eastern portion of Alutopek was a myth to him. So many rumors and stories. He wasn't sure what was real and what wasn't.

But in the heart of the Lahmora Swamp was Opal Lake. He recognized that from his vision. There was even an island, named Queen's Island. "That's where the Four Kings were." He said to himself. He placed his hand on the map, but felt no vision coming to him. His mind felt emptier since losing Blaridane. Even more so when he hoped to get a vision, and nothing happened.

He turned his attention to Samrons's desk. There had to be something there he could find. Maybe get a vision of his father? As he opened the drawer of the desk the door opened. The trainer entered, not noticing Rafik. His demeanor had changed. His head drooping and the slight wrinkles appeared deeper.

He heaved a sigh, sitting down on the bed. "I'm sorry, Rafik."

"What are you sorry for?" Rafik asked, inching away from the desk

"Jinuk sent a letter to the king, telling him what had happened at the Golden Gate. King Vanarzir will be here tomorrow." Samron said.

"I'll be gone by then, so that shouldn't be a problem." Rafik said.

Samron shook his head. "No. Jinuk is thorough. Detail oriented. He mentioned you. The king is expecting you. He wants to meet you."

"I can still leave. Say I escaped. Or died on the way here."

"No. Then he would send Kylix after you or want proof of death. Do you think Salina would cover for you?"

"I could get away from them. Xeo did."

"Xeo was up north, not in the Biodlay Desert." Samron said. "I'm sorry, Rafik. But you're going to have to stay. At least until after he leaves. Then we can get you out of here."

"But you promised." Rafik snapped. "You promised you'd let me go. You told Gorik you didn't want me here. You lied."

"I didn't lie, Rafik. I don't want you here. You shouldn't be here. But until the king leaves you are going to have to stay here."

"You can't stop me. My sister is stuck in a fortress with the undead. I don't even know if she is still alive."

"And Gorik is saving her." Samron said, cutting Rafik off. "We will still get you away from here. After the king is gone."

"No." Rafik said, clenching his fists. "No. I'm not staying. I trusted you."

"I'm sorry, Rafik." Samron said.

Rafik pulled a knife from his belt. "You can't stop me."

"Think about what you're doing." Samron said, not showing any sign of alarm. "This place has more Kylix soldiers than you can imagine. And you plan on just walking out when you don't even know the way?"

"I'll think of something." Rafik said, stepping closer to the door. His eyes had narrowed, voice colder. "And you better not try and stop me."

194

"I won't." Samron said as Rafik grabbed the door and opened it. "But they will." Two soldiers charged in, tackling Rafik before he could use the knife.

"You promised!" Rafik screamed. "You liar! You bastard!"

"Take him to his own room. Lock it. Guard it. Don't let him out. I'm sorry, Rafik." Samron ordered.

The soldiers didn't say anything, but hoisted Rafik up from below his shoulders and dragged him away. Rafik kicked and screamed, threatening the trainer. Nobody answered him or paid him attention. The soldiers they passed stood guard, and the ones dragging him remained silent. They dragged him up another flight of stairs and down several winding corridors before opening a door and shoving him in. Before he could turn around the door was closed, and the lock clicked into place.

Chapter 16: A Wall of Glass

Haitu, Biodlay Desert, Alutopek

Rafik banged on the door and yelled. He cursed, screaming at the Kylix, the king, and at Samron. He demanded to be set free, but nobody answered. The door wouldn't budge, and kicking it wasn't getting him anywhere. Cursing under his breath, he turned to face his new prison. The room was barren, with only a rug on the floor. No decorations, no furniture. He paced back and forth, randomly hitting or kicking the door. He was locked in. If he wanted to escape, he would have to climb out through the window. His stomach growled, but no food was ever brought to him. *'Least the window doesn't have bars on it.'* He thought to himself.

As his temper subsided, he began to think. Maybe it would be easier to escape once the king left? Where could he go? Samron was right. He knew nothing of the desert, let alone the city of Haitu. He had no friends, and the Kylix was around every corner. Even if he could escape, how could he meet back up with Gorik and Anza? If she was still alive.

He glanced down at the rug, fatigue setting in. It would be easy just to sleep on the rug. Wait until morning and see what happens. He shook his head, cursing himself and the thought of that. How could he think of sleeping when he was about to be forced into enlistment with the Kylix? No, he had to leave. He had to find a way out.

His attention turned to the window. He watched the soldiers marching back and forth. Others stood guard at certain doors. The Sekolah Fortress was like a labyrinthian castle, it seemed. It didn't look like the ruins of the Sarason Fortress or the Golden Gate. This place had a feeling of someone's home here. Walls were decorated rather than left being plain. Statues and suits of armor stood guard in corridors. Smells of baking bread wafted on the faint wind. The thought comforted him, as he believed homes were easier to escape from than cold military fortresses.

The eternal glow of twilight began to fade into darkness as light left the Black Wall. He recognized the few gleaming stars piercing through the wall in the northern sky. Most light, though, came from the torches around the fortress. It was now or never if he wanted to try and escape.

He poked his head out of the window, looking down. It was a far drop if he fell. Rafik prayed that falling wouldn't be his fate. "Oh well." He smirked. "If I survive the fall Krista can heal me." He stuck one leg out of the window, reaching for a thin strip of decorative ledge below. His toes touched, and he kicked down his other leg. He could just reach it, and he began to inch along the outer wall. The night air was cold, but stagnant. Not even the smallest of breezes touched Rafik.

Inching along another thin ledge he came to an end. He tried turning his head without slipping and noticed another ledge across from him from another tower. Rafik took a deep breath, counted to three, and pushed off the ledge, turning and gripping for the opposing wall. He missed one ledge but grabbed hold of a windowsill on another. Rafik bit his tongue, wanting to scream as his shoulder tried yanking free from its socket.

He made his way to a lower bridge, climbing over it as a soldier looked the other way. He blitzed to the door not guarded and dashed inside. Rafik froze, waiting for the soldier he sneaked passed to raise an alarm. Nothing. Through the darkness, he skulked across the corridor, darting between the shadows of torchlight. He made his way down the stairs, freezing as other soldiers marched along. More than once he had to wait in the darkness as two soldiers had a conversation.

At one hiding spot he sneaked behind a tapestry as a soldier walked by. He felt the familiar sensation of a vision and tried fighting it off. "No. Not now." He whispered to himself, shaking his head, banging it against the sandstone wall to keep him set in the present. He couldn't afford one now. The vision clouded his own, as he saw a bright day and people laughing. He shook it off once more, jumping out from behind the tapestry.

"Hey!" The soldier shouted, jumping in the air, and spinning around.

Rafik scrambled to his feet and sprinted out the door. The soldier gave chase, ordering him to stop. Rafik turned the corner, ran down another passageway and exited onto another outer wall. He glanced down and saw the city streets below. The soldier was getting closer. Without thinking Rafik jumped over the wall. He ducked and rolled, only looking back to flash the soldier a smirk of victory. The Kylix guard yelled for him to stop, but Rafik didn't answer and disappeared into the city.

Back in Datz every building was unique. Whether it be from the pattern of boarded up windows to the piles of rubble or chunks missing from entire structures. He could recognize where he was just by a glance of a building. Even the front of the farmhouse he and Anza had found he would have recognized in passing again. But here in Haitu, everything was identical. The streets were nothing but sand. Buildings were smooth tan stones or dried mud. Windows, doors, and walkways helped change the monotony. But to Rafik, it all appeared the same. He found some streets wider or narrower than others, but to him, there was no rhyme or reason for any of it.

There weren't any street signs, and he continued wandering forward, trying to follow the northern star of Quellor. That would get him home. It wasn't long until the Sekolah Fortress looming behind him were replaced with more sandstone walls and rooftops. While down one street he looked up and couldn't see the stars to find his way as the buildings were so tall, and not one could be spotted. It was at this moment he heard something down a nearby alley.

As the sound happened a second time, he recognized it. A sniffle. Somebody was crying down there. "Hello?" He called out, unable to see anybody. The sound didn't happen a third time, but Rafik inched his way into the alley. Maybe whoever was down here could help him get away?

'I should have stolen a sword from them.' He thought, going deeper into the alleyway. The thought triggered his hands to

itch and his mind wander to Blaridane. He didn't want any sword. He needed *his* sword. Then he wouldn't be running from the Kylix. He took on Skage's armored minion, he was positive with Blaridane he could conquer the Sekolah Fortress. Lost in thought, he almost didn't notice the silhouette of a figure. Right in the center, where light couldn't touch on either end, Rafik could just make out a girl sitting on the ground. She looked up at Rafik and he froze. Her green eyes nearly glowed in the dark. The fire behind them sparked something inside him.

Rafik gave a half smile as he approached. It wasn't her almost flawless skin or dirty blond hair, but the intensity in her eyes that caught his attention. "What's your problem?" He asked in the most confident tone he could muster. He bit his lip, clenched his fists, and closed his eyes. *'Why did I say that?'* He shook his head, hoping he hadn't upset her. *'Of all the things I could say to a cute girl.'*

The girl laughed, shaking her head. "Of all the things you could have said."

"I was just thinking that." Rafik laughed. "Well, it's not every day I find a girl crying in the middle of an alleyway." He leaned against the sandstone wall and slumped down next to her. "I'm Rafik."

"Kryn." She said.

The two didn't speak, just stared up into the night sky. A star twinkled into existence, beaming through the Black Wall, before getting hidden behind a wisp of a cloud. "Seriously." Rafik said, turning to Kryn. "What's your problem?"

"You really want to know?"

"I wouldn't have asked if I didn't want to." Rafik said. "I could have just walked on by and forget I even saw you."

Kryn laughed. "You would have come back. You've been going in circles for the last half hour."

"Yeah, I'm not from around here." Rafik laughed.

"I couldn't tell."

"So, are you going to tell me?" Rafik asked.

Kryn looked down at her feet. "It's my-my father." She bit her lip, fighting back tears. "Today is the anniversary of his death."

"I'm sorry to hear that, Kryn." Rafik said, putting his arm around her. "What happened?" He noticed how warm she was, almost like a furnace broiling inside her.

"King Vanarzir." She said, clenching her fists. Her voice turned to anger and stone. "He killed my father. Seven years ago."

"The Kylix killed my mother a while ago. Starting to believe they killed my father, too."

"I never knew my mom." Kryn said. "My father was out; when he came back our home was burned down. All that was left in the remains was me. The placed burned to the ground."

"Well Kryn, I think you have me beat in most tragic childhoods." Rafik smiled. He took her hand and squeezed. "You know what the bright side of that is?"

Kryn snapped her head around, noticing a small wisp of sand blow into the air. "We need to leave."

"What?" Rafik laughed. "I doubt there are any monsters here with all the Kylix around."

"We need to leave. Now." Kryn said, hurrying to her feet. She yanked Rafik up, nearly making him fall face first into the sand.

"What's wrong with you?" Rafik snapped, getting to his feet, and dusting himself off.

"Them." Kryn answered, pointing to the end of the alley.

"Oh. Those monsters." A Kylix soldier stood at the entrance. What made Rafik's heart beat faster and his blood run cold was the one beside them. A member of the Kylika. In the dark their eyes glowed an unnatural ghostly white. Without saying a word, the two ran, bolting the other way. A sudden gust of wind shot through the alley way, sand picking up and swirling about. The sand formed into a wall, cutting off one way they could go. The two turned the corner and fled down the street.

"I think they're after me." Rafik said, looking behind him and seeing a Kylix soldier chasing him.

"No." Kryn shook her head. "I don't think so."

They turned down another road and into another alley. They climbed the stairs leading to homes on the higher levels. Kryn led the way, darting around one pathway, running down another. Rafik followed, feeling as if he was going in circles. He didn't say anything. This was Kryn's home, not his.

By now there were three Kylix soldiers. Rafik and Kryn were able to stay one step ahead of them. The elite soldier, though, cut off their path more than once, suddenly appearing from the shadows. Rafik shoved him to the ground once, jumping over him as he sprang out between the two of them. He was like a ghost, as at the next turn the Kylika soldier was there.

Kryn yanked on Rafik's arm, pulling him down an alleyway. She cursed, coming to a dead end. "I thought we were one street over."

Rafik hunched over, gasping for breath. Kryn still stood tall, putting her hand against the sandstone wall. "If you were hoping for a secret passage," Rafik said between breaths. "We're out of time."

The three Kylix soldiers were at the entrance. The two on either end had swords drawn. "Get on your knees. Hands behind your head." The center one ordered.

Rafik looked up at Kryn, surprised she wasn't exhausted. "Think we can take them?" He cursed again, wishing he had grabbed a sword. If only he had Blaridane!

Kryn nodded. "But not them." Two Kylika soldiers appeared behind the three others. Their eyes glowing, sending shivers down Rafik's spine.

"That explains it." Rafik said. "Two of them. Those special soldiers."

"Kylika." Kryn said. She nodded and the Kylika returned the nod.

The two Kylika soldiers pumped their hands into the air creating a wall of sand between them. The sand inched forward, pushing Rafik and Kryn closer to the back wall.

"Stay behind me." Kryn said, shoving Rafik to stand behind her.

"Oh no. I'm not a coward. If we're going down, we are going to side by side. I can defend myself." Rafik argued, holding up fists.

"Not like this." Kryn said, barring Rafik from stepping forward. She held out both her hands as the sandstorm drew nearer.

Rafik opened his mouth to speak when he noticed her hands. They began to glow. A moment later both hands erupted into bright flames. Rafik held up his arm, blocking the intense light.

Kryn yelled, and the fire burst forward in a large stream, cutting through the sand like boiling water on snow. She split her hands and the stream turned into a wall. The light grew brighter, the flames hotter.

"You…you have talent?" Rafik said, trying to keep his jaw from falling to the ground.

Kryn nodded, not saying a word.

"You could have used this earlier instead of running all over Haitu?"

"I guess." Kryn shrugged, the fire beginning to fade from her hands. As the flames dispersed Rafik gasped. Standing in front of them was a wall of glass. It towered into the sky. On the other side they could hear the Kylix scream, making out faint shapes of them in the torchlight. The Kylix soldiers banged on the wall as the two Kylika disappeared into the city.

"Way to go!" Rafik laughed. He reached out to touch the glass, but it was still hot on their end. It glowed slightly, cooling just ever so slowly.

"Now we can get out of here." Kryn said, beginning to climb the back-alley wall. "Are you coming?"

Rafik took hold of her hand and climbed the wall, escaping with Kryn. "That was amazing. I've never seen anything like that!"

"You've seen people with talent before?"

"Yeah." Rafik nodded. "There's Ziri. She came with me to Haitu. She can poison people. And when I got here, I met Krista. And-"

"Ugh." Kryn groaned, cutting him off. "I'm sorry you met her."

"You don't like her?"

"You met her." Kryn said. "Pretty sure even Mahlix would muzzle her if he could get away with it."

Rafik laughed, imagining one on her. "Is she like that all the time?"

"Pretty much. She can be nice and likeable on rare occasions, but I'd like her more if she were not here." Kryn laughed. "And that's putting it nicely. I won't say where I'd prefer her to be."

"So, you know them, I take it?" Rafik asked. "Those Kylika?"

"Yeah." Kryn said. "They're the Sand Brothers. They don't talk much, but they're good kids."

"Aren't you just a kid?" Rafik asked. "Never heard someone our own age say that."

Kryn laughed, holding up her hand. A small ball of fire began to swirl within her palm. "You really want to tease me?"

"Yeah." Rafik smiled.

Her eyes flashed across Rafik. "I like you."

"I like seeing that smile better than your tears." Rafik said. "Glad I could help."

"Yes, you totally helped me feel better as I was hunted for being out after curfew." Kryn said, a half-smile on her face.

"All part of the plan." Rafik laughed, winking at her. "How come you can't be out, but they can?"

"Because of their talent." Kryn explained. "They take up guard duty often. Usually when something important is about to happen."

"I just got to town." Rafik said. "Didn't think I was *that* big of a deal."

Kryn laughed. "When something *really* important is about to happen."

Rafik nodded, smiling. "You're one of them. Kylika, right?"

203

"Yes." Kryn nodded. "I was the first one."

"I can't believe you're one of them." Rafik said, clenching his fists. "Just when I thought I could like you."

"Just for now." Kryn said. "I'm getting out of here as soon as I can."

"Why can't you tonight?" Rafik suggested. "We can escape north. Find my sister and hide away somewhere."

"No." Kryn said, shaking her head. "I don't hide. And why not tonight? Because the king is coming tomorrow. He will want to see all of us with talent. If I'm going to escape, I'd like to avoid having him know about it until I'm far away from him."

"Is he *that* bad?"

"You have no idea." Kryn said. "Rumors say he killed the last known Dragon Rider for his dragon. And his soul is so dark he can appear out of any shadow."

"Dragon Riders are a myth." Rafik argued. "Everyone knows that. And nobody can appear out of shadows."

"Just like nobody can control fire." Kryn laughed, snapping her fingers and small embers sparked to life, slowly drifting to the ground.

The two had started walking now. Rafik constantly looking over his shoulder but enjoyed the conversation with Kryn. They swapped stories, he told her about his favorite constellation, Quellor, and she told him of stories back home. She came from Sysinal. A city between the Akitung Jungle and the Biodlay Desert. Even he knew it was nicknamed the City of Warriors.

Rafik glanced up and noticed the Sekolah Fortress looming in the distance. They had been walking back here and he hadn't even noticed. "I'm not afraid of him, King Vanarzir. You shouldn't be either. With your talent you could burn him where he stands."

"Yeah, and die in the process." Kryn said. "You need to think. Not everything is as simple as you seem to think it is."

Rafik shook his head. "Maybe down here. But up north there was a kid who challenged the king to a duel."

"Really?" Kryn asked, not hiding her skepticism. "I hear the king is coming tomorrow, so I guess I know who won in that fairy tale."

"No. The king cheated. Xeo got away and they're hunting for him now." Rafik insisted. "They tore apart my home looking for him."

"Maybe there is hope. Or maybe he's just stupid." Kryn said. "King Vanarzir is more powerful than even your Quellor hero."

"I'd like to have hope."

"I do have hope, Rafik. Just not in fantasies. I have a plan."

"Well, what's your plan?" Rafik asked.

"They are training me here. I am learning about them. Their tactics. As soon as they let me out, leaving Haitu, I'm escaping. And then I'm going to find a way to stop them."

"Sounds like a good plan, I guess."

"My father taught me that. If you learn about your opponent, you're one step closer to winning."

The two walked in silence as the Kylix home grew closer. The main gate was flanked by soldiers standing at attention. Guards announced their coming. "Kryn and a boy are approaching."

"You sneak out a lot?" Rafik laughed.

"Almost every night." Kryn said. "Usually I can avoid the guards, and nobody minds as long as I'm back by morning."

"Thanks for the adventure." Rafik said. "This one was better than the last few I've had. And I'm still in one piece!"

Kryn laughed. "I don't know where you're staying. But you're safe inside there. Just don't try and escape without me."

Rafik smiled. "I promise."

Before turning down a corridor Kryn gave Rafik a hug. Rafik never thought possible he could walk on air. He didn't notice as the Kylix took him back to his empty room. He ignored their insults and comments. All he could think about was his new friend who had just put a smile on his face.

Chapter 17: Introductions

Sekolah Fortress, Haitu, Biodlay Desert, Alutopek

"Look at that hair."

"Disgusting."

"And that skin?"

"Yeah, what are you, a ghost?"

"You give people like us a bad name, looking like that."

Rafik turned the corner entering a large room. The Kylix directed him here, after jolting him awake as he curled up on the rug. He was to report here every morning for breakfast and instruction. The massive room felt more like a cave with the sandstone walls curving into a dome at the top. At the very top a bell hung, he imagined could fit a whole person inside. Torches dangled from the ceiling and echoes of children chatting filled the room. But he heard those phrases first, noticing the group of people in a nearby corner. He recognized the girl in the center, Krista, with two other girls and a boy teasing somebody trapped in the corner. Between them he recognized who they were bullying. Ziri. "Hey!" He shouted, pushing his way through rougher than he should have.

"What do you think you're doing?" Kryn shouted, appearing at Rafik's side. He didn't even notice her approach.

Krista turned, a scowl on her face. "Oh, it's you. I forgot. I guess she will fit in since you're still here."

"Leave her alone." Rafik snapped, taking another step, and standing in front of Ziri. She grabbed his arm, and he could feel her quivering.

"People already think we're freaks." Krista spat. "We shouldn't have anyone looking the part."

"You don't even know if she has talent." Kryn said. "And she doesn't look like a freak."

"I do too." Krista said. "I know everything that goes on here thanks to my dad."

"I don't care who your dad is." Kryn said. "Leave her alone." A flame flickered between her fingers faster than a moment. Just quick enough for Krista to notice.

"I'm surprised someone without talent is even standing up for you. Let alone a boy." Krista smirked, turning to Rafik. "You like freaks like that or something?"

"I have talent." Rafik said, clenching his fists. He would give anything to have Kryn's power of fire right now. He could hear Blaridane's voice screaming at him to cut her down where she stood.

"You do?" Kryn and Krista asked in unison.

Rafik nodded. "Ziri is my friend. And from what I can tell, a lot better of a person than you. Leave her alone."

"Guess you don't really know everything after all." Kryn laughed.

Krista threw her fist forward and Kryn caught it, pushing it out of the way and shoving her to the ground; her two friends catching her. She looked up and glared at Rafik and Kryn. "You'll regret this."

"They're coming." The boy with Krista said, after checking the doorway.

Ziri stepped forward, but Kryn held up her hand. Krista and her friends scattered into the crowd of other children. "Are you alright?" Kryn asked, putting her arm around Ziri.

"I'm fine." Ziri replied in her usual soft tone that was scarcely above a whisper. "Thank you."

Rafik smiled. "It's what friends are for. This is Kryn. I met her last night."

Ziri smiled. "I'm Ziri."

"Nice to meet you. And who cares what they think. I think you look amazing. Love that red hair!"

Ziri's face lit up like the sun. "Thank you."

"That was Krista and her friends. And her puppy dog." Kryn said. "They think they're in charge."

Rafik glanced behind him, noticing Kylix soldiers entering the room. They looked over the children, scanning the room before nodding to each other and stood guard at the door. "Puppy dog?"

"Taygin." Kryn said. "He's infatuated with Krista. She only lets him hang around because she can control him."

"Who would like her?" Ziri asked.

"Apparently Taygin." Rafik said, smiling. "Why are the guards at the door?"

"They always come. Breakfast is almost over. They won't allow anyone to leave."

"But we could before?" Rafik asked.

Kryn shrugged. "I guess. You won't get far. The Kylix are everywhere. They're like ants in Haitu. They're everywhere. And this is their home, so they're crawling on top of each other."

"I didn't realize there was that many."

The bell clanged, ending all other noise in the hall. Rafik, Ziri, and a handful of others covered their ears. Kryn laughed, as the ringing stopped. "You get used to it."

"What was that for?" Rafik shouted, rubbing his ears.

"Breakfast is over." Kryn said. "Time to get to training."

"But I just woke up." Rafik said, grabbing at his gurgling stomach.

"Shouldn't have been sneaking around last night then." Kryn laughed. "And right on queue."

Rafik turned to where Kryn was looking. Samron came walking towards the three. The scowl of displeasure obvious even from here. "The three of you, come with me. Now." He ordered while walking past them. Kryn took the lead, following suit close to Samron. Rafik and Ziri weren't far behind. He led them down a corridor Rafik didn't recognize. Kylix stood guard at every door.

"This isn't your office." Rafik said as the trainer lead them into another room.

"It is for now. Sit." He said, closing the door behind them. The walls were barren, save for the Alutopek flag, hanging behind Samron's desk. The trainer sat across from the three of them, heaving a sigh and tenting his fingers. "Who wants to go first?"

Rafik looked at Kryn who glanced down at the floor, to Ziri who stared at Samron completely oblivious. "I think it might help if we knew what we were supposed to be confessing."

"Everything." Samron said.

Silence.

"Alright, let's start with you." Samron said, turning to Ziri. "Trying to escape last night. You poisoned 16 guards. 16! Were you thinking of just walking out of here, poisoning anyone you come across?"

"I guess so, yeah." Ziri said, shrugging.

"I thought you wanted to be here. You told me you did."

"I said I wanted to help you." Ziri whispered. "I didn't want to join an army. I've hurt enough innocent people. I'm done fighting."

Samron sighed. "You are here, as part of the Kylix army. You won't be fighting innocent people."

"I don't want to fight." Ziri said.

"Well, too late now. You are here. And if I find out you're trying to escape again, or poisoning anyone else, you will regret it. The king is allowing those with talent to live, but only if they are willing to serve him. Serving him doesn't mean poisoning his own men. Does it? Does it?" He repeated when Ziri didn't answer.

Ziri shook her head. She muttered something under her breath, but nobody heard it.

"And you two." Samron said. "Running around all of Haitu. I've let you come and go as you please within the city, Kryn, but I guess I was being too lenient."

"I didn't want to get caught. You should be proud of me. Shows I can defend myself and evade capture." Kryn argued.

"Even the king knew you could when he brought you here." Samron said. "No. I could turn the other way when you didn't cause problems. Making an entire wall of glass, running around with the Kylix giving chase throughout the city. Those are problems, Kryn. If anyone catches you outside of the fortress again without my permission, it will be imprisonment. Even if the fortress itself is crumbling, unless I give the go ahead, you will stay and fall in the rubble."

Rafik watched Samron. In all his short time knowing him he had never seen the trainer like this. A vein throbbed on his neck, and the lines and wrinkles in his face all seemed to exude anger. Just like Ziri, Kryn nodded. She didn't mutter anything, but Rafik noticed wisps of smoke steaming from her hands.

"And you." Samron said, pointing at Rafik. "I told you I'd help you leave *after* the king's visit. But that wasn't good enough, was it?"

"My sister is still with Skage." Rafik snapped, shooting to his feet, his chair falling backwards.

"Sit down!" Samron said, raising his voice but staying in his seat. "How many times do I need to tell you that Gorik is rescuing her? I am sure she is safe by now."

Rafik shook his head. "No. I would know." He said, holding his hand to his heart. "I felt alone when my father died, only to find out later he was dead. I watched my mother die and felt the hole in my heart grow bigger. When Anza went missing that hole grew larger, but the feeling of loss isn't there. She is still out there."

"And if you keep this up that hole will get even bigger." Samron yelled. "Now sit down, Rafik!"

The two glared at each other, neither one blinking. Finally, Rafik picked up his chair he had kicked over in his outburst and sat down. He didn't lose eye contact the entire time with the trainer.

"Kryn, Ziri, you two are here until your time with the Kylix has expired and you are free to leave. Until then, better enjoy staying here. These walls are your home. Or prison. It makes no difference to me how you see it. As for you, Rafik. After the king leaves you will remain here until you learn respect."

"Ziri could poison you right here." Rafik said.

"Excuse me?" Samron asked.

"Ziri could poison you." Rafik repeated. "She could poison you, and Kryn could burn whatever is left, leaving no trace of you, and we could escape."

"Don't be such a fool, Rafik. You're smarter than that. At least that's what I was led to believe."

"I'll make sure he doesn't do anything stupid." Kryn said, putting her hand on his shoulder.

"We both will." Ziri agreed, doing the same thing.

"Good." Samron said, nodding.

"I'm leaving after he is gone." Rafik said.

Samron shook his head. "Not if I can't trust you."

"Ya shire." Rafik cursed. His glare was almost palpable as he imagined Samron being pushed overboard into the Tahlbiru Ocean. He wanted to say more, he wanted to lunge forward and throttle the trainer, but he sat still, glaring at him.

"Now, King Vanarzir is here already. Kryn, he will want to see you and Krista, as usual. He may also want to meet the newest members of the Kylika, Ziri and Rafik. As well as two others. Most likely after tonight's feast to celebrate his arrival and the trial."

"When is the trial?" Rafik asked.

"Could be as early as tomorrow. Until then, Kryn, take them to training. You will all stay there until I have someone call for you."

Kryn nodded, getting to her feet. They left, not saying another word.

"That's a strange man." Rafik said, punching the wall as they left. He could feel Blaridane's wrath course through him. The feeling of vengeance and anger surged. If only he had the sword. *'Samron wouldn't stand a chance.'*

"What do you mean?" Kryn asked.

"We traveled the entire Eko River together. He seemed friendly. Now that we're here it's almost like we're just problems to him."

"I've never seen him being friendly." Kryn said.

"Guess it was the charm to get us here." Rafik sighed, shaking his head.

"So, are we going to stay here?" Ziri asked.

Kryn laughed. "I'm more determined than ever to leave here now."

Ziri smiled. "I don't want to stay here."

"We'll think of something." Rafik said. "We just need to get through the king's visit first."

"And your introduction." Kryn smiled. "I'm looking forward to seeing your talent, Rafik."

Kryn had led them to a field of sand deep within the desert. Just small walls tapered off into the distance showing they were still within the fortress. "Whoa." Ziri gasped, seeing two geysers of sand explode into the air, make a sudden turn, and down on a person who held up their arms in defense.

"We call them the Sand Brothers." Kryn said. "You already met them last night, Rafik."

Rafik nodded. "Still amazing to see. But I like your talent better." He flashed a smile at Kryn, and as their eyes met, he darted his eyes to the ground.

Kryn laughed, snapping her fingers emitting small flames. "I'm quite fond of my talent. They say I'm the first to have the talent over fire."

"Really?" Ziri asked, mesmerized by Kryn's dancing flames. They flickered between her fingers, weaving in and around them, before darting into her palm and disappearing.

"I guess." Kryn shrugged. "I've never been to the libraries of Detnu to check. I know there haven't been any fire wielders within the Kylix. I was able to figure out that much thanks to the Hall of Records here."

Before Rafik or Ziri could respond a Kylix, soldier hollered and waved them over. "Who is that?" Rafik asked.

"Our trainer." Kryn answered. "His name is Mahlix."

"I thought Samron was our trainer." Ziri said.

"He was. Until he went all over Alutopek. Then Mahlix took over."

Even to Rafik with his tempered still flared, Mahlix was an imposing figure. The Kylix soldiers that had attacked Datz and

212

who he had seen until now were all slim, like the skeletons they portrayed. Not only was Mahlix large, but he also towered over other soldiers who stood guard. Being in the middle of the field of sand he was like an obelisk looming over everything. "Nice of you to join us, Kryn. I see you brought two friends." He said in a deep, booming voice.

Rafik scrunched his eyebrows looking at the trainer. His voice was deep but was nowhere near as intimidating. It was a soothing, loving voice. Like a father's. "I'm Rafik of Datz." He said, holding out his hand.

"Well, mighty fine to meet you, Rafik." Mahlix extended his own hand, nearly crushing Rafik's. "Now this session is for those with talent. Did Kryn tell you?"

Rafik nodded. "Yes sir. Still trying to learn to control it."

Mahlix laughed. "You came to the right place. Most of us here are still trying to learn how to control their talent. That's why we are out in the old battlefield. Can't break anything here."

"Are we just going to fight each other?" Ziri asked.

"I'm sorry, you'll have to speak up." Mahlix said, smiling and leaning over, putting his hand to his ear. "Hard to hear you from way up there."

Ziri smiled, repeating the question.

"Of course! How else will you become the best?" Mahlix laughed. "You have talent, which by the grace of the king has allowed you to become one of the Kylika soldiers. The greatest of all soldiers in the Kylix army. But you still need to train."

"What's the Kylika?" Rafik asked. "I never heard of them until I met Samron."

"It all starts back with the great King Emerald. He called his army the Kylix, which means soldier. But his elite group, the ones most feared, he called Kylika. Meaning soldier of power. Kylika is a name to be feared more than Kylix. You will be trained to take on any challenge. There is even a legend where a single Kylika warrior was able to fight off two dragons! Though, that is just a legend. Before Kryn and Krista, the Kylika were used to hunt down any magic user or those with talent and end them."

"End?" Rafik asked.

"He means kill." Kryn said. "Because some people think we're freaks. They used to slaughter us like animals."

Mahlix sighed. "That isn't the proudest time of the Kylix's history, I agree. But times have changed. By the grace of King Vanarzir that was changed. Now, enough history. This isn't a classroom, it's a sparring field. Let's get to it then, shall we?" He clapped his hands, rubbing them together. "Time for introductions!"

"I'll start!" Krista shouted from behind Mahlix. Rafik and Kryn clenched their fists, noticing her pompous stare and smirk.

"Great idea!" Mahlix boomed.

"I'm Krista. Mahlix is my father. And I have the best talent ever. The talent to heal. I can heal anyone. If I want to." She added. With a gleaming knife, she sliced open her hand and held it up to show it slowly stitch together. Her two friends were the only ones showing audible amazement at the feat.

"Who is next?" Mahlix asked. "Now I know that is a hard one to follow, but you should all be proud of your talent."

"I'm Ziri." Ziri whispered, taking a step forward. "I have the talent of poison. I can cure or poison anyone. Even Krista."

"No, you can't. I can heal myself."

"Heal, but not cure." Ziri snapped back.

"Is that a challenge?" Krista snapped. "Dad, she can't do that."

Ziri nodded. "If I'm going to be forced to fight, I'm going to make sure you know I can."

"During training I'm Mahlix." Mahlix said. "Now Ziri, you can challenge her, but not during introductions."

Kryn introduced herself next, showing off her pyrotechnics. Everyone but Krista cheered and asked to see more. Next were the Sand Brothers who were mute. They were twins, sandy blonde hair, and rail thin. There was a child who could levitate and another who ran quickly. One child claimed to be able to breathe underwater while another showed off their talent as changing to look like Mahlix, before turning back into the little girl that she

214

was. Another had one of the Sand Brothers throw a spear at them, only to suddenly have a bubble appear around the boy and the spear bounce off. Rafik was so amazed by everyone's talents he didn't even remember their names.

After three more children showed off their talent Mahlix turned to Rafik. "And last, but not least is our newest member."

Rafik nodded. "As I said earlier, I'm Rafik of Datz. I have the talent of psychometry." When Mahlix and the others scrunched their brows, whispering to one another, and shrugging their shoulders, Rafik continued. "It means I can look into the past."

"Everyone has a memory." Krista laughed. "Are we just handing out the label of talent now?"

Rafik glared at Krista. "I swear you're worse than Salina." He muttered under his breath. "No, it means I can look into your past. I'll touch something of yours and I'll see its most powerful memory. I can find your biggest fear, or most embarrassing moment."

"Well that is great, Rafik." Mahlix said, beaming. "Unlike your friends Kryn and Ziri, there, I don't think you can rely on your talent in times of battle, though. Maybe help in preparing for battle. I hope you know how to fight."

Rafik nodded. "I do. Give me a sword."

The boy with speed tossed Rafik a sword and dashed toward him with his own. Rafik ducked, rolled, and sprang to his feet catching the sword, blocking an attack as the speedster flashed away. He spun around in time to block another blow from him. The boy sprinted around, jabbing, and knocking Rafik over. "Not well enough, rookie." He laughed.

Krista and others laughed.

A fire roared within him. That wouldn't have happened with Blaridane. He wanted to get up and charge at him again. He didn't need just any sword; he needed his sword.

"You did do better than most." Mahlix said, helping Rafik to his feet. "Most can't even block one strike from Haloro."

Rafik nodded at Haloro. He waited to hear the familiar voice of Blaridane scream for blood and vengeance. Not hearing it, he felt empty, longing for that violent voice. As odd as it sounded, it comforted him, knowing he wasn't alone in a fight. Haloro returned the nod, saying something under his breath and smirking at him.

"Now, Ziri, I believe you challenged Kryn?" Mahlix said. "Everyone pair up with someone you haven't sparred with recently. Weapons are on the far wall. The odd man out will spar against me." He whistled a high pitch tune, and everyone scrambled.

Haloro wasted no time in attacking Rafik. Rafik ducked, parried, and dodged, but couldn't land a blow on the boy with the talent of speed. More than once he successfully knocked Rafik to the ground. In one fight Haloro hit him in the chest so hard Rafik flew back, sending up a cloud of dust as he crashed to the ground. Yelling in frustration, Rafik glared at Haloro who was already beginning to move on him again. Rafik threw his sword, scrambled to his feet, and jumped, punching the air in front of him. Just as he punched, Haloro had jumped to dodge the sword, and ran straight into Rafik's fist.

Rafik laughed as Haloro whined on the floor.

"You'll regret that!" He said, spitting out blood.

"I only regret not hitting you harder." Rafik laughed.

It was obvious that Ziri had never held a weapon before. Krista swung her sword at Ziri, and on first contact Ziri dropped hers. Krista didn't hesitate, swinging her sword again at Ziri's neck, stopping at the last second. "You're dead." She said, grinning. "Good thing I'm merciful. Even to freaks."

Ziri grunted, moving her bright red hair out of her face, and grabbed her sword. Krista swung her sword again. Ziri didn't drop it this time but didn't move fast enough for the next attack. She ducked, reached out and touched Krista's outstretched hand. Krista gasped, going pale, dropping her sword. "You're dead." Ziri whispered, she smirked, getting to her feet, and folding her arms.

"What did you do?"

"I'm not that merciful." Ziri said with a wry smile.

216

Beads of sweat streamed down Krista's face, her eyes rolling back into her head. She collapsed and those near them gasped, beginning to crowd around her. Ziri hunched over Krista, putting her hand on her forehead. Her eyes fluttered and her trembling stopped as she began to wake. "What…what happened?"

"I think it was the heat." Ziri said in her quiet whisper of a voice.

Krista noticed her, scrambling to her feet, screaming. "You poisoned me!"

"How could I?" Ziri asked, feigning innocence. "You were winning. Couldn't even touch you."

Mahlix hurried over, shoving everyone else out of the way. "Are you alright?"

Krista stared from Ziri to her father. "I…yeah, I'm fine. Ziri was right, it's just the heat."

Mahlix nodded. "Well, it's about time to be getting ready for the feast anyway. Rafik, you did better than I thought you would. But you should never throw your sword."

"My father used to say never and always are two words you always want to remember never to use."

"That's witty." Mahlix laughed, smiling.

"Thank you."

"Being witty doesn't win sword fights." Mahlix said. "If your father was in a sword fight, he is probably dead by now. Was he the one who taught you to fight?"

Rafik clenched his fists, glaring at Mahlix. How dare somebody insult his father! He knew if he held Blaridane he wouldn't be able to stop the cursed sword. And he didn't want to stop the thrashing either. "Some. Most of it came from Blaridane." He could imagine the sword's voice screaming at him to attack Mahlix. *'Cut him down!'* It would surely scream.

Mahlix's smile vanished. "Don't you be joking like that, boy."

"I'm not." Rafik said.

"Blaridane hasn't been seen in thousands of years."

"I had it until I came here." Rafik said.

217

"Don't play games, boy. That is not something to joke about."

"Good thing I'm not."

"Training is over." Mahlix snarled. "Get washed up for the feast. And if you want to keep making up stories about things you shouldn't be, you're going to really start hating your time here." He stomped away, not looking back.

"Is training usually cut short?" Rafik asked, watching him march away, growling under his breath.

Kryn shook her head. "He's usually calm. Takes a lot to upset him."

"Who is Blaridane?" Ziri asked. "I've heard you mention that name in your sleep."

"Just the name of my sword." Rafik said, brushing it off and heading to hang up his sparring sword. He noticed there wasn't anyone guarding these ones.

"Not just a sword if Mahlix acted like that." Kryn said. "You're not telling us something."

The group shelved the swords, spears, and knives they were using and began walking back to the inner part of the fortress. "You did that, didn't you?" Kryn asked once it was just the three of them.

"Did what?" Rafik and Ziri asked in unison.

"Poisoned Krista. You did that." Kryn repeated.

Ziri smiled. "Just to prove I could. Maybe she'll leave me alone now."

"Or you'll get a knife in the back." Kryn said.

"Is every day like this?" Rafik asked.

"What, fighting? No. Just most. We are taught history and how amazing King Vanarzir is. Math. Some are even taught to read, alchemy, or other subjects. But us Kylika? We may be powerful, but we're just tools for the king."

"But it's mostly fighting?" Ziri asked.

Kryn nodded. "Especially the Kylika. We are supposed to be vicious killing machines. Why would we need to know anything else?"

Rafik didn't answer. They walked the rest of the way from the battlefield in silence. A Kylix soldier stood inside the entrance, among the guards on either side of it. As the three approached he stopped them. "You two," He said pointing to Rafik and Ziri. "Come with me."

"Where are we going?" Rafik asked.

"You'll find out. Orders are to come with me." The soldier said.

"It's not like you're in trouble. That was already this morning." Kryn said, smiling. "It's alright. I'll meet you both before the feast."

Chapter 18: Dressed for a Feast

Sekolah Fortress, Haitu, Biodlay Desert, Alutopek

The Sekolah Fortress was like a labyrinth. Towers reached into the sky, basements leading to even deeper dungeons, and rooms larger than most homes in Datz. All of it spread over an oasis that watered the city of Haitu. It was a wonder to everyone. It had to take generations, and maybe some magic, to build all of this. Rafik believed one could spend a lifetime exploring the fortress and not even discover every room.

Some corridors were decorated with statues and armor, some tapestries, while others were barren. There seemed to be no rhyme or reason behind which part was decorated with what, but Rafik felt as if there was a pattern. He knew Anza would pick up on it. He thought of her and her attention to detail. She was always better at catching that sort of thing. A tear welled up as a memory emerged.

He had tried so hard to hide from Anza. Even double backed and climbed over ruined walls. But as he was out of breath, hunched over and slowly walking to where he hoped to hide from her, she was already there. She told him how she figured out where he would go, and even noticed him running around. It frustrated him then, but it made him smile now. "I miss you, Anza." He whispered to himself.

Ziri squeezed his hand, smiling. "We'll find her." She whispered.

Through one corridor, and down another. Up a flight of stairs and then up a spiral staircase. They were being led to the top of a tower. The steps didn't appear as worn as in other places, but it was a common place, Rafik noticed. At one point where they climbed the spiral staircase one beam of light from the window didn't meet with another, and they were hidden in darkness. It reminded him of the Sarason Fortress. He could still see Skage calling back his minion. Something didn't seem right with the memory. Like a dream, slowly trickling out of thought.

The soldier stopped at a door, moving to the side. "I'll escort you once you leave." He said, leaning against the wall.

Rafik opened the door, bracing himself for the worst. This fortress was filled with silent Kylix soldiers. Men and women dressed like the dead. It was a wonder this place wasn't built with bones like the inside of the Sarason Fortress. He took a deep breath, trying to imagine the foulest of things that awaited him and Ziri on the other side of the door.

"Hello!" A bubbly woman said, coming towards the two. A pencil behind her ear, a measuring tape draped over her shoulders like a robe. The room was littered with loose fabrics of so many different colors Rafik couldn't see the floor.

"Er...hello." Rafik replied, exhaling.

"New recruits, I see. New recruits, indeed." She said, clapping her hands together and dancing towards them. "And aren't you two the cutest."

"Yes, ma'am." Ziri whispered.

"My name is Nora. I help with the Kylix armor. Now, let's see here." Nora said, reaching forward. She used her measuring tape, reaching and jotting down notes.

Rafik's face lit up bright red, turning his attention to the ceiling as she measured the inside of his legs. "Um, what are you doing?"

"Taking measurements of course!" Nora said, slapping the air with one hand and giving a slight giggle. "How else will we figure out what size for your armor?"

"You make the armor?" Rafik asked, looking around the room. There wasn't a piece of fabric in here that even looked like it could be part of the Kylix attire, let alone metal armor. He'd seen enough of the soldiers to know their armor was made of that, at least.

"Oh, no, my husband does." Nora explained. "He's one of the smiths to construct the armor you probably saw as they rescued you from your homes. But I make other things. And help with the desert armor."

"Desert armor?"

"Of course!" Nora laughed. "You can't go lugging around the desert in full metal armor. You'd be cooked before breakfast." She finished jotting down her notes and folded the piece of paper. Her puffy grey hair bounced with every step walking away from the two and prancing back and forth. She zoomed from one pile to the next, sifting through fabrics. Like a bee fluttering from flower to flower. "Look at this." She handed the paper to Rafik and Ziri. The two unfolded it, looked at it, and returned it to her.

"What about it?" Rafik asked.

"Did you know it is impossible to fold a piece of paper in half more than seven times?" Nora asked. "According to legend, there were warriors who had armor made of paper. They would fold the pieces, connecting them. Supposedly it could stop arrows and spears."

"I never knew that." Rafik said. "So, our armor is paper?"

"Oh, not at all." Nora laughed. "That's just a legend. Can you imagine going to war in paper? We aren't origami soldiers!"

Ziri and Rafik laughed, imagining paper soldiers being washed away in rain.

"It's this fabric. It's specially crafted that when layered it is as durable as most armor." Nora explained.

"Then how come we don't use this armor everywhere?" Ziri asked.

Nora sighed. "It still has its weaknesses. But in the desert, it's better than nothing."

The rest of the visit was spent in silence as Nora rummaged through stacks of fabrics, pinning pieces together and making jokes that neither child understood. She shouted back to them as she worked, asking questions, or making random comments and jokes. Ziri smiled and tried speaking up to her. Rafik wasn't as interested. Several hours passed. Nora now focused more on her work than conversating. Ziri and Rafik fought to stay awake when Nora announced her completion. Two suits of skeletal armor. They swayed back and forth but looked like the armor Rafik had fought against in Datz. How she had made such morbid uniforms among such bright fabric was beyond him.

They fit over Rafik's clothes, and he looked just like any other soldier. His stomach turned. He saw ribs and hip bones, and not his skin. As he gawked in morbid fascination now being suited in Kylix armor, he felt air breeze through his armor. Nora screamed, swinging a metal bar at Rafik. He held up his hands, "No stop!" The bar clanged against his arm, bouncing back. He hardly felt that. "Woah." Rafik gasped

Nora laughed. "Now I won't have your helmets done yet. From what I understand you are both Kylika, yes?"

Ziri nodded.

The seamstress nodded, pulling her tape measure from her pocket, and fluttered around the two. The tape went one way and around another. Across the eyes, and from head to neck. More than once Rafik thought her measuring was just her way of being a nuisance, jotting down numbers and measuring every little thing. Ziri giggled, watching her.

"Well, this will do for now. Got to look our best for the king!" Nora smiled. "Word has it that he has great news! I'll have your helmets done by tomorrow."

The two left the room looking more like Kylix soldiers than either of them wanted.

"That was..." Rafik said.

"Fun!" Ziri finished. "She was fun. I like her."

"I didn't expect to meet someone like her here." Rafik said. "She was definitely different."

"I'd rather have her, than these guys. Especially measuring me all over."

The soldier glanced back as Ziri said it. Though he wore his helmet, she knew he was glaring from her comment. "I guess you're right. I don't think she had to get so close to...certain things." Rafik said.

"Well," Ziri laughed. "If they're making armor for us, she needs to know how tall we are."

"Maybe. I don't want to do that again."

Rafik watched the guard in front of him. It had been a little over a day since he had arrived. Everywhere he went he was escorted by a soldier. It felt like he was a child again. "Do they lead you everywhere too?"

Ziri shrugged. "It sure seems like it."

"The fortress is so large we don't want you getting lost." The soldier said over his shoulder.

"I thought it's because you don't trust us." Rafik said.

"We don't."

"Is there a map for this place? That could help." Ziri asked.

"Maybe put some signs up." Rafik added.

This time the soldier didn't respond. He led them through the fortress, snaking this way and that. "I think we're going in circles." Ziri said, pointing out a chip taken from the wall. They moved through barren corridors only decorated by the sconces that held the candles. If the soldier heard, he didn't make notice of it. A few seconds later, they were out of the barren halls and entering open walkways.

The desert air wafted through the breezeway. "That isn't too bad." Rafik said, holding up his hands. Heat poured onto him, the warm hair slithered into the gaps of his armor, but he wasn't cooking.

"She wasn't wrong." Ziri said, pounding her chest. "And still strong, too."

Rafik knew they were getting close. There were more Kylix soldiers near here. It seemed that once Ziri pointed out they were going in circles it went much faster. They rounded the corner and saw the corridor lined with soldiers on either side. It was like the hall of the dead as they stood motionless. Instead of the usual candles on the walls, lanterns hung from the ceiling. The soldier guiding them turned, taking his place in line.

"There you are." Kryn said, running to them. "Was beginning to worry about you two."

"Had to get new armor." Rafik said, tapping his gloved hand on his chest.

"Ah." Kryn said. "Welcome to the team, I guess. You get used to it" She was wearing her own armor, her helmet held under her arm.

"I thought the feast wouldn't be until tonight." Rafik said. "No complaints from me, though."

The three walked into the center of the Sekolah Fortress. The breakfast hall they were in could easily fit in here. It was another domed room with several hundred lanterns hanging from the ceiling. In parts of the dome were stained glass windows, casting twinkling colors to the floor below. The walls were lined with soldiers and painted on the walls were depictions of ancient battles and the Kylix military being formed. The familiar flag of Alutopek hung in the center and seemed large enough it could cover at least a dozen beds at once. There were six long tables stretching the entire span of the room, and benches for them. At the far end was a platform raised above the rest. A table going perpendicular from the others spanned the stage, with a large throne in the center.

Embedded with gold and jewels, and the arms ended with skulls. The throne lay empty, as the Kylika were the first to enter the hall. They were directed to sit at the main center table, closest to the throne. The others removed their helmets, placing them beneath the table. Minutes later other soldiers began filling the seats and other tables. High officials and teachers filled the remaining seats of the tables closest to the platform.

Rafik noticed Samron, not far from them. Across from the trainer was a very shaken up Jinuk. His hands twitched, eyes darting to the door with every newcomer. More than once Samron had to tell Jinuk to relax. A soldier came up, grabbing Jinuk's shoulder causing him to scream.

Talk stopped as two Kylix soldiers entered. They wore the usual black armor, but the bones were gold instead of white. Everyone got to their feet, Rafik and Ziri one of the last to stand. Behind the soldiers was King Vanarzir himself. As he passed the onlookers bowed their heads in reverence. His regal swagger of a walk exuded an air of authority. His armor was black with golden bones. A purple cape draped off his right shoulder. Horns didn't curl, but jutted outwards like a dragon's, and small spikes across the brow. Between the horns was a golden crown, miniature skulls emblazoned across the band.

The king removed his helmet as he climbed the steps of the platform, and he stared out across the hall. His piercing gaze sent shivers down Rafik's spine. There was no sign of his age, or any sign of weakness. Vanarzir's eyes appeared to glow an icy blue, darting around, analyzing everything. Once Vanarzir appeared satisfied, he nodded and sat down. The rest in the hall followed suit.

King Vanarzir cleared his throat, everyone turned to face him. Rafik tried noting any weakness he could see of the 200 plus year old man but saw nothing. His smile was devilish, like a thief finding long forgotten treasure. He stood, motioning for everyone to stay seated. "Welcome everyone." He said in a deep, strong voice. "It has been an adventure, and we aren't even finished."

Soldiers nodded, but nobody said a word.

He paused before continuing, surveying the room. "Before we commence this feast, I have an announcement to make." He motioned for two more gold boned Kylix soldiers who escorted a young woman into the room. Her dark hair glimmered in the light and eyes full of sorrow. She didn't look up as she made her way to the king. Her slender frame reminded Rafik of a scarecrow. "This is Valkayto. Kay for short. She will be my new wife, and your new queen. Her word is law as much as mine."

The hall erupted with applause, whooping, and whistling. Kay flashed a smile before returning to her saddened demeanor. She glanced up at the crowd, murmuring a soft "Thank you."

"She looks defeated." Ziri whispered to Rafik.

"I would be too if I had to marry him." Kryn replied. The two girls stifled a giggle, watching Queen Kay.

They were right, Rafik noted. She did walk and appear to have given up. But he saw something in her eyes. A fire. Was her demeanor a ruse, or the fire slowly burning out?

"The wedding will be in Detnu upon our return. I know your hearts will be with us." King Vanarzir said. "Now, there is more to announce, but as Queen Kay decided it, she will announce it."

King Vanarzir sat down in his throne, directing his attention to Kay. Queen Kay looked across the room, focusing her gaze on a soldier in the far corner. Rafik turned to where she was staring. It was a young man he had never seen before. His look of hurt and surprise showed that he knew the queen, though. "Thank you, King Vanarzir." She started. "I delayed the further enlisting for two years. It will be then that the Kylix will cross the Eko River in the east, and the Bomoku Mountains in the south, and finish collecting the children for the king's army."

Applause echoed through the hall, Queen Kay smiling at the reaction. The applause seemed to give her strength as she stood taller. Her golden eyes burned brighter. As the applause ended, she continued. "As of tomorrow, children 15, 16, or 17 will be sent home. Their enlistment has been revoked."

"Ya shire." Kryn spat. "I'm 14. Just one year off!"

"Same here." Rafik and Ziri said at the same time.

Other mini conversations erupted as cheers and applause followed. Queen Kay turned to King Vanarzir, her eyes narrowing. "And anyone ages five and six. They will be returned to their families as well. Their enlistment suspended for the next two years."

The king's eyes widened. Rafik noticed it wasn't what was supposed to be said. Queen Kay gave the king a look, as if challenging him. "Of course," King Vanarzir said, getting to his feet. "Any who wish to stay will be rewarded immensely, as well as their families, though. Think carefully before deciding. Your future, and your family's future, could depend on it."

"That means if they decide to go home something is going to happen." Kryn whispered.

"How do you know?" Rafik asked.

"He spent all this time gathering the children for his army, and now his wife is letting some of them go. No, this is a trap. Anyone who decides to go home is going to die. Mark my words."

"There is one more thing." King Vanarzir said, cutting out the noise. "Our wonderful trainer, Samron, has collected all children with talent west of the Eko River, and north of the Bomoku Mountains. This is a great achievement, as this is the largest group of them together since before the Purge during my father, King Arzir's time."

Kryn cheered at this, and the others with talent roared with approval more than the others in the hall. Rafik smiled, hearing he was part of such a select group that now wasn't being hunted.

"But their first test to prove themselves is soon approaching." King Vanarzir continued as the applause died down. "During his adventures, Samron discovered an enemy just beginning to show himself. A supposed necromancer in the Sarason Fortress of Datz. My newest commander, Jinuk, has confirmed this, being the only survivor at the battle of the Golden Gate."

Murmurs instead of applause made their way through the hall. It was obvious that the attack on the Golden Gate, let alone Skage's presence, was not known. "What's a necromancer?" Krista asked. She wasn't the only one asking that, Rafik noticed. He remembered seeing the ugly man enter that room in the Sarason Fortress. Cornering Anza in there and calling his lifeless armored guard of his. The corpses emerging to life within the Golden Gate. The chaos. The unstoppable force of unnatural power.

"The Kylika will take back the Golden Gate." King Vanarzir said over the murmuring. "The Kylika will stop this necromancer, and we can continue to build this great kingdom under the marvelous Black Wall. It will be their true test, that these are the most powerful warriors, and serve their king. But tonight, we celebrate my marriage and the gathering of this soon-to-be-great army."

He clapped his hands and servers poured into the hall. Some carried pitchers filled with different kinds of drink. Most carried platters of fruits, vegetables, breads, and meats. There were bowls of mashed potatoes and others with different kinds of gravy. Sausages and steak, chicken, and pork. King Vanarzir sat back down, taking a sip of freshly poured wine, and the feast began. The servers placed their trays and pitchers of wine, juice, and water throughout the tables.

Rafik's stomach growled, realizing he hadn't eaten all day. He could smell the succulent pork wafting towards him mingling with the freshly cooked breads.

Rafik reached for an orange when Kryn slapped his hand. She pointed up at King Vanarzir as everyone else stared up towards him. Nobody ate until the king had a bite of his own food. Nobody drank until he had a sip of his own. The moment he did the hall roared with conversations and laughter. "The king always takes the first bite." Kryn said. "If you're caught eating before him, you'll get punished."

"That's strange." Rafik said. "I would have everyone take a bite before me in case something was poisoned."

Kryn shrugged. "Just how it is."

Rafik nodded, grabbing the orange he was after and a couple of scones. He took a bite of the bread, his eyes rolling up into his head. "I love scones." He said to Ziri and Kryn. "My mother used to make them for Anza and I."

"What did you call them?" Krista asked from several seats away.

"Ya shire." Rafik cursed, noticing Krista. He held up his plate, showing her the light and airy fried bread. "Scones. Want to try one?"

Krista scoffed. "Those aren't scones. That's fried bread."

"In Datz we call them scones." Rafik said.

"You people are weird." Krista said, shaking her head. "No wonder most of you Datians died if you don't even know the proper names of things."

Kryn shot her hand to Rafik, holding his shoulder. "Leave her alone. She isn't worth getting in trouble over."

Rafik glared at Krista before turning back to the food. "You're right."

The feast continued without incident. Kryn showed Rafik her favorite fruit, a zutro melon, with a green, leathery husk and vibrant purple meat. Ziri even laughed and ate several plates, her voice never rising above the whisper Rafik had to concentrate on hearing. As the trays emptied the servers filled them up, refilling everyone's glasses as well.

"Are you excited?" Kryn asked.

"Excited for what?" Rafik asked.

"Dessert!" Ziri said in her form of a shout. The trays were being replaced with the sweet smell of fresh pastries, cakes, and puddings. Chocolate cakes, vanilla puddings, and snacks Rafik and Ziri had never seen before now littered the tables. The drinks were all replaced with sweeter beverages, too.

"You should have asked me before I ate everything in sight. I'm stuffed. Now I'm just ready to sleep." Rafik laughed.

"There's always room for dessert." Ziri said, smiling, digging into a chocolate pudding.

Kryn smiled. "I was meaning that we're leaving here. Going to stop that necromancer. We can save your sister!"

"And then leave the Kylix." Rafik smiled. "They won't be able to stop us."

"They'll try." Ziri sighed.

Kryn nodded in agreement. "Trying doesn't mean they'll succeed."

Rafik shook his head. "True. If we can get Anza and make it back to Datz there are tunnels we can hide in. Until they leave."

"Well, it's the beginning of a plan for after the Kylix." Kryn said. "That's more than I've had in a long time."

The feasting slowed, as fewer hands grabbed for seconds. Most talked amongst each other, ignoring what was left of the food. King Vanarzir stood up, waiting for all eyes to be on him. It didn't take long. His thin line of a mouth curled into a smile, looking over the Kylix army. "Some soldiers, by Samron's choosing, will join the Kylika in taking back the Golden Gate.

Anyone chosen, and survives, will become Kylika as well. This will be a dangerous battle for anyone. Those staying behind will continue as usual. But for now, everyone, have a wonderful night." He held out his hand and Queen Kay took it. They walked off, escorted by the four gold-boned soldiers.

"I thought Samron said he would want to talk to you and meet us?" Rafik asked.

Kryn shrugged. "He usually does. Probably will tomorrow or whenever everyone who gets to go home does."

Chapter 19: The Invisible Murder

Sekolah Fortress, Haitu, Biodlay Desert, Alutopek

The feast was more than Rafik could have dreamed of. The only time he had seen that much food in one place it was all fish. There was no way he could eat another bite. His stomach bulged from his meal, and a sense of fatigue washed over him. He believed he could fall asleep at the table if he didn't get up soon. As everyone stood up to leave, he started to wonder where he would sleep. The thought hadn't occurred to him all day. There was no special escort to his room from last night, so he followed Kryn out the hall.

"You can't come with us." Kryn said, stopping Rafik with a hand on his chest. "Girls are in one part, and boys in another."

"What?" Rafik asked, looking to Ziri who nodded in confirmation.

"You need to go with them." Kryn said. "Don't worry, you'll be fine."

Rafik nodded. "Well, goodnight." He turned and saw the boys heading down one corridor, and the girls up another.

"I can help you." A squeaky voice said from behind.

"Oh." Rafik said, noticing who it was. "You're Krista's friend."

"I'm everybody's friend." Taygin smiled. He held out a thin arm. "My name is Taygin."

"I know." Rafik said. He shook Taygin's outstretched hand, and noticed the strength hiding behind it. Looking at him, it wasn't much of a stretch to see the Kylix armor on him and believe he really was just skin and bones. "You were rude to Ziri."

"I think we got off on the wrong foot." Taygin laughed. "I had no idea you had talent. I thought you were just a nobody like me."

"Excuse you." Rafik said, pausing. "You believe you're a nobody?"

Taygin nodded. "Yeah, I'm just a Kylix soldier. Just another grunt for now. You're Kylika. Already powerful and amazing."

"A title doesn't make you amazing." Rafik said. "Your actions do."

"Which I'm sure you've accomplished more already." Taygin said. "You came from the north. I just came from Haitu. I was willingly given to the Kylix. Not even my family tried fighting to keep me."

Rafik sighed. The last thing he wanted to do was begin to feel sorry for someone who was picking on his friend. "You're just fine, I'm sure."

"One day I'll be great, Rafik." Taygin continued as they walked with the mob of boys heading to their rooms. "I'm going to be the greatest Kylix soldier ever."

Another boy overheard this and laughed, shoving Taygin into Rafik. "That'll be the day, wimp."

Rafik looked up to see Haloro laughing with other boys. "Hey!" He shouted.

Haloro turned. "Are you sticking up for this pipsqueak?"

"I guess I am." Rafik said through gritted teeth. "Leave him alone."

"He doesn't need you for protection, he has his girlfriend." Haloro said, and the boys laughed.

Taygin lit up bright red. "She's not my girlfriend!"

"You're right." Haloro said. "My mistake. She has standards." Again, the boys laughed.

"Did you tell your friends how I won in a sparring match with you?" Rafik asked. "Your friend here was so smart he ran straight into my fist. Should we show them?"

The laughing stopped, and Haloro's face soured. "You got lucky. Guess the weaklings got to stick together. What kind of talent is yours? Mine is actually useful."

"Yeah, running really fast. You can be the Kylix errand boy." Rafik said. "Leave Taygin alone." The crowd of boys laughed at Rafik's joke, and Haloro glared.

"Just wait until next time." Haloro said. He slunk forward, shoving his way through the crowd.

"Thank you." Taygin said. "Most don't really stand up for me."

"Don't mention it." Rafik said. "I hope you do become Kylika, just so you can beat Haloro in a sparring match."

"You really think I could?" Taygin asked, beaming ear to ear.

"He got to the Kylika because of his talent, not his skill. If you got in, you'd be one of the better ones. You could take most of them, I'm sure. Just keep practicing."

Taygin nodded, his smile never fading, as he led Rafik to their beds. The boys had a large open room, a fireplace on either side and littered with random pieces of furniture. Some boys hung around in groups, while others went to the beds leading off on either side of the room from the middle.

There was a young man in the far corner, sitting in the corner and fighting back tears. Rafik recognized him as the soldier Queen Kay was staring at. "Do you know him?" Taygin asked. "He's from the Nyler Peninsula, too."

"No." Rafik shook his head. "I'm from Datz. He's not. He seemed upset though when he saw the queen."

"Shouldn't be any surprise. He used to talk about a girl named Valkayto who helped save their home of Kristol. They celebrated their engagement just before the king arrived." Taygin explained. "Talk about moving up in the world."

Around the room there were small celebrations and even larger pity parties. Rafik overheard several older boys giddy for going back home. Others chimed in how jealous they were. The little ones smiled and cried, excited to see their parents again. One small boy eagerly said how he couldn't wait to get home since he missed working on the harvest. His little brother had died from a sickness the year before, and it was just his older parents working the farm. It was evident the boys who had been here longest had the same suspicion as Kryn. They warned the younger ones, telling them it was a trap. Most brushed it off, insisting they were going home.

Rafik wasn't sure if it was a trap, but hearing the boys' stories, he didn't want to take the risk. The stories they shared of King Vanarzir's revenge was ruthless. One boy told of the town butcher in the city of Mekina who refused to give up their son. The king ordered for the family to be butchered like the animals they slaughtered. Another told how while in the city of Astrid he burned it down until a family hiding their children gave them up. As the night grew later, the stories became more gruesome and horrifying. King Vanarzir was the monster everyone feared. Capable of anything and enjoyed tormenting the innocent.

Some young boys decided to say, but the boy who had missed the harvest insisted. He was going home. Those insisting on leaving repeated that the new queen said they could. The older boys had packed, and eagerly paced the room. Since it was King Vanarzir and Queen Valkayto's orders, they believed they were safe, unlike the younger children. They had to be. The tension between worry, jealousy, and excitement grew tighter. From no sleep, and the high emotions, some began to yell and fight. Rafik shook his head, deciding he wasn't going to be part of this, and went off to sleep.

He chose a hall to go down, unsure if there was a certain one he was assigned. If there was, nobody said anything. There were rows of beds stacked on top of each other. Three beds per stack, he counted, stretching into darkness. He heard distant snoring, and the occasional whisper. The farther he crept into the room, the fainter the shouting was from the common room. The only light came from stars that shined through the Black Wall and came down the sky light windows.

Rafik sighed, crawling into a bed against the far wall. It was a long day, and he was looking forward to going home. Even if he had to wait to go with the Kylix, he wasn't going to be stuck here forever. He thought of Anza, imagining her cowering in a dark corner, hiding from Skage. His hands itched, thinking of her fear.

235

"Skage will pay." He said to himself, clenching his fists. He could hear the voice of Blaridane calling for him. The moment he got the sword again, he would kill Skage, and chain the sword to his wrist. Nobody would ever take away his sword again.

First there was a scream. A blood curdling scream that makes the blood run cold. Rafik jolted up, hitting his head on the upper bed. He noticed others had done the same and were hurrying to the door. A few younger kids cried, another shouted how they think they're going to be sick. Rafik pushed his way through and gasped.

The little boy, so eager to go home, lay dead on the floor. Blood still flowed from his slashed throat where stocks of wheat and barley were stuffed. A scythe clutched in his hands, and the look of utter fear were in his dull, lifeless eyes.

Rafik could see the boy's body cracking, shuddering, as it came to life and screamed, attacking everyone. It thrashed about, using the scythe, and taking others, only for his victims to rise again. The imagery jolted out of his mind as Taygin grabbed him.

"Are you alright?" He asked.

"Yeah." Rafik said. "Just had a bad thought. Who did this?"

"I'll give you one guess." Haloro said. "I hope you're not that dumb to know who."

"Joyless Jinahka." Taygin muttered.

"Who?" Rafik and a couple others asked.

"Joyless Jinahka." Haloro said. "The ghost of Sekolah Fortress. If he even senses you feeling joy, he will murder you."

"I doubt he's real." Rafik said, trying to think of any reason why a murderous ghost couldn't exist. Before Skage, he didn't think a vengeful spirit would be possible. But now? It wasn't so outlandish at all.

"What's going on?" Mahlix said, pushing aside some boys as he came forward. He gasped and ordered everyone to look away. "Did anyone see anything?"

"Maybe Rafik could actually use his talent?" Haloro suggested. "If he's not faking."

Rafik glared at Haloro, the pompous demeanor about him made Rafik want to punch him. And he wasn't even holding Blaridane! "I can try. Do you want me to, Mahlix?"

"Yes. That would be great. What do you need?" Mahlix answered.

"Nothing." Rafik said, kneeling beside the boy. "I didn't even know your name. I'm so sorry." He whispered, looking up and down at the body. He needed an object. Something that was present during the murder. He closed his eyes and yanked the scythe from the boy's icy grip. He urged for something to happen, but not even a drop of a memory was present on the tool.

"Well?" Mahlix asked.

"I knew he was faking." Haloro laughed. "He's even more pathetic than Taygin! No wonder they're friends."

"This wasn't the murder weapon." Rafik said, ignoring Haloro. "If it were, I know I could see it. This was just placed here after."

"That's just an excuse." Haloro said. "Mahlix, he's lying. He doesn't actually have talent."

"Shut up." Mahlix growled.

Rafik put the scythe down and reached for the wheat seemingly sprouting out of the boy's throat. That was enough. Rafik gasped, as the events unfolded to him.

It was the common room, but nobody was in here. Rafik looked around, and all the boys had gone to bed by now. But there was a voice, coming from somewhere. It called out for the boy, Rafik assumed, hearing the boy's name for the first time. "Nayflin" The voice was just above a whisper, and as it repeated the name it dragged out the name, calling the boy to him.

Rafik looked under chairs and tables, near the fireplaces, and up the chimneys but there was nobody in the room. He saw the scythe laying on a table, far from where the boy was found. The voice called out for Nayflin again. And again. And again. From the darkness he could see the small boy emerge from the darkened hall.

Nayflin yawned and was yanked by an unseen force. Rafik gasped at the sudden movement. The small boy flailed, trying to break free from the invisible grasp. Out of thin air the wheat and barley emerged and shoved into the boy's throat. Rafik gasped, looking away from the gruesome scene. He didn't want to watch the boy be held by something unseen and murdered. He couldn't. "I'm sorry." Rafik cried, shutting his eyes tight. He covered his ears, trying to drown out the struggle Nayflin made.

It was a minute later he opened them after he heard Nayflin collapse to the ground. Something stood over the boy, he could feel its presence, as the plants were pulled through the hole in his throat. The scythe floated through the air, and into the boy's hands. The room fell silent, and the memory faded.

"What did you see?" Mahlix asked as Rafik's eyes fluttered to life.

"I-I don't know." Rafik said. "Does anybody here have the talent to be invisible?"

"Invisible?" Mahlix asked.

Rafik nodded. "Unless you believe in ghosts, whoever killed him was invisible." He relayed what he saw to Mahlix and the group.

"Joyless Jinahka!" several boys muttered, nodding in agreement with one another.

Haloro scoffed. "You're still just making it up. You wouldn't have said that if you hadn't heard the story."

Mahlix scratched his chin, looking at the boy. He opened Nayflin's mouth and saw bits of the plants still in his mouth. "I guess that proves you did see it." He said.

"Do we have anyone who can be invisible?" Rafik asked again.

"What? No." Mahlix asked. "Not that I know of. If we did you would have met them yesterday."

The boys began mumbling. There was somebody with the talent of invisibility somewhere. And they were monsters. "How do we know it wasn't Rafik?" Haloro asked.

"One person cannot have two talents." Mahlix said. "Everyone prepare for your day. Finish packing if you're leaving or go get breakfast. Including you, Rafik."

The young boys excited to leave last night now agreed in unison they were staying. Even some of the older boys agreed to stay. If this was King Vanarzir, like Kryn suspected, his goal was achieved. Nobody was going home.

The echoing chatter of children was replaced with somber silence. The great room where they all ate breakfast just the day before, now stood quiet. Few who spoke did so in low, hushed whispers. There was only one thing everyone was talking about. What happened?

Meeting with Kryn and Ziri, Rafik learned the girls had a similar experience as well. Just like with the boys, it scared most into staying. There were no witnesses and no idea who it could have been. Kryn spoke first, blaming King Vanarzir. "It has to be him."

"Not that ghost everyone else was saying?" Rafik asked.

Kryn scoffed. "That's just a story to scare first years. In my time here this has never happened. Seems suspicious it did right after the king allowed some people to leave."

"How can a 200-year-old man move so silently?" Ziri asked.

"Do you know if the king can turn invisible?" Rafik asked.

Kryn scrunched her eyes, tilting her head. "Why?"

"I had a vision, seeing Nayflin's murder." Rafik explained. "But nobody was there. It was like he was murdered by ghosts."

"Hhmm," Kryn hummed, poking at her porridge. "He stole everybody's talent and created the Black Wall. I'm positive somebody with that power could be invisible if they wanted."

"But you don't know for sure." Ziri said.

Kryn shook her head. "Guess not. But I know it was him. It must be. Who else would kill children?"

Rafik shrugged. "I don't know. But somebody can be invisible, and we have no idea who. How have they stayed hidden?"

"Because they're invisible." Ziri added, smiling.

Kryn laughed. "You've cracked the case, Ziri!"

Their laughter echoed through the silent hall, causing others to stare. Taygin glanced over at the three, and as their eyes met with Rafik's he darted back to his breakfast, finding immense interest in his grey porridge. Krista slapped his arm, getting his attention. She had clearly made a snide remark she expected him to laugh to.

Rafik heaved a sigh and shook his head. "We should go say goodbye."

Kryn nodded, getting up and leading the way. "They should be going to the docks. I can't believe some of the kids are still leaving."

"Most aren't." Rafik said. "If it was the king,"

"It was." Kryn interrupted.

"If it was the king," Rafik repeated, "His plan worked."

It was a somber air through the fortress. Even the soldiers standing guard at doors seemed more slumped forward than standing straight. There was no laughter from the children, or conversations from the soldiers. News spread throughout the fortress quicker than lightning could strike the ground. Two children murdered within the Sekolah Fortress. Home of the Kylix army. Supposedly the safest place in all Alutopek. Yet two murders occurred, and no suspect. Even with Rafik's talent it didn't lend to any answers.

Rafik hated to admit it, but Kryn was right. He hadn't been here long, didn't know either victim. But from what he gathered, neither had any enemies and both were young. Innocent even. There was no motive behind it, other than to strike fear into others, keeping them from leaving. The only man who wanted them here was the king.

"The most frustrating part," Rafik started, grumbling. "Is that even if it is him, there's nothing we can do."

"Welcome to my life." Kryn sighed. "He's been like that ever since I met him."

"Where are we?" Ziri asked, stopping. "This doesn't look like the docks."

Between being lost in thought and talking about who the invisible suspect could be, they had gotten lost. They were nowhere near the city of Haitu, or the docks, but now overlooking a massive sand dune that stretched into the sky as high as it was round. It was a mountain of sand even Kryn hadn't seen before. She turned around, looking one way then another, then down the hall they came from. "We took a wrong turn, but I don't recognize this place. That dune has to be new?"

"Who or what could make dunes like this?" Rafik asked. "That's bigger than some of the foothills near Datz."

Kryn shrugged. "Probably doesn't matter. On the other side is just going to be more sand."

Just then there was a roar from the other side of the sand mountain. It caused some sand to slide down, the walls to shake, and even the air rattle. Rafik and Ziri froze where they stood, their hair standing on end and unable to move. If it were possible, Ziri's face got even paler from the monstrous noise. Kryn, on the other hand, perked up. Like a child hearing a mother's call from a far distance. She froze, listening, waiting to hear it again. And it did, roaring even louder and angrier than the first.

"Come one, let's go check it out." Kryn said. She took five steps before noticing Rafik and Ziri were still frozen in place. "Hello?"

Neither said a word, just shuddered, staring at the mountain like it was the Hound of Soboribor, or the boogie man himself.

"Hey!" Kryn said, waving her hand in front of them. She snapped her fingers, emitting flame between them, snapping them out of their fear induced stupor.

"What?' Where are we?" Rafik asked.

"What happened?" Ziri asked.

241

"I don't know what happened to you two," Kryn said. "But there's something on the other side of that hill."

"It looks more like a mountain." Rafik said. "I thought we were going to the docks?"

"Well, we're here now." Kryn said, taking a deep breath. "Come on." She hurried up the sand mountain, not waiting for her friends.

"Ya shire." Rafik cursed and started after her. "You can stay there if you want."

"I'm not being left behind." Ziri insisted, muttering under her breath.

Kryn reached the top of the mountain first, gasping, and ducking back down. She stared down at Rafik and Ziri with wild and wonder in her eyes, a grin growing on her face. "I knew it. I knew it, I knew it, I knew it."

"What are you talking about?" Rafik asked through panting breath. Climbing a sand mountain in a hurry was a lot harder than scaling other hills.

"Look." Kryn said, half giggling. "I can't believe it." She turned and peeked again.

Rafik made it to the top and gasped. Down below, in a crater deeper than the side they had just climbed, was the king. Flanked on either side by the Sand Brothers standing guard. The king was yelling at Queen Kay, though they couldn't hear what. Beside her was a large container, sewn together with bits of leather and furs, a chain bolted to the top, leading to a great black dragon.

The dragon's eyes burned a fiery red. Long fangs jutted out of its mouth like an unexplored cave. Spikes grew out above its eyes, meeting in the center and running from its head to tail, gradually getting smaller. At the base of the neck was a gap with an empty saddle in place. Unlike the stories Rafik had heard, this dragon didn't have front legs, just two massive wings with claws at the end. Whoever cared for it did a poor job, as it appeared thin, nearly starving.

It roared once more, petrifying Ziri and Rafik until Kryn shook them awake again. Kryn pointed at footprints made in the

242

sand near the dragon. They had suddenly just appeared, as if the figure jumped off the dragon. The footsteps walked from the king and back to the dragon. "I think the murderer is with them."

"If it's the king, yeah." Rafik said. "He's right there."

"No." Kryn said, shaking her head. "Look at the footprints."

"Those were there before." Ziri said. "I think."

"How did you not notice them suddenly appearing?" Kryn asked.

Rafik pointed at the black dragon, hand trembling. "I'm a little distracted by that to notice something like a footprint, Kryn. I thought dragons were extinct."

"I thought they were fake." Ziri said.

Kryn shook her head, smiling. "No, they're real alright."

Queen Kay entered the container and closed the door. The dragon roared again, expanding its wings, and lunging into the air. It flew higher, and higher, only stopping as the container started lifting off the ground. Another flap and it dangled in the air. The Sand Brothers began moving, shifting their hands back and forth, creating a sandstorm. The mountain was collapsing and the dragon flying away, deep into the Biodlay Desert.

The king and Kylix soldiers started back, the Sand Brothers sinking the mountain of sand.

"Hurry." Rafik shouted. "If they catch us, we're dead!"

The two others nodded and sprinted for the fortress, each of them still grappling with what they had just seen. The sand fell beneath them and a wave of it toppled over them. The three fumbled, almost swimming through the sand before making it back to the surface just at the fortress entrance. Rafik turned and saw the Sand Brothers notice them. The king hadn't yet. They scrambled inside as a small flurry wisped behind them, covering up their escape. Rafik nodded and waved to the brothers as they disappeared back into the fortress.

"I knew they were real." Kryn said. "And not just the sand dragons people talk about here."

"Sand dragons?" Rafik asked.

Kryn nodded. "According to legend the dragons died out. All of them. And the ones that survived became smaller and more monstrous. Like giant lizards. The sand dragons are supposedly what's left of them."

"Aren't giant lizards dragons?" Ziri asked.

Kryn shrugged. "I guess it's the same difference as a long knife compared to a short sword."

"How come it didn't freeze you?" Ziri asked.

"What didn't?"

"When it roared," Ziri said, "Why didn't you freeze up like we did?"

Kryn shrugged. "Probably because I'm not afraid of them."

"You will when that thing comes after you." Rafik said. "It would scare anybody." He felt the familiar itch in his hands, and the void in his head. Now that there was a dragon, he needed Blaridane. Between the two of them, he was confident he wouldn't freeze from its roar. *'One day soon.'* He thought to himself, clenching his fists. No sword was the same after using that. It didn't matter to him that it was evil. The sword was his, and he would be prepared for its attempt to control next time.

Chapter 20: The Hall of Records
Sekolah Fortress, Haitu, Biodlay Desert, Alutopek

"His name is Skage." Rafik said as they ate lunch the following day. In honor of the two lives lost, classes and training had been cancelled the rest of the day. To nobody's surprise, most had agreed to stay in the City of Sand. Only six children left. Everyone anticipated to hear some gruesome fate that awaited each of them. Even two days after the murders it was all anyone could talk about.

Rumors swirled back and forth as to who did it and why. Others claimed they heard what happened to the six that left. Each version got more grotesque than the last. Even the older children who had warned of something like this happening were still somber.

The three sat on a wall looking over an open plaza area of the fortress. All Kylika soldiers were exempt from classes to prepare heading north. Though it was encouraged to continue sparring and training, nobody did. They watched other Kylix soldiers march around the square as the elders barked orders at them.

Kryn continued gushing over the dragon. She would burn impressions in the sand of the dragon, and only talk about the monster until they had heard when they'd be leaving north. "And he can raise the dead?"

Ziri nodded. "It was horrible. The way they moved. And nothing could stop them."

"I can stop them." Kryn smiled, a ball of flame appearing in her palm.

Rafik shook his head. "No. Some were even on fire and they still attacked. Fire didn't do anything to them. Some even didn't have a head and they still attacked us."

"Well I'm useless." Kryn sighed.

"Not as much as I am." Ziri said.

"Stop. Both of you." Rafik said. "On some ships it takes several men to work the rigging. Dozens sometimes. On their own they are useless. But together, they can help steer the vessel over oceans. We just need to work together."

"Do you know anything else about him?" Kryn asked.

Rafik shrugged. "Skage was defeated once before. I don't know by who."

"Probably the Kylix." Kryn said.

"It was a long time ago." Rafik said, shaking his head. "I don't think it was them."

"The Kylix was founded by the Four Kings. I thought everybody knew that. Unless you think he's older than that?"

Rafik shook his head, remembering the stone in the bag that had King Roobino's memory. If Izamar had it, and Skage was his apprentice, it couldn't have been before that. "No, I think you're right. Probably right after the Four Kings."

"If only we could go to the Grand Library in Detnu." Ziri suggested. "I hear everything is in there."

"We don't have to." Kryn said. "Everything the Kylix has been involved with have a record here in the Hall of Records. We could look in there. See how they defeated him."

"And you're just telling us this?" Rafik asked, jumping from the wall. He held out his hand to help Ziri and Kryn down, his hand lingering a little longer with Kryn.

"I'm sorry, I've been distracted thinking about a dragon I saw fly away."

"Maybe the Hall of Records will have something on the dragon, too?" Ziri suggested.

"Couldn't hurt to check." Kryn said.

"Let's focus on Skage first. Then dragons." Rafik sighed.

"I don't think you understand how glorious that dragon is. He's probably the last of his kind. Shame King Vanarzir has control over him."

"Lead the way." Rafik said, giving an exaggerative bow and hand gesture for Kryn.

246

"When we leave here and go north," Kryn said, smiling. "I expect a grand tour since I've had to guide you two everywhere across this fortress. I swear you two are like babies sometimes."

Rafik laughed. "I can show you around. I think you'd love it up north. Even when it's cold I bet you'd stay warm."

Kryn nodded, beginning to lead them through the maze of corridors. "I've only been cold once, and that was just after my father died. Don't want to experience that again."

The group fell silent after this, looking around. Rafik was trying to memorize where they were going, but everything seemed the same. The Hall of Records was on the far end of the fortress Rafik hadn't been to yet. A narrow walkway slowly grew outward to a large expanse, lined with potted cacti. Ahead of them was a separate building surrounded by columns. Rafik was surprised to see even Kylix soldiers here were standing guard. It had a different feel from the rest of the fortress. For starters, it was its own building. The architecture was different too. More advanced, in a way, with arches, columns, and ornate designs carved into the stone.

"Have you been here before?" Rafik asked as they approached.

"Once." Kryn said. She took the steps two at a time. "They don't like me here." She waved a fiery hand about and the three laughed.

Upon entering they found a librarian behind a desk reading a book. "Not often children come in here. Let alone three." She smiled, getting to her feet. She was thin, almost like a skeleton. More than once she pushed back her sleeves to reveal a thin, bony hand. She didn't wear armor but long robes that devoured her, making her scrawny arms and fingers look even smaller and longer. "How can I help you?"

"Do you have any records of the Kylix fighting a necromancer?" Rafik asked. "His name might be Skage."

"Skage?" The librarian asked. "A report was filed about him just yesterday."

"No, ma'am." Rafik shook his head. "Anything older? This necromancer was defeated a long time ago."

She furled her brow, crossing her arms. "Now how would you know about that, but not anything else?"

"Just stories." Rafik said. "From where I'm from."

The librarian nodded, still eyeing the three. "I haven't heard of anything. But as you can see," She said gesturing to the large expanse of rows of books. "There is a lot to read here. I doubt anyone has read it all. You are welcome to look. No horseplay, though."

"Thank you." Rafik said, taking a step closer to the shelves.

"You!" The librarian shouted, grabbing at Kryn. "I recognize you."

"I didn't do anything." Kryn said, holding up her hands.

"Nothing yet." The librarian snapped. "Having you in here is like having a torch next to whale fat. Just a matter of time before it catches fire. If there is even a spark within this library, I'll see that you will be punished thoroughly. It's bad enough your kind is allowed now. But your power of fire. That is even more unnatural and dangerous."

"We're also 'her kind.'" Rafik said, stepping between Kryn and the librarian.

The librarian took a step back in exaggerated disgust. "All three of you?"

Ziri, Rafik, and Kryn nodded. "All three of us." Kryn smiled.

"Go. Before I change my mind." The librarian said. "But I'll be watching you three."

"Then have fun watching us read." Rafik said, turning to go deeper into the library.

"I wish I had the talent to sprout a third eye or something to give them something to stare at as we just sit here." Kryn said.

Ziri laughed.

There were some shelves that had dates, while others were dedicated to entire authors. The books varied in size, most of them looking ancient and brittle. "Oh, look at this one." Kryn said, grabbing a thin leather book by the spine. It was smaller than most others. "*The Adventure of Prince Vanarzir.* I didn't know King Vanarzir served in the Kylix."

"That was 200 years ago. I doubt anyone living knows what he did before being king." Rafik said. "Now come on, we need to find something about Skage."

"Interesting." Kryn said, ignoring Rafik and flipping through the pages. "Says here he wasn't part of the Kylix. Prince Vanarzir, his friend named Swayfir, and a band of Kylix soldiers were tasked with finding the 'World beneath the world.'"

"Did they find it?" Ziri asked.

Rafik paused from his search and looked at Kryn.

Kryn shrugged. "It doesn't say. Says they were gone for 12 years. Took a whole squad of Kylix with them. Only Prince Vanarzir came back. On the day his father, King Arzir, died. The next day the Black Wall was created."

"12 years?" Ziri gasped. "I wonder what happened."

"Look at this one." Kryn said, shelving the former book and grabbing the next. "*Diary of Nekvaz.*" On the cover was the outline of a dragon, with the constellation of giants shining above it."

"We don't have time to look at every book." Rafik said. "Obviously, this is the stuff from 200 years ago. We need to go to the beginning of the Kylix."

Kryn nodded. "You're right. Let's go. But I'm saving this one for later." She glanced back to make sure nobody was behind her before stuffing it into her armor.

"What are you doing?" Ziri asked.

"It has a dragon on it. I'd like to know more." Kryn responded, brushing off her armor, hoping there wasn't a bulge where the book was now hiding.

"It's just the cover. It might not even have dragons in it." Rafik said.

"Guess I'll learn about Nekvaz, then." Kryn laughed. She noticed another figure in a robe wandering the shelves. The figure kept glancing towards them before disappearing behind shelves of other books. "Let's keep going." She said, telling the others of the robed figure as they left for the depths of the library.

The three made their way to the back of the library, still several years away from the Four Kings. A staircase led into darkness. They glanced back at the librarian; a clear pathway stretched from where she was to here. She was distracted, reading a book again. "After you." Rafik smiled.

Kryn held out her hand, a small flame sprang to life. "I know where I'm staying next summer." She said, making her way to the bottom. It was cold enough their breath could be seen in the flickering fire from Kryn's hand. There were more shelves, with even more books. If the ones upstairs looked ancient, these looked archaic. Straps of leather were all that remained of some covers. Ziri touched one book which no longer had a cover and it fell to pieces. Rafik grabbed another and the book disappeared in a cloud of dust.

"If we find it, will we even be able to read it?" Kryn asked.

"One can only hope." Rafik sighed. There was no rhyme or reason why books were crammed together down here. Time periods mixed with others, and the handwriting was hard to read on most. He grabbed another book and was thankful it didn't fall apart.

"Is this it?" Ziri asked, holding up a book. It was another leather-bound book, emblazoned with the title 'The Four Jewels of Alutopek.' The cover had a sapphire, ruby, white crystal, and emerald glued to it. Each shined like miniature suns over a map of Alutopek. The Four Jewels was a common nickname of the Four Kings. Rafik nodded, amazed the detail still vibrant on such an ancient tome.

She placed the book on a nearby empty shelf and turned to the first page. It began with the familiar story everyone knew. Prince Emerald banished from the Rantyak Islands. Told to only come back if he conquered Alutopek.

"We already know this. Flip to the end." Kryn said.

Ziri carefully lifted each page with the tips of her finger, holding her breath with every turn. Finally, they made it to the last page. "That's a lie!" Rafik snapped.

It told of how King Emerald was the last of the Four Kings, the remaining died of old age. And with him being the last one, he united all Alutopek under one banner. After doing this he gave the throne to King Bones.

"How do you know?" Kryn asked. "Everyone knows this is what happened."

Rafik shook his head. "But that's not true. I saw it. The Four Kings were all killed on Queen's Island."

"Your talent?" Kryn asked, skeptical.

Rafik nodded. "Before losing Anza I was trying to learn to master my talent. One of my visions was the last day of the Four Kings. They were betrayed by their own army. And it sounded like they weren't good people, either."

"Interesting." Kryn said, scrunching her brows together and looking at Rafik. "So, you're saying the Legend of the Four Kings is wrong?"

"At least the ending." Rafik said. "He might not even be a prince of the Rantyak Islands."

"Well, in either case, I'm guessing this Skage isn't in here?"

"I don't know." Ziri shrugged. "I was just trying to get to the last page like you suggested."

"Go through and see if you see Skage's name." Rafik said. "Kryn and I will keep looking."

Kryn grabbed a nearby candle, dusting it off. "Here." She said, lighting the candle and handing it Ziri.

Beside where Ziri had found the book of the Four Kings Kryn pulled out the next one. It was *The Accomplishments of King Bones. First King of Alutopek.* "How is he the first king if Emerald was?" Kryn asked.

"Because the legend we all know is wrong." Rafik said again. "What kind of name is King Bones?"

251

Kryn shrugged, opening the book. The first page turned to dust in her hands. "Says here he made the Kylix army the official army of Alutopek, deeming it a part of his heritage. Wasn't that Emerald who did that?"

"Anything about Skage." Rafik asked, irritated he hadn't found the book. He wanted to find the answer and leave as soon as possible. Anza was still itching in his mind. He couldn't relax while she wasn't safe.

Kryn shook her head. She skimmed the page, trying carefully to turn to the next one. "Yes! Right here...Oh."

"What does it say?"

"Almost nothing." Kryn sighed. *"The Grey Fox led the Silver Council to investigate and put an end to rumors of a necromancer at the Sarason Fortress. King Bones offered aid. They politely declined, stating magic must defeat magic."*

"And with magic gone, I guess there isn't a way of stopping him?" Ziri said.

"No. There's us." Kryn said. "Maybe that's why Vanarzir is sending us. He knows more than he's letting on?"

Rafik didn't move. A tear welling up. His heart ached harder now. He was so sure he could find the answer how to stop Skage. Save his sister. Now that hope was gone. A cold, hollow chill swept through him. He couldn't hear what Kryn or Ziri were saying, if anything. An image of him standing over the grave of his sister filled his mind.

Ziri reached for Rafik. He whipped his arm away from the sudden touch, being pulled back into the present. "Rafik." She said in her whisper of a voice. "Rafik, are you alright?"

"I'm fine." Rafik lied. "What's the Silver Council?"

Kryn and Ziri shrugged. "My guess is some sort of magic army." Kryn suggested.

"Think we'll hear about them in any of these?" Rafik asked.

"No." Ziri said. "These are about the Kylix, not a different army."

"Guess we'll have to wing it." Kryn said.

252

"How can we beat him? We don't have a plan." Rafik said. "We can't just wing it. If he kills any of us, they become his puppet."

"Think about it." Kryn said, smiling. "If we have a plan, he could mess with it. Screw it up. If we don't have a plan, he can't twist it."

"That's a funny way of thinking about it." Ziri smiled. "I like it."

Rafik laughed, staring from one friend to the other. "Let's go, before the librarian comes looking for us."

They left everything as it was, leaving the basement in silence. The three didn't say a word as they walked past the several shelves. They noticed the librarian, snoring behind a book. The robed figure, now with his hood down, combed through the shelves they had been searching earlier. None of them had seen the old man before. His ring of grey hair around his head was thin, and wrinkles set in showing the long life he'd lived. Thick eyebrows nearly covered his eyes. As the man noticed the three, he dashed out the library, not saying a word, and stuffing a book into his bag.

"He runs pretty fast for an old man." Kryn laughed.

"He just stole a book." Rafik said.

"That's what happens when you're sleeping on the job." Kryn said, laughing as they left. "Guess it happens often." She patted her armor, eager to start reading this person's history.

The librarian snorted back to life, fumbling with the book she was attempting to read. "Get out of my library if you're going to be so loud!" She ordered.

"See, nothing gets passed her." Rafik said, and the three giggled, leaving the library.

Rafik looked up at the ceiling, lying on his cot. Ziri and Kryn were playing cards while he thought about the Sarason Fortress. There were 11 Kylika. The fastest way to the fortress would be going through the Golden Gate, and that was riddled with Skage's minions. And they still didn't know how to defeat them. Maybe once they reach Skage, though, Kryn could burn him, or

Ziri poison him? If what the book said was true, magic must defeat magic, their arsenal was limited.

One thing itched in his mind. The names King Bones and Grey Fox. They just seemed wrong. Almost like nicknames than their legitimate ones. Something in him burned at wondering who these people were. Like he knew who they were but forgotten their faces. For the countless time Rafik spoke up, asking, "Have either of you heard of Grey Fox?"

For the countless time both Kryn and Ziri replied in unison, "No."

It wasn't much of a surprise. Neither of them had heard of the Silver Council. Why would they know one of their members? He wished he had his bag still. He could ask Izamar. He should know since he was alive during that time. As his thoughts turned to Gorik, he wondered if his uncle survived the Golden Gate and the Sarason Fortress or became one of Skage's countless minions. The three jumped with a start as the door opened. A Kylix soldier marched forward demanding Rafik. When he asked why the Kylix turned and began walking away, saying over his shoulder "For the trial."

Rafik looked at Ziri who smiled, jumping from her seat. He hurried after the soldier, Ziri and Kryn not far behind. The soldier led them back to the Great Hall where the feast was the previous night. It had changed now. Almost like a stage was built on the far end of the hall, the king's throne in the center. The long tables were gone, replaced with individual seats, a cage off to the side. Soldiers surrounded the cage and lined the front of the stage. Across from the cage was Samron, sitting at a small table looking over scrolls.

The soldier led Rafik to stand in front of the king as Kryn motioned for her and Ziri to take nearby seats. "Are you Rafik of Datz?" The king asked. Rafik turned to look at the prisoner. "Don't look at her, look at me."

Rafik whipped his head around to face the king. The icy blue eyes glared at him, making Rafik fidget, adjusting his weight from one foot to the other, rubbing his arm. "Yes sir. I am."

254

"And do you know why you are here?"

"A trial?" Rafik asked.

King Vanarzir nodded. "That woman," He said pointing to the cage. "She is accused of trying to kill you. Tell me what happened."

Rafik nodded. "I was in the Sarason Fortress." Rafik began. "Trying to find my sister when I was attacked. A large hulking suit of armor blocked the room she was in. At the same time, some men I had never seen before arrived, and tried killing me, Salina, and the suit of armor. They failed, the armored giant killing almost everyone. I saw Skage appear, calling back his henchman just as it had crushed me. Leaving me to die. It left and Salina appeared from out of the shadows. She stabbed me with a knife. I felt horrible. Worse than being crushed, but like a fire spreading through me."

"I see." The king said, scratching his chin. "And you survived how?"

"My friend Ziri." Rafik said. "She has the talent of poison. She removed whatever Salina stabbed me with. I could hardly move until I arrived here when Krista healed me."

King Vanarzir nodded. "And where was Ziri during the fight?"

"I can answer that one." Samron said, getting to his feet. "My lord, she was with me. We had arrived on the Sarason Fortress just a little earlier, coming to rescue Rafik."

The king looked from Rafik to Salina. "Did anyone see her stab you?"

"No." Rafik said. "It was just her and I at that point."

"She claims you fell on a spear." The king said. "Samron arrested her, but with no witnesses it is just her word against yours. Who should I believe?"

"Me. I'm telling the truth." Rafik said.

"But she claims to be telling the truth as well."

"I wouldn't fall on a spear."

"And most women wouldn't hurt a child, let alone kill them." King Vanarzir said. "I feel we are at a fork in the road,

Rafik. If I side with you, I could be condemning an innocent woman to death. If I side with her, you wouldn't be much better. I don't like liars."

"I'm not a liar!" Rafik yelled.

"You will speak when I tell you to speak." The king growled. "I've had enough of bratty children trying to better their superiors to last a lifetime."

Rafik looked the king in the eyes, clenching his fists. In the far reaches of his mind he could hear Blaridane's voice screaming to kill. If only he had the sword, he could end him now.

"My Lord." Samron said, raising his hand and getting to his feet again. "If I may?"

The king nodded. "If you must."

"Thank you, King Vanarzir." Samron said. "Now this boy is remarkable. He comes from a family of sailors, but managed to fend off the suit of armor, and the men. Both Salina and Rafik have said were there. He survived the attack on the Golden Gate while crippled, no less. And on top of all that he has talent. In the time I have known him he has been nothing but honest. I walked into that room with Salina standing over him. She tried killing him."

"She could have been trying to administer aid." King Vanarzir reasoned.

Rafik glanced at Salina, a smirk on her face. "She tried to kill me."

"This boy." King Vanarzir said, gesturing in the air and staring at Samron. "He's the one you mentioned. Can look into the past?"

"He is." Samron said.

"Having such a power, it would be hard to trust someone who is a liar."

"I'm not a liar!" Rafik screamed, taking a step forward. The Kylix soldiers brandished their weapons, pointing them at Rafik.

"One more outburst, and this trial will be over as you'll be dead." Vanarzir said. "Just because you have talent, doesn't mean you get to talk to your king like that."

256

Rafik glared at the king, their eyes never parting from staring into the others. Finally, he nodded. "I'm sorry, My Lord."

"That's better. Now, has he been initiated into the Kylika yet?"

"No, My Lord. Not yet." Samron said.

"And you can do what they say? See into the past? You have been able to already?"

Rafik nodded. "I saw a vision of the Four Kings."

"Interesting." King Vanarzir said in a steady tone, stroking his chin. He sat on his throne silent for several minutes as Rafik and Salina stood there. "That can be quite useful. Shame you won't ever use it again."

"I'm sorry?" Rafik said, his eyes widening.

"There is no evidence. Just one's word against the other. The penalty for Salina's supposed crime is death. I don't like liars wasting my time, either. Both of you will be executed. This will be a lesson to anyone who tries to spin a story to me. You better have evidence to back it up. Tomorrow morning you will be executed."

"What?" Rafik, Salina, Samron, Kryn and Ziri all said at once."

"I didn't do anything!" Rafik yelled.

"No, but there is no way to tell she did either." King Vanarzir said. "Too bad I just passed sentence, or I would have the guards drop you where you stand for this outburst, boy."

Rafik's mind screamed for him to run. To bolt out of the room and escape. But his body stayed still like a mountain. He didn't do anything. Salina tried killing him and now the king was finishing the job. Samron tried saying something but the king cut him off. He couldn't hear what was being said, lost in his own thoughts. He didn't notice as two Kylix soldiers dragged him away, or when Kryn swore she'd save him before leaving the room.

The next moment he was fully aware he had no idea where he was. It was dark, cold. A torch was hanging far from him. Between him and the torch were several cages. He couldn't tell if he was in one. Rafik lifted his hand and felt the heavy chains on his wrist. Looking down he saw the outline of the chains extending back to the wall. The armor Nora had made him was gone, replaced with a thin layer of clothes. The holey garments he wore in Datz seemed warmer and thicker than these ones.

"You're awake." A familiar voice said, still dripping with venom.

Rafik turned, noticing Salina in the cage beside him. "Where am I?"

"In the bowels of the Sekolah Fortress." Salina said calmly. "Waiting for execution."

"But I didn't do anything!" Rafik screamed, the flood of memories coming back to him.

"Call it the sins of the father." Salina mused. "If I'm going down, I'm happy to bring you down with me."

"What are you talking about? You have always been a bitter old hag." Rafik said.

Salina laughed. "Oh, Rafik. You clueless boy."

"If I'm that clueless, fill me in. Might as well know why you've been wanting me dead."

"Your father." Salina said. "Your very, very handsome father. Believe it or not, he loved me for a time."

Rafik snorted. "You?"

Salina ignored him, continuing her story. "And then your mother moved to Datz. Nobody moved to Datz. She had to be a witch. Drane was smitten and forgot about me. Gorik egged him on since he and I never liked each other. When my father passed, I was distraught. Your father was the one who said I was unfit to rule. King Vanarzir made the council. I should have been in charge. Not me with two others. I was happy to hear he was lost at sea. A pathetic life lost in the abyss of the ocean."

"My father wasn't pathetic." Rafik said.

"Oh, he was. Always talking about doing what's right, all the while hiding a drinking problem." Salina laughed. "I'm sure it was you and your sister that led him to drinking in the first place. Most children do that, you know. Lead their parents to drink and anger. And then there was you. Questioning *my* authority. Leading the others to safety in the pond and the tunnels. You're just like your father."

"Thank you." Rafik said.

"That wasn't a compliment." Salina said.

Rafik wasn't sure how much time had passed. In the darkness it was hard to tell the difference between a minute and an hour. Salina had tried goading him into more arguments, but he ignored her. They were both sentenced to die, he wasn't going to please her with conversation.

A hooded figure emerged from the far end of the hall and sat beside the cage door of Rafik. "Hello, Rafik." Samron said, lowering his hood. "I would ask how you are doing, but I can only imagine."

"What happened?" Rafik asked. "I didn't realize I was on trial."

Samron shrugged. "The King is angry today. I will try and talk with him, but it doesn't look good. I may be able to convince him to save you, if you admit Salina didn't try to kill you."

"But she did!" Rafik yelled. "She should admit it."

"She should," Samron said, casting Salina a look of disdain. "But she won't. Her ilk only tries to save themselves."

Salina laughed. "It's what the boy deserves."

Samron didn't reply. "Your friends are in trouble."

"What happened?"

"After they dragged you away Ziri poisoned a couple guards and Kryn tried burning her way to the king. They're both being held in separate rooms until after the execution."

"Are they going to die too?"

"I don't think so." Samron said.

"You also thought I would be on my way back to the Sarason Fortress." Rafik argued.

"Yes." Samron chuckled. "Seems like fate has different plans. Just don't give up, Rafik. We will think of something."

Chapter 21: Sand Dragons

Dragon's Roost, Biodlay Desert, Alutopek

Coming from the Nyler Peninsula, Gorik knew mountains. He lived beside, on, and in them. Though he loved the sea, seeing a mountain reach into the sky always brought a sense of comfort. The sea called him, but the mountains were his home. Far in the distance there was a peculiar sight. It was like a mountain with the top half sheared off. It was out of place as there was nothing but sand for miles.

Seeing it in the distance there was an increased oomph in his step. Almost there. He loved the sea. But not this sea of sand. His peg leg dragged behind him as he slowly made his way farther. The bag he carried hit against his hip. He glanced down; thankful Rafik had left it with him. If he couldn't hide out in there, he was positive he would have died days ago from the heat.

"Just a little farther." Gorik said to himself again.

The glowing light from the Black Wall beat down on Gorik. He had tried moving at night but felt as if he was going to freeze to the bone. More than once he cursed the desert. The mountain grew closer as Gorik felt weaker. Walking through the desert was next to impossible. His food and water he got from the Golden Gate was almost gone. How he would return to civilization was something he tried to avoid thinking about.

He stopped, sitting on the burning sand that he was growing so used to and unscrewed his leg. A few sips of rum and he was back pressing forward. A small mound of sand shifted near him. Gorik shook his head, believing it to be a trick of the mind. There was no wind to make anything move. Behind him something slithered. As the flat-topped mountain grew nearer Gorik could hear the shifting sands. He turned, watching the large lump move closer.

At the last moment Gorik jumped out of the way. A massive mouth erupted just where he was standing. "What was that?" He screamed, another lump moving towards him. He scrambled to his foot and peg leg, moving out of the way. Another mouth tried grabbing at him. A third mouth narrowly missed Gorik.

He looked around, trying to find where another bulge would be charging him. Nothing happened. The sands were just as calm and silent as ever. "Ya shire. These damn mirages are going to kill me." Gorik said, dusting himself off. He continued toward the mountain, cursing under his breath.

It was several minutes later that Gorik saw something atop a dune he was heading towards. It was large, dark like the bark of a tree, and had piercing orange eyes. The beast stood on all four, its mouth large enough to eat a man. "Sand dragon." Gorik said in awe. The scaly creature's body rippled with muscle. Just beneath the one three slender sand dragons emerged from the sand.

"Ya shire." Gorik cursed. There was no way of out running them. Nowhere to hide. The one on top, largest of the four, roared causing sand to slide down the nearby dunes. The other three burrowed back into the sand. A shiver ran down his spine from the roar, nearly freezing him. Gorik could see three lines slithering their way towards him.

The center dragon moved in faster than the others. Gorik jumped out of the way as it launched itself into the air, its slender body glistening in the desert light before plunging back into the sand. Gorik rolled out of the way of the other, as a fourth slender dragon ambushed him from the back. He screamed as the dragon bit down, yanking off his peg leg.

"My rum!" Gorik yelled, sitting up. The sand dragons circled him like sharks in the ocean.

The four emerged, growling and glaring at Gorik. None of them moved to pounce but just stood guard around him. The bulkier of the dragons arrived, walking calmly into the circle. Gorik swallowed, unsure if he should make eye contact with the monster or keep his eyes on the sand.

He heaved a sigh as it just sniffed him and turned to roar at the mountain. The others following suit. Gorik opened the bag, scrambling to get in. He let out a grunt as he crashed onto the floor, looking up to make sure the dragons didn't follow him. He could hear muffled roars from above, but nothing more.

"Are we there?" Izamar asked.

Gorik shook his head. "Dragons. Dragons are out there."

"Real dragons?" Anza asked, pressing herself against the frame of the portrait trying to see up the trap door. "I want to see."

"Oh no you don't." Gorik said. "They took my leg!"

"You've always had that one leg." Anza said.

"No, my drinking leg." Gorik said. "I have no rum. I can't walk. We're stuck in the middle of the desert surrounded by dragons."

"Were you born with one leg?" Izamar asked in the calmest voice Gorik had heard.

"No. I lost it."

"So, there was a point where you had to move around with one leg?" Izamar asked.

Gorik nodded. "Yes."

"Then you can do it again." Izamar said matter-of-factly.

"I am not hopping across the desert." Gorik said, pushing himself up, leaning against the back wall.

"You shouldn't have to." Izamar said. "I'm guessing you have never run into a dragon before?"

"Have you?" Gorik asked, trying to hold onto his temper.

"Several times!" Izamar said. "And all dragons have one thing in common. They're hoarders. They take treasures back to their lair often."

"How does that help?"

"Simple. You just crawl out of the bag when they're sleeping and hobble out of their den."

"And then hop across the desert." Gorik cut in.

Izamar shook his head. "No. Dragons, even sand dragons, have lairs. They don't hide all day in the sand, or in the middle of the forest. They have homes. A cave. An abandoned castle. They will take us back to the one mountain in the area."

"Dragon's Roost." Gorik said.

Izamar smiled. "Exactly. All you need to do is crawl out, and you can escape into the safety of the secret oasis here. I could even help you get back your leg if you make it."

"You just have random legs in your hideout? Wait, you said if. If I make it?"

"Well with your attitude now you're setting yourself up to fail. So, they have your leg. That's just one less body part you have to worry about them biting off."

"Because they already did!"

"And they can't do it again." Izamar smiled. "Now I am positive you can do this, Gorik. You've come this far."

Gorik sighed. "I guess I don't have much of a choice."

For the next several hours Gorik hopped from one end of the room to the other. If he had to escape a dragon's den on one leg, he wanted to make sure he actually could. Anza's laughs of him toppling over soon turned to words of encouragement. It took some repositioning, but he found a way to hop without losing balance. Soon enough he was able to hop all over the room without having to rebalance or lean against something.

"I think I'm ready." Gorik said, half out of breath.

"At the base of the Dragon's Roost there is a line of runes running across the outside wall of the mountain. Follow those and it will take you to the entrance." Izamar said.

Gorik nodded and began to climb the ladder. He turned, looking at Anza stuck in the portrait. "If I fail. What will happen to her?"

Izamar glanced at the portrait of Anza. She was fighting off sleep and failing. "She'll stay in the portrait. Forever."

"She won't age?"

"No." Izamar said. "She will remain as she was when she was placed in there."

"Wish me luck." Gorik said, after a short pause. He wanted to say more, but wasn't sure what to say. Anza was counting on him. He stuck his hand out first, waiting for any sort of movement to investigate the sudden weight in the bag. Nothing. He inched farther out but felt only the cold air of the desert night. As his head popped out, he froze, a deep growl hummed from beside him.

'Ya shire.' He thought to himself, wincing.

The growl faded before returning with one just as loud. He dared a look, slowly turning to the source of the noise. It was one of the slender sand dragons, sleeping. Gorik dragged himself out of the bag and hobbled onto his foot. Far away he could see a dim light shining in the darkness. One of the stars twinkling through the Black Wall.

Gorik kneeled, scooping up the bag and waited. There were more growls echoing throughout the cave. Nearby a dragon shifted, causing a pile of unseen treasure sprinkle down. Nothing else moved. He jumped; thankful his landing didn't echo among the snoring. Another hop, and another.

Every hop got him closer to the star that seemed so far away. He hopped again, lost his balance, and fell. The dragons didn't stir. Gorik paused, his eyes slowly adjusting more. All around him were piles of treasure. He could make out coins, cups, and jewels in some piles. Swords, spears, and shields in another. There was more than one pile of bones with human skulls scattered about. There were the slender ones, but the bulky one he couldn't see yet. He grabbed tight of the bag and stood back up.

Three more hops and he was at the entrance. Not a single dragon awoke or disturbed. He turned, leaning against the wall to catch his breath. Just above his head were the runes. The runes looked ancient, even he couldn't read them, let alone which way they went. Taking a guess, he moved forward, jumping along, leaning against the rocky mountain side for support.

Light began to glow in the east and Gorik still hadn't found the entrance. A wind whirled around him and a roar echoed along with it. The dragons were awake. Gorik cursed and tried hopping faster. Turning behind him, he noticed one of the slender dragons stamping towards him. Its nose was to the sand, not looking up and seeing Gorik.

He prayed he would find the entrance when he hopped again, his hand grabbing thin air above him. A few more hops, and just above him was a small crevice he could squeeze through. He jumped, hoisting himself into the hole. Moments later the sand dragon sniffed by and pawed at the mountain side. It roared, getting on its hind legs to sniff into the crevice. The runes glowed and the dragon howled, getting back onto its legs, growling, and whimpering away.

"Take that." Gorik laughed, spitting out the hole. "Now try and make me your dinner! Or breakfast, now."

He turned looking down the tunnel. There was a light at the end, but no discernible features between where he was and there. The crevice opened and rose upwards the farther he made his way. It wasn't long before he arrived at the light. Gorik gasped, shouting at the sight.

"Hey!" Gorik yelled into the bag. "Hey we made it!"

Dragon's Roost was surrounded by smooth red stones. There was no ceiling, as he saw the glowing light of the Black Wall above him. There were trees everywhere, a stone tower in the distance. In the center of it all was a mound, water streaming down one side into a pond. The pond came to where Gorik stood below. A carved ladder on the smooth mountainside. He shook his head, jumping into the pond below like a boulder.

The cool water enveloped him and Gorik gasped from the sudden cold. He kicked and paddled to the surface, spitting out a mouthful of water, and gasped for air. Once on the shore he crawled into the bag and announced, "We're here."

"I see you chose to jump." Izamar laughed. "I did too."

"When can I get out of here?" Anza asked. "Swimming sounds so nice right now."

"Once I find a way to get you out of there." Izamar said. "Now, Gorik, did you see a tower?"

Gorik nodded. "I did."

"Good. I need you to make your way there. Take the stairs to the basement and come back once there." Izamar said.

Gorik climbed back out the ladder and stretched, the cool air of the oasis a blessing after trekking for days through mountains of sand. He took off his shoe and soaked his foot in the running stream. The cool water was like a drug. Once again, he jumped in, doing backstrokes from one end to the other.

On one end where he had left the bag, he saw a movement and dived underwater. If the dragons had found a way in, he wasn't going to make it easy to get to him. He stayed there, unmoving, until the creature came towards the pond and got a drink. He splashed out of the water, kicking himself for being so scared. The rabbit that he had mistaken dashed away. "I'm glad nobody was here to see that." Gorik sighed, crawling out of the pond. He left his shoe by the pond, grabbed the bag, and hopped towards the tower.

He could see chickens and rabbits wandering around, and even a tortoise. He felt back at home, a small grove of trees like the forests of the Nyler Peninsula. The grass tickled his foot, which he preferred over the grains of sand digging their way into him. The tower was peculiar in construction. It stood atop a large square chicken coop held up by stone columns. The door locking them in had long since rusted and fallen apart. Grass grew through the remains entangling it. There was a wide and deep ladder, almost like it was trying to be a staircase, leaning to the higher portion of the tower. That portion was circular and slowly grew bigger the higher it got like a mushroom.

"How is that possible?" Gorik asked himself, noting that the caged chicken coop spanned the entire bottom of the tower. He popped his head into the bag. "You said take the stairs to the basement?"

"Yes." Izamar nodded. "Take the ladder, enter the tower, and head downstairs."

Gorik shook his head, debating on the sanity of the wizard stuck in a mirror. Before climbing the ladder, he walked the expanse of the caged area. Rows of chicken coops, but no sign of stairs leading to even a lower level of animal homes. "There are no stairs."

He returned to the ladder and slowly made his way up them. The ladder was so far inclined he could jump from rung to rung. He made his way to the door, a small window in the center.

He peered in, and sure enough, there were stairs leading downwards. Inside the tower it twice as large as the secret room of his bag. He looked up, seeing the stairs lead upwards along the wall but no other platform. As he turned to make his way down the stairs, he noticed a boarded up well. "Magic makes no sense." He shook his head, pushing open the door.

The stairs seemed to wind down as much as they did upwards. Far below the chicken coop that was the base of the tower. A single door loomed over him at the bottom of the stairs. It was at least twice as tall as him, a keyhole off to the side. He turned the knob, but it didn't turn.

"Please tell me you have a key." Gorik asked once he was in the bag.

"Oh, that's right." Izamar said. "The key is at the top of this tower."

"Are you serious?" Gorik sighed, imagining himself hopping up all those stairs, and then back down. The slump in his shoulders apparent as he turned to leave.

Izamar laughed. "No, I'm joking. I was curious how you would react. The key is a decoy. Knock three times and whisper the name sekolah."

"Sekolah?" Gorik asked. "That's the name of the Kylix fortress in Haitu."

"It means school." Izamar said. "It's from the Bone Hunter language."

Gorik nodded, as if he understood who the Bone Hunters were, and left the room. Without wasting time, he knocked three times on the door, leaned into the keyhole and whispered "Sekolah." A resounding click echoed throughout the tower and the door inched open.

He always wondered what a wizard's hideout would be like. Never would have thought it would be far away in the middle of nowhere, almost impossible to reach. He always envisioned it to be a mysterious laboratory of some sort. Vials of colorful liquids corked and shelved while others were on tables, ready to be used. A podium to hold a book and a stack of other books nearby. Loose parchment scattered about. Chalk drawings of strange runes and symbols littering the walls. Maybe an owl or cat skulking about.

"Oh." Gorik said, peering into the room, the disappointment apparent on his voice. It was a room with nothing special. Bookcases lined the walls and a table in the center. The only peculiar thing were full length mirrors where the bookcases weren't and even behind the bookshelves. He tossed the bag on the floor, kicked open the flap and jumped in.

"We're here." Gorik said. Anza let out a noise of excitement.

"Good." Izamar said, clapping his hands. "Good. Now I need you to do one more thing before I can help you. I need you to take this mirror and place it on the gap in the wall."

"What gap?" Gorik asked. "There are mirrors everywhere."

"Well there is a spot that doesn't have one." Izamar argued. "Place this mirror there. And don't drop this mirror, or you came here for nothing."

Gorik nodded. "Not sure if I'm the right guy for the job. Having one leg." He laughed, jumping to Izamar.

"I believe in you." The wizard said.

Gorik reached forward, picking up the mirror and turning. He saw his reflection stare back at him as he made his way back across the room. Once at the ladder the mirror shot out of the trapdoor. Gorik crossed his fingers that he wouldn't see shattered glass everywhere when he got out.

Thankfully, that wasn't the case. He sighed, grabbing back a hold of the mirror, trying to find the gap it had to fit in. Just behind him near the door was the gap, big enough for the mirror. As the mirror fit snugly into place a golden beam lined around the top and bottom of the mirrors in the room.

"There we go. Thank you, my friend." Izamar said. "Now, let's see." He moved to the next mirror and Gorik gasped, watching him move from one mirror to the next. The wizard moved behind bookshelves and he could have sworn he saw a book on one of them move. He returned a few moments later holding a large tome.

"Are all of these wizard books?" Gorik asked.

"Wizard books?" Izamar said, smiling. "Spell books, potion books, and history books, mostly. Do those constitute as 'wizard books?'"

"The first two at least." Gorik said.

Izamar opened the book and flipped through the pages, humming softly. "Ah, here we go." He looked at Gorik, whispering words that sounded like hissing from a snake and light growls of a wolf.

"Hey, what's going on?" Gorik asked, his skin itching. He felt a burning sensation at the end of his lost leg. It intensified and a moment later a leg shimmered to life.

"I promised a leg, didn't I?" Izamar asked. "It's only temporary. But hopefully you can find another peg leg by then."

"Th-thank you!" Gorik said, a tear trickling down his face. He jumped in place, stomped the ground, and rubbed his new leg.

"Of course!" Izamar said. "Now I need you to go get Anza. You can hang her above my mirror. With any luck we'll be able to get her to be in the mirrors of this room instead."

Gorik nodded and jumped back into the bag, smiling ear to ear. "Notice anything?" He asked Anza, a large grin on his face as he danced and twirled.

"You've gone crazy?" Anza asked.

"No." Gorik said, stamping his new leg.

Anza looked him over once and gasped. "Gorik you have a leg!"

"Sure do. Two of them to be exact." He reached over and grabbed the portrait, taking Anza up the ladder. "And with any luck, you'll be out of this picture in no time, too."

It was an hour later that Anza had escaped the portrait and was in the mirror with Izamar. "I am sorry." Izamar said, sighing. "This is the best I can do for now."

Anza laughed, running around the room. "I'm happy I can move now. Do you think you'll be able to let me out?"

"I hope so, yes." Izamar said. "This piece of magic, I'm not sure of its source. Skage was my apprentice once. A horrible one. Obsessed with the dark arts, but not the rest. And even in that area he could only summon undead spiders. But when he returned, he was powerful. Changed. Becoming the monster you saw in that portrait. He had to have had a new master. If I can find the right piece of magic to counteract this curse, I should be able to."

Gorik nodded. "I'll help." Gorik offered, grabbing a book.

"I will too." Anza said, mimicking Izamar and taking a book off the shelf.

"Who is Grey Fox?" Gorik asked, after closing one book and grabbing another.

"Why?" Izamar asked, not looking up from his own book. In the reflection Anza and he were sitting at the table beside Gorik.

"He's written a lot of these books, it seems." Gorik said.

"Probably most." Izamar said, agreeing. "It is his library."

"But isn't this your library?" Anza asked.

Izamar nodded. "After locking away the dark objects your brother discovered, my name was taboo. Nobody was to know it. And in time everyone forgot it. I was Gray Fox, Sarafin became Jester, and Furen became Bones."

"You said their names!" Anza laughed.

Izamar shrugged, giving a sigh. "I feel it is time to drop the nicknames. Your brother saw to that."

Gorik and Anza read through other books. They were able to skim through some but had to skip over entire portions as they couldn't read the ancient runes. He was beginning to believe he was of no use, looking for the answer as one book was solely written in those runic symbols.

"I recognize this!" Anza said, pointing at her book and jumping up in her seat. "It was at the Sarason Fortress!"

"What is it?" Izamar asked, moving to sit beside Anza.

"The Kymu-Guiden Talisman." Anza said. The picture of the spider engraved talisman was the only thing she recognized on the page. All the names of the relics were in that unfamiliar rune language. "Skage had me find it before he tricked me."

"Are you sure?"

Anza nodded. "Positive. He said once I found it, he could bring back my mom."

"With that talisman I'm sure he could." Izamar said. "It's a legendarily dark object. Most wizards in my time believed it to be just a myth. No one in ages had even seen it."

"What does it do?" Gorik asked.

"To those who can't control the dark arts it's said to curse the user with a horrific death. But if you're like Skage being a necromancer, it increases the user's power tenfold. But only if they are concentrating."

"Wait." Gorik said. "So that is how he is able to raise the dead from so far away? Like at the Golden Gate?"

"It's possible." Izamar said. "But he would have to see what he's doing."

"The spider." Anza said. "The spider on the fortress has a telescope connected to it."

"That is the answer." Izamar said. "If he uses the talisman while looking at a certain place it could work."

"So, we just need to break his concentration and the dead would stay dead?" Gorik asked.

Izamar nodded. "In most cases, yes. Skage is…he is something else. Always obsessed with magical relics, artifacts, and treasures. I wouldn't be surprised if he had found a way to keep his powers going, while moving on or focusing on something else. When the other magic users at the time went to confront him, he disappeared. On the telescope there was a snowflake pendant. We confiscated it and gave it to Furen for safe keeping. We weren't sure why it was there, but thought it was a nice gesture to give to the new king of Alutopek."

The wizard held up his hand, scratching his chin, his eyes closed. "You have an idea?" Gorik asked after a long minute of silence.

"Yes, That's it!" Izamar grinned. "Why didn't we think of that? Anza found the Kymu-Guiden Talisman in the telescope. That would do it, yes. The snowflake pendant stops magic from

271

being altered. That would include when no longer concentrating. He's combining relics. We searched for years trying to find him, until I found a portrait of him. It gave off an unnatural feeling. So, to be safe I hid it away in the bag in the wardrobe. I suspected it may be him but couldn't find a way to do anything about it."

"You could have burned the thing." Gorik suggested.

Izamar nodded. "I considered it. But that may have allowed him to escape. I hoped he would be lost forever, imprisoned in the hiding hole he created for himself."

"And I let him out." Anza said.

Izamar nodded. "Yes, well, we all make mistakes."

"My mistake caused people to die." Anza said. "I deserve to be in here."

"No, we'll get you out of there." Gorik said. "Right, Grey Fox?"

"Yes." Izamar smiled. "We just need to keep looking."

"Could you use the talisman?" Anza asked. "You're already dead."

"I enchanted this room so I can read these books from the Mentor's Mirror." Izamar said. "I'm not sure if I could use such an item."

"You said Skage was weak?" Gorik said, beginning to pace the room after another couple hours of searching through books.

"Yes." Izamar said. "Magic comes from the heart and willingness to learn. Skage just wanted power. Obsessed with death. Because of this I didn't teach him all that I knew. I anticipated him to be an amateur necromancer at best. Not a scourge on Alutopek."

"And he needed the talisman before breaking free." Gorik stated.

"According to Anza, yes." Izamar said.

"What if he is only powerful because of the talisman? We take that away from him and we can stop him." Gorik suggested.

Izamar scratched his chin, which turned to a smile, and then a laugh. "Gorik, I think you may be right. It would definitely impede on his plans, at least."

"Is there a way to send a message to somebody here?" Gorik asked. "A carrier bird or something?"

Izamar laughed. "Witches and wizards don't use birds to carry letters. We use crystal balls to communicate with one another. Or send one of our students with a message."

"We need to tell Samron how to stop Skage." Gorik said.

"I fear the only way to get to them would be you having to go." Izamar said.

"If you don't mind?" Gorik asked, looking at Anza.

Anza shook her head. "I know you'll come back for me. And who knows, maybe I'll get out of here soon and meet you back home."

Gorik glanced at Izamar. He looked down, shaking his head. Gorik frowned. "Maybe. But if anything else, I'll be back for you. And I'll have Rafik with me."

Anza smiled. "I miss him. He would love this place." She turned to Izamar. "Um, what am I going to do in the meantime, if Gorik is leaving?"

"Same thing you are now." Izamar said. "Instead of looking for a spell to free you, you will read every book."

"But I can't do magic." Anza said. "And magic is gone. Not to mention I can't read most of these runes."

"As I said earlier." Izamar said. "Magic comes from the heart and willingness to learn. You may not have heart to perform magic now, but you have all the time in the world to learn. You could be the first witch Alutopek has seen in years."

Anza's smiled went from ear to ear. "Can you imagine Rafik's face? He would be so proud."

"Yes, he would." Gorik smiled. "You would be an amazing witch."

"Thank you." Anza smiled. "But I can't read most of these."

"Looks like I have a new student." Izamar laughed. "And already I like this one more than my last."

"I promise I won't go evil and summon the dead." Anza said.

Izamar laughed. "Good. I think the world has had enough of that."

"You said my leg is temporary?" Gorik asked. "I have to walk through the desert again. I don't want it to suddenly disappear."

"That would be so funny!" Anza laughed, imagining her uncle's leg suddenly disappearing and his falling into the sand.

"It will go away in a year." Izamar said. "You have plenty of time. I'd suggest getting a leg sooner, rather than later, for preparation."

"Of course!" Gorik laughed. "I already miss my rum." He stamped his new leg on the ground several times. "This thing is durable, but I need my drink."

The three laughed, as Gorik scooped up the bag and left. It had been a long adventure, but the end was in sight. He was positive the wizard would find a way for her to get out sooner or later. And she was safe, tucked away where Skage couldn't get her. Now he just had to worry about Rafik. He prayed his nephew wasn't getting into trouble. *'Fortunately, Samron is with him to keep him safe.* He thought to himself.

Chapter 22: The Gallows

Sekolah Fortress, Haitu, Biodlay Desert, Alutopek

Rafik didn't sleep. He couldn't tell time but felt that a lifetime had passed down here already. Salina was snoring. He thought it odd that she was so calm to be sleeping just before being killed. Then again, she had already spent a couple days in the dungeons.

The torch on the wall flickered out long ago, leaving the two in darkness. Salina had tried scaring Rafik before she fell asleep, but just managed to annoy him. There was a waving light growing brighter in the distance. "Kryn?" He asked, a tinge of hope in his voice.

A soldier turned the corner, Ziri walking alongside him. "Five minutes." He said, leaving Ziri at the front of Rafik's cage.

"Morning." She whispered. Down here her voice echoed so Rafik didn't have to strain to hear it.

"Morning." Rafik said. "Where's Kryn?"

Ziri shrugged. "Probably still locked up. After they took you away Samron had Kryn taken before she could kill the king. I was sent away but released since I don't appear as angry as Kryn. She's fuming like a dragon!"

"I'm sorry, Ziri." Rafik said, unsure of what else to say.

"No. I'm sorry." Ziri said. "I should have tried harder to break you out."

"Then you'd be in the same boat as me." Rafik said. "No. Since I won't be able to see my sister," He choked, thinking of Anza. "I need you to save her. Keep her away from the Kylix."

Ziri nodded. "I promise."

Silence permeated through the dungeon. Even Salina had stopped snoring. "Do you think we can beat Skage?"

Rafik nodded. "Nobody is invincible. I know you can, Ziri."

"Hey, Rafik." Ziri said, fighting back tears. "Thank you."

"For what?"

"For being my friend. You were my first friend." Ziri said. "Thank you."

"Hopefully, your next friend won't die so soon after." Rafik said, trying to laugh.

"The king is sending us off after...after it happens." Ziri said. "Says we need to watch because if we try to run away that's what will happen to us. Samron left, though. Says he is meeting us in Sysinal."

"Why did he leave?" Rafik asked.

"Rumor has it somebody else with talent is there." Ziri said. "I hope it's somebody who can stop people from summoning the dead. He took one of the Kylika with him, too."

Rafik smiled. "If only it were that easy."

Ziri paused, wringing the bars that were between the two. "I-I'll miss you, Rafik."

"Don't say that. Not yet." Rafik said.

The rest of the time was spent in silence. They held each other's hand, not wanting time to continue. "Times up." A soldier said, whistling and beckoning for Ziri to return.

"She your girlfriend?" Salina asked as she left.

"Shut up." Rafik snapped. "I was hoping I wouldn't have to hear you again before I die."

"Life is full of disappointments. Better get used to it. Oh, wait. I'm sorry." Salina snickered.

Rafik imagined Salina on her knees, head bowed, and him taking the axe that would remove her head. His daydream was cut short as a few more soldiers appeared. "It's time." One of the soldiers said, dangling the keys and laughing. "Been a long time since we've had a proper execution. Now we get two of them."

The other two soldiers brandished their swords. "Any funny business we'll stick you." One of them said. They opened the doors, yanking both Rafik and Salina to their feet. They marched in silence out of the dungeons and to a short trip to an open area. It was surrounded by tall balconies. The only other doorway was across the yard. In the center of it was a contraption Rafik had seen only once before. A handful of stairs leading to a platform with a trapdoor. A beam hanging over the platform with a rope dangling down.

"Welcome to the gallows." The soldier behind Rafik said.

Rafik looked around. The balcony was lined with skeletons staring down at him. In the center was the king, glaring down at him. He was the only one not wearing a helmet. "I'll give you one last chance." He said in a voice as thick as mud. "You two tell me what happened. Truthfully. Or both of you will hang."

Salina opened her mouth first. "I was trying to save him. Right, Rafik?"

Her look of desperation bore into Rafik. He had never seen her like this. He thought it was probably the first time she ever was as well. His gaze moved to the crowd of skeletons about to be watching him die. There, opposite of the king, were the familiar monster skull helmets of the Kylika. One of the smallest of them lifted their hand, waving. He smiled, hoping that was Ziri. He turned to look at the king. His eyes appeared to have sunken in as just black holes were there. A glint of the icy blue eyes glimmered every time he blinked. With everyone in full Kylix armor he couldn't recognize anyone. They all stared at him. Like corpses awaiting another member into the brotherhood of the dead.

Finally, Rafik shook his head. "The truth is what I said before." His voice shaky, but with every word it grew firmer. "Salina tried to kill me. If it wasn't for Ziri and Samron she probably would have succeeded. I'm not going to lie to save someone who tried to kill me. Even if that means I die, too."

King Vanarzir laughed, a deep joyless chuckle. "You have honor. Guess there's no sense in telling you that will get you killed. Still no way of seeing who is being honest. So, both of you will pay for lying. Hang until dead. You can go first." He pointed at Salina.

Salina's head dropped, the color washing away from her face. The soldier behind her shoved her forward. She inched closer, step by step. Each foot was encased in stone. Slowly, ever so slowly, she made her way up the platform, turned, and stood in the center. As the soldier placed the rope around her neck, she glared at Rafik.

"You may give your final words now." The soldier said. Salina cleared her throat. "I'll see you in Soboribor."

Another soldier pulled a lever on the other side of the platform and the trapdoor gave way. Salina's body dropped as everyone gasped. Rafik turned away but the soldier behind him forced him to look. He watched as her body twitched, the last noises she made were gasping for breath.

He had seen some nightmarish things in Datz as they tried to escape. The monster in the tunnels with the chains. And the dead rising at the Golden Gate. But seeing Salina hang was probably the worst. The way she moved and jerked. He paled, realizing that would be him in just a few moments.

The yard fell silent, no one saying a word or moving. Salina's body swayed, twitching once more before finally coming to a stop. It was only then that the king ordered for her to be taken down. The king turned to Rafik, shaking his head. "You had potential, boy."

Rafik looked around, hoping Kryn could use her fire and save him. Or the Sand Brothers swooping in. He wouldn't even mind Krista or Haloro saving him now. A soldier stood under Salina and picked her body up. Another removed the noose. They tossed Salina's body to the side like trash and beckoned for Rafik.

Every step his vision narrowed. He didn't notice those around him now. He saw his father and mother in the distance, smiling. He saw little Anza running into their arms. The image faded and he saw Gorik eating dinner with them, all of them somber. He recognized that night. It was the day after he learned their father had died. He saw his mother fall to the volley of arrows. Saving others in the pond. He saw Anza run across the dark room with spiders, going back into the bag as he fought the suit of armor.

Rafik gasped, stopping and the soldier behind him walked into him. "Get to moving." He snarled, shoving Rafik.

"She's alive?" Rafik whispered. "She's alive!" He never saw her leave the bag. But Skage walked across the room. Skage escaped the bag. But where was Anza? Before he realized it, he felt the rope tighten around his neck.

"You may give your final words now." The soldier said.

Rafik looked over to the Kylika. "She's alive. She's not in the tower. She's with Gorik."

The soldier nodded and Rafik shut his eyes, wincing. He didn't hear the lever be pulled or feel the ground give beneath him. After a second, he opened his eyes. The soldiers in the yard with him had their swords brandished, slowly surrounding Salina's corpse lying beside the gallows. He saw Salina, the look of malice burning through the cold dead eyes. A knife stabbed into the back of the Kylix soldier at the lever.

Salina growled that unnatural sound, charging forward at the other soldier. The soldier she had killed began to stir and moved after another soldier. Rafik yanked off the noose and jumped off the platform. King Vanarzir yelled, ordering to attack the dead. Soldiers screamed in panic while others jumped from the balconies charging for attack.

Rafik didn't stick around to watch. Being sentenced to death he didn't want to find out what would happen if he survived. He crossed the yard through the other door. He had no idea where he was going, but anywhere would be better than where he was. Turning another corner, dashing down a corridor, and turning another, he found himself in front of an unguarded door.

On the other side was freedom. He pushed through the door and made his way into the streets of Haitu. Far away there were other screams. Rafik guessed others were discovering the dead were coming back to life. A noise caught his attention. A couple soldiers were chasing after him. Rafik slammed the door shut and sprinted away.

He had never seen this many people in his life. There were some in bright colored clothes, and others garbed all in black. Some with dark skin and others pale like Ziri. Others were hairier than bears and others looked softer than silk. He pushed his way through the crowd, hearing only tidbits of people shouting the goods they were selling. He ignored those who shouted at him, not looking back.

If one were to see the city from the Eko River it didn't seem that big. But running through it was something else. How could there be this much city? So many people and so many things to spend money on. He saw the large rock wall at the edge of the city, leading to the river. The natural barrier blocked the boisterous noises coming from the other side.

Rafik pushed his way through. "Where are you going?" A Kylix soldier asked, stepping in front of Rafik. "All kids go to the Sekolah Fortress."

"I know." Rafik said. "I left my armor at the fortress."

"Ah, we got a runaway." The soldier laughed. "Should have kept that to yourself."

"No." Rafik said, thinking quickly. "Some of us are leaving, heading north. I was sent ahead to get ready."

"Do you have any papers?" The soldier asked.

"No. It was an order from the king himself." Rafik lied. "Do you really want to question him? I'm sure he'd love to hear why a lowly Kylix soldier was preventing the Kylika from leaving."

"Now, now." The soldier said, raising his hands. "Don't get too hasty. Can't be too careful, you know."

Rafik nodded. He entered the docks waving away the guard and looked around. He just had to find a boat heading north now. A yell caught his attention. He turned, noticing the Kylix soldier who allowed him entry pointing at him. "Ya shire." Rafik cursed. He didn't notice the sky grow dark as the soldiers gave chase, he bolted and jumped into the Eko River.

Kryn paced back and forth in the windowless room. Her outburst at the trial got her sent here. Even King Vanarzir seemed surprised at how angry she was. If it weren't for Samron, everybody would have incinerated trying to take Rafik away. There was no way of knowing what time it was in the room, let

280

alone if the execution had occurred yet. She prayed a miracle would happen. Anything to save her friend.

As she turned to walk the length of the room again the door clicked open. Shouting and panic entered the room. "We need your help." A soldier said, turning to leave before getting a response from Kryn.

She hurried after the soldier, the noise getting louder. "Stop him!" The king shouted.

Kryn entered a balcony and saw the chaos below. Salina and two other soldiers were attacking others. Salina had at least a dozen arrows sticking from her. One of the Sand Brothers kept blocking her with walls of sand, but she fought through it. Kryn jumped off the balcony, using her fire to slow her fall. A fallen soldier charged her. Without thinking she burned the soldier and turned to the others.

The burning soldier stepped forward, unfazed. Haloro sped by, blocking the soldier from attacking Kryn. "What?" Kryn said, looking back. "They weren't joking."

Another soldier came to life beside her, screeching and wailing like a banshee. It hurried to its feet and charged at Kryn. She parried his jarring movements and kicked him to the ground. Standing over him, she removed the helmet and blasted a fireball into his face. It didn't move for a moment, before returning to life. The noise was even worse now, gurgling through singed and cooked flesh.

She noticed other soldiers discovering similar events as a headless soldier scrambled back to life, flailing around. Mahlix joined fighting with the Kylika, blocking blows, and kicking the dead away. He had given up trying to slay them, and only defending himself and others.

A deep voice sounded on the wind and the morning light grew dark. Everyone paused, spinning one way and then another, trying to find the voice. The fallen soldiers and Salina collapsed to the ground. Wisps of silvery smoke escaped them. The smoke slowly trailed upward, spiraling and curving, entering the palm of King Vanarzir. The king stood over everyone on the balcony.

Wind blew, causing his robes to flow in the wind. "Dark magic indeed." He said in his deep voice. "Where is the boy?"

Everyone searched, peering under the finally lifeless corpses and throughout the arena. Ziri removed her helmet and made her way to Kryn. "I think he escaped." She said.

"Gone, My Lord." A soldier said. "Not among the dead."

King Vanarzir nodded. "Kill him on sight. He is now an enemy of the kingdom. This Rafik of Datz. Spread word. As for the Kylika prepare to leave. We'll need to stop this menace before he grows too powerful."

The Kylix spread throughout the city. Some people claimed to see a boy like Rafik. According to reports, he had made his way to the docks. From there no one noticed. It was as if he vanished in thin air. Stowaway was the conclusion.

"Do you think he did it?" Krista asked as they boarded a ship to head north.

"Did what?" Kryn asked.

"Raise the dead like that? He said he had talent, but we never saw him use it. And who ever heard of being able to look at objects' memories? Objects aren't alive. Maybe that was a lie. Then he used his actual talent to get away."

"Are you thinking everybody in the north can just raise the dead?" Kryn asked, gritting her teeth, clenching her fists.

"No. But maybe he is the necromancer we have to kill." Krista said. "How could one so far away summon the dead all the way down here? Doesn't make sense."

"Guess we'll find out soon enough." Kryn said. She walked away from Krista and sat next to Ziri. It wasn't long after the boat set off. A handful of Kylix soldiers helped steer the boat as the Kylika sat in the center. None of them had left the Sekolah Fortress since they were brought here. It was as exciting as it was nerve wracking. After watching what the necromancer was capable of, none of them believed it would be as easy as they first thought.

"Stowaway!" A soldier shouted as they entered the first canyon passed Haitu. His announcement echoed for several moments before fading away.

"Rafik?" Kryn and Ziri asked, springing up.

The soldier kicked over a barrel. Potatoes and a boy came rolling out. He coughed as he got to his feet, brushing himself off from the dirt that had collected on him. "I want to fight." Taygin said with a squeaky voice, taking a step forward and stepping on a potato, falling. The soldiers laughed.

"You can't even stay on your feet. This is a dangerous mission, boy. Kylika only."

The mousy boy shook his head. "We can't turn back now. And obviously I have talent, or I couldn't have sneaked onto this boat, right? Not under all your watchful eyes, of course."

"Prove it. Right now." The soldier demanded.

Taygin squirmed, looking from side to side and rubbing his arms. "Ugh, I-I can't."

"Pathetic." The soldier laughed. "What's your name?"

"Taygin, sir." The boy said.

"Well, Taygin." The soldier sighed. "You are right. We aren't turning around. So, lucky for you. I'll make sure I put you on the front lines of the first battle."

Taygin's face paled and the soldiers nearby laughed.

"You can sit with me." Krista said, holding up her hand. "You always do."

Taygin nodded, moving to sit beside her.

"That boy is going to die." Kryn said. "Probably in some embarrassing way, too. He's going to slip on a water droplet and crack his head or something."

Ziri shrugged. "Hopefully, he'll learn before that."

"Where do you think Rafik is?" Kryn asked.

Ziri shrugged. "His last words were saying that she's with Gorik."

"His sister?" Kryn asked.

"I think so." Ziri said. "So, I bet on his way to try and find him. But if he just jumped on a random boat he could be anywhere on this river."

"He could have hidden somewhere in Haitu." Kryn said.

"No," Ziri said, shaking her head. "I don't think he would."

Kryn looked back towards Haitu. The city and fortress were long gone. A twinge of excitement crept through her. She hoped she would find Rafik again, but leaving the desert was something she had been waiting years for. She drifted off to sleep dreaming of the marble columns of her home, the raucous crowd, and thunderous applause.

Chapter 23: The Fallen Order

Eko River, Alutopek

The water of the Eko River wasn't nearly as cold as the Tahlbiru Ocean. Being cooked under the desert heat, Rafik loved the water. He was thankful he didn't have his armor, as he was certain he would have sunk. He didn't look back once but hoped he may have found a ship he could climb aboard, but to no avail. As night loomed ahead, he shivered on the banks of the Eko River. Winter had crept in by now, and even though it was hot during the day, it was well below freezing during the night.

He sat up, pointing out the constellations. There was a twinge of guilt in his stomach. He had left Haitu, but at the cost of abandoning Ziri and Kryn. The three of them had grown close, and he hoped he could finish the adventure with them, and rescue Anza. "I'm coming for you." He said to himself for the countless time. It wasn't like he had much of a choice, though.

Rafik replayed the day's events again in his head. How Skage's power could reach this far south would have worried him if he hadn't realized Anza was with Gorik. She was safely in the bag, most likely hiding, and that was why Gorik hadn't noticed. He wasn't really one for snooping into what could be magical. Escaping Haitu was a personal disappointment. If he had Blaridane he could have defended himself. He could have made a difference and made King Vanarzir cower in fear. Now, even though it wasn't intentional, he owed the necromancer. Though he was about to be executed, so most likely wouldn't have his sword anyway. Just the thought of Blaridane in his hands sent a ripple through him. His fingers itched, and his mind turned from Anza to the cursed sword. He needed it. He needed them both.

His arms ached. Legs cried out with every step, but he kept moving forward. It didn't occur to him until now that he was free. No longer a prisoner of Samron, King Vanarzir, or the Kylix. Though he planned to reunite with Anza, and craved getting back Blaridane, he could do anything he wanted. Start a new life. Make a new name for himself. The Kylix were after Rafik. But he could hide and change his identity. He could be Frippit of Datz, and nobody would question it.

The thought of the name made him smile. It was a name Anza had made up for one of her stuffed toys he had made her. It always struck out to him as a silly name, and he tried imagining what the person with the name of Frippit looked like. The distracting thought helped him move forward, until his imaginings turned to reality. The sword. Blaridane. He didn't have to be a made up nobody if he had the sword. He could be invincible. A new warrior to defeat the king.

His shivering got worse as the night went on, thinking of the sword as he wandered northward. He was certain he was going to freeze to death. Even the water of the river seemed to chill him to the bone now. As he fell back in defeat into the sand, he saw it. A ship on the horizon. The torches lit, showing something was there. Rafik, determined it was now or never, jumped back into the water.

The water bit at him, freezing him. Ignoring the chilly river water, he swam towards the ship, realizing they had put an anchor down for the night. Thanking the gods, he made it to the ship. He didn't care if anyone saw him climbing the anchor. He just wanted to be dry and warm again. "Hello there." A whimsical voice said.

Rafik spun around, teeth clattering. "Hi." Just his luck, he had made it onto a Kylix ship. He was face to face with a Kylika soldier, the helmet beneath her arm.

"They're looking for you, Rafik." She said. "But you're safe with me."

"Um…thanks. Who are you?"

The girl took a step back and her face changed. It contorted and shimmered, caved in and ballooned out. Rafik gasped, watching as the girl standing in front of her now became a large, hairy, dark-skinned man. "You don't remember me?"

"You're part of the Kylika." Rafik said, glancing back at the river water. It didn't look too horrible now. "I don't remember your name, but I recognize your talent."

286

The man smiled, giggling a little before replying and shifting back into a little girl. "My name is Pyla."

"Nice to meet you, Pyla." Rafik nodded, still shivering. "You said I'm safe. Where am I?"

She handed him a blanket he eagerly wrapped himself up in. "You're aboard the *Fallen Order*."

"That's a weird name for a Kylix ship." Rafik said.

"It's not a Kylix ship. It's a refugee ship." Pyla explained. "It runs along the river, picking up those who escape the Kylix."

Rafik nodded. "So, where are you going? I see you're just anchored here."

"Yes," Pyla said, smiling. Her voice was almost hypnotic to listen to with her accent. "Just for the night. We are heading to Borlo, and from there into the Lahmora Swamp. Maybe the Bomoku Mountains. Both places the Kylix don't have that strong of a grip in."

"You're escaping?" Rafik asked.

Pyla nodded. "Yes. Samron took me to Sysinal, and on the way there he flagged down the *Fallen Order*. He told me to prepare once arriving there."

"Prepare for what?"

"War." Pyla said, the smile leaving her face. "We have two years to prepare before he starts collecting children again. It's time to stand up to him. Fight back."

"And Samron told you this?"

Pyla nodded. "He knows I've been wanting to escape for a couple years. This was his opportunity to let me go. Said he would claim I died fighting the necromancer."

"Samron helped you?"

"Yes, that's what I said." Pyla insisted. "I thought I could trust you. Do you not know about him?"

Rafik shook his head. "I don't know anything about him. When I first met him, he seemed to want to help. Now it just feels like he wants me in the Kylix."

"He doesn't like the king." Pyla said, turning to look out onto the water, gripping the side of the boat.

"Nobody does." Rafik said, turning to stand beside her, his shivering slowing.

"He's in a dangerous position, training the Kylix but also trying to lead a rebellion." Pyla said. "He shared with me what happened seven years ago, when the first attempt was made."

"What happened?"

"Nearly everyone died." Rafik said. "A man he called Gorik got away. But nobody else. Samron didn't have time to warn them. It was a slaughter."

"I know Gorik!" Rafik smiled. "I didn't know he was in a rebellion."

"I doubt he told many people." Pyla said."

"My father died seven years ago. Gorik was with him."

"Was he part of the rebellion?"

Rafik shrugged. "I don't know. Gorik said he got drunk and fell overboard."

"You'll have to ask him." Pyla said. "Will you help us, Rafik?"

"With what?" Rafik asked.

"The rebellion." Pyla said, a hint of a laugh at the end of her whimsical voice. "I can't imagine you'll be safe many other places now. Deserting the Kylix. Surprised you made it this far."

Rafik looked northward, then to Pyla. "I can't." He sighed. "I need to go north and find my sister."

"Family is important." Pyla said, nodding. "We have two years to prepare, Rafik. Don't take too long finding her."

Rafik smiled. "I won't. I think she is with Gorik."

"You can stay on the ship for tonight." Pyla said. "But we are continuing to head south once light hits the wall."

"Thank you." Rafik said, nodding. "I'll jump overboard by then."

Pyla giggled. "I like you, Rafik. I hope our paths cross again."

"They will, I'm sure." Rafik said. The two watched the moonlight glow through the Black Wall. It was a full moon, and it lit up the river like shimmering, liquid silver. The sands and distant red rock gave everything an otherworldly feel. "I'm sorry, but I have to ask."

"Oh." Pyla said, pulling herself away from her own thoughts. "What's that?"

"Your talent." Rafik said. "You can literally be anyone. You could hide from anybody you don't want to meet, and nobody would know. So why this?"

"Why what?"

Rafik gestured at all of her. "Why this. Why do you choose to look like that?"

"Because this is who I am." Pyla said with an innocent smile. "This is me. Yes, I can pretend to be other people, look like different people, but this is who I am. And I don't want to spend my life wearing a mask. I want to be me."

"I see." Rafik said, nodding, unsure of what to ask now. With her tone and answer, he felt like he crossed a line. Like asking something personal to a stranger. Which, she was. He barely knew her. "I'm sorry for asking." He finally stammered.

She took a deep breath and let it out slowly. "It's fine. Good night, Rafik." She wandered off, not looking back at him.

As he stood on the deck alone, he turned northward once more. A gust of wind sent a chill through him, and he gripped his blanket tighter. "I'm coming for you, Anza. And you, too, Blaridane." His hands wrapped around the railing, knuckles turning white. He wanted that sword. Almost needed it.

He stood there for several minutes before making his way to the lower decks. He found the galley and stocked up on food, even found a sword tucked away in a corner. He found more blankets, and wrapped the food in them, tying them to the end of his sword. If he was going to be going alone from here, at least he had some supplies now.

"Hey! You!" Rafik woke with a kick to his leg, leaning against the railing of the deck, wrapped in the blankets he had. He opened his eyes and lurched forward, seeing a Kylix soldier standing over him. "What are you doing? I don't recall you being on the ship. Stowaway?"

"Oh, um, I" Rafik stammered, getting to his feet.

"Relax." Pyla said, coming from below deck. "I helped him aboard last night."

"He's coming with us?" The soldier asked.

"No." Pyla said. "He's heading north to find his sister."

"Well, we're heading south." The soldier said.

"I told him. He's leaving the ship once we set off."

"Why are you dressed like a Kylix soldier?" Rafik asked.

"We're nearing Haitu. Camouflage." The soldier said. "Make sure he leaves." He marched off, checking the rigging of the sails.

"I didn't think the Kylix had a navy." Rafik said, stretching and yawning. "Was thinking about that last night."

"They don't." Pyla said. "Just about a dozen ships that were mostly converted from traders. Minus the *Fallen Order*."

The Black Wall began to glow in the east and shouts were called to raise the anchor. It was Rafik's queue to leave, and he stood on the rail, taking a deep breath, and turned back to Pyla. "Thank you." He flashed a smile, and before she could respond he was in the water.

"What are you doing?" She yelled to him.

"Swimming to shore." Rafik said, starting his way back to the sand of the desert.

"We could have rowed you to shore." Pyla shouted.

Rafik stopped mid stroke and turned. She was laughing at him, and a couple Kylix soldiers were lowering a dingy and were shaking their head. With cheeks bright red, Rafik swam away and continued to shore.

It didn't take long for Rafik to dry off. Trudging through sand he made his way northward, the heat beating down on him. He imagined Datz, the cool air and sea breeze cutting through the streets. He never thought he would miss the bitter cold winters, but anything beat the stagnant heat of the desert. It was like he was being cooked slowly. The canyons offered some cooler temperatures, but the heat still burned into him.

Hours had passed since leaving the *Fallen Order*. There was a trading ship on the other side of the river, he doubted anyone noticed him walking along the shore. There weren't many ships on the Eko River, something he wasn't surprised about. Trading with the south usually stopped during the winter in Datz. They probably could handle the cold as well as he could handle the heat.

The afternoon glow of the Black Wall bore down on him, and it wasn't long before he started seeing things. Mountains and pine trees in the distance. Even a lake. After running to them the second time, he realized they weren't real. "Ya shire." He cursed, doubling over, trying to catch his breath. He sat on the riverbank, dunking his head in the water and soaked his feet. At this rate, Skage will have taken over all Alutopek. The desert went on forever. More than once he considered floating down the river.

On the bright side, there was no sign of Haitu behind him. He turned, looking up the river. There, just on the horizon, was a dot on the river. It hadn't been there before, and it seemed to be come closer. Slowly, ever so slowly, it inched toward Rafik. It was too small to be a ship, but it was something, he was sure. After watching for several minutes, Rafik brushed himself off and continued to Datz. He couldn't spend all day watching a dot on the river grow closer.

It was an hour later, entering another canyon, when Rafik turned around. The dot had now taken shape. An older man in a canoe, paddling down the river. "You there!" The man shouted, paddling towards Rafik.

Rafik paused. He had seen the man before. His ring of thinning grey hair, thick bushy eyebrows, and deep wrinkles in his face were like a dream to Rafik. He knew he had seen him, but where? The older man stood up as he made it to the shore. It struck him where. And the memory sparked within Rafik. Back at the Sekolah Fortress. It was the old man he had seen in the Hall of Records. His eyes widened and he turned to run. The man shouted for him, but Rafik didn't stop. The next moment there was a sting in his neck and his world went dark.

It was the warmth Rafik noticed first. The stagnant, dry heat that permeated the desert. He was beginning to think he'd never feel the cool air of his home again. The next thing was the crackling of a flame behind him. He could hear the fires chatter as it devoured the wood. He couldn't tell how much smoke there was. It was darker than shadow from what he could see. He grumbled, trying to move, and noticed the rest of his surroundings.

His eyes adjusting, he could make out a cave wall, reddish in color. He was in a chair, bound and tied. He tried turning his head and could see a hooded figure out of the corner of his eye. The figure tended the fire, stirring a cauldron full of something bubbling. The figure noticed Rafik and turned him around in the chair.

"You're awake." He said.

Rafik recognized the voice of the old man. "What happened?" He didn't remember getting here. Last he remembered was the man stepping out of the canoe.

"You ran." The old man, said. "And I didn't know who you are."

"I saw you at the Hall of Records." Rafik said.

"Yes. Which is why you're tied up."

Rafik paused. "What are you going to do to me?"

"I'm not sure yet. What's your name, boy?"

"Xeo." Rafik lied. "Maybe you've heard of me."

"Xeo?" The man asked, nearly gasping. His eyes widened, nearly peeking through his thick eyebrows. "Yes, I've heard everything about you." The man stepped forward, brandishing a knife.

Rafik started to protest when he cut the ropes, freeing him instead. "Oh, thank you."

"Anything for a friend." The man smiled. "I know your sister. My name is Paris."

"My sister never mentioned you."

Paris laughed. "I'd be surprised if she did. We met after she was taken."

"Where is she?"

"Probably Detnu by now. Off to be wed. If not already. I do lose track of time often. All things considering." Paris laughed, glancing over at the boiling liquid in the cauldron.

"Detnu?"

"Oh, you've been missing for some time." Paris said. "Though I must know what you were doing in the Sekolah Fortress. We thought you were still up north, Xeo."

"I got hurt." Rafik said. "Samron found me and took me to Krista. She healed me and I escaped."

Paris nodded. "I see. Well, your sister made a deal with the king. She would go with him if her home was safe. Vanarzir agreed, until you challenged him to a duel. After you escaped the king ordered for your home to be burned down. And he forced your sister to join him.

Rafik could hear Blaridane's voice within him. Together they could have beat Vanarzir, and not run away. His skin itched and crawled, wanting the sword in his hands. He needed it. "All because of me?" He finally asked.

Paris nodded. "You were the first to challenge the king and almost win. He had to do something."

"It takes months to get to Detnu from Kristol." Rafik said. "How did she get there so fast?

"Very observant." Paris smiled. "According to your sister, she was taken by a black dragon."

"A black dragon?" Rafik asked, trying to sound skeptical. He had seen that dragon fly away with her in it. Its roar sent a shiver down his spine. "Dragons aren't real. The ones that are, are nothing more than wolf-sized lizards with bad tempers."

"That's what they've become." Paris nodded. "Yet she insisted it was a large black dragon. Rathsa was its name."

"How?" Rafik asked. He imagined the monster he saw terrorizing the people of Alutopek. Death on wings, turning everything to ash. "Surely someone would have seen it."

"The king is mysterious." Paris said. "I've been trying to learn about him for years. But all I get is darkness. It's as if he were a mirage; never truly there. But I know that isn't true. It can't be. Magic doesn't work like that."

"Studying him? And what do you know about magic?"

"Oh, I know more about magic than any other man alive at this point, I'm sure. For example, there are four sources of magic, and have their own hierarchy." Paris explained. "Though I believe a fifth can be debated."

"Have you heard of the Silver Council?" Rafik asked.

"How do you know about the Silver Council?"

"They were mentioned in the Hall of Records." Rafik said. "I've never heard of them."

"The Silver Council was the highest order. In ancient times, magic users were governed by the Silver Council. They determined magical law and worked with kings and queens to better lives. They disbanded some time ago, though."

"How do you know all this?"

"Oh! I'm so sorry, Xeo. Sometimes I ramble on, thinking you know enough to follow along. I am a Bantrita."

"A storyteller." Rafik nodded. "Is all of what you say just stories?"

"A historian. Truth seekers" Paris corrected. "My brotherhood records all of history, documenting everything. The libraries of Detnu are filled because of us. We have vaults all over Alutopek with records. After Vanarzir became king he outlawed and banished us. Relegating what's left of the once proud organization as nothing more than storytellers. Very few remain."

"Do you stalk people and interview others?"

"Of course not!" Paris laughed. "How could you ever get the truth by asking everyone?" People only convey what they want to. You'd never get a full, let alone accurate, story."

"You know," Rafik started, smiling. "Never and always are two words you always want to remember never to use."

Paris laughed. "I like you, Xeo. No, I will show you what we do. Come here."

Rafik followed him to the cauldron. Steam wafted off the pinkish orange potion. It looked like liquid sunset captured within. The fire had been extinguished while they were speaking, but the concoction still bubbled as if the heat were still there. It gave off an unnatural but enticing glow. He reached out his hand and felt the cold potion tickle at his fingertips. It was colder than the Tahlbiru Ocean. "Magic?" He asked.

"Magic." Paris confirmed. Without warning he plucked a hair from Rafik and tossed it into the brew. It frothed and swirled before changing to a clear sheen. Colors bubbled up, exploding into a scene. It was like a moving portrait.

Rafik clung to the edge of the cauldron, mouth agape. The colors slowed and formed. Seconds later he was watching himself in the Sarason Fortress. Skage had crawled out of the bag. Anza was still in there. He knew it. He watched himself get beaten, the sword being ripped from his grasp from Skage. He felt his side burn, watching himself be stabbed and poisoned. Ziri and Gorik arrived, saving him. The vision ended as Gorik said Rafik's name.

"Call me crazy," Paris said, the joy in his voice gone. "But I don't believe you are Xeo."

Rafik turned and saw Paris's eyes narrowing, brows creased. The frown sank into his face like sagging jowls of a hound dog. He raised his hands in the air, noticing the knife Paris held. "I can explain."

"I don't like liars." Paris snapped. "It seems your story is quite interesting. I'll be happy to learn more. Though your story ends here." Paris lunged forward. Rafik sidestepped and pulled on Paris's extended arm. The old man fell to the ground. He spun around, throwing the knife at Rafik. It missed the boy by inches.

Rafik picked up the knife and kicked over the cauldron, sprinting away deeper into the cave. "I'm not the bad guy!" He shouted over his shoulder. He came to the end of the cave, lit by a campfire in the center. The light he was following was this, and not the outside world. He found his sword and blankets with a single book on it. He recognized the outline of a dragon, and the constellation of giants. "Diary of Nekvaz." He read aloud. This was the book from the Hall of Records Kryn took.

He grabbed the book and felt the memories of the author flood into him. He fought off the urge, watching flashes of someone's memory. He tried pushing them away, and the memories merged with reality. He was still in the cave, but now surrounded by pine trees. He would blink and now he could see himself entering a foggy landscape, the roar of a dragon behind him mixing with the screams of Paris.

"A liar and a thief." Paris said, snatching the book from Rafik's hand. "You may not be the enemy, but you aren't good."

"You can't keep me here." Rafik said. He could already see how he would do it. Use the knife, lunge forward and slash at the throat before making his escape. How much more powerful he would be if he had Blaridane! He was confident Paris would already be dead if he did. "Let me through, and I'll let you live."

Paris shook his head. "I can't allow that." The storyteller whistled a tune. Moments later five men arrived. Three with bows and two with swords. "Drop the knife."

"Ya shire." Rafik cursed, glaring at each of the men. He threw down the knife and spat on the ground. This wouldn't have happened if he had Blaridane. "You cheated." Nodding at each of the archers.

"No, just prepared."

Rafik was led back to the room with the cauldron tying him back up to the chair. The five guards didn't say anything and disappeared into the cave.

"They may not be so kind next time." Paris said. "What should we do with you, Rafik the lying thief?"

"I'm not a thief." Rafik said.

"You tried stealing my book." Paris said, holding up the diary.

"That isn't yours." Rafik said. "You stole it from the Hall of Records."

"Just like your friend stole a book, too." Paris said.

296

"What? I don't know what you're talking about." Rafik said.

"You really want to keep lying, thief? I saw her hide a book. No, this was waiting for me at the Hall of Records." Paris corrected. "Your friend has the decoy. What should we do with you?"

"I'd love it if you let me go." Rafik said. "I have places to be."

"Do you think this is a game?"

"Not at all." Rafik smiled. "I just know something you don't."

"And what's that?"

"You need me."

The laughter from Paris echoed throughout the cave, ringing Rafik's ears. "I need you?"

Rafik nodded. "Your brotherhood needs me."

"And why is that?" Paris asked. "The brotherhood doesn't look kindly on liars and thieves."

"I'm not a liar or a thief." Rafik said. "You need that potion to tell your stories."

"History!" Paris corrected. "Our history."

"You need that potion." Rafik repeated. "I don't."

"What do you mean?"

"Did you ever wonder why I was frozen when you found me holding the book you stole?"

"Attack of conscience?" Paris asked.

"No." Rafik shook his head. "I can see things into the past. And I was having a vision just by holding the book."

"Really now?" Paris laughed. "And what did you see?"

"I'm not sure." Rafik said. "I was trying to fight it off so I could escape. I heard a dragon's roar."

"And you know what a dragon sounds like?" Paris asked. "You could have just said that after seeing the cover."

"I do, actually." Rafik said. "I've seen one."

Paris glared at Rafik, pacing back and forth. "Yet you were arguing about them and magic when we first spoke."

"That was when I was Xeo." Rafik said. "I doubt he has seen dragons or magic."

"You are a liar." Paris snapped, wagging a finger at Rafik. "Your lies and trickery won't work with me."

Rafik sighed. "I can prove it. Give me the book."

"No."

"Why?"

"You'll run off with it."

It was Rafik's turn to laugh. He moved back and forth, rattling the chair before it fell on its side. "Yes, I can just sprint out of here the second you give me the book."

Paris muttered under his breath, cursing, before grabbing the book. "Alright, tell me who is Nekvaz." He tossed the book to Rafik, who could barely grasp it with his fingers. His vision blurred, as he wondered who Nekvaz was.

The room was vast, filled with shelves and shelves of books. There were monks frantically scribbling on parchments beside a smaller cauldron the one Paris had in his cave. Stained glass windows caused colored light to sprinkle the tops of tables and books. A handful of Kylix soldiers surrounded a boy with messy hair and icy blue eyes at a table, studying ancient maps.

"You look busy." A deep voice said, causing the boy to jump. The Kylix soldiers turned, but nobody was there beside him. The boy shrugged it off and continued tracing his finger along a trade route when the voice came again. "I'm sure I can help." Again, the boy turned, as well as some soldiers. And again, nothing.

The boy closed the book, and a figure appeared out of thin air, sitting beside him. The boy jumped, causing his chair to crash to the ground and echo through the large library. "Who are you?" The boy asked.

Kylix soldiers turned, swords drawn and pointing at the man holding a peculiar helmet away from his face. His dark skin made his crimson hair look even brighter. "A friend." He said. "My name is Nekvaz. But my friends call me Nek."

"I'm Prince Vanarzir." The boy said. "Can you help?"

Rafik gasped. The old man with the icy blue eyes that sentenced him to death. He tried smacking him in the back of the head, but his hand went through him like all his other visions. He was a ghost. And no matter how bad he wanted he couldn't throttle young Vanarzir.

Nek nodded. "I've been watching you for quite some time. You're looking for something."

"Yes." Prince Vanarzir said. "I'm trying to find the World Beneath the World. Have you heard of it?"

"The land of the Immortals." Nek said. "I have. And I know how to get there."

Rafik's vision blurred, and his stomach lurched.

"Well?" Paris asked, yanking away the book. "You should have seen enough by now to know who he was."

"I was still in the memory." Rafik said.

"I don't care. Who is he?" Paris said. "If you're right, maybe we could use you."

"His friends called him Nek. He was friends with King Vanarzir."

Paris nodded. "It may seem you know something. Tell me, can you read this?" He opened the book and saw runes he'd never seen before jotted down on the pages.

"No." Rafik shook his head. "I don't even recognize those."

"I doubted you would." Paris said. "Tell me, Rafik, what were you doing in the Hall of Records with the Kylix."

Rafik shared his story, from losing his mother, to the tunnels and watching Skage return. He shared how he made it to the fortress, and Samron seemed to lie to him. How King Vanarzir sentenced him to death, and he escaped from Skage's ambush on Haitu.

"I'm heading to Trinkit to find a translator. The runes are of the Dragonborn." Paris said.

"Why don't you go to the Dragonborn?" Rafik asked. "Might be easier."

299

"The Dragonborn don't like outsiders. If Nekvaz was one, but friends with Vanarzir, he had to have been an exile. They hate exiles more than they do outsiders." Paris explained. "I would like to avoid there if possible."

"Why did you steal it from the Hall of Records?"

"I didn't steal it." Paris insisted. "Xeo's sister, the soon-to-be Queen Kay, was given the book by an invisible man on her way to Detnu. She brought it here in hopes the Bantrita would find it."

"Why?" Rafik asked.

"That's what I was about to find out before you ruined the potion." Paris said. "Why is this book so important, and who is Nekvaz? But you answered the last question."

"Do I get some sort of reward?" Rafik asked, glancing down at his bound arms and legs, still laying on his side in the chair.

Paris laughed. "How would you like to come to Trinkit with me? You can find your sister, I'll find a translator, and then you return to me. You are right, Rafik. My brotherhood needs you."

Chapter 24: Escaping the Dead

Eko River, Alutopek

Rafik skimmed his hand along the water's surface. It had gotten colder since traveling with Paris. And they were making good time. With the blankets and food they had, the two would paddle down the river during the day, and float down it at night. The only time they got out was to stretch their legs. It was a tight fit in the canoe, but it beat walking along the riverbank and in the sand. After a few seconds of the cold water, he pinched his arm.

"Thinking of it again?" Paris asked. "The sword?"

Rafik nodded. Since leaving they had shared their stories. Paris told him that every time he thought of Blaridane to pinch himself, to help kick the craving. "I don't think it's working."

"It takes time." Paris said. "Doing that helped me get out of my more...unhealthy habits. That sword should be destroyed."

"Could you look into its past?"

"Oh, I'm sure I could." Paris said. "I just need to make a new potion and have the sword. I don't have conjuring abilities to summon the moments I want to see. I'm surprised you can't."

"It was like it was alive." Rafik said. "I could see flashes of memory while it fought, but the rest of the time it was quiet and cold. Like a living thing."

"It's an abomination." Paris said for the countless time.

Rafik nodded, but his mind drifted. He could feel Blaridane calling for him, the closer they got. Skage was a necromancer. A wizard. He didn't need swords. He used magic. But Rafik, he needed a sword. He could use it. And deep within his mind he could hear the sword beckoning him, wishing to be in his grasp once more. Not on the wall as another's prize. "I guess." He finally answered.

"Would you consider joining the Bantrita?" Paris asked.

"What?" Rafik asked, being yanked from his daydream of the sword. It seemed that ever since he realized Anza was safe with

Gorik all he could think about was Blaridane. "Oh, I never thought about it."

"With your talent you could be an amazing one." Paris said.

"What about the king?" Rafik said, taking a bite of an apple. "He outlawed all of you."

"Look around, Rafik." Paris said. "There is so much unrest in Alutopek. The people east of the Eko River are preparing for war. The king is taking everyone's children to try and prevent that. He created the Black Wall, stealing everyone's talent but you're proof now even that is fading. There's unrest in the Timlin Forest, and the Gateway Mountains has pockets of rogues. And now hearing about this Xeo child. The king's power, whether he wants to admit it or not, is fading. I'm sure by the time you are my age he will be gone."

"Do you think the new king would allow the Bantrita?" Rafik asked.

Paris smiled. "If there is no king, Queen Valkayto would become ruler. And I'm positive she would."

"Oh." Rafik said, nodding. "I don't know. When I had Blaridane I loved fighting. The blood pumping, heart racing. It's like my senses on overdrive and everything is going so fast, but slow enough I can see my way through with ease. I love that feeling. I'm not sure if I could stare into a magical potion all my life, documenting things that have already happened. I want to be the one to make things happen."

"I understand." Paris said, nodding. He tossed the paddle to Rafik. "With your talent I doubt you would need the potion. And we don't spend all our time doing that. Sometimes we're treasure hunters. Even I enjoy a good adventure from time to time."

"Treasure hunters?" Rafik laughed. "I've never heard that before."

"My mentor saw in a vision of a chalice that could grant anyone who drinks from it the power of invisibility. It fascinated him, and he spent the rest of his life searching for it. Traced it all the way to Datz before the trail ran cold. Almost like it ceased to exist. Our role is to document everything. That includes the whereabouts of treasure."

"So, you're saying that you know where all the treasures in the entire world are?" Rafik asked, guiding the canoe away from a rock jutting out of the river.

Paris laughed. "It would be ignorant to say we know where everything is, but we know enough."

"I'll think about it." Rafik said.

"Please do."

He pretended to concentrate on paddling. After a day with Paris, he started liking to paddle. He didn't have to pinch himself while thinking of Blaridane, and he could daydream all he wanted. Reuniting with Anza was one of his favorites. *'Hang in there, Rafik.'* He thought to himself. *'Just a little longer.'*

The rest of the day was mostly silent. The two took turns paddling, sightseeing, and napping. There wasn't much else to do in a canoe in the middle of the river, in a desert. Everywhere looked the same, and the canyons were so far between them it was mostly just sand. The chilly evening air surprised them both. Clouds swirled above them, and thunder rumbled in the distance.

"I didn't think it rained in the desert." Rafik said, holding out his hand and waiting for the droplets to hit.

"It does along the river in the north." Paris said. "Not sure of anywhere else. And only during the winter."

"It doesn't snow?" Rafik whipped around, eye wide.

"Nope." Paris shook his head. "Too warm. A lot of places don't get snow. This one looks different, though."

"What do you mean?" Rafik asked.

"Look up there." Paris said, pointing at the storm clouds. "They're swirling. They usually just move eastward.

Rafik shrugged. He hadn't studied storm clouds enough to worry when one swirled instead of blew. Clouds were clouds, moving endlessly above him, out of reach. As the rain started pouring, he tucked away the paddle. They each wrapped themselves in the blankets, floating down the river.

The storm raged, causing the canoe to jostle and lean one way and then another. More than once they both thought the canoe would capsize. But the small sturdy boat continued down the river. The darkness prevented them from seeing anything ahead. They only noticed a Kylix ship anchored just before hitting it. It took the two of them pushing themselves off the boat to stop it. They heard shouts from the Kylix ship, but within moments the voices were drowned out by the pattering of rain and roaring of thunder. They continued down river, secretly praying they would be safe.

They couldn't tell as the darkness and rain prevailed how long they had been floating now. The storm refused to stop or slow to a drizzle. It relentlessly came down on them like the gods themselves were trying to wash them away. The glowing light of the Black Wall never came, but through flashes of lightning they could see it. Just ahead was the twin towered fortress of the Eko River. The Golden Gate.

Rafik didn't remember arriving there the first time, but recalling the dead screaming and attacking at him flashed into his head. "We need to get out." He yelled over the storm.

Paris shook his head. "We can take shelter in there. Make our way to Trinkit after the storm."

"No." Rafik said. "The dead are in there."

Paris's face paled. He had remembered hearing Rafik's stories. "Maybe they're dead again?"

Rafik shook his head. "I'm not going in there."

The river picked up speed, pushing them closer to the Golden Gate. Rafik could see the gates open from when he and the others escaped. The river was too fast, and the two were nearing the fortress. Rafik jumped into the river, breaking free of the soggy blankets and swam to shore. Paris called for him to come back, as he entered the Golden Gate.

"Paris!" Rafik shouted just after a rumble of thunder. He stood on the shore just outside of the Golden Gate. His hands were trembling, teeth clattering. The few clothes he had on clung to him, weighing him down. It was windier here, as the freezing winds cut into him, chilling him to the bone. Maybe hiding in a fortress filled with the dead would be better than freezing to death outside. "Ya shire." He shook his head, and inched his way to the door, legs trembling.

"Help me!" Paris shouted.

It was the first thing Rafik heard as he opened the door. Rafik hurried inside, heart racing even faster. He watched the corpses slowly get to their feet. Their screams were muted by the storm, pouring down around them. He glanced over and saw Paris in the canoe, a dozen of the undead crowding him. Rafik charged forward, shoving two into the water.

Paris screamed, holding out his hand. "Help me!"

Rafik yanked on his hand, pulling him out of the canoe and onto the fortress floor. More of the dead began dragging themselves towards them. "We need to get out of here."

"How are they alive?" Paris shouted. "That's not possible."

Rafik dipped and weaved between the dead as they lunged for him. Paris, while trying to reel in his fears, followed suit. The two made it out the door, slamming it shut. The dead pounded on the door, trying to break free. It wasn't long until the pounding stopped. "I told you we shouldn't go in there. Did you not believe me?"

"I-I believed you." Paris said, teeth clattering. He pulled out his hair, taking out chunks of the so few he had, "It's-It's another thing seeing it."

"Well, we're safe. And almost to Trinkit. We need to keep moving or we'll definitely freeze." Rafik said.

Paris nodded, and screamed once more as he walked away from the door. A handful of corpses fell through, the door swinging open. They were dead once more. "I take it back."

"Take what back?"

"If we survive this adventure." Paris said. "I'm done. I'd rather stare into a potion the rest of my life."

Rafik laughed.

The storm didn't stop as the two walked to Trinkit. They didn't stop, Rafik from worrying that if he did, he would freeze and die; Paris from wanting to get himself as far away from the living dead as possible. More than once the Bantrita looked back, fearing the dead were behind him. With every growl of thunder he jumped, taking an extra step or two in haste.

"Just imagine being in there while you couldn't walk." Rafik laughed.

"They can't be stopped. How can you stop the dead from waking up?" Paris asked.

"By stopping the man doing it." He pointed at the tower in the middle of the Tahlbiru Ocean. He could just make out the tower with the spider. It was easy to see the spider, though, as the red eyes glowed with a hateful hunger that chilled him even more.

"I'm not going there. That was enough. And how do we know Trinkit isn't full of them?" Paris asked. "I'll risk working with the Dragonborn instead of the horde of the dead."

Rafik smiled. He kept calm, imagining Blaridane at his side. The fury wasn't there, but the thought alone was enough to help him move forward. His hands itched for the blade, but he kept the thought to himself. He looked at the Sarason Fortress again. Anza wasn't there. But his sword was. She was safe with Gorik. He just wanted his sword.

Trinkit was always off limits to Rafik. It was too unsafe of a place for children. His mother worried he would be taken and enslaved, his father always worried he would be lost to the darkness of the city. Surprisingly, he never wanted to travel there. He held some animosity towards them. After the Black Wall, Trinkit flourished while Datz crumbled away. It was almost like the favor of the gods now shined on Trinkit instead of Datz. But now, seeing the city come in to view, those feelings were gone. He didn't care if the city was run by monsters. He just wanted to be dry again.

The city couldn't be seen from Datz, and he rarely sailed close enough to it. He could see the silhouette of temple steeples in the center of town, and buildings of varying heights surrounded it. There wasn't anything ominous or evil about it. As they approached, he noticed a wall, hastily built, guards standing in front. They pointed their spears at them, telling them to freeze.

Rafik shook his head, smiling. "We already are." He shouted.

Paris glared at Rafik. "Now isn't the time for jokes."

"Who are you?" The guard asked, ignoring the joke.

"I am Paris Bantrita, and this is Rafik of Datz."

"Bantrita?" The guard asked. "Don't get many storytellers here anymore."

"We need shelter from the rain."

The guard nodded. "Come on in. We just had to make sure you weren't one of the dead."

"You were able to stop them?" Rafik asked.

"No." The guard said. "We defended our city. Then they just stopped. We have scouts reporting they're roaming all over the Nyler Peninsula. Most haven't made it passed the Bruin Fortress. But we get some."

Rafik thanked the guards allowing entry and entered the city. Gorik had told him how the streets were littered with drunkards, women of loose morals, and the downright nasty. He wasn't sure if it was the storm, or the fear of the dead, but the streets were quiet. Only the occasional guard marched along the walkways. The streets, now muddy and large puddles made each section of the city its own miniature island in some places.

"This way." Paris said, leading Rafik to the heart of the city.

The temple could be seen from any direction, with its spires and towers reaching into the sky. He wondered if the one in Datz ever looked this impressive. "Are we going to pray?" Rafik asked, noticing they were getting closer.

Paris shook his head. "I don't know where to find a translator. So, we're going to Pirate's Alley."

"If you don't know where to find one, why there?"

"Here's a great piece of advice. Pirate's Alley has everything." Paris smiled, jumped over a large puddle, and helped

Rafik across. "If you can't find what you need here, it doesn't exist."

The sign of the Silver Shark swayed, being beaten relentlessly by the storm. The arm sticking out of the shark's mouth still pointed at the door. The aroma inside was what Rafik expected the entire town to smell like. Dozens of different perfumes permeating through the air, with an underlying aroma of alcohol. A crowd of boisterous men grabbing at women and laughter erupting from all corners. How anyone could speak in here, let alone have a conversation, was beyond him.

After speaking to the barman Paris turned to Rafik. "Well, Rafik." He sighed, putting his hand on the boy's shoulder. "It's been an adventure getting here. It would be irresponsible of me to leave you in a place like this, though I doubt you want to continue any further with me. My translator is on up ahead, and you are hellbent on reuniting with your sister and that sword. Don't deny it. I know you still crave its power over you. If you change your mind, you can find me with this." He flipped Rafik a golden coin.

Rafik caught it in midair. There was a book on one side, and a cauldron on the other with the four points of the compass along the rigid edge of the coin. "Thank you." Rafik said, looking up. Paris was gone, lost in the sea of people within the tavern. He turned around, glancing from one face to another, and didn't recognize anyone. "Excuse me."

The barman turned and gave Rafik the once over. "What can I do you for?

"I'm looking for someone. A sailor." Rafik said.

"You've come to the right place. Plenty of them here, boy." The barman said. "Where's your parents?"

"Dead, sir." Rafik answered. "I'm looking for Gorik of Datz. Has a peg leg, bald, shorter than usual."

"Ah, Gorik! He's a friendly fellow. If you're looking for a new dad, can't go wrong with him, I say." The barman smiled. "Let's see, Gorik." The barman looked around before snapping his fingers and yelling. "Oy! You!" He pointed at a woman handing drinks to a man. "Have you seen Gorik?"

The woman shook her head. "Not for a long time."

"Thought not." The barman said. "I haven't seen him for a couple months. Left here with Samron and Ziri. If you know those two?"

Rafik nodded. "I know them. Thank you."

"Hold on!" The barman said, as Rafik turned to leave. "It wouldn't sit well with me with you leaving. 'Specially with storm out. You can stay here until the morning. Oy!" He called over the woman he had asked for Gorik. "This orphan doesn't have a home. Take him to a bed for the night."

The woman nodded, and took Rafik's hand, leading him up the stairs. "You'll be safe here for the night." She said, opening one of the several doors. "Here's the key. Don't lose it and stay inside. I'll go fetch you some supper."

Before Rafik could thank her, she was gone. He closed the door, locking it, and turned to the bed. It called to him more than any sword could. The soft pillow and mattress topped with thick, heavy blankets. He stripped off his wet clothes, throwing them near a smoldering fire, and jumped into bed. It wasn't long before he was asleep.

Chapter 25: The Convocation

Sysinal, Akitung Jungle, Alutopek

Gorik hooted with excitement, sprinting across the sea of sand. The dry air failed to tire him. Nothing could deter him as he ran for the first time in seven years. He never thought he would have ever missed running. But feeling the wind break across his face as he hurried across the desert proved otherwise. He had two legs again, and he wasn't going to squander this gift a second time around.

He didn't notice the sand dragons that caused so much strife before, though he never looked back to check either. He knew he was making better time leaving the Dragon's Roost than he did getting there. Izamar and Anza would find a way to get her out of the portrait while he told everyone how to defeat Skage.

He would make his way to Sysinal. A city on the other side of the Eko River and home to the best fighters. He had only been there a handful of times. They were one of the first cities to reject King Vanarzir. Their ruler was whoever was strongest. He had heard rumor on his travels several years ago that a young girl almost became that, having an extraordinary talent. What happened to her nobody knew. He guessed that like so many other fighters, they fell during battle.

It wasn't until a full day later that Gorik began to tire. He made camp, cooking a chicken he had taken from the Dragon's Roost. The cold desert air was bitter, and his breath lingered in front of him. It wouldn't be long now until winter was here. He had never spent a winter in the desert, but he didn't want to experience one either. He imagined snowstorms pouring down on the desert, only to melt away during the day. He knew Haitu never received snow, but this far north, he wondered. The days were getting shorter and the nights longer. If there was going to be snow, it would be any day now.

A few days later he had reached the banks of the Eko River. Just beyond he saw the dunes hiding the Warrior City. He paced back and forth along the bank, trying to find the best place to cross. It was along one of the bends that the current appeared slower and shores closer together. Without wasting a moment, he jumped into the river and swam across. His arms and legs screamed with fatigue and on the other side he had to lay and rest on the sand.

Gorik woke with a start, a blunt jab at his side. As he reached for a sword a man stepped on his arm. "I would have thought you'd be much more cautious than sleeping on the banks of the Eko River." His attacker growled.

Gorik looked up at the bald man pinning down his arm. He smiled, noting the moon tattoo over his left eye and emerald gem embedded on the top of his right hand. Another tattoo of a dragon wrapping itself around a sword was on his arm. "Shallon! So good to see you."

Shallon smiled, extended a hand, and helped his friend up. "Tell me, did the Datians make it to Emerald?"

"I'm afraid not." Gorik said, his joyous mood turning to one of somber. "After our meeting I arrived home as the Kylix finished their attack. We fled. They left heading east."

"And why aren't you with them?" Shallon asked.

Gorik recounted everything that had happened as the two walked towards Sysinal. He mentioned Dragon's Roost, but not its location. It was Izamar's secret he entrusted Gorik with. Didn't want to betray a wizard's trust, after all.

"Ya shire." Shallon cursed. "I told you magic wasn't completely gone. Glad to see you have your leg again. Almost thought you a specter because of it."

"I am quite fond of this leg." Gorik laughed, patting his new appendage. "I thought you were heading to Lynn?"

"I was." Shallon said. "Until I got this." Shallon held up a scroll, handing it to Gorik. It was mostly blank save for random letters written in silver.

Gorik studied the scroll. "A convocation at Sysinal?"

Shallon nodded. "The Soniky are returning."

311

"We'll see." Gorik laughed. "Traveling with Samron, I was thinking it may happen. But going through the desert on my own, I had time to think. The trainer will just lead everyone to their deaths. Just like last time."

"Only one way to find out." Shallon said. "I am going. And maybe we can shake things up."

"I'm listening." Gorik flashed a devious smile, looking up at his giant friend.

"It's a convocation. It's time to decide our future, and who to lead it."

"I like the way you think." Gorik chuckled. "Well, I'm already heading there anyway. Might as well join you."

"I must say." Shallon began after the two had walked a distance in silence. "It's nice walking with you with both your legs."

"I'm quite happy about it." Gorik laughed. "But I do miss my rum. Would have liked if the wizard made me taller, too."

"I would have thought that stuff would have killed you a long time ago." Shallon said.

"Yes, well, we can't all be sober like you. Somebody has to be the bad example."

The two erupted into laugher, climbing the final dunes of the desert. The white marble city of Sysinal stood on the edge of the Biodlay Desert and Akitung Jungle. The lush greens were a sight for sore eyes, after traveling through sand for weeks. Echoes of cheers could be heard from here. The entire city was one massive coliseum. Long ago it was a place to hold annual sport, but now it was home to warriors. Legends said the city used to spread across the edge of the two regions, but slowly nature reclaimed the city. Now only the coliseum remained. It stood as tall as a mountain and glistened in the glowing light of the Black Wall. It was like a fallen star as the midday light made the white marble shine. Roars of cheering adoration echoed from the arched windows far up into the sky. At the base was a ring of more arches, most of them bricked up.

The entries that weren't bricked closed had warriors in different kinds of armor, and some patched together from differing suits. Most had little armor but held a spear or sword that looked like it could cleave stone in two with how strong the warriors were.

"Names." The guards demanded. "Shallon of Emerald and Gorik of Datz." Shallon said.

"Do you wish to enter the fights?"

"No." Gorik said.

"Very well. Leave all weapons with us." The guard said. "You can pick them up when you leave."

The two turned in their swords and were allowed entry. There were rows of markets and brothels, some on top of the other, all circling around the fighting arenas. Only fighters or those in competition were allowed onto the sands of the arena. The two made their way, circling through the coliseum. There were metal smiths, homes, jewelers, bakeries, butcher shops and training areas. They turned down a spiral staircase and into the dungeons of the city. A long walk across a dark corridor and they came to a door bolted shut.

Shallon wrapped on the door making a rhythmic pattern. The door opened, and Samron appeared. "Gorik? I'm surprised to see you here."

"Not as much as I am seeing this letter." Gorik said, holding up the scroll.

"Where is Anza? Please tell me you didn't bring her here?" Samron asked.

"No, she isn't here. She's safe. Where is Rafik?"

Samron's face turned grim. He looked down as he opened the door further. "We will have to talk about him after this meeting."

"What happened?" Gorik insisted, grabbing Samron's robes.

"After the meeting." Samron insisted. "Now everyone, find a seat."

Gorik looked around and saw a long table filled with only half of what could fill it. Maybe a little more than a dozen, he

313

guessed. He recognized some from the last time a meeting like this had occurred. Some new faces. He shook his head. "We're all dead if this is it."

"The time has come." Samron said. "The time has come to stop King Vanarzir. I know we tried in the past. But I am certain of it this time."

"You were last time." Gorik said. A few of the others grunted in approval.

"I have been serving in the Kylix in hopes to find a weakness. To bring down the king. His recent campaign to take the children and force them into the army has soured many. His brutality has scared so many into submission. But now, my friends, now is the time."

"And why is that?" Shallon asked.

"As some of you may have heard, there is a necromancer in the Sarason Fortress." Samron said. "His power is great. I've witnessed it myself."

"Yes. We stopped the fighting arena because of that unnatural ability." One woman, Annorla, spoke up. Gorik hadn't seen her in nearly seven years. Her golden skin and fiery amber eyes glistened in the torchlight. She still looked just as beautiful, and just as intimidating.

"Indeed." Samron said. "Now the king is sending his Kylika, the soldiers with talent, to defeat Skage. We need to do it."

"Us?" Annorla asked. "Why?"

"This threat is exactly what the king needs to prove how great he is and why all children should be enlisted. But if we defeat this monster, we prove to everyone we don't need the king. We don't need his army. We can take care of ourselves." Samron explained. "This is our chance to inspire others."

"We just need to take on an unholy wizard who can raise the dead." Another interrupted. "And how can we defeat such a being?"

"I-I know how." Gorik said.

314

Samron's eyes widened before his face melted into that of relief. "Much of this convocation was to figure out a way to defeat him. So, by all means, please tell us." He gestured for him to talk.

"The necromancer's name is Skage. From what I understand he is a shoddy wizard at best. He relies on relics for his power. Mainly the Kymu-Guiden Talisman and snowflake talismans. If we get those talismans, we can stop Skage."

"The trick is getting to them. That'll be next to impossible." Shallon said, glancing down at his emerald embedded into his hand.

"I don't think so." Gorik said. "While on my way here I thought of an idea. He relies on the talismans. He will use its powers to summon his minions to fight us. While he's doing that a couple of us could sneak into the fortress and take out Skage. He would be too distracted with the battle to notice us."

The others murmured with the news. Samron smiled from ear to ear. "So, it is decided. The Soniky will return to defeat this necromancer and start the rebellion."

Gorik raised his hand. "I will support this. But I make one recommendation before I commit."

"And what's that, old friend?" Samron asked.

"I demand a new leader." Gorik said.

"I second this." Shallon said.

Samron gasped, glaring at the two men. The others in the room raised their hands, nodding their approval. "So be it." He spat with venom. "And who do you recommend lead this newly formed rebellion?"

Kryn eagerly handed the guards her sword and two knives concealed on her back. A storm slowed their arrival, and more than once thought their ship may capsize. But she was finally here. Home. It had been too long since she was home in Sysinal. The smell of blood and sweat mixed with baked goods flooded her with memories of her home. Of her father. She recognized the small shops and some of the people still selling their wares. They were granted to go anywhere in the city so long as they didn't cause trouble and were back at the ship by morning. It was then they would sail to the Golden Gate with Samron to begin the fight Skage.

"Where are we going?" Ziri asked, trying to keep up. Everyone appeared tough. Even those without weapons seemed as if they could snap a person in two if looked at the wrong way.

"To see a friend." Kryn said. "I hope she's still here."

The smell of baked goods gave way to metal and the air echoed with clanging of hammers. Three stores in on the main level of Sysinal she found the shop. She knocked on the door. "Come in." A voice said, from the back.

Kryn pushed the door open and removed her helmet. "Hi." She said, biting back a smile.

"Hi." Annorla said, glancing up from her work. Her eyes widened, looking Kryn up from head to toe and seeing the skeletal armor. "Can I help you?"

"I-I think so." Kryn said, smiling. "This is my friend, Ziri."

"Nice to meet you." Annorla said, nodding. Her piercing amber eyes felt as if they bore into Ziri and Kryn. Her ebon hair glowed from the nearby furnace fire. "And you are…?"

"I was hoping you would remember me." Kryn said. She frowned, turning to leave. "Sorry to waste your time."

"Kryn?" Annorla asked as Kryn turned the knob to leave. "Child of Fire, Kryn?"

Kryn spun around, a smile wider than Ziri had ever seen. She squealed and before Ziri knew where she went, she was in Annorla's arms. "Aunt Annorla!"

"I thought I would never see you again!" Annorla said, embracing Kryn, tearing up. "What are you doing here?"

"We are stopping here before heading up north to fight a necromancer." Kryn said. "Ziri, this is my aunt, Annorla. Well, not my actual aunt, but close enough."

Annorla smiled, still looking Kryn up and down. "I remember when you were just a little thing. It was cute. When she was a baby and sneezed, little sparks would shoot out of her nose making her laugh. You had the cutest laugh."

316

"Yeah, well, I don't laugh much anymore." Kryn sighed. She looked around the shop and noticed the furnace dying. Several bags and chests were on her desk in the backroom. "Are you going somewhere?"

"I am." Annorla said, pulling out a black ring that hung on a chain around her neck. "Thanks to this the king hired me to build a new fortress in Syro."

"I thought you don't like using that." Kryn said.

Annorla shook her head. "No, I don't. But I don't think I'll have to use it much. I'm not that inept."

"What is that?" Ziri asked.

"This is my blood metal family ring." Annorla said, rolling it around her fingers.

"Blood metal?"

"It's a lost art." Annorla nodded, twirling the ring between her fingers. "Back before magic had died, some magic users would hire an unsavory blacksmith to forge them a weapon. While making it they would put a curse on the weapon and infuse part of their own body within it. Usually blood. If done right the weapon would only work for the magic user, or their heir. This ring was made by my ancestors, and so only I can access its knowledge of all who wore it."

"That's amazing." Ziri said.

"Sometimes." Annorla said. "Other magic users made blood metal objects to try and possess others hoping it the key to immortality. It's a type of dark magic that is best left forgotten."

"I'm glad I found you before you left." Kryn said. "How long will you be there?"

"The king wants it done in four years. I think I can get it done sooner than that." Annorla said. "After that I'm not sure where I'll go. I don't want to be in Sysinal forever. I don't do much fighting anymore."

Gorik stepped out of the back room, stretching. "Thank you for letting me sleep here. After all this is over, I'm going to gut Samron myself."

Annorla turned. "Of course. Gorik, this is my niece, Kryn, and her friend. No need for that talk while she's here."

"Didn't know you had company. I'm sorry. Ziri." Gorik said, nodding. "Yes, I've met you before." His face turned sour.

"Hi Gorik." Ziri said, flashing a half smile.

"Tell me." Gorik said, stepping into the room. "Did you watch it?"

"Watch what?" Ziri asked.

"Don't play dumb with me." Gorik snapped. "Samron told me what happened. Rafik sentenced to death."

Ziri nodded. "I saw it. They hanged Salina first. When it was Rafik's turn Salina came back to life. Through the chaos Rafik escaped."

"What?" Gorik said, narrowing his eyes, but the smile appearing hopeful. "Are you sure?"

Ziri nodded. "We never found him. Last people who saw him were on the docks. I thought he would be trying to find you."

"Well we don't really have a home anymore to meet up again with." Gorik said, smiling. "Where is that boy?"

"I don't know but I hope he's safe." Kryn said. "King Vanarzir marked him for dead like they did that Xeo boy."

"They haven't found him either. Hopefully Rafik will be just as lucky." Annorla said. "What are you going to do?"

"Stick with the plan." Gorik said, staring firmly into Annorla's eyes. "Going to fight Skage."

"We are leaving tomorrow." Kryn said.

"I know. That's why I am leaving later today." Gorik said.

"Can we come with you? Maybe we'll find Rafik?"

"No." Both Gorik and Annorla said in unison.

"It is too dangerous for children." Gorik said.

"Even if those children have talent." Annorla added. "Let the adults handle it."

"Then why did the king send us?" Kryn asked. "If adults are supposed to handle it."

"I have my guesses." Gorik said. "But that is a conversation for another day."

Ziri tugged on Kryn's armor, pointing at a bag slung over the door of the backroom. As Gorik gave Annorla a hug goodbye she led Kryn to the bag and opened it. A moment later both disappeared into the hidden chamber in the bag.

"Where did they go?" Annorla asked.

"Probably trying to find a way to join me or off to find Rafik." Gorik said.

"Without saying goodbye?" Annorla asked.

"Well, they are kids." Gorik reasoned. "I'm sure they'll be back."

"I didn't even hear them leave."

"Ziri is always quiet." Gorik said. "Probably teaching your niece how to sneak around. Oh, I almost forgot my...bag."

"Something wrong?"

"I wasn't planning on showing you this. Least not yet." Gorik said. He grabbed the canvas bag from the door and opened the flap. "Look at this." A moment later he disappeared in front of Annorla.

She gasped, picking up the bag. A second later she fell over, dropping the bag as it bulged with sudden weight. Out came Gorik, Ziri, and Kryn.

"This bag belongs to Rafik." Gorik said, helping Annorla back to her feet. "He found it. Let me borrow it to find his sister while he got healed."

"That's amazing." Annorla said, still looking at the bag.

"Yes. And not a toy to stowaway two children to a dangerous deathtrap of a fortress." Gorik scolded.

"Where's Anza?" Ziri asked. "She should be in there."

"How do you know?" Gorik asked.

"Rafik said she was." Ziri answered.

"She's safe." Gorik said. "We just need to defeat the necromancer now."

"Tell him, Aunt." Kryn insisted lifting her hand and emitted a ball of flame. "I can take care of myself."

Gorik nodded. "How were you able to beat Salina and the soldiers she was able to kill?"

"We-uh-we didn't." Kryn said. "King Vanarzir stopped them. Not sure how he did that."

"Interesting." Gorik said, giving Annorla a suspicious look. "See? Even you and your fire couldn't stop one. We are going up against an army."

"Why hasn't he tried attacking here?" Ziri asked. "He did at the Golden Gate and Haitu."

"He did." Annorla said. "Over a month ago under a full moon. The dead couldn't escape the arena and after several hours they just collapsed."

"That's weird." Kryn said. "Wonder why?"

"You don't worry yourself about that." Gorik said. "If everything goes well you won't need to worry about it."

It wasn't long after Gorik left Annorla. He took the bag, making sure Kryn and Ziri weren't trying to follow him. Shallon joined him as he arrived at the city gate. "Are you ready to do this?" He asked. A third man, Brohl, joining them.

"As ready as I'll ever be." Brohl said.

Shallon nodded. He was taller than most men. Next to Gorik he looked like a giant. They walked out of the gates of Sysinal, retrieved their weapons, and hopped on a boat leading to the Golden Gate. Besides Annorla, who was heading to Syro, they were the only ones who agreed to the mission. Sneak into the Sarason Fortress and stop Skage.

After talking with Kryn and Ziri he was more eager to stop Skage. He didn't want kids being sent to the slaughter. And he didn't want Skage to get the power to control those with talent. He imagined an undead Kryn burning the forests around Datz to the ground.

It wasn't until the following evening that they arrived at the Golden Gate. A storm raged, not letting up once and soaking everything with freezing rain. The only sound within the fortress was the roaring of thunder. The dead remained motionless. Silent. Nothing stirred, and the smell of death was even stronger than when Gorik was last here. He looked up in the sky, not seeing a sign of the moon. It was darker than they had anticipated.

"Hopefully, this plays in our favor." Brohl said. "Think the dead have better sight than the living?"

"Remember." Gorik said. "It's not the dead, it's Skage. If he thinks we are here, he will bring the dead to life. We need to be careful. And stay in the darkness."

Chapter 26: Night of the New Moon

Trinkit, Biodlay Desert, Alutopek

"Wake up boy!" A man growled, kicking open the door.

Rafik jumped up, raising his fist, with a dazed look on his face. "Who are you?"

"You don't get to sleep all day. Not today." The man said, examining the door to ensure it wasn't broken. "The name's Rahgo. The barkeep told me to collect you." His gruff voice didn't match his frame. He looked tough, tattoos across both exposed arms, but not weathered like the voice would imply.

"I'm looking for Gorik. Do you know him?" Rafik asked.

"That's nice." Rahgo said. "Follow me."

"Do you know Gorik?" Rafik asked, hurrying after Rahgo who was already leaving.

The man spun around, slapping Rafik, sending him to the floor. "You don't be asking me questions, boy. It's your lucky day. If you live."

'If I live?' Rafik thought, getting to his feet, and rubbing the side of his face. He could already feel a mark burning from the hit. He followed Rahgo, taking him to the main floor of the Silver Shark. There were men and women, all suited for battle, but also having the same tattoo on the top of their hand. An anchor, the shaft of which being a sword. They were sailors.

"So, you're the new recruit?" A woman asked, stepping out of the crowd. "I'm Farra. You'll be serving me now if you live."

"What?" Rafik asked. He turned to face the barman who nodded.

"Any orphan who comes in here gets taken aboard a ship." He explained between yawns. "They paid handsomely for you, too."

"You can't do this!" Rafik yelled. "I'm leaving." Not looking back, he moved for the door.

Rahgo reached out, spun Rafik around and slapped him to the ground again. "You aren't going anywhere. You're part of the crew, now. Farra's crew."

Farra nodded. She tucked her dark hair into a hat and finished buttoning up her dress. She wrapped a trench coat around herself, hiding her feminine figure. "He's right, boy. And if you don't want to be bruised and bloody before the battle even begins, you'll listen to me."

Rafik shook his head. This couldn't be happening. He was so close to the sword, and to his sister. He couldn't be taken now. Not like this. "I'm looking for my sister." Rafik said. Rahgo raised his hand and he flinched, preparing for a swat that never came. "Just let me find her first. And I'll join you."

Farra shook her head. "No deal, kid. I have a better deal."

"What's that?" Rafik asked, inching deeper into the room. The crew circled him. There wasn't any escape now.

Captain Farra pulled out a map and unfurled it, taking knives to pin it open. It was a map of Trinkit, the surrounding area, and the ocean. Rafik noticed the parts of the ocean wasn't nearly as detailed as Gorik's chart. It barely had any markings of where sandbars, rocks, and other obstacles were. "It's the night of the new moon," she started, looking at each of her crew members. "And we were paid to do a job."

The sailors roared in agreement. Rafik watched each one's face contort with menace. Their violence etched on their faces. He noticed the tattoos on Rahgo were of corpses and treasure. He guessed it told the story of his life. The life of a mercenary.

"Those things are going to attack. And that means the dead are coming too. We need to be prepared for the worst. We will have two guards at each entrance, and the rest of us on the docks. That should be enough to stop anything trying to break into this city." Farra continued. "You, boy."

Rafik stood up straight, staring into Farra's eyes. He noticed her cold eyes matched her hair. "Yes?"

"Usually, we take the orphans and don't let them see land until we can trust them. But it's your lucky day. If you survive fighting with us, we'll let you go. Do you know how to fight?"

"I do." Rafik said, nodding.

"Without a magical sword?" She added.

Rafik's jaw dropped, his brow scrunched, and head tilted. "What magic sword?"

"No need to play dumb." Captain Farra said. "It's amazing what storytellers will say when you get drink in them. We know all about you, Rafik of Datz."

"I know how to fight." Rafik snapped, cursing Paris.

Farra nodded. "Good. We don't need to babysit you in battle, then. You'll be on the docks with Rahgo."

"I will make sure you don't try and escape, boy." Rahgo laughed. "I don't believe half of what I heard of you."

"I'm glad." Rafik smiled. "That means you are twice as smart as you actually look, but still half stupid." He ducked as the man punched him. With the hilt of a knife, he got off the dinner plate he jabbed it into Rahgo's arm and held the knife at the sailor's throat. "Does that answer your question?" He could feel his heart racing, blood pumping through him. The voice of Blaridance screamed within him, fainter, but present. He was getting close to the sword. He could feel it. And once he had it, nothing could stop him.

Captain Farra smiled. "Your wit can't save you in battle, boy. And now you have Rahgo to worry about, reclaiming his reputation. He's just as bad as the king now, being bested by a boy."

Rahgo snarled, kneeing Rafik in the gut. "You won't survive the night, boy."

"I wouldn't be wishing that. With the dead coming back to life." Rafik said.

"Rafik is right." Farra said. "We need to protect each other. The Taktor are relentless."

"Taktor?" Rafik asked. "Here?"

"Aye. Every new moon." Farra nodded.

"They're real?" Rafik asked.

"Oh, they're real." The barman said. "Been plaguing Trinkit since the end of summer. And now the dead are coming."

"How can we stop them?" Rafik asked.

"Simple." Farra said. "We imprison them. The Taktor come from the sea. And like fish, they will die if they stay on land for too long. We need to try not to kill them but take them prisoner. Have them dry out and die in the cells of the prisons here."

Rafik had to admit, it was a good plan. In all the stories he heard of the Taktor they never remained on land. He wasn't sure why, but what Captain Farra said made sense. It was worth a shot. She continued to explain the plan, which everyone agreed to. "Now what?" He asked, as the meeting had concluded.

"Everyone can prepare and do what they want until this evening." Captain Farra said. "Except you. To ensure you don't escape or run away, you're staying in here."

The crew came and went, slowly filtering out of the tavern. Rahgo sat at the door, watching Rafik. "Are you afraid?" He asked, sitting at the bar.

"Me?" The barman asked, wiping down the bar. "Oh sure! But the Silver Shark has stood firm for centuries. I doubt any sea creature can take this place down, let alone the entire city."

"It's raining out." Rafik said. "Storm hasn't stopped since I made it here."

"It is strange." The barman nodded. "With the dead returning, Taktor attacking, and this storm, I think magic is back. And we just have to roll with it."

"If it's raining, they could stay on land longer." Rafik said.

"We'll keep them dry." Rahgo said, kicking up a fire in the far part of the tavern. He poked at the embers, tossing another log onto the dying flame. Slowly, the fire licked at the log before biting, and the fire was alive once more. "Even if we have to spit roast them doing so."

The day dragged on as Rafik wandered the tavern. There wasn't much to do or explore, as most of it was locked. He resolved himself to a corner watching the patrons of the Silver

Shark. There were all sorts of people in here. He watched them interact, slowly getting drunker and more rambunctious. Late morning gave way to afternoon. He saw Paris and another man enter the tavern. The storyteller avoided eye contact with Rafik while they were there. It wasn't worth bothering him. He was already a prisoner.

The afternoon hours faded, and the patrons became more boisterous. Women joined in, laughing, as the men bought them drinks. The women would take the men upstairs, only to return a little later. There were two separate card games going on around Rafik and a separate game of dice. He didn't think he had seen that much gold in one place in his life. The patrons yelled, cheered, laughed, cursed, and roared with every game. The drinks flowed and the women cheered the winners on.

"Maybe one day you'll be playing cards." Rahgo said, handing him a plate of food. "If you don't die tonight."

"You think I will?"

Rahgo took the seat opposite him and grabbed the fried fish on Rafik's plate for himself. "Maybe." He said, half spitting out the fish he was devouring. "If you do, no hard feelings when we destroy your corpse."

Rafik laughed. "Yes. No hard feelings."

Above all the noise, the music, and clinking of glasses a bell rang from the temple. The Silver Shark fell silent by the third toll. Eyes darted around, looking for something that wasn't there. Others distracted themselves with their drink or became suddenly interested in the designs etched into their dinner plates.

"What's that?" Rafik asked.

"It's time." Rahgo said, lighting up. He took another drink before yanking open the door. "Let's go, boy. Earn your freedom!" The patrons cheered Rafik, Rahgo, and two others as they left, wishing them good luck. Even a couple of women promised their attention if they returned.

Rain still poured down, and the muddy roads were now becoming shallow rivers. They stayed on the boardwalks, making their way to the docks. The bell echoed throughout the city. "Good of you to join us." Captain Farra said, fastening another sharpened post towards the ocean.

They were all hiding behind the hastily built wall. The sharpened posts secured to it. "How many do you think are going to attack?" Rafik asked.

Captain Farra shrugged. "Not sure. Just need to be prepared for anything."

Wave after wave of the Tahlbiru Ocean crashed down on them. Some went over the wall, drenching them further, while others hit the wall, rattling it. More than once Rafik thought the wall wouldn't even stand for the storm, let alone an attack. Another large wave splashed down on them, and as the water subsided, he saw it.

The arms and legs appeared longer than that of men. Razor sharp fins jutted out of their arms and legs. His head was bald, with more, shorter fins running from his brow to the back of his neck, converging into one larger fin. Their skin a pale green, and jagged teeth filled their mouths. Their lidless eyes were as black as the nighttime sea and looked just as foreboding. The Taktor got to its feet and roared, sounding like a combination of a wolf's growl and the drowning of a man. It raised its arm, and Rahgo dashed forward, stabbing it through the chest.

"Don't kill them!" Captain Farra yelled. "You fool of a man, don't kill them."

"Sorry, Captain." Rahgo said, lowering his head, yanking his sword out of the Taktor's chest. His triumphant smile gone.

"Toss it back into the sea before it has a chance to kill us." Farra ordered.

Rahgo nodded, and just as he threw him over the wall Rafik could see him begin to stir. Another Taktor emerged, leaping out of the water, and stuck himself on the spike. A few moments and he collapsed on it. Another five came out, howling as the thunder roared. The dead Taktor screamed to life, wriggling himself on the spike to slash at his living brethren.

"If you believe in the gods, boy, best start praying." Captain Farra said. "We're going to need it."

327

Gorik kicked a body with his leg and it didn't stir. He climbed the fortress wall and looked out over the ocean. The Sarason Fortress stood darker than the rest of the ocean. The eyes of the spider glowed in the direction of Trinkit.

From where they were, he could see the faint outline of the city. It helped as the lighting flashed across the bay. Torchlights could just be made out at the dock. If he concentrated hard enough, he swore he could hear the temple bells indicating an attack. Though he could have easily just imagined it or be part of the rumbling thunder. The howling winds and thunder easily deafened him. More than once he thought Shallon had screamed for him when they were nowhere near each other.

"I think Skage is attacking Trinkit." Gorik said as Shallon stood at his side. "Poor bastards."

"What does he want with Trinkit?" Shallon asked. "It's a place full of drunks."

"The dead don't need drink." Gorik said. "Gaining numbers for his army is my guess."

"On the bright side, we should be able to get to the fortress without him noticing." Brohl said. "I found us a canoe."

The three wandered the fortress in darkness. They didn't want to draw attention of the necromancer with sudden torchlight. Brohl had found the canoe, they just needed to open the gates. It was Shallon who finally found one wheel. At the top of the fortress overlooking the Tahlbiru Ocean there was a wheel, a chain dangling down a shaft made just for it. "The other one must be on the other side of the fortress." Shallon guessed.

"I'll get it." Brohl offered. He walked the expanse of the Eko River. He faded from view in the darkness before making it to the other side. Several minutes later the chains clanged, shifting. Shallon started turning the wheel and Gorik could see the gate slowly rise into the fortress wall below him.

"Let's go!" Gorik said, clapping his hands together.

It was a small blessing the dead Taktor couldn't make it over the wall. Only a handful of the living made it on the other side without being cut down. As soon as any made it over the wall there was a small skirmish before being defeated. Other fighters hurried to chain them, yanking them away from the battle.

This only lasted a few minutes as the screams of war changed to the screams of help. Taktors scrambled over and around the spikes, avoiding their dead who were now actively attacking them. Rahgo pushed others back, screaming that they didn't deserve rescue. Captain Farra yelled at him again, ordering them all to help the Taktors over the wall. Instead of fighting each other, they pushed back the dead.

"We can't keep doing this." Rahgo yelled. "You people need to go back into the sea. What are you doing?"

Rafik hurried to the imprisoned and helped unshackle them. "We need all the help we can get." Rafik said.

"Agreed." Captain Farra said. "Truce?" She held out her hand to a nearby Taktor. He glared at Rahgo before nodding, shaking her hand.

The temple bells clanged louder, announcing a new attack. "The dead are coming!" echoes came from within the city. "The Bruin Fortress has fallen!"

Captain Farra's face paled. "Fall back! Into the city!" Taktor and man hurried into the city, the thunder rumbling as if laughing at their retreat. Rafik hurried to the walls with the others, seeing the horde coming from the west.

"Where did Skage get so many?" Rafik asked.

"Who?" Captain Farra asked.

"Skage." Rafik said. "He's the necromancer responsible for all this. In the Sarason Fortress." He pointed back at the spider tower, burning red eyes glowing.

"The necropolis." Farra said. "Some of them look like they've been dead for years. He awakened the dead. All of them."

"We need to get to the Sarason Fortress." Rafik said to the men and Taktors that were near him. "Skage is there. He's doing

329

this. See those eyes?" He pointed at the spider fortress with the glowing red eyes. "If we don't stop him the city will fall."

"We can't cross if the dead Taktor are guarding it." One of the men said. "This is your fault! I don't even know why we saved you." He pointed his finger at one of the Taktors leaning against the wall. He was panting, gasping for breath. He grabbed a man's canteen and splashed his face with the cool liquid.

"Do you understand me?" Rafik asked, kneeling, and handing him his own. The cold rain poured on them, but he still gasped for air.

The Taktor nodded.

"Can you get me to the fortress?" Rafik asked. "I need to try and get there, at least."

The Taktor looked up to the tower. The red eyes added a light of fear, like the spider was piercing into his very soul. "Not with them there." He said in a strange and garbled voice. "No man would last swimming from here to there with Taktors anyway."

"We have to work together." Rafik said. "If any of us want to survive this, we need to stop fighting each other. Why are you trying to attack Trinkit anyway?"

"We need more land. More food." The Taktor said. "Since the Black Wall, our people have been dying. Now we need to return to the land or starve. Our crops are dying, and fewer fish swimming. Surely you have noticed less fish?"

Rafik nodded, recalling Gorik mentioning having to sail further and further for fish. "You know of the Black Wall?" Rafik asked. "I didn't know it went underwater."

"Even the gods know about the Black Wall." The Taktor said.

"I'm a sailor." Rafik said. "If you get me to the Sarason Fortress I'll help you and your people get food."

"How can I trust you? Nomad and Taktor have always been enemies."

"Nomad? You can't. But we need each other." Rafik said, holding out a hand. "My name is Rafik."

"Inakus." The Taktor said, shaking Rafik's hand. The Taktor smiled, revealing a row of serrated teeth.

"How are we going to get there?" Rafik asked.

"Who said you're going?" Rahgo snapped, visibly shaken as he watched the dead drag themselves closer. "You're stuck with us. Or you die. That's the deal."

"I've been to the fortress." Rafik said. "If Paris told you everything you should know that."

"He's right." Captain Farra said. "Do you think you can defeat him?"

Rafik shrugged, remembering the hulking armored warrior that mangled his body. "I don't know. But maybe I can distract him long enough for the dead to become dead again."

"It's the best shot we have." Captain Farra said.

"Can you take me there?" Rafik asked.

Inakus shrugged. "With my fallen brothers waiting for us in the water, it will be tough."

"You can dry up." One of the other men snapped, noticing Inakus and Rafik's conversation. "We wouldn't be stuck in this mess if it weren't for you."

"Now isn't the time to blame others." Captain Farra snapped. "And if you haven't noticed that horde of dead coming towards us is all men. Not Taktor."

The man shook his head. "You won't see me working with some fish freak."

"That's fine." Rafik said. "Not everyone is cut out to be a hero."

"Excuse me?" The man roared. "You watch your tongue, boy!"

"No, you watch yours." Rafik snapped, raising his sword. "None of you have even tried to learn why the Taktors started attacking. All you see is someone different than how you look."

"Of course. They're nothing better than a fish who think they have the brains of a man." The man said.

"Look on the other side of that wall." Rafik said. "Do you really think it matters what we look like or who we are, if death is coming for us all? We need to stop Skage. Then, if you want, we can start hating and killing each other again."

The man spit at Rafik's feet. "I'd rather join the dead."

Before Captain Farra or Rafik could say anything Rahgo hurled a punch at the man, knocking him out. "He can just sit there, then."

Rafik smiled, turning to Inakus. "If we can get around, could you get me there?"

The Taktor ran his fingers over the fins on his head, thinking. "Yes."

"How are you getting passed the dead Taktor?" Captain Farra asked.

"It's easy." Rafik said. "The dead Taktor are at the dock, and a horde of the dead from the west. We head back towards the Golden Gate. Start swimming along there."

Captain Farra laughed. "Seems too easy."

"Because we still need to make it there." Inakus said. "We just know where we're getting into the water."

Gorik, Shallon, and Brohl tossed and turned in the Tahlbiru as they tried rowing the canoe to the fortress. One wave would push them back towards the Golden Gate while another tossed the boat to the side, nearly capsizing it. They continued rowing forward, trying to make their way to the glowing eyes of the spider. It was like taking two steps forward, and one step back. Even Shallon was tiring out rowing to nowhere.

"This is hopeless." Brohl shouted above the howling wind. "We can't make it."

"We will." Shallon growled, pulling at the oars harder, forcing themselves forward. "The sea doesn't stop me."

A wave crashed onto them, soaking them even more than the pouring rain had. "No, but it may kill you." Gorik laughed.

Shallon cursed and continued pushing towards the fortress.

"Look!" Brohl shouted, pointing at the fortress.

The massive spider statue atop the ruins of the fortress began to turn. The sound of grinding stone echoed among the thunder and gave Gorik the shivers. The stone spider's eyes faded to darkness once more. "I didn't know that moves." Shallon said.

"Learn something new every day." Brohl said, actively shivering. "This whole thing gives me the willies."

"Because it isn't right." Shallon said, glancing down at his hand with the emerald. "None of it is."

"There she is." Gorik smiled as they made their way around the ruined fortress and the *River Lizard* came into view. "Was worried the necromancer did something to that, too."

"Isn't that just another boat?" Brohl asked.

"It's my boat!" Gorik snapped. "Besides, Annorla put one of her inventions in it. I can run the whole ship myself if I wanted."

"That's impossible." Brohl said.

"And yet there it is." Gorik laughed. He jumped onto the dock and tied up their boat. He helped Shallon and Brohl off and they looked at the Sarason Fortress.

"I don't like this place." Brohl said, shivering.

"I don't either." Gorik said. "And I'm sure it won't feel much better until it's over. Now, you ready?"

"As ready as I'll ever be." Shallon said, brandishing a thick two-handed sword. "Been a long time since I used this."

Chapter 27: The Necromancer

Sarason Fortress, Tahlbiru Ocean, Alutopek

"We need to watch out." Ziri said, pointing at the Golden Gate. "It won't be easy getting through there."

"That's why you have talent." Samron said, peering through his telescope. Since meeting back with the king's army, he had been bitter and hostile towards anyone. His scowl and frown appeared natural on his face, hidden in shadow beneath a hood. For the trainer of the Kylix, it was peculiar he didn't wear his armor.

"Yeah. Because that helped back in Haitu." Kryn said, snapping her fingers and watching the flames extinguish from the rain.

"The trick is not to die." Krista interrupted. "That's why you have me."

"That's right." Samron smiled. "You're the most important one here. Keep everyone healed. Don't let anyone die."

Krista glared at Ziri with a twisted smile. "I'll do my best. I just hope I can get to everyone."

"I can help." Taygin smiled. "Help you get to everybody."

"She doesn't need a bodyguard." Kryn scoffed. "She can heal herself."

"Some people don't like her." Taygin said, glaring at Ziri. "She needs protection."

"Some people actually have a brain." Kryn whispered, causing a fit of laughter between her and Ziri.

Taygin and Krista glared at the two. "Enough." Samron ordered. Thunder roared, and the rain poured, pattering against their armor. The storm hadn't let out, and some were starting to think the rain would flood the world if it didn't let up.

The Golden Gate loomed in the distance, drawing closer by the second. The river's gate of the fortress was still open. "Just as I left it." Samron said. The Kylika sailed into the fortress, hands on their weapons. Small wisps of flame slithered out between Kryn's fingers. The stench of death hit them as they drifted into the fortress. The winds were calmer here from the walls, letting the smell of rain give way to putrid death and decay. Bodies in various stages of decomposition littered the ground. More than one Kylika ran to the edge of the boat and threw up. Everyone removed their helmets and covered their noses.

A fireball shot from Kryn's hand at a nearby corpse, lighting it up. The smell of burning, rotting flesh was even worse. The downpour of rain snuffed it out moments later.

"Kryn!" Samron yelled.

"What? If I burn them to dust before they wake up, they can't harm us, right?" Kryn said.

Samron shook his head. "That only works if Skage doesn't notice the fire before they're all gone. You wait until I tell you to attack."

"The dead don't look too bad." Krista scoffed. "I thought I was supposed to be scared and be in a battle. Not die from the smell of Kryn's horrible cooking."

"You know," Kryn said, tossing a fire ball between her hands. "Fire is so hard to control sometimes. Would be a shame if I accidentally caught someone else on fire. Again."

"You did?" Ziri asked, laughing.

"Yep." Kryn nodded. "She thought she could beat me. She was wrong."

"You even try, one more time." Krista spat, eyes narrowed, her lips thinning.

"It's not like you couldn't heal yourself. Probably only hurt for a second." Kryn said, turning away from the rest. She lit the corpse on fire, and this time it held, ignoring the cold rain and Samron's anger. She watched the body as it broke apart. Some pieces slid into the Eko River in a wisp of smoke.

"This might be easier than we thought." Haloro said, jumping off the boat as it was tied. He darted around from one end of the fortress to the other. "Nothing is alive here. Just fallen soldiers."

"Maybe Skage is already defeated?" Ziri suggested, thinking of Gorik.

"I don't think so." Samron said, shaking his head.

"Think we can go on ahead?" Kryn asked. "We aren't doing much good here."

"No." Samron said. "Climb the fortress walls. Look towards the Sarason Fortress."

Haloro was first, using his talent of speed to sprint to the top before anyone had even taken five steps. "That place looks creepy." He hollered down to Samron.

The spider's eyes began to glow. Clicking like popping knuckles came from the fallen as they began to twitch. One by one each of them screamed, thrashing about. "Look alive, people!" Samron shouted, kicking one corpse getting to its feet into the Eko River.

Kryn set fire to those around her. The Sand Brothers swirled sand from the desert, smashing the column of sand into each corpse. Krista screamed, hiding behind Ziri who she shrugged off. Ziri hurried to join Kryn, holding a knife.

"You'll be alright." Kryn said.

Ziri nodded, holding her knife tighter. "I hope so."

"I have a plan." Kryn whispered. "Once they all attack follow me."

The fallen Kylix soldiers came to life and moved like puppets on a string. Slow at first, but gaining speed, chasing after anything that breathed. The Kylika soldier with the talent of water breathing jumped into the river as the corpses followed. Samron helped pull her out moments later. The soldiers that had fallen in clamored to get out but couldn't grab hold of the ledge. Another Kylika soldier that could levitate hovered over the dead, making them run into one another.

Krista hurried and healed one of the Sand Brothers, dodging an axe coming down on her. Samron fought off four more, narrowly missing a spear to his neck. He fell back into one of the rooms, out of sight from the others.

"Now." Kryn said. She ran up the fortress steps leading to the outer wall. Three fallen soldiers followed. She blasted the stairs with flame, causing them to fall off as they were set ablaze. "Can you swim?"

"What?" Ziri asked.

"Can you swim?" Kryn asked again, kicking off her boots.

"Yes I can. Why?"

"We're jumping." Kryn said, grabbing Ziri's arm and flinging herself off the fortress wall. With a large splash that nobody noticed they landed in the freezing waters of the Tahlbiru. Ziri gasped, water filling her lungs. She sprang up out of the water, coughing. Kryn followed.

"We-we can't swim that far!" Ziri said even now her voice was still little more than a whisper. Her teeth chattered and every kick of her feet in the cold water were like knives stabbing into her. The icy water of the Tahlbiru churned, shoving her around like a grain of rice. Her body shivering, treading water, trying to stay afloat and away from rocks. Going back to the Sarason Fortress seemed more tempting than staying in the freezing ocean.

"I always wanted to try this." Kryn said, smiling. She grabbed Ziri and with her other hand shot flame outwards. They didn't budge.

"T-try what?" Ziri asked, looking at the steam curling upwards from beneath the sea.

"I thought that would propel us forward." Kryn said. "Ya shire."

"K-kryn we ne-need a b-b-boat." Ziri said through clattering teeth. "We can't-t s-stay here. It's f-f-freezing."

"I'm sorry, Ziri." Kryn said, kicking her feet. She dunked her head into the water, holding her breath. Her fire kept sparking and steaming, but not doing much else. Every time she tried there was nothing more than a dying spark. Then she saw it. Something lurking below her. It looked like the shape of a man. She imagined it was the dead, swimming to snatch her and Ziri. The sudden fright caused the flames to shoot from the bottom of her feet and hand. Kryn grabbed hold of Ziri and began zooming towards the Sarason Fortress. A trail of steam billowing behind her.

Inakus laughed, looking at Rafik. The boy's eyes were still wide with shock. His body shivering. "The water isn't that cold." He said.

"Y-you l-live in that." Rafik said, trying to calm his shaking. They had left Trinkit and turned straight to the ocean. Rafik wasn't sure what happened next. Inakus yanked him, telling him to hold his breath over his shoulder, pulling him into the water. He could have sworn he saw an underwater city. At one-point other Taktors with lifeless eyes began chasing them. As Rafik would begin to run out of breath he would squeeze Inakus's hand and he would jump into the air like a dolphin, diving back in. The bitter cold air made the water feel colder, and soon he was dreading needing to get breath.

The Taktor swam to the Sarason Fortress faster than he thought possible. What would have taken him hours to swim, if he were even successful, Inakus did in a fraction of it. "Under an hour." He bragged when Rafik mentioned this.

There was a small entrance underwater. They swam through and Rafik recognized the room they had entered. The floor was at more of an incline, sinking slowly into the frigid water. Beside the glimmering door was the well. Though the wood pieces boarding it up were now shattered and scattered across the floor.

"We're here." Inakus said, heaving a sigh of relief. "The belly of the beast."

"That's different." Rafik said, picking up one of the broken, rotted pieces of wood. "Wonder what happened?" He tossed the piece into the well but didn't hear a splash or even it hitting the ground. His teeth clattered, looking around the ruined, dank room. "How can-n you live d-down there?"

"You get used to it." Inakus said. "I just don't understand you land dwellers."

"Wh-why?"

"Those things in the air." Inakus said. "What do you do if you want to chase one? We see sharks and other fish and just chase them. You can't do that."

338

Rafik smiled. "N-n-no. We can't-t f-fly. We s-stay on our feet."

"How horrible is that?" Inakus asked. "Always having to be on your feet to move. No wonder you have noodle arms."

"Y-you know what n-noodles are?" Rafik asked.

"Of course! We might live underwater, but we don't just eat fish." Inakus said, flashing a smile. "Though we do like meat."

Rafik laughed. "I-I do t-too."

"Those are grass chompers." Inakus laughed. "We must like meat more than you."

The water began to churn and bubble. Steam filled the room and Rafik enjoyed the sudden warmth. A moment later Kryn and Ziri popped up, gasping. "Wait!" Rafik said, holding up his hand as Inakus moved to attack. "I-I know them."

"Rafik?" Kryn asked, spitting out water. Without another word she charged forward, hugging him. "I thought I'd never see you again."

Ziri moved to hug Rafik as well, holding him tight. "We were happy to hear you escaped."

"Thanks." Rafik smiled. "Not sure if I'm in a better place." He gestured to his surroundings, looking around the room.

"What is this place?" Ziri asked. "It doesn't look like the fortress from last time I was here. And who are you?"

"Ziri, Kryn, this is Inakus. He is a Taktor. He helped me get to the Sarason Fortress."

"Pleasure. And welcome to the Sarason Ruins." Inakus said. "When the Black Wall was created, the island it rested on collapsed. But the dark magic of the spider protected part of the fortress. Preserving it as if it were still in ancient times. Before the cataclysm."

"Skage." Rafik said.

Inakus nodded. "I held up my part of the bargain."

"And I will mine." Rafik nodded. "We will stop Skage, and then I will help find food for you and your people."

"Well, I'm not sure how dry it will be up there." Inakus said, a twinge of guilt in his voice.

"No worries, my new friend." Rafik smiled. "Thank you. We got this." He beckoned for Kryn and Ziri to follow and he entered through the glimmering doorway. "I'll meet you back at Trinkit."

Inakus nodded, diving back into the water, not watching as the three children disappeared through the shadowy doorway.

"Wow." Kryn said, noticing the difference instantly. The dark ruins were replaced with an expanse of elegance. The tapestries and suits of armor between the jutting rooms.

Rafik noticed the rooms, remembering the last time he was here. The panic and fear he had in finding his sister. "Follow me." He said, leading the way. He silently prayed, thanking the gods Anza wasn't stuck here but safe with Gorik.

They sprinted up the spiral stairs, not saying a word as they hurried forward. "That man is ugly!" Kryn said, pointing at the bust of Skage at the end of the hall. "But where's the door?"

"That is Skage." Rafik said. "And trust me, he looks uglier in person. There was a portrait of him I saw. I don't know how he did it, but his skin is even a shade of purple." He pointed up, showing Kryn the spider shaped doorway with the chain coming down like a piece of web. "We need to go through there. Took me a long time to figure that out."

"Gorik almost broke the bust of Skage trying to find where to go." Ziri said, stifling a laugh. She ran and jumped for the chain, just barely grabbing it. Nothing happened, as she dangled there, holding onto the chain. "Uh, a little help."

Rafik smiled, pulling on Ziri's legs. The doors swung open revealing the entrance to the House of Spiders within the Sarason Fortress. "After you." He said, gesturing to Kryn.

"Such a gentleman." Kryn smiled, holding out her hand to light the way.

"Yeah, you would think that. It's just because you have the light." Rafik laughed.

Kryn laughed. "I thought it was because I'm a better fighter than you."

"I didn't think I had to admit that." The two laughed, trading glances.

While climbing the countless stairs the memories the last time he was here flooded Rafik. He didn't even remember leaving this place before. He had fought off people he still didn't know who they were and survived an enchanted suit of armor with a corpse inside. He turned, smiling at Ziri, remembering her saving his life from Salina. The clanging of a battle already in progress grew louder and pulled him from his thoughts.

"Who is up here?" Kryn asked, hurrying the rest of the way.

There hadn't been any undead minions or other signs of something within this tower. Something the three didn't notice until now.

The giant suit of armor was fending off a bald man none of them recognized. An emerald shimmered on his right hand. From what it looked like he was handling the suit of armor well. Gorik, and another man they didn't know with darker skin were fighting the spider that was hanging from the ceiling before. How it came to life Rafik had no idea. Though he had one guess. Across the room were the giant doors he saw Skage enter what seemed like a lifetime ago.

"Gorik!" Rafik shouted.

Gorik turned and the spider swatted him with one of its legs. "We'll check on him." Kryn said. "Ziri, go check on Gorik. I'll help with that spider. You go find Skage. Maybe you can sneak up on him."

Rafik nodded, running between the two battles. Kryn shot a fireball, catching the attention of the enchanted mechanical spider. Ziri hurried to Gorik's side. "Get the talisman." Gorik said, trying to get to his feet.

"What talisman?" Ziri asked.

"Skage has a talisman. Has a spider on it. That's how he is doing all this. Take the talisman, you stop all of this. Gorik said. "Go. Kryn, Brohl, Shallon and I will take care of these two."

341

Ziri nodded and darted towards the door. Halfway there the doors clanged shut. The doors didn't budge, and she couldn't find a way of opening them. "Watch out." A voice shouted. Ziri turned and saw the suit of armor sliding across the ground towards her. She pulled out a knife, took a deep breath, and joined the battle.

The moment Rafik entered the room the doors slammed shut behind him. He looked around, unsure of whether he should be amazed or worried. There were rows and rows of shelves filled with books. Some strange figurines and crystals scattered about. A map of Alutopek on a wall and tables filled with even more books. Hanging from the center of the room was a telescope. Next to the telescope on a higher platform was the necromancer, Skage.

Below Skage, on the main level with Rafik, were two boys. One with dark, shoulder length hair, the other short, almost shaved bald. They looked nearly identical with the same honey-colored eyes that glowed in the torchlight. They didn't seem to notice Rafik, as they were talking amongst themselves.

It was then that he noticed the necromancer appeared to be in a sort of trance, his eyes closed, one hand touching part of the telescope. He continually muttered under his breath. "Who are you?" Rafik asked, approaching the two.

"We could ask you the same thing." The boy with shorter hair said jumping, turning, and pointing a sword at Rafik.

"You really think he's the enemy right now?" The long-haired one said.

"Could be his apprentice." The other replied.

"Yes. The apprentice is going to ask who we are instead of just trying to kill us."

"Maybe he's a dumb apprentice."

"I'm not dumb. And I'm nobody's apprentice." Rafik said. "Who are you?"

"I'm Tragi." The long-haired boy said. "This is my brother, Xeo."

"Wait." Rafik smiled. "The Xeo? The one who fought the king and got away."

Xeo laughed, standing up straighter and puffing out his chest, smiling, winking at Rafik. "I see my reputation precedes me."

"Yeah. Thought you'd be taller." Rafik said. He smiled as Xeo frowned.

"I like you." Xeo said. "We were sent to try and stop him." He pointed at Skage who still hadn't noticed them.

Rafik nodded. "We can just push him over the ledge."

"That's what I said!" Xeo laughed. "See. Two against one."

Tragi groaned. "Then he can be your twin."

"Or you all can be dead." A deep and strange voice said from above. Skage glared down at the three boys. He held out his hand and Blaridane whistled through the air. "I won't waste my magical ability to kill you. Not when I have this."

"That's my sword!" Rafik said. "I found it!" He could hear Blaridane's voice call to him in his head. This time challenging him. Telling him to prove his worth. His hands itched, and a seething anger boiled within him. How dare somebody else use *his* sword!

"Then come and get it." Skage challenged.

Rafik could hear Blaridane's voice taunt him. It was now fighting him, defending his new champion. His blood boiled and he snarled, slashing at the necromancer who blocked every blow with ease. He wasn't sure what Xeo or Tragi were expecting, but he didn't anticipate Skage to be as good of a sword fighter. Even with Blaridane. He hoped the sword would want him back. Stop defending Skage and let him win. Allow him to be the champion of the sword. The sword gave no recognition to Rafik and attempted to slash at him like the sword did for him to so many faceless soldiers.

The necromancer managed to fend off all three of them. Between the three they managed to land one blow on Skage, and gained ground, fighting him back into a corner. Once there Skage muttered something and placed his free hand on the back wall. An explosion blasted the wall and Skage leapt out in the cloud of smoke.

Tragi was the first to go through the hole and Skage kicked him inside. Rafik was next, with Xeo not far behind. They climbed onto the metal exterior of the spider, the storm raging around them. Lightning flashed, blotting the blackened waters with light. Thunder roared and Skage laughed. "Dark magic always summons storms. Soon this world will be one large hurricane I control." Skage laughed, a lightning bolt striking near Xeo's side.

"Stop talking and just fight." Xeo snapped. "If I wanted to hear old men talk all day I would have stayed back in Kristol."

Skage sneered, jabbing his sword forward at Xeo as Tragi entered the battle. Rafik recognized more of these the moves. It wasn't Skage fighting. It was Blaridane. He saw the necromancer's eyes closed as he began muttering under his breath. "Go for the sword."

"What?" Tragi and Xeo said in unison.

"It's the sword." Rafik said. "Skage isn't even paying attention. It's the sword. Get it out of his hands and Skage won't fight. He can't fight."

Tragi and Xeo shrugged but didn't question it as they changed their method of attack, now aiming for the arm that carried the blade instead of Skage's heart.

Inside the House of Spiders, the suit of armor was once again swatted across the room. One arm was missing, but it didn't stop the thing from pressing on Shallon. The suit of armor spun, swinging the hammer. Shallon raised his sword to help stop the blow. His sword shattered, the pieces flying across the room, and the giant fell back, grunting.

The mechanical spider pressed on the other four. Ziri tried moving around, trying to cut at the spider's legs with her knife. Kryn kept using her fire, keeping the spider at bay, but not doing any damage. The spider growled and reared up on its hind four legs. As it crashed down it swatted with its front legs, sending Gorik and Brohl flying in opposite directions.

Brohl landed on his feet, skidding to a stop, and charging the spider again. Gorik hit his back against the wall and gasped. He hunched over, gasping for breath. A moment later he heard Shallon yell. He looked up and saw the broken sword fly towards him. He didn't feel any pain as broken pieces of the blade struck his heart. He didn't hear Shallon yell out his name, and he didn't see the floor as he fell towards it.

Shallon screamed, rage building and his emerald glowing. A fire grew in his eyes. The suit of armor swung his hammer again and Shallon grabbed it mid swing. He lifted the hammer, with the suit of armor still holding onto the handle and began to spin. He let go of the hammer and the suit crashed into the spider.

"Get the talisman." Gorik muttered to Shallon as he approached.

Shallon nodded, taking the hammer from the suit of armor still trying to get up. The spider didn't budge. He made his way to the door and smashed it down with the hammer, twirling it in his hand.

"Gorik." Ziri said, kneeling by his side. "Gorik."

"Take this." Gorik said, reaching in his pocket. He gave Ziri a metallic stone and two bottles of ink, and Kryn the bottomless bag.

"Gorik, you're going to be okay." Ziri said, squeezing his hand.

"No. Not this time." His breath was shallow, getting slower and slower. "Find Anza. Dragon's Roost."

Tragi kneeled, hacking with his sword at Skage's legs. The necromancer jumped and Xeo went high. At the same time Rafik slashed, taking off his arm holding the sword. Skage screamed, snatching at his stump of an arm. Rafik broke from the fight, scrambling for Blaridane. He grabbed the necromancer's arm, wrenching Blaridane free, and threw Skage's arm over the side.

"No!" Skage screamed. "No!"

345

'*KILL!*' The familiar voice screamed inside Rafik. He fought the urge but welcomed the angry voice. His fighting companion. '*Kill boy! Kill!*'

"Way to go." Tragi said, smiling. "Wasn't so bad after all."

Skage growled, holding out his other hand as a stream of lightning shot at Rafik. The boy collapsed, sliding off the statue. Both Xeo and Tragi jumped forward, grabbing Rafik as he went over the edge of the spider. Blaridane wrenched free of Rafik's limp grip and fell, landing on a ruined wall far below. The necromancer got to his feet and laughed, holding out his only hand. "I can always make myself a new arm. But you won't be around to-"

"To what?" Xeo asked as the ending of the sentence never came. They pulled Rafik up and turned. Skage held his heart, falling to his knees.

"What happened?" Tragi asked. "Did you do something?"

"No. You would have saw me if I did." Xeo said.

Below the four of them Shallon swung the hammer, crushing the telescope. The talisman cracked, falling out of its crevice, and bouncing to the ground. There was a rumble. The whole tower shook, nearly twisting in place, and they collapsed to the ground, feeling the room shift and fall.

"It's the fortress." Brohl said.

"Finally collapsing." Shallon nodded, agreeing. "What it should have done 200 years ago. We need to get out of here."

"What about Rafik?" Kryn asked, looking around.

"He's not in here." Brohl said, looking around the room. "He must have stopped Skage. That's why this tower is falling apart."

Shallon shook his head, looking down at the cracked Kymu-Guiden talisman. "No. Not quite." With a forceful swing and a scream of anger, the hammer fell onto the talisman, shattering it to pieces. The tower shifted and rumbled more, dust falling from the ceiling.

"Did he go through there?" Brohl asked, pointing at the hole in the wall. Smoke still simmering off the burning edges.

Ziri hurried over, craned her neck out of the hole, and frowned. Down below was nothing but waves of the sea. "He would have fallen into the ocean."

"Well let's get out of here before we join him." Brohl said.

Shallon held his new hammer over his shoulder, Gorik slung over the other. They rushed down the stairs, the room crumbling behind them.

"We can't go back that way." Xeo said, trying to reach the hole. The spider shifted, dislodging from the fortress as it writhed and shifted.

"That's fine." Tragi said, smiling. The necromancer's body was burning, evaporating into dust, and melting a hole into the spider. Tragi jumped in first, and Xeo lowered Rafik down to him. They carried him, noticing the suit of armor had turned to dust as well.

The twins hurried across the room, down the stairs, and to the ruins of the fortress with the well. Everything crumbled behind him. Walls reduced to dust and rubble, and the stairs collapsed with every step. "Wake up." Xeo said, smacking Rafik. "Wake up."

"Guess he's coming with us?" Tragi said.

Xeo shook his head. "We aren't allowed to."

"We don't have a choice. Can't leave him here." Tragi said.

"Guess you're right." Xeo said. They each grabbed an end of Rafik and climbed into the well. Neither looking back as they disappeared. The fortress collapsed above them, crashing into the ocean.

In Trinkit as the hoard of the dead fought against the living, slowly breaking their way into town they collapsed. The dead at the Golden Gate fell where they stood. Everyone looked towards the Sarason Fortress, realizing it was over. The burning red eyes of the spider faded, and the spider fell from the tower, shattering to

347

pieces as it made its way into the depths of the Tahlbiru. The tower fell, first shifting as one and then crumbling to pieces, sprinkling the ocean with rubble and ruin. From Captain Farra and Rahgo, to Samron and Krista at the Golden Gate, cheered with the collapse. It was over. The necromancer was gone.

"How did that happen?" Krista asked.

Samron smiled. "It wasn't because of the Kylika." He answered. He watched as the dead collapsed, finally remaining dead. No more haunting, ear-piercing screams. Their jarring movements now just a memory. And, he was certain, a vision in his nightmares for years to come.

Chapter 28: The World Beneath the World

The Dark Tribe Tunnels, World Beneath the World

It had been a full day since Skage was defeated. Kryn and Ziri rummaged through the ruins of the fortress. Inakus even searched the depths of the Tahlbiru. The spider had crumpled away, falling into the ocean. Only pockets of ruins of the fortress remained jutting above the surface. There was no sign of Rafik or Skage. It was as if both had faded away from existence.

With a telescope Kryn had found she watched the Kylika sail back to Haitu. No one had come to search for her or Ziri. She hoped they believed her to be among the fallen. Finally, she would be free from the king and his army.

"I think he's gone." Ziri finally said, sitting against a slab of rock. "What are we going to do?"

Kryn fought back a tear. "If we can't find him, we need to find his sister. We owe him that much."

"And what are these for?" Ziri asked, holding up the stone and bottles of ink.

"I have no idea." Kryn shrugged. "But it seemed pretty important to Gorik."

"Any idea where Dragon's Roost is?"

"No idea." Kryn said. "Shallon didn't even know before he left."

Shallon and Brohl didn't stick around after the battle. Brohl had left for Sysinal and Shallon to Datz with Gorik's body. It was just her and Ziri scavenging through the ruins. She was unsure how much longer they could stay looking. On the following night snow had begun drifting down. Although Kryn couldn't feel the cold as much as Ziri, even she felt the bitter chill settle in the air. The midday glow of the Black Wall failed to give a lick of warmth.

"We'll find her." Ziri said.

Kryn nodded. "Yes, we will. Then we'll have to tell her about her brother."

"One step at a time. We have to find this Dragon's Roost place first." Ziri said.

Rafik awoke to darkness. If he were dead, it wasn't anything like he had expected. The darkness felt thick like a cloud. Like the tunnels under Datz. He sensed others nearby, but he couldn't even see his own hand. "Ugh. What happened?" Rafik asked, trying to sit up. His heart beat faster, nearly bursting from his chest. His whole front side stung, and every movement caused sharp pains. Last thing he remembered was Skage screaming from losing an arm.

And Blaridane.

He had the sword. He remembered it's welcoming violent voice, melding with his own mind. His spirit. Finally, he was whole again. Then, nothing. The sword wasn't with him now. He couldn't hear its voice call for him. The emptiness within filled him. He was alone again. No sword. No sister. Stuck in a void of darkness.

A light flickered in the distance. "He's awake." A voice shouted. A silhouette of a boy grew closer. "Welcome back to the world of the living."

"What part of the world of the living am I in?" Rafik asked, laying back down, grabbing his head.

"Tunnels below Datz." Tragi said, setting the torch in a sconce and sitting beside him.

Rafik bolted upright, ignoring the discomfort. A searing pain shot up to his head as he got to his feet, causing him to fall back down. "We can't be down here."

"Relax. You're safe." Tragi said.

"Better than the fortress that collapsed above us." Xeo said, entering the room from some entrance Rafik couldn't see. "No way of going back through there."

"I got this, Xeo. Go back with the others." Tragi said, shooting his brother a glare.

Xeo nodded, holding up his hands in surrender and disappearing once more.

"You don't understand. There's a monster down here. Has chains for fingers." Rafik said, moving his fingers like tentacles. He turned, eyes darting from one side to the other, trying to peer into the darkness.

"Oh, Tiris." Tragi said.

"You know him?"

"We ran into him earlier." Tragi said. "After Agam scared him with a blast of fire it grabbed Xeo and I. Told us we could go if we bring back a man with black diamond eyes."

"It spoke to you?" Rafik asked. "That thing just tried to kill us. We went through these tunnels to escape the Kylix. Ran into him instead."

"Yes. But only briefly." Tragi said. "Then it left. Heard it scream a while later. Guessing that was you?"

Rafik nodded. "I suppose so. It's still out there."

Tragi nodded. "Supposedly he can't be killed. Cursed from what Agam says. He managed to kill half of Agam's men on their way to us."

"Who?" Rafik asked.

"Master Agam. You'll meet him soon." Tragi said. "He and about a dozen others saved us after Xeo tried to duel the king."

"And they kidnapped you?" Rafik asked. "That doesn't seem much better."

Tragi shook his head, smiling. "No. The Kylix chased us. They were relentless and we had no food. Then they appeared and we followed. They agreed to help us on one condition. One of us would be trained as a warrior. The other a peacekeeper."

Rafik nodded. "Are you the warrior?"

Tragi shook his head. "They let us decide. Gave us each a book they claimed to be scripture and whichever one felt something from reading it would be the peacekeeper. The other the warrior. Xeo always gets to be the warrior, so I threw my book in the river when they weren't looking and claimed I had lost it. I figured if I didn't have the book, and Xeo did, I'd finally be the warrior. Couldn't exactly be a peacekeeper if I didn't have the book to keep the peace. That night the book was by my bedside, still wet from the river."

Rafik's eyes widened. "Did that really happen?"

"Of course!" Tragi said, nodding. "Gives me the chills just thinking about it, see." He held up his arm to show Rafik the goose skin running up his arms. "I'm supposed to be some sort of peacekeeper. That's why I was chosen to talk to you first."

"And why is that?"

"They want to train you as well. Learn to fight like a real warrior."

"I already know how to fight." Rafik said.

"But do you know how to win in a battle? A war?" Tragi asked.

"I think my sister was in that tower." Rafik said, choking back tears. My uncle, Gorik, was in that tower. My friends. Everyone I cared about."

"As my brother pointed out," Tragi said. "It's all gone. They're all gone. We didn't see anyone else, and we barely escaped. I'm sorry, I don't know if they made it out."

Rafik gritted his teeth. He could have sworn he saw Gorik with two legs, rather than his peg leg. His memory was already distorted from that fight with Skage. A tear trickled down his cheek, imagining his sister. Anza, running for safety as the tower crumbled atop her. Gorik stuck in a battle with the suit of armor, Kryn and Ziri helping him. All of them just to be crushed as Xeo, Tragi, and him defeated Skage. None of that would have happened if King Vanarzir didn't try and take away children in the first place. It was he who had to pay.

He clenched his fists, his nails digging into his skin. Rafik nodded. "I want to fight. I want to stop the king. But I need to find my family. My friends."

"Rafik." Tragi sighed. "I try to stay positive. But even I can't imagine anyone else surviving the collapse. We barely made it."

Rafik nodded. "Alright."

352

Tragi smiled. "I'll go tell the others. You sit tight, try and get some rest."

As Tragi left, Xeo entered the room. "Couldn't help but overhearing." He smiled, sitting next to Rafik. "You're joining us?"

Rafik nodded. "I guess so."

"The way you fought back there, I'm excited to see how you'll be."

"We can be sparring partners." Rafik nodded. "Since your brother is going to be a peacekeeper."

A mischievous grin flashed across Xeo's face. "Yes indeed."

"What's so funny?" Rafik asked.

"I really didn't want to be a peacekeeper. I like fighting. I saw him throw his book into the river. After he left, I fished it out and put it by his bed. You should have seen his face!"

Rafik burst out laughing, his chest screaming in pain in doing so. "Would have been funny to see."

"You ready to meet the others?" Xeo asked.

"I thought your brother said to stay here?"

"Come on, Rafik." Xeo said, grinning. "We are being trained to fight against the king. Might as well start rebelling against the little things, too."

Rafik smiled. "You got a point."

"Besides. I'm the older of the two. Not taking orders from my little brother." Xeo added. He held out his hand and Rafik grabbed hold. As Rafik tried getting to his feet he felt his heart pumping. With every beat a pulse of pain coursed through him. Xeo grabbed Rafik's arm, putting it around his shoulder. "Don't worry, I got you."

With every step a searing pain shot through Rafik. He leaned against Xeo, and he led them to a light he hadn't noticed before. The tunnels were just as cold and damp as he remembered. The darkness seemed to consume the light, though. The light didn't stretch out but stayed in pockets like golden orbs.

The two made their way to the nearest pocket of light. Rafik gasped, noticing Tragi sit with beings he had only heard about. One figure stood up. Crimson feathers intertwined with their hair and ran along their arms. Massive wings jutted out of their backs. And their faces had beaks protruding out. They were the complete figures the monster stalking the tunnels once was. "There's more of you?" He asked.

The birdman walked forward. The feathers bright red and orange like solidified fire danced from the firelight. In a voice that sounded like crackling flames he spoke up, holding out his hand. "Welcome, Rafik. I am Agam. Master of Fire."

Rafik took the hand and shook it. "This isn't possible."

Agam smiled. "Oh, it's more than possible. It's real. We're *Immortals*." He had said something else, but a deep voice like thunder spoke the word Immortals instead. "The one you encountered is a cursed figure. It doesn't represent us."

"Oh." Rafik said, unsure of what else to say.

"The boys tell me you helped defeat Skage?" Agam asked.

Rafik nodded. "I think so. Don't remember much of it."

"He cut off his arm!" Xeo said, slapping Rafik on the back.

"Xeo and Tragi brought you down here." Agam said. "Rescued you from the cursed spider tower collapsing."

"Thank you." Rafik said. "Don't know if I had already thanked you for that. I don't know how I can repay you."

Agam smiled. "We are more than happy to help. No need to repay us. Tragi tells us you agreed to train with them?"

"Yes. If my sister isn't here anymore, there isn't anything else stopping me."

"I'm sorry, Rafik." Agam said. "Sayros over there doesn't even know where your sister is. He's the best life tracker alive. If she's alive, she's found a way to hide from him, which has never been done before.

Rafik glanced over at the Immortal Agam had gestured to. Where Agam had orange and red feathers, Sayros was jet black. Like the monster with the chains. The small light in his eyes glinting in the fire light unnerved him. "What about Gorik?"

354

Sayros closed his eyes, his lids fluttering about. He finally opened his eyes and shook his head. "Gone." He said in a raspy voice.

Rafik closed his eyes, biting his lip. He wanted to run away, destroy everything, and scream, but he couldn't move. Gorik was gone. His sister. Everyone he ever cared about, gone.

"I know you are angry, Rafik. And rightfully so." Agam said. "Stay down here. Train with Xeo and Tragi. Get trained and then bring down the king and the Black Wall that looms over everything."

"I already agreed to." Rafik said.

Agam smiled, taking Rafik around the shoulders and leading him back into the darkness. He felt a cold breeze waft across him. He held out his hands, unsure of where Agam was leading him. They hit a wall a moment later. "Let me help you." Agam said, hoisting Rafik over the wall.

Orbs of light scattered across the darkness. He saw towers and figures flying around. "Welcome to Mahparry. The world beneath the world." Agam said. "You are safe here."

The fear of the unknown faded and filled with awe and wonder. Rafik had never seen anything like it. The light emanated warmth, and a feeling of calm that he needed. Slowly, ever so slowly, he felt something creep back into him. Hope.

About the Author

Growing up in haunted houses, exploring forgotten forests deep within mountains, and spending the last ten years writing and sharing fantasy and horror stories online, T.S. Colunga has a unique way of storytelling. She is best known for her YouTube channel, Terra's Tales, and her e-book horror short story series, Lakewood Stories. She lives and works from home in a small town tucked away on the foothills of the Wasatch Mountains in Utah. Although she sees herself as quite independent, she gets bossed around by her two dogs, Gus and Rowdy, daily.

If you would like to contact her, email her at tscolunga@gmail.com.

Acknowledgements

Before thanking anyone else, I need to thank the amazing artist, Dragolisco. He did the cover for Reign of Shadows, as well as another piece of promotional artwork for it. I love his work and cannot express enough gratitude towards him. I highly recommend you check out his other artwork! I promise you won't be disappointed. Another thanks to Trevor who helped finalize the cover.

This story took a long time to write, and so many people helped get me to this spot. My beta readers, Elan, Luanna, and Matt really helped this book shine. My writing friends, Ben, Cara, and Michelle Savage offered so much encouragement and inspiration. If you ever get the chance to check out their work, you won't be disappointed.

Before continuing I need to thank Pauline. She is by far the main reason you read this story, and any others of mine. She has pushed me to do and be my best and encouraged me to break out of my comfort zone. Pauline kept me on track to get my work done, and to get it out there for others to read. She is the real MVP, and I wouldn't be here without her constant pushing. Thank you so much!

I'd love to thank Gus and Rowdy, but they didn't help at all. While sitting down to write this, both have been scrambling for my attention. And this was after playing with and taking them to the park. But I wouldn't have them any other way. Even if they kick me out of my own office chairs.

And thank you to Karessa. A former boss, and now good friend. Thank you for believing in me.

Most importantly is you. The person reading this book. Hopefully, you have enjoyed it and can't wait for more. I've always wanted to share my stories and inspire others. I am so thankful you took time to read my story. I appreciate that and look forward to sharing more stories in the future as well.

Made in the USA
Coppell, TX
27 March 2021

52467570R00208